WHITE WARRIOR'S WOMAN

Rand swept Kimi off her feet and into his arms. "You are mine and I will have you. I have thought of nothing else since last night."

She opened her mouth to say she was not yet ready to leave the dancing, but his lips covered hers, making her tremble.

He smiled ever so slightly. "You want me, too." With that, he carried her through the camp and into his lodge.

"Oh, Hinzi, are you sure?" she asked. "Are you sure you want to stay among the Lakota?"

"I only know that I want you. I can think no further than that. Tomorrow must take care of itself. Still, I have never known such freedom," he whispered. "To live as a warrior without the restraints of civilization, wild and free. This is what every white man secretly dreams of."

She looked at him, so tall and virile. He was what every woman dreamed of, she thought. To be carried off by him and pleasured without thought of anything but the ecstasy and the passion . . .

GEORGINA GENTRY

SIOUX SLAVE

ZEBRA BOOKS
KENSINGTON PUBLISHING CORP.

There is a large photo on my wall of a moment frozen in time for all eternity of a handsome, green-eyed, black-haired man lifting and whirling a petite and deliriously happy bride. This novel is for our daughter, Erin, who loves the song, "Greensleeves," so much that it was part of her wedding music. And also for Mark, our son-in-law. May you two always be as happy as you are in that portrait.

ZEBRA BOOKS

are published by

Kensington Publishing Corp.
475 Park Avenue South
New York, NY 10016

First printing: September, 1992

Printed in the United States of America

Prologue

1864. A year of bloody Indian wars on the Plains. As the Civil War dragged on, even the warriors realized that the bluecoat soldiers were having difficulty defending the wild frontier country. There weren't enough Union soldiers to send against the South and fight Indians, too.

Faced with this reality, Northern leaders made a tough choice as they looked at all the Johnny Rebs languishing and dying of disease in army prisons. Were these former enemies desperate enough to volunteer to join the Union army and go West to fight Indians? Six thousand of them said yes. History refers to these Confederates who donned blue uniforms as "Galvanized Yankees."

Imprisoned in the grim Union stockade called Point Lookout was a handsome, wealthy Kentuckian named Rand Erikson. Perhaps if the arrogant lieutenant had known what he was in for against the fierce warriors of the Seven Council Fires of the Teton Sioux, he might have chosen to stay in the Yankee prison camp. As it was, to escape the hellhole, he joined up. . . .

One

Early Spring, 1865
Dakota Territory

Today she was to wed the warrior, Mato, but Kimimila did not love him. No matter: at least now there would be meat in the lodge and her elderly mother would be well cared for.

In her tipi, Kimi sighed as she brushed her long black hair, holding the porcupine tail comb with her left hand. She listened to the drums and singing drifting through the camp. Her father had accepted the many ponies before he was killed in the last war party against their enemy the Crow. Kimi had voiced no objections, because Mato was a good hunter and her parents were old and had no other children to look after them.

Kimi reached for the bright ribbon from the trader to twist into her braids and pulled on the soft, beaded doeskin shift. She traced the outline of her spirit animal, the butterfly, in the beadwork. *Kimimila*. It meant "butterfly" in the Lakota language of the Seven Council Fires of the Teton Sioux.

Tonight she would be back in this lodge on the soft buffalo robes with the burly warrior called Mato: the Bear. She thought with regret how much older than she Mato was. Other warriors had made offers, but Mato was her father's friend. And the ironic thing was, all the wealth of her ponies was gone. The hated *wasicu,* the white soldiers, had run them off months ago.

She hummed her spirit song absently, wondering what else she could do to delay, even as Wagnuka, (whose name meant "Woodpecker") stuck her wrinkled face through the tipi flap. "Daughter, why are you so slow? The whole camp has already begun feasting and dancing."

Did she dare say she didn't want to go through with the marriage? No, she shook her head and steeled herself. Her family's honor was at stake, and besides, she and her mother had no male relatives to hunt for them. Mato's family had died of the white man's spotted disease the last time it had swept through the Plains like mounted death. It could be worse; she could be a second wife in some warrior's lodge.

"I am ready," she said dutifully in Lakota and stepped outside. Although Wi, the sun, shone brightly, Tate, the wind, made the early spring day seem cool.

Across the circle of the camp fire, she saw Mato waiting, his homely face smiling as he saw her. The people surrounded her, teasing her, remarking what a great warrior he was, the women wishing her many children to replace the family Mato had lost. Everywhere in the Sihasapas camp, small children ran about laughing and playing, sniffing the good smells from the big kettles, knowing that today there would be feasting and dancing. There was no formal wedding ceremony among her people, but Mato had decided today would be a good time, since yesterday's hunt had been successful and there was plenty of food.

Mato. He looked like a bear, all right. If only he

weren't so paunchy and almost old enough to be her father. She wished now that one of the younger warriors had been rich enough to offer more ponies. Her heart pounding with nervous dread at what she knew would come later today when the two were alone, Kimi forced herself to return his smile. For just a moment she glanced over at her mother and caught an expression that seemed uncertain and troubled. Had Wagnuka guessed her feelings? Was she wishing that there were another man for her only surviving child? Kimi was eighteen winters old, past time to be wed.

Kimi hardly remembered the festivities except sitting next to Mato and the way he ate huge bowls of food, the grease of the hot meat smearing his hands and broad, ugly face. He also had a bottle of the white man's firewater that he had gotten from a fur trader. Whiskey. The whites had brought more trouble with them than just the Long Knives with their new forts.

Time passed. Kimi pretended not to see him glancing sideways at her, hoping to catch her eye so he could signal that they should sneak away to their tipi. He belched loudly and put one greasy hand on her knee.

Others noticed and nudged each other, the men exchanging knowing looks, the women giggling modestly behind their hands. Kimi felt the blood rush to her face, but she took a deep breath of the scent of burning brush from the big fire and pretended to watch the dancers. She intended to put this off as long as possible.

Even her mother was beginning to appear slightly embarrassed that her daughter still sat by the fire although drunken Mato had grown more bold with his hints. If they didn't leave the celebration soon, Kimi would humiliate her mother. As a dutiful daughter,

9

she must make the next step now. Her legs felt almost wooden under her as she rose.

Her man stumbled to his feet and followed her to the new lodge near her mother's. Inside the light was dim.

"Woman, today you will begin making a fine son for me." Mato belched and rubbed his hand across his greasy mouth before he took off his finely decorated shirt. He smelled of old fat and smoke from a hundred camp fires.

She stared at his bare chest, thinking how much more brown his skin was than hers. No words of love or tenderness, she thought, her mouth dry, her heart sinking. To the warrior, she was only a mare to be bred, and he was the stallion. What was it she had yearned for? She wasn't even sure. Not that the plain, heavy man hadn't been honest with Kimi. Mato had lost a whole family of children, and he expected her to replace them for him as rapidly as possible.

Now he hesitated, obviously waiting. She reached up to untie the drawstrings of her fine, soft doeskin, but her hands trembled so much that she couldn't seem to untie it.

He smiled. "It is good that a maiden be modest the first time her man sees her body."

Was it that? Kimi swallowed hard. There had been troubled nights when she had dreamed of a young man's muscular, virile body warm against her own, his hot hands on her breasts and thighs, his wet mouth claiming hers.

Mato made a sound of impatience, reached out, took the strings from her fumbling hands, and untied it. Slowly the dress dropped to the ground, leaving her standing there naked, except for the medicine object hanging between her full breasts.

His expression changed and his eyes swept over her

hungrily. He nodded approvingly. "Your skin is so light and soft," he whispered, and his hands cupped her bare shoulders. "You are worth any gift a man would give to have you in his blankets, Kimimila." His breath smelled sour with white man's whiskey and she drew back.

"No, you have put me off long enough, even for a shy bride." His voice sounded tense with lustful wanting, and he dug his fingers into her bare shoulders, pulling her closer. "I have lost all my family, but you are young; you will give me many fine sons. Perhaps instead of my dark skin, they will favor their mother, maybe even with eyes like hers."

He pulled her up against him. Kimi felt the hard maleness through his breechcloth against her bare body, and she couldn't control her trembling.

Mato laughed and hiccoughed. "Enough of this maidenly modesty. I intend to mount you continually until your ripe body swells with my child. I am not as young as some of the other braves, so I cannot humor you too long. By the time of deep snows, you will give me a son. This, your old father, Ptan, my friend, would expect from you."

Yes, of course she must do this because it was as her old father Ptan ("Otter") wanted. A Sioux woman could divorce her husband, maybe she might have even refused to marry her father's friend, but she felt her family's honor was at stake since she couldn't return the ponies. Besides, at the moment Kimi didn't see any better alternatives. Mato was a good hunter. She and her mother would be well fed.

Reminding herself of this, Kimi forced herself to relax against his bare chest as they stood there, his arms going around her roughly. His greasy hands felt hot on her bare back. She closed her eyes, wishing he were young and virile and that this first time was already over. Yet how different would it be with any other man? As a woman, she was not expected to do anything, she thought, except be there as the receptacle for his seed.

Her breasts felt crushed against his bare, brown chest as he held her against him, his mouth hot on her neck. *Relax and let it happen,* she reprimanded herself, but deep inside, some little independent part of her resisted.

"I have been waiting a long time to make you mine, Kimi." His hands stroked her bare back.

From outside, there was sudden noise and confusion: the sounds of a horse galloping into camp, a warrior shouting, people yelling questions, dogs barking.

Mato pulled away from her and turned toward the racket, muttering, "What is happening?"

Kimi drew a sigh of relief that she had been given a short reprieve before this brave took that to which he was now entitled. "Had you better go see?"

The shouting outside continued. Mato frowned, listening to the Lakota words. "Something about a bluecoat patrol. Perhaps I had better find out."

Turning, he picked up his buckskin shirt and pulled it on even as Kimi crossed her arms over her full breasts.

He grinned. "Later tonight we will continue and there is not an inch of you that my body and mouth won't know, so do not be so shy before me." He reached for his weapons. "For now, I had better see what this trouble with the *wasicu* is about."

Mato strode through the tipi flap as she breathed a little prayer of thanks to Wakan Tanka, and reached for her dress. Trouble with the bluecoats had slowed over the long cold winter as the snow fell across the desolate plains and the sacred Pa Sapa the whites called the Black Hills to the south. A war party might count coup or steal a few horses from the

Long Knives patrol, but the main thing was to make sure the soldiers didn't find the camp.

Kimi dressed and went outside to stand by her mother. Already in the spring afternoon warriors were painting themselves and their ponies, readying their weapons. Mato galloped up, weaving slightly on the back of his pinto pony.

An old man protested. "I feel uneasy about this war party. There has not been proper time given to making medicine."

Mato smiled and caused his mount to rear, its china eyes rolling as it danced and snorted. Red paint handprints on its white shoulders signified that its owner had killed an enemy in hand-to-hand combat. Mato himself wore a warbonnet with trailing eagle feathers, each one showing a brave deed or coup counted. He had changed into a buckskin shirt decorated with enemy hair.

Wagnuka's old face furrowed with worry as she glanced at her daughter. "White soldiers always are looking for young women to steal and carry back to their fort to amuse themselves. Perhaps they come looking for Kimimila."

One of the other warriors shook his head. "I think they seek nothing in particular," he said in Lakota. "Long Knives forever go on patrols. They just wander in circles unable to follow the track of even a big buffalo herd."

Mato held up his rifle reassuringly. "My woman need not be afraid; Sioux warriors will not let the soldiers find this camp, rape and burn and kill as they did our Cheyenne brothers at Sand Creek last winter. We will die rather than allow that to happen to our people!"

The other braves set up a yelp of agreement.

One Eye, Mato's friend, frowned. He, too, was a Shirt Wearer. One Eye might have been handsome

13

except that he had lost the sight in his right eye fighting the Crow enemy, and now wore a patch over it made from a scrap of red blanket. "Mato, my friend, since you have just taken a bride, you have no obligation to go on this war party."

The Bear laughed in drunken derision. "I should stay and enjoy a woman, safe in my blankets while my friends gain honors and count coup on the *wasicu?* There will be horses to steal, scalps to take." He grinned drunkenly at Kimi. "Should I go, woman?"

Kimi hesitated, dreading that time when he would take her virginity. "Do whatever your heart tells you to do."

Mato nodded with pleased approval. "Spoken like a proper wife. There will be many coup to count today and war honors to relate around the fires by our sons." He wheeled his horse around. "Kimi, I will bring you back some shiny brass buttons, some blue cloth to decorate yourself with."

Even then Kimi thought if she begged him not to go, her new husband might change his mind about accompanying the war party. She hesitated. Mato was stubborn. Perhaps he would not listen anyway to a mere woman while his thoughts were on war honors and fresh scalps to show off at a victory celebration. Already they were hearing reports of the coups counted by warriors such as Crazy Horse, Sitting Bull, and Red Cloud among the other clans of the Teton Sioux. Kimi pushed her misgivings from her mind. Countless times she had watched her father ride out with the war parties. The Seven Council Fires of the Teton Sioux had many enemies. They had fought against the Snakes, the 'Rees, the Crow and the Pawnee who raided and killed her people at every opportunity.

Years ago their enemies had begun to scout for the

14

white wagon trains that crossed the prairies, and finally for the soldiers who seemed to push farther and farther into the sacred hills of the Pa Sapa and the buffalo country that belonged to the mighty Sioux by right of conquest.

The women and children gathered to watch as the war party rode out, cheered on by old men too feeble to ride the war trail anymore and young boys who had not yet become men. The women made the trilling sound to encourage the warriors and sent them galloping out of camp.

"Wakan Tanka nici un," she whispered in Lakota. *Good-bye and may the Great Spirit go with you and guide you.* Kimi stared after them a long moment, feeling both proud that her man was one of the bravest of the warriors, even though he was not as young as some of the others. Yet her pride was mixed with relief and then guilt that it would postpone that time before Mato took her virginity and really made her his woman.

The women broke up into little groups, talking of past war parties and booty that had been theirs. This evening when the warriors returned, there would be much feasting and gathering around the fire while the braves recounted each coup and happening. Old warriors then would tell of past glorious times when the Sioux were the undisputed rulers of the Plains; when they and their allies, the Cheyenne and the Arapaho, the Comanche and Kiowa, controlled the whole prairie from the Land of the Grandmother the whites called Canada to the Rio Grande of the Mexicans. Not so long ago, enemies trembled at the mere mention of their names. Now their enemies rode boldly for the gold of the white soldiers who had invaded Sioux domain and acted as if they might even dare to stay permanently, although the white chiefs denied it.

Absently humming her spirit song, Kimi reached up to touch the small fetish hanging between her breasts. Her mother had never told her where she had gotten it, but it must possess powerful spirit magic because it was such shiny metal like Wakan Tanka's own sun, Wi.

There was always work to do in the camp, and Kimi tried to help women burdened with children or old people too frail to dry meat or scrape a hide. She went about her chores and looked forward to the evening's victory celebration, even if it must be followed by Mato's thick body lying on her small one. Perhaps if she closed her eyes when he took her, she could pretend he was the strong, virile warrior of her troubled dreams.

Why had he been unlucky enough to end up stationed at Fort Rice, Dakota Territory? This was no place for a Southern aristocrat! Swearing under his breath, Randolph Erikson shifted his weight in his saddle as the patrol rode across the bleak prairie.

"Because it was either volunteer to join the Union Army or die in that hellhole of a Yankee prison camp," he drawled aloud as he took off his hat and brushed his blond hair back.

"Huh? Lieutenant, did you say somethin'?" The rednecked lout riding next to him glanced over, startled.

"I'm not a lieutenant anymore, soldier," Rand drawled. "The damn Yankees wouldn't let any of us Confederate officers keep our rank."

The other soldier guffawed good-naturedly and spat tobacco juice that dribbled down his chin and onto his saddle. "Now you've learned how poor white trash lives, I reckon, with not even one slave to polish your boots. If I'd had all that, I'd have fought

16

to keep it, too. I'll bet you was a purty sight in your fancy uniform at all the balls and soirées."

Rand didn't answer, concentrating instead on the others of the patrol riding ahead of them across the endless prairie. "Reckon I've changed a little since being in Point Lookout. After that miserable trip here and all these months at Fort Rice, reckon we had it good in that Yankee prison and didn't know it."

The other nodded in understanding. "Fort 'Lice' would be a better name."

Seven months in Dakota Territory. Maybe he had changed a little from the arrogant, spoiled plantation owner's son he was. Rand blinked pale blue eyes against the afternoon sun, not wanting to think about his miserable existence since he'd been captured.

Instead, he remembered olden, golden days before the war on his parent's Kentucky estate. With money and social position, Randolph Erikson's biggest worry was whether the fox hunt might be called off because of rain or if he might have to choose between a ball at the capitol or an elegant dinner at the nearby Carstairs' estate.

The other sneered. "What did a young dandy like you do in the war?"

Rand flexed his wide shoulders. "I was a liaison for the colonel, carrying messages. I reckon I never did much real fighting."

The other spat tobacco juice again and wiped his mouth with the back of his hand. "I knowed you was quality the first time I laid eyes on you at the prison: hatin' to have to mix with poor redneck trash, swaggerin' when you walked. God, I don't even know what I was doin' in this war. I never had me no money to own no slaves."

"Oh, we own slaves, I don't even know how many,"

17

Rand shrugged, "but you know Kentucky was a border state, didn't go with the Confederacy, and Lincoln only freed the slaves in the rebelling states."

The other looked at him, scratched his mustache. "Then what the hell was you doin' fightin' anyways?"

"I reckon my answer is about as foolish as yours," Rand admitted as they rode through the late afternoon. "I thought it would be a grand adventure."

The other man snorted with laughter. "Reckon you found out different, didn't you?"

"Yes, I surely did." Rand cursed softly under his breath, remembering how he had expected this war to be a lark, an adventure to amuse the ladies with over drinks on Randolph Hall's veranda. He had never thought any further than how dashing he would look in the gray uniform. Father had tried to talk him out of it, but Mother, with her deep Southern sympathies, and his fiancée, Lenore Carstairs, had secretly encouraged him. After all, it was going to be a short war that the Confederates would win out of sheer gallantry. Lenore had said he looked so handsome in the uniform, and she gave a ball in his honor.

Instead the great adventure had turned out to be hell with the hinges off. The young blueblood had never before known hunger or pain or terror such he had experienced. The irony of it all was that he was captured carrying a dispatch in an area that was supposed to be controlled by the Confederates.

Rand flexed his shoulders again, trying to find a comfortable position in the saddle. Lieutenant Colonel Dimon led the patrol across the gray-green buffalo grass toward a small creek where stunted willows grew. Rand had lost track of where they were; somewhere near the Knife River, maybe. At least they would get a minute's rest while they watered the horses.

"Hey, Rand, you suppose there's any Injuns out ere? We ain't seen any, and we're ridden clean hrough that area where we might have seen Hunkpapas and Sans Arcs."

"Maybe we'll be lucky and not see any. Dimon's a lory hunter, but medals don't mean much to me."

The other man shuddered. "After what them Eastrn Sioux did to them settlers in Minnesota, I've had ome nightmares about bein' taken alive."

Taken alive. Rand didn't want to think about it. Three years ago, after years of starvation and misreatment, the Santee Sioux had revolted. When it vas over, eight hundred white people lay dead. In the argest mass execution in American history, the govrnment had hanged thirty-eight Sioux warriors.

Rand frowned. "The Yankees forgot to tell us bout that possibility when they were looking for olunteers."

"Do you suppose the war is over yet so we can go ome?' The last we heard, it looked like Lee was igh surrounded."

"Who knows?" Rand shrugged. "If Dimon knew, e wouldn't tell us; afraid we'd all desert and leave."

"Why didn't your rich folks bribe someone and get ou out of Point Lookout?"

Rand made a noncommittal grunt. In truth, he'd ent a couple of messages and hadn't gotten any anwers. Maybe his mail wasn't getting through. Now hat he was stuck in the Dakotas, mail was almost mpossible to send and receive anyway. Maybe that vas why he'd heard so little from Lenore.

"Rich boy, what you gonna do when the war's over?"

Rand didn't bother to answer the ignorant lout. What was he going to do? As expected, he'd go back o Kentucky, marry the Carstairs heiress and return o the aimless, idle life that being one of the local gentry afforded him. Somehow now that he thought about it, that life didn't seem as appealing as it once had. As much as he hated to admit it, the freedom of this trackless wilderness and wild, windswept prairie was beginning to grow on him. He was even beginning to feel a little empathy for the Indians, who, like the Southerners, were fighting against invaders and a changing way of life.

They rode toward the thicket along the creek. Rand thought how a fine cheroot and a tumbler of good Kentucky bourbon would taste about now on the spacious flagstone veranda of his family plantation. Beautiful, dark-haired Lenore Carstairs might be there to visit.

Maybe it was that sixth sense that some men seem to have that sent a sudden warning prickle up Rand's neck as they rode into the willows. Whatever it was, he cried out a sudden alarm and reined in his rearing bay mount, even as the brush ahead of them seemed to explode with gunshots. Startled horses neighed and reared as men around him toppled from their saddles.

Young Colonel Dimon shouted orders, but no one seemed to hear him over the thunder of guns. Horses screamed and kicked while riders fought to control the terrified mounts. The men appeared ready to panic and retreat in disorder. Without even thinking about it, Rand found himself coolly shouting orders. He might be considered an arrogant and privileged dandy, Rand thought grimly as he directed the men around him to dismount, seek cover, but he was no coward.

"Get down!" Rand shouted again, then swore softly under his breath at that fool young colonel leading his patrol into this. Dimon was not yet twenty-five, and he lacked common sense. Rand was not much older himself; he wondered now if he would live to be a day older than that. "Don't give them a target! Keep calm, men! Make every shot count!"

He hit the ground, crawling through the damp dirt with his rifle to a vantage point behind a dead log. The trooper who had ridden next to him crawled up close. "What do we do, Rand?"

He started to answer even as the man screamed out. The soldier looked at him with wide eyes, tobacco juice dripping from his mouth and blood pumping with each beat of his heart through the ragged hole in his blue uniform and into the new green grass of spring. Rand reached to help him, saw it was no use. The redneck rebel who had tried vainly to save his life by joining up with the Yankees had lost his gamble.

Around Rand men reloaded and fired, the scent of blood and burnt powder so thick it gagged and choked him. The little patrol was outnumbered; Rand had been in battle enough to realize that. He aimed, pulled the trigger and missed. The corporal nearby brought down an older, war-painted brave wearing an eagle-feather warbonnet from his pinto pony. That Sioux looked big as a bear, Rand thought. Would he be next to spill his life blood upon the ground?

Gunshots and shouts roared in his ears. The smell of acrid powder and warm blood hung on the late afternoon air. All around him men screamed as they fell. Rand flexed his shoulders and swore silently. Had he come all this way from Kentucky only to die in a faraway wilderness against red men who were only trying to defend their land against white invaders?

All that mattered now was staying alive. Rand reloaded his rifle. A cavalry horse screamed and half reared as it was hit, and then went down. Somewhere over the noise and screams and shots, Rand heard the bugler blow retreat. He rose from the ground, looking for his horse.

A pain like a red-hot saber burned through his thigh. He was hit! Rand fell, cursing, grabbing at his leg, shouting at the patrol not to leave him. In the smoke it was hard to see anything. Over the noise and shouts, the soldiers seemed intent only on saving their own lives, scrambling for the few horses that hadn't bolted away or been killed.

Rand shouted for help again, but already he saw the soldiers were mounting up in panicked disorder, the Sioux warriors shrieking triumphantly as they crossed through the willows in pursuit.

The old timers always said it was better to kill yourself than be taken alive by the Indians to be tortured to death. He was out of ammunition and fast losing consciousness from pain and loss of blood. With sheer willpower, Rand struggled to hobble toward the retreating soldiers. He gripped his thigh, trying vainly to staunch the hot blood running between his fingers. Ironic somehow, he thought weakly. He'd been at Fort Rice since last autumn and had never killed or wounded a single Indian, yet he would die here, a victim of their revenge against white Yankees. He would have been better to have stayed in the Yankee prison with the other captured Confederates.

The soldiers had mounted up, were galloping away as Rand tried to hobble after them, but the remaining horses had bolted. Out of ammunition, all he could do was hide. Rand burrowed down behind some low bushes, listening to the warriors moving through the brush.

He took off his gun belt and used it to make an awkward tourniquet. It would be dark in a couple of hours. Maybe if he lay very still the braves wouldn't

22

ind him. At night, he might have a chance, although it was a long way back to the fort. He wouldn't think about that. He'd think about staying alive.

In the past long winter, out of sheer boredom, he'd learned a little of the Lakota language from an old drunken Sioux who hung around the fort. He wished now he hadn't. He could understand enough of the shouts to know the warriors were looking for more than scalps and extra guns. They were looking for revenge.

Abruptly, one of the painted braves stood over him, his painted face grinning with triumph. Over one eye, he wore a patch made of a scrap of red fabric. *"Hoka hey!* I have found one of their wounded!"

All Rand could do was lie there and look up at him, hoping the brave meant to kill him cleanly with that big lance he carried.

The warrior shouted to the others and gestured. "The bluecoats have killed my friend, Mato! We will take this yellow-haired captive back to camp for Mato's widow to avenge his death!"

Two

The warriors were returning. Kimi, working on a pair of beaded moccasins in her tipi, heard shouting throughout the camp. She sighed as she laid her work aside and looked toward the blankets. What she had managed to delay must soon take place unless Mato was too weary from the fight or there was a great victory to celebrate. She could only hope he would drink enough of the white man's liquid fire that he would not bother her tonight.

A Sioux woman could leave her man; it was part of Sioux custom. However, there was no other man in this camp that had turned her head. Maybe she was better off to be Mato's only wife rather than the second wife of another warrior. He was a good man, just a little old. She would try to be a dutiful wife to him and produce a son quickly. That would insure that her mother would be well cared for.

Kimi paused as she stood up, feeling a sense of foreboding because she didn't hear shouting or victorious trilling from the people outside. She reached to touch her spirit charm hanging around her neck before leaving her tipi to stand in the twilight with her mother. Together they watched the war party riding slowly into view.

Aihee! Yes, there must be something wrong; the warriors were not shouting triumphantly and galloping their horses in the way they should be if all had gone well. No, the men rode with their shoulders slumped and several looked bloody and wounded. None wore the customary black victory paint.

Her mother made a small noise of alarm. "One is missing. I thought more rode out."

Around them, a murmur went through the crowd that waited in the big circle as they, too, seemed to realize something was wrong. Mato. She didn't see him among the riders.

Kimi put her left hand to her mouth, guilt sweeping over her.

Abruptly, her mother cried out and a sympathetic murmur ran through the women as they turned and looked toward Kimi. Oh, no. She shivered with apprehension, said a little prayer to Wakan Tanka. She promised she would be a good wife, she would not regret her husband's age, if only . . .

A warrior led a pinto horse with red hand prints on its shoulders. But another crimson smeared the horse's white coat and dripped in a crooked trail from the limp body thrown across its back. Mato.

She was a widow before she had ever really been a wife. The impact of it hit her and she screamed along with the other women as they ran forward, surrounding the weary men as they slid from their horses.

"Mato. Mato!" She shouted, crowding close. Maybe he was only unconscious and wounded, maybe—

His friend, One Eye, looked down at her, shook his head sadly. "Your husband died a brave death, trying to get some brass buttons for you to decorate your dresses."

25

Tears flooded her eyes and she wasn't sure whether it was grief or guilt. Mato was dead and she had never pleasured him. Now she never would.

Around her, women set up shrieks of mourning. Her mother sang a mourning song, tearing at her hair and clothes, slashing her skin with a small knife. She handed the bloody knife to Kimi, but it fell from Kimi's numb fingers as she pushed forward to touch Mato's arm. Already his body was cold.

One Eye muttered, "Kimi, we brought back a captive for your revenge. You may do with him what you wish."

"A captive?" She turned and looked toward the rest of the war party. A tall, blond soldier sat his mount, sweat and grime and blood smearing his torn blue uniform. He reeled in his saddle, looking barely conscious. Hinzi — Yellow Hair. "Did — did he kill Mato?"

"Does it matter?" One Eye snapped. "I think the bluecoat who fired the shot had dark hair. But this is the one we captured, so he is the one who will pay!"

Already people had gathered around the trussed soldier, throwing horse dung at him, striking at him with sticks, spitting, yelling taunts. "Kill him! Strip his flesh in small bits! Make him scream and beg for death!"

"Be still!" One Eye thundered. "As leader of this war party, I have given this captive to Kimi. It is for my friend's widow to decide how the Hinzi should die."

A nodding murmur of approval ran through the crowd. "Hoka hey! Yes, it is only just. In her grief, the widow will think of more terrible things to do to him than any of us."

Yes, she would enjoy killing him all right, Kimi thought grimly as she pushed through the crowd and looked up into the soldier's blue eyes. Maybe punishing him would lessen the guilt she felt. His fair skin looked pale, the thigh of his blue pants was wet with blood. He might bleed to death and do her out of the pleasure of torturing him, Kimi thought, as she glared up at him.

The soldier looked down at her and their eyes met. He tried to say something through cracked, dry lips, reeled, fainted, slid from his horse, and landed in a heap at her feet. Her people pushed closer, shouting for her to kick him, hit him with her fists.

Kimi hesitated. Even though he was an enemy, her heart softened with pity for a brief moment. Then she turned and saw her own man hanging dead over his horse. Steeling her emotions, she knelt and turned the wasicu's face to look at him. Under all that gun smoke and blood, his own woman probably considered him handsome. "If we don't do something to keep him alive quickly," she said to One Eye, "this captive will die and do me out of the pleasure of revenge."

A murmur of agreement went through the crowd. "Aiyee! Of course he cannot be allowed to escape Mato's widow's wrath."

As she touched his face, the soldier opened his sky-colored eyes slowly and looked up at her. Their gazes met and a feeling like the surging lightning of summer storms coursed through her. *Hate*. The passion of hate, she thought.

She knew a little English from her mother and tribal people who had occasionally traded with the whites. "You. You die soon." He tried to reach to

27

her with his bound hands. Kimi listened closely as he gasped the unfamiliar words of his language. She couldn't understand it all, but she understood a little.

"Help . . . help me," he whispered, looking up at her, and then he fainted again.

She looked around. Her people were watching. She would not let herself pity him when her own man was not yet properly mourned. "The Yellow Hair begs me to help him, not knowing who I am." Kimi stood up. "Stake the captive out by my tipi. I'll see to his wound. He must not be allowed to die until I have time to take my revenge, after the ceremony is over for Mato."

One Eye nodded and gave orders. "Yes, this is how it should be." He, Mato's stout friend, the *Akicita* called Gopher, and several others half carried, half dragged the big man through the camp, leaving a trail of blood behind.

Kimi stared after them, listening to her mother wailing with grief behind her, nodding to the sympathetic murmurs of the women. Much as she hated to touch the pale body of this captive, if someone did not do something quickly, he would die. She would not allow him to escape her revenge so easily when he had just destroyed her future. She could not even look forward to Mato's child.

Torture. She had no stomach for it, and the Sioux seldom resorted to it, but for the tall *wasicu* she could make an exception. Besides, when she thought about the loss of a good warrior and the plight she and her mother now faced her anger grew, fueled by the guilt she felt over Mato. This soldier would pay.

While others took the body from his pinto horse, Kimi followed the warriors back to her tipi.

Her mother trailed along behind, weeping and pulling her hair in grief. She had cut off the tip of her little finger. When Otter had been killed, Wagnuka had sacrificed two fingers to show her grief.

Kimi wasn't sure what emotions she felt; anger, yes, guilt that she hadn't really loved her new husband, fury at the white soldiers for invading the Lakota lands.

She was numb as she watched the warriors rip his shirt open, spread-eagle the big, unconscious man on his back, and stake his hands and feet down to pegs driven in the ground so he lay helpless. He didn't look as if he would survive, even though he was a magnificent specimen of a male. His breath came in shallow gasps, his naked, brawny chest moving as he breathed. Unlike Indian men, this wasicu had much hair on his chest, as blond as his head.

It was not fair, Kimi thought as she stood looking down at him. He was alive and her man was dead. Why couldn't it have been the other way around? The Hinzi's manhood was visibly prominent in his tight blue pants. She tried not to stare at it as she went into her tipi, came out with some old scraps of trader's cloth, some ointment and a water jug.

As much as she hated to touch his bloody white skin, she could not let this soldier die. Later she would take more time with his wound. Now she only hastily bound it so he wouldn't bleed any more.

Her mother and some of the other women stood by, wailing and making trilling songs of grief. Old Wagnuka had slashes on her arms and legs and had hacked away her long gray hair.

"Daughter, I will help the women begin to prepare Mato's body while the men cut willows and cottonwoods for the burial platform. You get some of his weapons and favorite things."

Kimi could only nod numbly as she went back into her tipi. Inside, she broke down for a long moment and wept, wondering as she did so if it were for Mato or for her own plight as a widow.

Trembling, she picked up the new blanket that had been her marriage blanket. Mato should have taken her virginity on it tonight. Instead, it would be his burial wrap. She selected some of his personal possessions to send with him to the Forever Place where he would look on the face of the Great Mystery tonight.

Now in mourning, she tore her clothes and hacked recklessly at her long ebony braids with a small knife. Keening in a traditional sorrow song, she gathered up the things and her knife and went outside into the growing twilight.

The chanting and the drumbeats drifted through the camp in the chill spring dusk. Tonight her man would sleep alone and cold on his burial platform instead of in the warm, naked flesh of his bride.

The women stood outside, silently waiting. Kimi paused and looked down at the spread-eagled soldier, shivering in his near-nakedness on the ground. She nudged him with a contemptuous small foot, knowing this big man was powerless as a trussed stallion, awaiting her pleasure.

There was one more thing she must do. She laid down her bundle and made small cuts on her arms, felt the sting of the knife, smelled the coppery scent of her own blood running red and warm down her arms.

This is for Mato, she wept. *Soon, Hinzi soldier, your blood shall run, too.* She held her arm out

30

and let it drip red drops on the brawny, naked chest. His blue eyes flickered open and he looked up at her. For a long moment he looked deep into her eyes and it sent an unaccustomed rush of feeling through her.

The man licked his dry lips and tried to speak. "W—water," he gasped, and then he said it in Lakota, which surprised Kimi, *"Mni . . ."*

"Mni!" she sneered, struggling to think of white man's words. She wanted to be sure he understood. "This is what you get instead of water." She held her bloody arm up triumphantly and motioned to the drops on his pale skin, still wet and warm from her arm.

"Iyokipi," he whispered in Lakota. *Please.* How did he know some of her language?

"No!" she shouted in the little English she knew so he wouldn't mistake her meaning. "The dead don't need water."

He muttered white man's curse words under his breath. "I—I'm not dead."

"You will soon wish you were," Kimi promised.

She handed her bundles to the waiting women, watched her mother lead them away to take care of Mato's body. She would see if she could keep this hated wasicu alive before she went off to join the mourning as twilight turned the sky pale purple and gray.

When she looked down at him the soldier had closed his eyes, and she wondered if he were unconscious or couldn't face the stark truth of her words. Kimi hesitated, his pain and plight pulling at her heart. Then she reminded herself that soldiers like this one were causing much trouble and misery for her people, and steeled her heart against softness. His half-naked body shivered in the chill darkness of the coming night.

She squatted next to him, examined the wound in his thigh. His eyes opened as she took out her small knife. The sudden apprehension on his handsome face told her he expected she was going to stab him, but he didn't beg. Whatever he was, this wasicu was proud. No, more than proud, he looked arrogant.

As she ran her hands over him, hating to touch him, the Yellow Hair pulled against the ropes binding his arms to the stakes like a wild stallion fighting to escape. She finished cutting away the dirty, bloody shirt, watched the muscles of his bare chest and arms ripple as he strained and pulled. His handsome pale face contorted with the effort and the pain it must be causing him.

He was an unusually big and powerful man, Kimi noted, but he would not be able to pull free. One Eye had driven the stakes deep in the ground. Even though it was chilly in the growing darkness, perspiration gleamed on his virile, muscular body. The furry hair on his chest was as light as the golden hair of his head.

She had never seen fur on a man's chest like this; Indian males were almost hairless on their bodies and many plucked the few hairs from their faces and eyebrows.

As she touched him, he stopped struggling and shivered. Hinzi was not as cold as Mato was at this moment, she thought bitterly. But if she did not keep him warm, the weak flame of life that flickered in his great chest might go out and do her out of her pleasure. He would not escape so easily into a merciful death. Kimi went back to her tipi, got an old buffalo robe, brought it to throw across the soldier and tuck it in around him, except for the thigh she must treat.

His eyes flickered open again and he smiled weakly at her, *"Pilamaya . . ." Thanks.* "W-water?" His lips formed the words, but he seemed almost too weak to speak.

Kimi scowled back. He must not get the idea that she meant him well. Later she would take revenge on this trussed up, helpless stallion and maybe that would make her feel a little better. Did he know what was coming? Was he going to be alive by then?

She looked at his wound again, decided it had stopped bleeding. She poured a little of the water into a horn spoon, dribbled it between his dry lips. He licked his mouth eagerly, looked up, obviously wanting more. She didn't give him any more. Instead she placed the water skin where he could see it; only a few inches from him. So near and yet so far. There was no torture like thirst, Kimi thought, and then wondered why she knew that.

He glanced at it, then at her, puzzlement furrowing his face. Then he seemed to realize what she was doing. An arrogance came back to his features and he spat a white man's word at her, "Bitch!"

She recognized that word. The warriors had learned it among the soldiers and traders. Still she started with surprise at his reckless arrogance. Helpless, wounded and staked out, and he dared challenge her like that. Kimi grabbed her knife and brought it up. She would kill him for his insult. Then she saw his expression in the growing darkness and realized he had been hoping to goad her into killing him quickly and mercifully. The white soldier must have guessed what was to be done with him.

Kimi shook her head. No, he wouldn't escape so

easily. As she lowered the knife and stood up, she couldn't help but admire his bravery. Looking at his handsome face and big, brawny body, she almost regretted the waste of such a virile male. Somewhere he surely had a woman who waited for him to return to pleasure her with that big manhood.

It was shameful to even be thinking such thoughts, Kimi flushed as she turned away. She should be thinking about her own man, sorrowing for him—not imagining the scene of this white soldier coupling with some eager girl as she dug her nails in his shoulders, begging him to go still deeper.

She felt the blood burning her face at her thoughts. She would geld him as part of her vengeance. This stallion of a man would pleasure no more women. But all this must come later when there would be time enough to take vengeance on this defiant *wasicu*. Staked out like he was, he wasn't going anywhere.

Making wailing sounds of sorrow, Kimi went to help with the ceremony honoring a dead warrior to whom she had been a wife in name only.

Later in the darkness, Kimi stood looking up at the burial platform. The paint horse, Mato's favorite, the one he had ridden that day, had been killed beneath the platform. The brave warrior would have a mount to carry him across the wide, starlit sky as he rode forever with those dead who had gone before him. She wondered if the big bear of a man had finally been reunited with the wife and children he had lost? She hoped so. The thought made her feel a little better somehow.

"Waken Tanka nici un," Kimi whispered in Lakota. *Good-bye and may the Great Spirit go with you.* The last time she had said that, she was sending her husband off to war. Now she was saying good-bye for eternity.

She sank to her knees beneath the burial scaffold, singing a mourning song to the dark sky. She had never felt so alone and bereft before. Yes, she had. Puzzled, Kimi searched her mind for the memory, but it eluded her somehow. It was a very small thing, no doubt; something from her childhood. But as far as she could remember, her past was one of happiness, of being pampered by two doting old people.

From the camp, the sound of drums echoed and the big fire in the center of the encampment glowed red against the black sky. Kimi wrapped her arms around herself and took a deep breath of the scent of the smoke drifting on the cool spring night. Somewhere far away, a solitary lobo howled. He sounded as lonely and miserable as Kimi felt. She buried her face in her hands suddenly and gave way to great, racking sobs and cleansing tears, unsure whether she wept for herself, or for Mato.

This would not do. She must be brave as any warrior's woman would be under these circumstances. It was a good thing to die in battle against enemies of the people, better than slowly starving as some of the conquered tribes were doing.

Touching her medicine object for reassurance and squaring her small shoulders resolutely, Kimi stood up and wiped the tears from her face. She was responsible for her old mother. In a few days she must think about the future. Perhaps there was a young warrior in another camp who had need of a wife.

She considered Wahinkeya, Gopher, Mato's other good friend. Stout Gopher already had a wife and a young son he doted on. He might want a second wife. He was a good enough hunter to feed two families. Somehow, being the second wife did not appeal to Kimi. Yet many great warriors who hunted well had several women. As much work as there was to do, it lessened the labor for the household. Often, the warrior married his first wife's younger sister. Kimi had no younger sister: no other kin but old Wagnuka. Her mother had often told her how the Great Spirit had given her a child after they had lost several little ones and had given up hope of ever having a family.

She smiled, remembering the often told story of how her mother had seen a bright *kimimila,* a butterfly fluttering above the prairie flowers and knew somehow that it was the sign the Great Spirit, Wakan Tanka, would soon bless her tipi with a girl child.

And now it was Kimi's responsibility to look after her old mother. Kimi stood up slowly. Tomorrow was time enough to think about becoming some brave's wife.

She started back toward the camp in the darkness. She wondered with sudden curiosity if the soldier had a wife, whether she was pretty, and what she would think if at this moment, she knew her young, handsome man was a captive in a Sioux village.

What did it matter? He was to be killed tomorrow. Kimi trudged back to camp, absently humming her spirit song that had always comforted her when her mind was troubled. She didn't want to think about the soldier. She was weary and sad; she didn't even really hate him anymore. Men were born to be warriors. They fought each other continually. It was the way of things. Suddenly she hoped he had already lapsed into a merciful death. She didn't want him to suffer torture, even if he were the very man who had killed Mato.

The Teton Sioux seldom took captives or resorted to torture. Usually they killed them and mutilated the bodies. If the captives were very brave, they might free them or adopt them into the tribe, or even ransom them. Like the other tribes, they had learned soldiers might trade food and tobacco to ransom a white captive.

To die the way she wanted this captive to die would be slow, agonizing and shameful. She had heard of warriors cutting off a prisoner's manhood as a beginning. The lobo howled again, and somewhere in the distance another wolf answered. New grass and spring prairie flowers felt soft beneath her moccasins as she walked. From the pony herd, a colt nickered. All around her were signs of spring and new life.

All Kimi had was death. She paused, looking back over her shoulder at the burial platform silhouetted starkly against the moon. Faintly the sound of drums echoed from the camp, accompanied by the chanting around glowing camp fires. The slight breeze mingled the scent of smoke with the fragrance of the prairie flowers.

She swallowed the lump in her throat. Never had she felt so weary and depressed. Never had she felt so alone and vulnerable. Tonight was to have been her wedding night, and she should be asleep now in the arms of a man. But the soldier's woman was sleeping alone, too. The thought should make her feel better, Kimi thought, but somehow it didn't. She could only pity that unknown *wasicu* girl.

Sometimes her own soft heart surprised her. It was not good that a woman of the Lakota give sympathy to the enemy who was so set on destroying the Sioux or driving them slowly from this land.

Her own medicine song came to her mind again as it always had when she felt sad. Wagnuka had told her the spirit animal, *kimimila,* the butterfly, must have given it to her as a special gift. Kimi hummed it to herself now as she avoided the circle of the fire, headed for her tipi. The medicine song had always comforted her before, now she willed it to drive the sadness from her heart.

The soldier lay staked down by her tipi, where he had been left for tomorrow's pleasure. He lay very still and Kimi broke off her song, wondering suddenly if he had died? But he stirred slightly at the sound of her approach, and his blue eyes flickered open. He seemed to be struggling with the effort of forcing words through his cracked lips. No longer was he arrogant and defiant. "Please . . ." he managed, "please . . . water . . . *pilamaya.*"

His voice had a soft drawl. Somehow it surprised her that it seemed familiar to her. Of course it meant he came from a certain part of the white man's country. Hadn't she heard the Sioux speak of some of those with the soft, drawling voices among occasional traders and mountain men who passed through their land?

Kimi pursed her mouth, thinking. The warriors had said those with the drawling voices now dressed in gray and fought against their brothers in blue. Yet this one with the soft accent wore blue.

The soldier didn't look as if he could survive the night, Kimi thought, and her heart went out to his plight in spite of herself. She reminded herself he must not be allowed to die. Kimi knelt by him, reached for the water skin. She poured a little between his lips and she paused to watch him swallow greedily. She must be careful not to choke him with too much at a time.

He licked his lips, looked up at her with pleading in the sky-colored eyes. "Please . . ."

She poured a little more between his lips, enjoying the fact that the big, powerful man was helpless and bound, having to beg her for whatever he needed. He was her captive, her slave to do with as she wanted at this moment. She could do with him whatever pleased her and no one would care.

She tried to remember whether she knew the white word for what she needed to ask. Somehow, her mother had seemed to know a lot of *wasicu* words and had taught Kimi a few. "Enough?" she asked finally as she remembered it.

"Enough." he nodded weakly. He didn't appear defiant now. He was too weak. "What — what is to be done with me?" He spoke in a mixture of white words and pidgin Lakota.

Should she tell him?

He must have seen the hesitation in her face because he demanded suddenly, "Tell me."

"You will not order me about," Kimi snapped back in a mixture of Lakota and the few white words she struggled to remember. "You are a captive; a Sioux slave."

"Slave? God in heaven! Not me! Not now; not ever." His arrogant drawl and the distaste on the aristocratic face showed his dismay. "Slaves are black."

The South. He was from some place called the South. Kimi tried to remember how she would know that, then dismissed the thought. "Here you are the slave, *wasicu*. I must know this. Did you

39

kill the warrior called Mato?"

His furrowed brow told her he didn't understand her words—at least not all of them.

"Kill," she repeated the word in English, and made the sign talk for killing. "My man. Did you kill him?"

The realization of what she asked crossed his pale eyes and he shook his head. "No, I kill no one."

"You lie, *wasicu* soldier!" She shouted it at him as she stood up. Of course he would say that, now that he was at her mercy. He would plead innocence. "Tomorrow you die!"

Kimi whirled and entered her tipi. It would serve him right that he die. She stood there a long moment, decided she couldn't bear to sleep alone in this lodge she had planned to share with Mato. She went the few feet to her mother's tipi. Her mother was already asleep at the far side of the big lodge. Now Wagnuka raised up on one elbow. "Daughter, what is wrong?"

"Nothing." Kimi settled down on her own blanket. "It does seem a shame to kill the *wasicu* when he is big and strong and the two of us have no man to hunt for us or do heavy work. We should keep him as a slave."

"It does seem a waste, but our people do not keep grown men captives. Yet, the soldier would suffer more if he were kept as a slave and worked with as little mercy as most show a horse," Her mother grunted and dropped back off to sleep.

The camp grew quiet as time passed and people left the fire to go to sleep. Kimi lay in her blankets, thinking what should be happening on her wedding night with Mato. She thought again of Hinzi, Yellow Hair, spread-eagled and staked down on the ground outside, wounded and in pain, awaiting his death on the morrow.

He was a brave man, Kimi thought with grudging approval. When she had told the man of his coming death, he had not begged for mercy or showed terror or cowardice. No doubt he would die with the same courage. The Sioux respected a man who could die well.

Tonight she should be losing her virginity. Instead she slept alone while a big, brawny, half-naked stallion of a man lay staked out on the ground, awaiting her whim. When she finally slept, she dreamed that she went outside and stood looking down at him, pulled the buffalo robe away from his magnificent body. The soldier lay naked and helpless, staked down. He was hers to do with as she chose.

She studied his big manhood straining against the tight blue pants. Yellow Hair was built as big as a stallion. *I was supposed to be given a man's seed tonight, but because of you, he is dead.*

She felt an unaccustomed stirring where her thighs joined. On this spring night, in many lodges, young wives were sighing in passion as their virile brown men spread their thighs wide and mounted them. But with her blood running hot at the thought, she would be unsatisfied and sleeping alone. No son would take root in her womb tonight.

Soldiers often used Indian girls for their pleasure, she thought, it was only just that he be used as her docile stud, to give her pleasure; to put seed in her womb.

Of course. Why not? He was helpless and staked

out. Hinzi was no danger to her. She could do anything she wanted with him and no one in the camp would object. It was her right as the dead warrior's widow.

The thought both shamed and excited her. Stirring restlessly, she knew she should be mourning for her dead warrior. Yet in her dream she couldn't control this urge to reach out and run her hand across the soldier's naked, hairy chest, down to his navel. His white skin was warm to the touch. She felt his pulse beating strongly in his hard belly.

Or was that her own pulse pounding in her ears? Had she no shame? What was it that drew her to have erotic thoughts about this *wasicu?*

She imagined taking out her small knife, cutting away his pants so he lay naked. She imagined that she put her hand on his manhood as it hardened and throbbed. He groaned aloud, writhing beneath her fingers. He was built big, Kimi thought, big as a buffalo bull or a mustang stallion. Surely a male like this one was virile enough to end all those troubled dreams she had had these past months.

In her mind, she took off her doeskin shift with tantalizing slowness, knowing he watched her undress. She stood looking down at him, as naked in the spring moonlight as he was And he was helpless, staked out for her use and pleasure.

You are my slave, my captive, she whispered to him as she arched her back so that her breasts jutted out with ripe promise. Ever so slowly, she ran her fingers up and down her own naked thighs, up to stroke her nipples. His gaze followed her hands as if he wished those hands on her flesh were his. His manhood seemed to throb as she went down on her knees beside him.

42

You will please me as I order you to do. If you pleasure me enough, perhaps I will give you a trinket as the soldiers do Indian girls they use.

In her troubled dream, she saw him studying her breasts and he ran his tongue over his lower lip. Kimi took a deep breath, threw back her shoulders so that her full breasts stood out. *Do you like them? No man's hands have ever cupped them, caressed them. Would you like to put your mouth on them?*

Please . . . He struggled against his bonds but he was tied securely, as a stallion might be crosstied to permit his safe use by a mare. Kimi ran her thumbs around the circle of her nipples with deliberate motions and his blue eyes seemed to follow every move.

Kimi bent over him, reached out and ran her thumb across his nipples and he arched his back and moaned aloud. *Please . . . oh, please . . .*

She clasped his iron rod of maleness in her hand and wondered if her small body could sheath that hard sword.

Then, leaning forward, she put one hand on each side of his blond head. That made her breasts hang just above his reaching, eager mouth.

Kimi smiled at his efforts to reach her breasts. *I'm going to use you now, slave. You look like prime breeding stock. This is my first time to couple with a man. I order you to make this pleasurable for me. If you do, perhaps I'll give you a trinket or an extra coin. If not, I may geld you or take a quirt to you.*

Oh, please, don't, mistress. I'll pleasure you; I promise to do just as you ask.

See that you do, yellow-haired stud. Feeling almost heady with her power over this big male animal, Kimi straddled him and leaned over so his mouth could reach her breasts. She almost cried out in her pleasure at the sensation of his hot, wet mouth sucking her nipples. *Yes. Yes. Oh, Yes!*

And now to make use of the soldier's big sword. For only a moment, Kimi hesitated, looking down at the size of it. He was built to give a woman pleasure. Her body felt wet and eager to be bred. With delectable slowness, so as to make it last, she slid down on him, sheathing his big sword in her velvet place. She felt it hit against the silk of her virginity. She would have to take him deep in her depths.

Only for a moment, she hesitated. Then she gritted her teeth and came down on him hard, taking him all the way up under her ribs as she straddled him. Kimi felt her maidenhood tear away, felt the sudden flash of pain and the warmth of her own blood running down his rod. He felt so good throbbing deep within her body as she began to ride him, her breasts brushing tantalizingly against his lips.

Arch your back and go deep; pleasure me, white soldier.

But now he was arrogant again, laughing at her desperate need. *No, bitch, you pleasure me, beg me for it; beg me; say please . . . please. . . .*

Kimi came awake with a sudden start, sat up, breathing hard, felt the perspiration on her face. She looked around in the darkness and heard her mother snoring. It had only been a dream, but so real. It almost seemed she could hear him begging for her favors.

What had awakened her? Kimi strained to hear.

Old Wagnuka snored loudly from her side of the tipi. No, that hadn't been it. The camp lay very still in the middle of the night. The remembrance of everything that had happened yesterday rushed back to her. Instead of losing her virginity to her husband, she dreamed of mating with his enemy. What kind of shameless woman was she? One who had a great capacity for passion, she thought, and now she might never experience that mystery.

A sound: a very soft moaning. "Please . . . please . . ."

Yes, that had been what awakened her from her troubled dreams. The soldier. No doubt he was in pain from his wound and being tied spread-eagled for hours. For a moment, she almost weakened at the thought of his suffering. No, she would ignore him. He deserved no better. He moaned again. Kimi frowned and sighed. If he didn't stop, he would wake her mother or maybe some of the others. She lay back down and tried to sleep. Hinzi moaned again, a little louder this time.

How could she sleep if the captive kept that up? She would go out there and stuff a rag between his lips to mute him. Yes, that was a good reason to go outside and check on him. Of course she didn't care if he were in pain; she wouldn't let herself even think about that. It was only important that she make him be quiet so he wouldn't wake the camp. She crept quietly from the lodge. It was still dark outside but the air had turned cooler. She looked down at the captive.

"Be silent!" she snapped in a mixture of Lakota and a few English words. "You will awake everyone and so be killed sooner."

"Water," he whispered, and cursed softly in that soft drawl, "Some water . . ."

"Be still, I said."

Hinzi looked unaccustomed to begging for any-thing. She wondered suddenly if he had been a high officer or a wealthy man, used to ordering people about, expecting others to obey his every command? She had a feeling women begged for his caresses as he had begged her in her troubled dreams. She leaned over him, as she reached for the water skin. "Beg me for it and perhaps I will give you a little water."

"Go to hell!" He glared up at her. "If I were free," he snapped, "you would be the one begging."

"Ha!" She threw her head back disdainfully and laid the water skin to one side. "Big talk for one tied up like a bull waiting to be slaughtered!"

Before she realized what was happening, his right hand shot out and grabbed her by the throat. He had worked that one hand loose from its bounds, she thought in that split second as she struggled with him. If she could only scream and bring people running to her aid.

The same thought must have flashed through his mind, for he dragged her down to him by sheer brute strength, blocking her cry with his lips.

In fear and fury, Kimi tried to break his grip, pull away from his mouth so she could scream, but in their struggle, his mouth was on hers, his teeth cutting her lip. No longer was she worried about screaming; now she only wanted enough air to breathe as his iron hand tightened on her throat.

"Please . . ." she managed to gasp against his mouth, choking slowly.

"Beg," he demanded against her mouth. "Untie me!"

He was as proud as she was, Kimi realized as she struggled. She tasted blood from her cut lip even as he forced his tongue deep into her mouth, muffling her cry.

In silence, they struggled. As hurt as he was and with only one hand free, he was still a powerful, virile stallion of a man. She had underestimated his strength and desperation, thinking him too wounded, too bound to be dangerous.

Mouth to mouth, they struggled. Kimi gasped for air as she fought, beating him about the face with her small fists. His hands were big and powerful enough to break her neck, she realized that. To save her life, she would have to submit, or his powerful hand would choke her breath off. If she untied him, he would be a danger to the whole camp. She would let him kill her before she endangered her people. If she only had a weapon—a skinning knife, anything. Her blows about his head and brawny chest seemed useless. His only chance was to ignore the blows of her fists and force her to free him, and he seemed to realize that as much as she did.

"Untie me and you'll live!" His breath was hot against her mouth as she fought to get away from his strong hand.

She couldn't even get enough air to refuse. All she could do was fight and shake her head. He was going to kill her, Kimi thought. He had nothing to lose in this desperate gamble. Yet to save her own life, she couldn't endanger the sleeping camp.

Kimi did the only thing she could think to do. She brought her fist down with all her small strength, striking the wound in his thigh.

He gasped in agony and passed out.

Three

With a sigh of relief, Kimi pulled free of the unconscious man and rubbed her bruised throat. That
had been a dangerous trap, caused by her own soft
heart. Her mother was right; the *wasicu* were not
to be trusted. They were as cunning and full of
tricks as a badger. No wonder Wagnuka had made
her stay out of sight every time a trader or trapper
had come to their camp. She said they hungered
for pretty Sioux girls.

But what of her own hungers? Without thinking,
she ran her fingertips across her lips, remembering
the hot, sweet taste of the soldier's mouth, the
warmth of his hand, the feel of his naked, hairy
chest against her when he held her close.

She must stop thinking of that, Kimi admon-
ished herself sternly. Perhaps the sooner this bluecoat was dead, the better.

She studied him. Could she blame him for doing
whatever it took to try to save his life, knowing
what lay ahead of him at dawn?

It would soon be light and the warriors would be
coming for the captive. Kimi took his big hand in
hers, more than a little aware of the power of that
hand as she tied his wrist down to the stake again.
He must have unbelievable strength, to have been
able to break that thong. Maybe it had been

48

strength born of desperation. She was fortunate he hadn't snapped her neck.

Absently Kimi brushed her left hand across his lips, wondering if he had put his mouth on many girls' mouths. No man had ever kissed her before. Immediately, she felt angry and guilty because of the emotion that raced through her at the memory. What kind of woman was she anyway, that the taste of a man's mouth could excite her and set her blood pounding like a mare in heat, while her own husband lay newly dead? Her face burned as she remembered her torrid, troubled fantasy. Had she no shame? This might be Mato's killer staked out here.

Dawn came slowly from the east, with all the pale, soft colors of prairie flowers. Around her the camp began to stir, dogs barked, babies cried. Women called to each other as they stoked up their camp fires and began to prepare food.

The soldier stirred slightly and moaned. Kimi wished the warriors would come for him and get this over with. Yet she dreaded the ordeal. Since he had first looked into her eyes and tried to talk to her, since his lips had brushed hers, he was no longer just a hated enemy; now he was a living, breathing human being.

Kimi stood up even as she heard the warriors approaching, led by One Eye. The battle-hardened warrior smiled without mirth. "So, Kimi, are you so eager for your revenge that you are out here waiting for us?"

What should she say? What *could* she say? "Of course. He—he deserves to die."

With mixed feelings, she watched the braves cut the soldier's bonds and dragged him to his feet. The Yellow Hair was conscious now and only moaned once when they hauled him upright. He could not stand alone and would have fallen, had not Kimi rushed forward, let him lean on her. He stared down into her eyes and she felt so guilty that she looked away and did not meet his gaze.

A frown crossed One Eye's handsome face. "You should have let him fall and be dragged like a dog through the camp for all to sneer at." He gestured to two of the biggest braves to shoulder the weight of the tall soldier. Hinzi tried to fight them, but in his weakened condition he was no match for the warriors. They half dragged, half carried him to the big camp circle. Kimi followed along behind, unsure what she was supposed to do, although she had already decided she didn't want to take part in his execution.

Most people had eaten, and they gathered curiously in the circle to watch what would be done with the captive. His thigh was bleeding again, Kimi winced as she noticed. What difference did that make to the brawny, half-naked man? In a few more minutes, he would have many other agonies to worry about. Even injured, he was still strong enough to strike several blows, scattering his enemies. Though he struggled, the braves raised his arms above his head and lashed them to a framework. He wore only the ragged blue pants, and someone had taken his boots. His feet barely touched the earth, and now they tied his ankles to two stakes driven wide apart in the ground.

Kimi hesitated. Should she leave so she wouldn't have to watch? What would everyone say if she left? They expected her to relish this vengeance because of her husband's death, and didn't this enemy of her people deserve this pain and humiliation? Wi the sun rose above the horizon.

Light gleamed on hair as golden as the sun itself. Hinzi. Yellow Hair. Tonight that fine scalp would hang on a lodge pole for a victory celebration and dancing.

The soldier tried to stand, but his injured leg wouldn't support him. He hung helpless and suspended from his wrists. With his ankles tied to stakes, he couldn't move anyway. Kimi stared at the rippling muscles of his broad back and wide shoulders. Her own skin where it was protected from the constant sun was much paler than the other Sioux, she realized that, but the yellow-haired soldier had the fairest skin she had ever seen. It was tanned only where it had been exposed to the sun.

Gopher stepped forward with a knife. "The wasicu wears clothes like a man, but a soldier is no better than an animal—a dog, a horse. He should not be allowed the dignity of covering himself."

With a quick motion, the stout brave cut the blue trousers from the soldier, threw them away, leaving him naked while the women laughed behind their hands. "Look at the Hinzi. He's big as a stallion. Kimi, it is only right that you make the knife stroke."

They expected her to geld him. Often when a warrior killed an enemy, he cut off his man parts. Sometimes as an insult, they left them stuffed in the dead enemy's mouth. It added insult to injury because any man valued his manhood more than he did his life. Gelding was what was done to horses, even among the whites to keep inferior stock from reproducing or make them tractable, docile work animals. Did whites geld men? Maybe some of their black slaves she'd heard the warriors talk about.

51

Were the Indians any less civilized than the *wasicu* then? Life was hard and merciless for the Indians: kill or be killed, even when they wanted to live in peace.

From where she now stood, Kimi could only stare in fascinated horror at the evidence of Hinzi's maleness.

One Eye put a sharp knife into her numb hand, pushed Kimi forward into the circle formed by the curious onlookers. Someone had started a fire nearby. Kimi's mouth felt so dry, she couldn't swallow. She looked from the blade in her hand to the naked, helpless soldier. The muscles rippled in his lithe body as he seemed to see the knife in her hand and pulled at his wrists, struggling to break free. Perspiration stood out on his handsome face in great beads.

For the first time, she saw fear in his pale blue eyes, not fear of death or pain, but fear for the loss of his maleness. Such a waste, Kimi thought, to geld a fine specimen of a man like this one. He wasn't going to beg for mercy, no matter what she did to him, that much was clear.

He began to swear and fight the thongs that tied him. "No! Damn you! No!" He pulled at his bonds again. Kimi took a deep breath of the smoke from the camp fire and watched him struggling to break free. The hard muscles of his belly rippled as he twisted against the thongs, and she saw the lean power of his hips. This one could drive hard and deep into a woman, make her know he was there, have her arching herself up, clawing those lean hips and the corded muscles of that strong back, begging him to plunge deeper still.

"Kimi, get on with it!" One Eye snapped.

She started, terrified that he might have read her

thoughts. Had she no shame? She looked from him to the waiting crowd, at the soldier fighting his bonds. She stared at the camp fire, looked at the naked soldier and knew that next they would see how well he withstood fire without screaming in pain.

She couldn't do this. She *must* do this. Kimi forced herself to approach Yellow Hair, knelt on one knee before him as he fought to break free, shouting and cursing, but not begging for mercy.

The people yelled encouragement; "Finish it, so we may begin the torture! Who will be first to put a burning stick on that white skin?"

The crowd roared approval at the remark, looking forward to the entertainment to come.

Kimi paused uncertainly. Suddenly she wanted to throw down the knife and run away. Very slowly she looked up into the soldier's stoic, angry face. His expression was pale but grimly determined as he set his mouth in a hard line. His eyes widened as he looked at her. What was it that surprised him so? That a woman could take part in such a thing? Lakota women were as brave and savage as their men. To survive against the tribe's many enemies, they had to be.

Yet she had a sudden feeling that she could cut him slowly to small pieces with her knife, even cut off his manhood and throw it in his face, and he would not whimper or beg for mercy.

There was sudden confusion on the far side of the camp and Kimi looked around, relieved for any diversion that would postpone the inevitable.

Somewhere an elderly woman shouted, "Tatanka Iyotake of the Hunkpapas and some of his warriors have come to council with our chiefs."

The crowd turned, abruptly more interested that

53

Sitting Bull was in camp. Kimi breathed a sigh of relief.

One Eye frowned. "We will see what these leaders think we should do."

Some of the Hunkpapas dismounted and came forward.

The short, stocky Sitting Bull, wearing the scarlet sash of his Strong Heart society, paused to look. "What is happening here, my friend?"

One Eye spoke with respect. "As you see, Tatanka Iyotake, we make ready to geld and kill a bluecoat soldier. You have arrived just in time."

"One Long Knife is of little concern," the leader shrugged, "I come to discuss future plans."

Even though, as a woman, she really wasn't supposed to speak, Kimi saw her chance because she knew now she couldn't bring herself to torture the Hinzi. Perhaps her status as wife of a respected warrior who had been killed in battle would cause the braves to overlook her impudence.

"It seems to me we are in too big a hurry to kill the captive," Kimi blurted to the important leader. "Yellow Hair would do better as a hostage to insure the soldiers won't attack this camp. Later we might even trade him to them. They won't give us cartridges and tobacco for a dead man."

The Strong Heart nodded. "For a woman, you think and speak well."

"No!" Some of the men of yesterday's war party protested and pushed forward. "No, we brought back this captive; we demand the right to test his courage by fire and blade!"

Kimi whirled on them. "You would question the wisdom of Strong Heart warriors? Perhaps he is right. Alive the soldier might be used as a hostage protect our camp or trade to the soldiers. Dead, he is worthless to our people."

A murmur of agreement ran through the crowd at Kimi's words, though many were grumbling at the talk of losing the morning's entertainment. She saw the hesitation on One Eye's face and knew that even he saw her wisdom. "What should we do with him in the meantime?"

Kimi shrugged carelessly as if it mattered little to her, although suddenly it mattered a great deal. "Hinzi might be useful as a slave. With my husband dead, I have need of a beast of burden to carry wood and water."

One Eye frowned. "The whites geld their beasts of burden to make them docile and tractable. Even if we don't kill him, that's what you should do with this soldier. Let him live so he might be of use as trade goods or as a hostage, but take his manhood."

"He is already weak from loss of blood," Kimi argued coolly, "he may not survive the knife."

Judging from the murmur of the crowd, the people seemed to agree with the warrior that the virile white male should be gelded.

The important warriors who had just arrived seemed to have more important things on their minds. "We are here to council and smoke. Anyway the woman is right; he might not survive the loss of blood. It is fitting that he be given to Mato's widow as a slave until he is ransomed . . . or a meeting of the Wicasas, the Shirt Wearers, decide to kill him."

An even greater murmur of agreement ran through the crowd. Sitting Bull, Red Cloud and Crazy Horse of the Oglalas, were gaining the peoples' respect. "Yes, give the soldier to Kimi to

55

be used as a slave! The *wasicu* will not attack our camp if they fear to kill one of their own. As a hostage, he will insure the safety of the people."

Kimi stood there holding the knife, staring up at the big, naked soldier tied hand and foot before her while the warriors discussed it. What would she do if they changed their minds? She could not go against her people, yet the unspoken plea in his blue eyes touched her woman's heart. Finally it was decided that the question as to what to do with Hinzi should be postponed. Until a final decision was made, the soldier should be given to Kimi to be used as a slave.

One Eye argued, "It is not seemly that a man occupy the tipi of two women." However, even as he said it, he cut the ropes and the soldier collapsed in a heap.

"Hinzi is not a man, only a slave," Kimi sneered. She walked over, nudged him with her moccasin contemptuously. "He is no danger to anyone right now. He can't escape, he can't even stand alone."

It was true, and everyone seemed to recognize that fact. Two warriors lifted him up out of the dirt and half dragged, half carried him back to Kimi's marriage tipi with the curious trailing along to watch.

Kimi stopped and put her hands on her hips as she considered. "He might not survive another night outside in the cool air. Bind him again and tie him to a stake inside the lodge."

She stuck the knife in her clothing and followed the warriors as they dragged the soldier into the tipi she would have shared with Mato. She went inside and stood watching as they tied his hands together, drove a stake in the ground above his head, and tied his wrists to it.

"Tie his ankles, too," Kimi said, remembering the soldier's attempt to escape before morning. She had told no one about that, but she wasn't sure why. Yes, she was. Because it would mean his death.

Wagnuka frowned and shook her head. "Daughter, you will regret this. It is not seemly to have this naked man in your lodge."

"Man? Hinzi is only a beast of burden," Kimi laughed coldly. "What are you so afraid of, Mother?"

The old woman hesitated. "I—I—nothing. I only know that the whites always bring our people grief. To have this one here will surely bring us even more trouble—or more soldiers. We should have killed him so we wouldn't have to worry about him escaping and bring troops back to our camp. I will get us food." She went outside.

Kimi knelt by the half-conscious man. His thigh still bled a little. It looked bad to her. If it weren't cleaned and bandaged, he could lose that leg, and a slave with a bad leg was useless as a horse with a broken leg. The beast always had to be destroyed. She looked at him lying there, his eyes closed. She had mixed feelings toward him now because of the bravery he had just shown though seriously injured. He was no white devil; he was only a man after all, with all the weakness and wants of any man.

His eyes flickered open and he looked up at her, seemed to struggle to find the words. "Thanks. *Pilamaya*. You saved me back there."

Kimi shrugged, understanding more of his drawling words that she had thought she knew. She answered coldly in a mixture of Lakota and English. "Don't thank me yet. They were right, you know.

57

A gelded slave is a more submissive, more docile animal to deal with."

Just a flicker of anger and defiance flashed through his blue eyes and he cursed softly under his breath. "If I ever get loose, you cold chit, we'll see who's submissive and who's the master."

"What? What did you say?" She must have imagined his words. It was unbelievable that he might still be so arrogant and defiant when he was helpless in her power.

He smiled ever so slightly. "I think you understand more English than you let on."

Maybe she did. Kimi didn't question that. Many of her people had learned to speak a little. She took a deep breath to control her anger and brushed the hair from her eyes. "You're filthy! I wouldn't keep a pet dog as dirty as you. You will smell up my lodge." She got a gourd of water and a little of the soap weed the tribes farther to the south had given her. Now she knelt by him and hesitated.

There was pain in his handsome face, but a trace of defiant triumphant still. "Don't be afraid to touch me. I'm tied down and harmless."

"I am not afraid of you," she snapped. "If I were, I'd geld you. I still might."

A flicker of fear crossed his face although he struggled to keep it immobile. Men, she thought. What was it about men that made their manhood more valuable to them than their lives?

She took the soap and a scrap of his ragged uniform and began to wash him. His skin felt warm under her hands. When she washed across his wide chest, his eyes closed, and he smiled ever so slightly and his maleness hardened. Kimi felt her face flush like fire. He was much bigger when aroused than she could even have imagined. She heard her mother coming, grabbed a buckskin garment that had belonged to Mato, threw it across his maleness to conceal it. She could only be thankful that the lodge was semidark.

Wagnuka entered, stared at their captive curiously. "I brought some stewed meat as a gift to you from Gopher. I think he would consider taking you as a second wife when a little time has passed to make it respectable." She gestured toward the captive with a sneer. "Do you intend to waste it feeding him?"

"He'll hardly be of any value as either a slave or a hostage if we let him starve to death," Kimi said carelessly as if it didn't much matter to her one way or another.

Her mother snorted in disgust and handed over a steaming gourd. "He doesn't look like he'll survive. No matter. I have told some of the other women I will help with the tanning of some hides." She left the lodge and Kimi listened to her footsteps fade away.

Kimi held the gourd and took a few bites with the horn spoon. The meat tasted hot and delicious. The soldier watched each bite that went into her mouth.

"You must learn to be obedient," she said, seeing that he watched her. "If you beg nicely like a puppy, perhaps I will give you a few bites."

"Go to hell!" Only a muscle twitching in his temple betrayed his anger.

"Very well, you may watch *me* enjoy it." She answered coldly and continued to eat. The scent of the cooked meat filled the lodge and he sighed and turned his face away. He looked weak and she remembered he was wounded and really should be fed to give him strength, but she steeled herself. When this slave learned to obey his mistress, then she would feed him.

She ate half the bowlful, waiting for him to change his mind and beg. She decided she could be as stubborn as he was. His face looked pale in the semidarkness, but he did not ask. Kimi hesitated. If she did not give him something to eat, in his weakened condition, he might die.

"Here," she lied, "I find I have more than I can eat after all." She put her arm under his head, lifted him and held the horn spoon out to him.

He shook his head. "I—I do not beg."

Kimi was the one who now wished she knew some of the white man's curses so she could use them. "Eat," she commanded, "before I change my mind and let you starve."

She held the spoon to his lips, and he wolfed it down so fast she was afraid he would choke. After a while, he looked a little stronger and sighed with apparent relief. Kimi was only too aware of the warmth of his head on her bare thigh where the doeskin shift had scooted up.

He shivered ever so slightly.

"Hinzi, are you cold?"

"I do not beg for clothes, either." His voice, though weak, was defiant.

"I need a fire anyway for what I must do next." She went about building a small fire in the fire pit, pulled the bloody bandage off, and looked at the wound. It looked bad. Kimi pursed her lips, shook her head.

"What—what are you going to do?" There was sweat on his face again as if he had already guessed.

"That wound must be cleansed and it keeps

bleeding." She took her knife and laid it with the blade in the flames.

"What do you think you're doing?"

"I'm going to sear that wound to stop the bleeding."

"No, damn it, no! I want an army doctor!" He tried to pull loose from the stakes that held him, but they were driven deep.

"Stop that! You're making the wound bleed again."

He only struggled harder and began to curse in that Southern drawl.

"You must not make noise, that will bring everyone running and they might change their minds. I'll try not to hurt you."

"Don't give me that! You're looking forward to it, you savage little bitch!" He fought the thongs that held his powerful muscles prisoner.

Kimi hesitated, a little afraid of his strength and his fury. If he managed to pull free, his expression told her he wouldn't hesitate to kill her. Yet she had to cauterize that wound. "I'll give you some leather to bite on. White men put bridles on their beasts of burden."

When he opened his mouth to protest again, Kimi put a leather strap between his teeth and tied it in place even as he tried to spit it out. He would need that leather, she thought almost sympathetically, to keep him from biting his own tongue when that hot steel touched that wound.

"Stop fighting. You don't realize how lucky you are." Kimi picked up the hot knife gingerly. "The others wanted to geld you; I'm trying to keep you from losing your leg."

He struggled to get the leather out of his mouth, fighting to break free. His blue eyes flashed fire at

61

her, amid muffled threats of what he would do to her if he got loose.

Kimi hesitated, looking from the wound high on his thigh to the glowing blade in her hand. "You're helpless; you can't stop me. If you don't lie still, I might accidentally put this burning knife on your manhood."

At those words, he stopped struggling and lay still as death.

Kimi gritted her teeth as she knelt by him and looked first at his naked manhood, then at the bloody wound on his thigh. She wasn't sure she had the nerve to do this, but it had to be done to stop the bleeding. She felt a little sick and swallowed hard. She looked down into his eyes. His virile, muscular body shone wet with perspiration. Very slowly she lowered the glowing knife toward the wound. She thought he would turn his face away so he couldn't see her do it, but he glared into her eyes.

Kimi took a deep breath, stilled her shaking hand, and applied the fiery knife against the wound in Hinzi's thigh.

He groaned, gasped, and bucked against his restraints, but he was powerless to stop her. The hot blade sizzled in the wet blood and the smell of burning flesh almost gagged her. She was going to be sick. No, she couldn't get sick, she had to finish this for his own good. Out of sheer desperation, she kept the glowing blade against the wound while his muscular, naked body arched and struggled against his bonds. Then mercifully, he fainted.

Kimi sighed heavily with relief and shook all over. At least now she could finish what needed to be done without worrying about him breaking free.

After she had applied healing herbs, she wrapped

his thigh in a scrap of trader's cloth. She took the gag from his mouth, reached for some cool water, and began to bath his face very gently.

His eyes opened slowly as if he weren't sure where he was as he looked up at her. "Lenore? Lenore, darling?"

A woman. He looked up at her and called some white woman's name. For some reason, it annoyed her. "I am called Kimimila—butterfly."

His face twisted with pain and anger as he seemed to realize where he was. "I must be delirious. For a moment, you almost looked like . . . Damn you, you little savage!"

"You are either very brave or very reckless," Kimi said, "I should beat you for your words."

A look crossed his face and Kimi shook her head. "Don't think about trying to escape. You can't even walk and it's a long way to any soldiers' fort. Your only chance of surviving is to be very obedient and behave like any slave so that you anger no one or they might change their mind and order you killed."

He didn't answer, either too weak or perhaps turning over the wisdom of her words in his mind. Anyway, staked out as he was, he didn't have a great deal of choice in the matter. As a man, all this must gall him, she thought—especially as a white man who seemed as if he were used to having people obey his orders without question.

Rand looked up at the girl. In the semidarkness, her face was shadowed, but from his hazy memory of the camp circle, he knew that she was pretty. In his delirium he had mistaken her for the elegant Lenore Carstairs. Lenore had black hair, too.

Wouldn't his fiancee be furious at the comparison? There was something unusual about this savage little bitch that pulled at his mind: What was it?

An unusually pretty Indian girl, he thought, with ebony braids and dark skin, but not nearly as dark as the others. His throbbing leg made his mind a blur.

At least he was alive, if only temporarily. Maybe that was something to be grateful for. He had fully expected to be gelded, scalped alive, and then slowly tortured to death with fire. From the mixed bits of Lakota and English he'd heard, he understood they were keeping him alive as a hostage and maybe to be used as a slave.

Rand shuddered at the thought. How ironic that a man who was heir to one of the biggest plantations and thoroughbred farms in Kentucky, complete with several hundred blacks, was a slave himself in this camp.

Rand tried to clear his mind enough to think about his options. Even if he got the ropes off, he couldn't travel far with that wound. He needed to bide his time until his leg healed enough to escape.

He watched the girl finish with the bandage. She resumed washing his body. He pretended to be unconscious so he could observe her without her realizing he did so. Very pretty and probably not more than fifteen or sixteen and a widow in mourning, judging from the cuts on her arms and her torn clothes. The Indians mated them young, he thought in disgust. A girl that age back home would be in school.

He felt her washing his naked skin and sighed. It felt so good, even though he was trussed and couldn't move. He was at the mercy of her whims, he knew. Whatever she did to him, probably no one in the camp would care or question. If she decided later to slash his throat and let him bleed to death, or geld him, torture him, or whatever, no one around here knew or cared that he was Randolph Erikson of Randolph Hall plantation or that he came from money and social position. In this camp, he was going to be a lowly slave, and he was helpless to do anything about it until his leg healed. A man who couldn't walk could not escape.

Her hands moved gently down his naked body as she washed him. He closed his eyes, tried to forget the throbbing pain of his thigh and concentrate on her hands touching him. In his mind, he imagined her as the slave, doing as she was ordered, washing every inch of his body while he lay back lazily and enjoyed it. It was also very arousing to have his wet, soapy flesh stroked by her small hands.

When he managed to escape, he might kidnap this girl and take her with him. Kimimila. Butterfly. Her small hands caressed his skin. Yes, Butterfly was a good name for her. If she were in a fancy brothel, she could earn good money for herself doing just what she was doing at this very moment, tantalizing a man with her velvet touch. He should be ashamed of himself for what he was thinking. It wasn't gallant at all. Besides she wasn't much more than a child.

He had not had a woman in a long time. Even with his leg aching, he looked at this girl's full, ripe lips and remembered the hot, honeyed taste when he had pulled her mouth down on his to shut her up in his futile escape attempt. Girl? She had a woman's body. As she moved, he saw the swell of her full breasts beneath the soft doeskin of her shift.

He must not think about that right now, or what he would like to do to this girl. He wouldn't even need to tie her up to enjoy the fantasy he imagined. He'd humble her all right. She had ordered him to beg like a dutiful dog. He knew about women; he had charmed enough of them. Before this was over, he intended that *she* would be the one who was doing the begging.

However, all that would take time—time for his leg to heal so he could escape. In the meantime, he would have to behave like a whipped, dominated pup, which didn't sit well with his upperclass arrogance.

When he finally got the chance, he'd teach this dark-haired little chit about obedience and domination. For now, all he could do was pretend to obey—to behave like a gelding so she would let down her guard. He would charm this Indian girl into helping him escape when he was up to it. Indian girl. Abruptly he remembered what it was that had tugged at his mind when he stared into her eyes—that incredible fact. Now he looked up into her face to make certain. The sunlight streaming through the tipi flap reassured him that he hadn't been either blind or crazy.

Indian girl? Rand's eyes widened and he cursed under his breath. She might be a half-breed, but no more than that. She looked down at him, and he almost smiled as he saw her face in the light. He had almost begun to believe he had imagined it, but now, there was clearly no mistake. Kimi had bright green eyes.

Four

Kimi struggled for the white words and finally spoke in a mixture of English and Lakota. "Hinzi soldier, what are you staring at?" She glared at him. "What is it?"

He seemed to recover his composure. "I—I, nothing," he said humbly and gave her a weak but engaging smile. "I reckon you are right. I'll do whatever you want, and hope that eventually the army will ransom me. Forgive me for staring. I haven't seen such a pretty girl in a long time."

She searched for the English words, bristling with annoyance at his attempt to flatter her. "Do you think me some stupid whore to be bought cheap as the soldiers do the Pawnee or Crow chits that hang around the forts?" She didn't trust him in this new meekness. She checked his bonds.

"I'm too weak to escape," he whispered, "even if I weren't tied up like a horse."

"Remember that," she cautioned. "You wouldn't get very far on that leg before you were recaptured. Besides, you are a slave, a hostage, which makes your position around this camp even lower than a horse."

Kimi touched the spirit object that hung between her full breasts under the doeskin shift, then reached for the quill work she was doing on a pair

67

of fine moccasins. She was completing them out of habit. They had been meant as a gift for Mato. She felt ashamed and guilty that she had not even given her husband very much thought since his death. Her thoughts and emotions had been concerned only with the white man.

She sneaked a look at him. He seemed to be drifting off to sleep. As young and strong as he was, that leg should heal enough for him to get around in a few days. Then he'd be a real threat if she didn't watch out.

In more than one way. Kimi tried not to look at the curve of his mouth, tried not to remember the taste of his lips when he had grabbed her in his escape attempt. She ought to turn the captive over to others to guard. But One Eye or any of the other families might mistreat him, and after all, with that wound, if he didn't get good care, he could still get gangrene and die. A dead hostage wasn't of much value or much assurance to the camp against attack.

He was asleep now, and she stared at him, thinking another girl might think him handsome. No doubt he was used to having any woman he wanted, playing with them as a bobcat might toy with its prey before devouring it. This Hinzi had obviously decided to try his charm on her, to get her to help him escape. Out of vengeance, she might play along, let him think he was charming her, but she was not the stupid little fool he seemed to think Indian girls were.

She went about her chores and let him sleep. Outside, when others asked about him, she shrugged and said she supposed he would live, as if it didn't much matter whether he did or not.

Only her mother seemed tight-lipped and hostile.

"I wish we had killed that soldier! Kimi, you should turn this prisoner over to the Shirt Wearers or the chiefs to look after. There might be talk with you spending so much time caring for him"

Kimi bristled. "Who would dare say such a thing? Our family reputation is without stain and I have only just buried a respected husband. I think only of the good of our people."

Wagnuka looked ashamed. "You are right. It's only that I fear . . ."

Kimi waited for her mother to finish, but the old woman only bit her lip.

"What is it you fear?" Kimi prompted.

"Nothing. I have said too much already. I fear to lose you, daughter."

"Is that it?" With her left hand, she patted her mother's arm reassuringly. "You think I would be swayed by some soldier's lying tongue? I have heard what happens to the Indian girls they seduce and keep around the forts for their pleasure."

"No," she shook her gray braids, "It's not just the soldiers. If the whites decide to take you away—"

"Mother, I will never leave you." Kimi put her arm around the bowed, thin shoulders. "Now stop worrying about this one wounded soldier. He's too weak to be of any real danger. Maybe later if the braves decide not to offer him for ransom, we might trade him to another tribe. Ever since the attack at Sand Creek a few moons ago, the Cheyenne have been eager to kill white soldiers."

"Your father joined them in a revenge raid only a little more than one moon later," Wagnuka remembered. "They nearly destroyed the town the whites call Julesburg. He spoke well of one big half-breed Dog Soldier, Iron Knife. Yes, our brothers, the Cheyenne, would deal harshly with any *wasicu* right now."

Kimi shrugged carelessly. "Perhaps should we run across the Dog Soldiers in our summer hunts, we will trade them the soldier for their revenge. It matters little to me."

Her mother nodded and shuffled off, apparently satisfied that her suspicions were unjustified; that it didn't matter one way or another to her daughter what happened to the Hinzi.

When Kimi returned to the tipi later, he was awake. "Feeling better?"

He pulled at his thongs. "I'd feel much better if I could free my hands for a little while. My muscles are cramping." He seemed to force himself to give her a charming smile.

Arrogant, dangerous, and trying to appear harmless. He must think of her as just another stupid squaw, Kimi frowned. She made no move to untie him.

"Why do you hate me so much?"

The question caught her off-guard, and she shook her ebony braids. "It is your people who hate mine. The soldiers come into our land, try to tell us where to live, what we must do, kill, hurt us—"

"I would never hurt you, Kimi, believe that." His handsome face seemed sincere, his drawling voice gentle.

"Your tongue is as forked as the snake's!" Kimi almost screamed it at him. "Yesterday, you helped kill my man!"

A look of sudden realization crossed his face. "So that's what this is all about! Believe me, Kimi, I didn't kill him. At heart, I'm not even a blue-coat."

70

"You wear the uniform. Do you take me for a fool?"

He looked weak and a little weary. "I reckon in your position, I wouldn't believe me, either." He moaned softly. "My — my leg hurts. If you would untie it, it wouldn't hurt so bad."

"Why should I care whether it hurts you or not?" Yet she felt a little tug at her heart for his pain, despite herself.

He stared at her a long moment. "I don't think you are as hard-hearted as you want me to believe. I saw the look on your face when the warrior handed you that knife."

"I still might do it. Don't goad me." She glared back.

"I think not," he said softly. "A good stallion is of more value than a gelding."

Kimi laughed bitterly. "Not to me."

"How do you know?" he whispered. "Have you ever ridden a stallion?" He stared deep into her eyes and his expression sent a heat running up and down her back that shook her a little.

She looked away first, furious at his double meaning. "I am a widow, of course I know."

"I think the circulation is giving out in that leg," he muttered. "Even a gelding is useless if he loses a leg."

That alarmed her "Maybe," she said grudgingly, "maybe I can at least untie your legs. After all, you are too hurt to escape."

"Pilamaya," he whispered. *Thank you.*

She untied his feet, too aware of the warmth of his body against her hand. Then she reached out and touched his forehead. "You're burning with fever."

He smiled weakly. "Perhaps I'll die and you'll

71

lose your valuable slave. . . ."

It was a possibility, Kimi thought, as she studied his wan face and watched him lick his dry lips. "Here, I have water."

She had to cradle his head against her to lift his face up so he could drink without choking. The heat of his fevered flesh seemed to burn through her deerskin shift and into the softness of her breasts. She had a sudden vision of his face cradled against her bare nipple, his lips opening against it. . . .

"You blush," he said, "why?"

"Nothing!" She put his head back down and pulled away from him. She must not think about that anymore. Perhaps it was only natural that a woman who had only yesterday been a wife, but had never been mated, should think much about a man's touch. "Why do you say you are not a blue-coat?"

"I wear the uniform. I am not really one of them," he said. The dim light gleamed on his yellow hair. "Have you heard that the white men now fight each other?"

Kimi nodded. "Yes, but we do not understand it. Sometimes we hear that those in blue fight those in coats the color of smoke."

"I was one of those in gray," Hinzi drawled with a sigh. "I was captured, locked in a bluecoat prison with some of my fellows. Many died or lost their minds. I began to think I might die, too, if I didn't get out."

Kimi nodded in sudden understanding. "We have heard about the soldiers' cages. Sometimes they put our warriors in them, too. Those who escape say it is a living death."

The soldier nodded. "It is. I watched men die

72

around me. Finally some of us were given a chance to save our lives by joining the bluecoats and coming West. I have no designs on your land. Those who wore gray only want to keep those in blue out of our country and live as we lived before."

"So now you invade my land and kill my people."

"It doesn't make much sense, does it?" he asked ruefully. "I wasn't sacrificing my life for a cause or even for love."

"No sacrifice is too great for love," Kimi whispered. She thought about her mother, her people. She had never known that kind of love with a man. She didn't even want to think about it.

The soldier looked listless and ill. A sheen of sweat gleamed on his handsome face. She reached out slowly and put her hand on his forehead. His fair skin burned with fever. She wished she could get a shaman to look at his wound, but a lowly captive was beneath the dignity of any important Lakota. Like a mongrel dog of no value, it mattered little to anyone whether this soldier slave survived. Why should it matter to her?

But of course it didn't, except for his value as a hostage. "Hinzi, are you hungry?"

He shook his head. "Not really."

"You must eat. I'll get you some broth." She went out, came back with some steaming meat broth, sat down by him.

He smiled. "I could feed myself better."

"I remember what happened last time you got an arm free," Kimi said wryly.

"I haven't forgotten either; believe that." His look seemed so earnest that she was almost touched. Then she remembered also that whites were no more to be trusted than a sly coyote. She began to spoon the broth between his lips.

"Left-handed," he said. "You're unusual in more ways than one."

She felt flustered in spite of herself. "No doubt you have kissed so many Indian girls, you wouldn't know one from another." She spooned broth into his mouth.

"Not many, but a few," he admitted with a shrug. "There are several who hang around the fort."

"Pawnee or Crow tramps!" Kimi sneered. "Their men sell themselves to the whites as scouts, their women trade their bodies for a little whiskey or a few trinkets."

"A man has needs," he said and his gaze swept over her body. There was no doubt what he meant.

She finished feeding him the broth and watched as he drifted back off to sleep. Needs. Did women have needs too? She looked at his prominent manhood and sighed. Kimi reached out and put her fingertips on his forehead ever so gently. His skin felt like fire. He moved restlessly in his sleep, writhed in a way that dislodged the bandage. What was it he saw in his dreams? She hummed her spirit song and it seemed to calm him. He stopped thrashing about and smiled ever so slightly.

Did he dream of another woman? Kimi looked at the virile, half naked man, wondering suddenly how it would feel to have this stallion make a woman of her? Then she felt her face burn and was relieved his eyes were closed so that he could not see her flush and wonder what had caused it.

For the next several hours, when she was not busy with chores, she checked on the delirious soldier, bathing his big body with cool water. She was glad no one saw her do this. Wagnuka would not approve of her touching the man's body. Not that he could harm her; his arms were still securely tied. In spite of his size and strength, he was a helpless prisoner, and she could do anything she wanted with him.

The thought that he was not really a bluecoat made her hate him a little less. Or was he lying? When he seemed restless, Kimi stroked his face and hummed her spirit song to him.

"Lenore . . ." he whispered, "Lenore . . ."

A white woman's name. The thought annoyed her. She was doing everything for him, and yet he dreamed of another woman, a civilized woman far away.

In his delirium, he twisted again and Kimi took a cool cloth and stroked his face, sponging his half-naked body, trying to quiet him. If he kept moving and twisting, he might tear open that leg wound, and he was weak from loss of blood already.

She tried not to look at his manhood or his mouth. Kimi brushed her left hand across her lips absently, remembering the taste and heat when he had put his lips on hers to stifle her cry of alarm.

"Lenore . . ." he whispered again.

Lenore. What did the name mean or did it even have a meaning? Hadn't she heard the word before? Of course she had. Maybe he had whispered it last night when he was off in the Spirit World. Ever so gently, Kimi touched his face and hummed her song to quiet him, wondering as she did so what he saw in his dream.

Rand twisted restlessly, trying to make some sense of the kaleidoscope of images that blurred and ran through his fevered mind. Hot. He was so hot. He tried to put his thoughts in order, but they ran together in a tangled vision. Where was he? What was happening to him? In his troubled mind, he drifted back. . . .

Lenore Carstairs was the most beautiful and richest girl in the county, Rand thought, sitting next to her on the wicker settee near the camelia bush in the big glass conservatory.

She touched his face with her fan and pouted. "For pity's sake, Rand, dear, it looks like you could see me more often."

Through the French doors that opened into the mansion, soft sound of old Mrs. Carstairs' piano floated on the early spring air. Lenore hummed the tune absently and played with the lace of her emerald silk dress.

"Lenore, I know there hasn't been much action around here, but in case you've forgotten, there's a war going on."

Lenore shook her ebony curls and fluttered her fan, flirting with heavily lashed golden eyes. "Now don't get testy with me over your little old war," she cooed. "After all, you didn't have to go. Most of the other rich boys paid a substitute."

Had she always been so frivolous and empty-headed as she seemed now? *Frivolous and empty-headed.* That was also a good description of himself when the war began. Rand winced when he remembered why, with Kentucky staying with the Union, he had decided to join the Confederate cavalry. He had thought the Rebels more dashing, their uniforms more attractive. Still he didn't really believe in slavery, although his parents owned several hundred slaves. Talk about frivolous! Rand had thought of war as only an exciting adventure for a bored rich man's son. He was three kinds of a fool. Since then he had seen blood and misery and death. The grand adventure had become a horror.

"For pity's sake, Rand," her cooing voice became strident. "Are you listening to me?"

He nodded without speaking. Suddenly it was amazing how much the wealthy heiress sounded like his mother or his sister, Vanessa. Less than a year ago, he had been too madly in love with Lenore to even notice such little failings. For the first time, he noticed the beauty had large feet. Maybe he was the one who was changing.

"I declare, Rand, what ever are you thinking?"

He gave her his most charming smile. "Why, I was just thinking what a lucky man I am to be engaged to the prettiest girl in Kentucky, and wishing this war was over so we could have that big wedding."

Lenore's golden eyes peeked at him from behind her fan coquettishly. "You are so gallant, Randolph Erikson, and so dashing in that gray uniform. Reckon you could wear it at the ceremony, maybe we could walk out under crossed swords and all?"

Rand slapped his riding quirt against his leg. "I've got other things to think of right now, but you plan the wedding any way you want. Will Judge Hamilton walk you down the aisle?"

"Reckon he will, since he's a long time friend of Grandmother's."

"It may be a while before we can schedule this wedding, my dear." Rand shook his head. "Things don't look good for the South."

Lenore whacked him on the arm with her fan. "For pity's sake, Rand, don't sound so gloomy! After all, Kentucky stayed with the Union, so even if the South loses, you'll come out all right."

He managed to stifle the urge to grab the fan out of her hand and tear it up. Instead Rand leaned out to pick a snowy blossom off the big camelia bush, tucked it in her low-cut bodice. "Not nearly so creamy white as your skin," he gave her a charming smile.

She fluttered her fan and giggled. "You are such a rake, you little ol' charmer, you! This was my mother's favorite flower. I thought I might use camelias in my wedding bouquet or do you think magnolias would be more elegant?"

"Whatever you want." Abruptly the white flowers made him think of all the dead faces he had seen, pale and bloodless, the eyes staring sightlessly at the sky.

"Randolph, dear, you're frowning." She touched his face with her fan. "Whatever are you thinking?"

He blurted his thoughts. "I was thinking how silly it sounds to be discussing the proper flowers for a wedding when not too many miles away, men are dying by the thousands. None of the people we know seem to care as long as their rich, idle life doesn't change."

"And what's wrong with that?" Lenore pouted prettily. "You are beginning to sound like my grandmother. Did you know she has freed all our slaves and is actually paying them to work?"

He admired Elizabeth Carstairs. Besides having been a prominent widow in this county for all these years, she seemed to have a steel to her backbone and an independence that her granddaughter

78

lacked. "When this is over, Lenore, I think all the slaves will be freed, so maybe it just makes good business sense to do so now."

Her pretty mouth dropped open. "Why, you sound like an abolitionist! I'll bet your mother doesn't know you feel this way!"

"No, and I'd just as soon you didn't tell my sister. She'll report it right back." He turned the quirt over and over in his hands. Vanessa was Lenore's best friend, and since the two big plantations were only a few miles apart, the girls saw a lot of each other.

She sighed as if she thought him tiresome and a bit stupid. "Rand, dear, one of the reasons Kentucky stayed with the Union, as did the other three border states, was that Lincoln isn't trying to do away with slavery. His purpose is to force the states that seceded back into the Union. His Emancipation Proclamation only applies to those states."

He reached out, brushed a wisp of ebony curl away from her flawless face "You are so naive. Believe me when I tell you that when this war is over, there will be sweeping changes. There won't be any more slaves."

She went deathly pale. "But that will change all our lives!"

"Maybe our lives need to be changed."

"But all our friends like it just the way it has always been, fox hunts and gala balls, trips to Louisville and Memphis. Why, I've hardly been able to buy anything nice since this stupid old war started."

"A shame that the elegant ladies have been inconvenienced." He tried to keep the irony out of his voice, but he knew some of the women in the hardest hit areas of the South were living on cornmeal, sweet potatoes, and maybe even an occasional rat. "A rich man's war and a poor man's fight," Rand muttered.

"For pity's sake, don't be so gloomy." Lenore reached out, picked a blossom from the big camelia bush.

It was steamy hot in here among all the flowers and ferns. Rand ran his finger around the gray collar of his uniform. This giant white camelia, growing directly in the ground by the wicker settee was Lenore's grandmother's special interest. It had been here since the conservatory was added to the east wing of the mansion when Rand was a small boy at neighboring Randolph Hall.

He reached to kiss her. "You're right, my dear. I wouldn't want to burden such a ravishing belle with such terrible problems. After the war so we can have the biggest wedding the county has ever seen."

"Rand, really!" she pulled away from him. "After all, we aren't married. It isn't quite nice—"

"I do apologize," he pulled back. "Sometimes I forget myself. You are so very pretty." *A doll,* he thought, *an empty-headed china doll.*

She simpered behind her fan. "Have you met your sister's new beau? Perhaps we can have a double wedding."

"I've met him." He stood up, slapping his leg with the quirt. "If it pleases y'all to do so. Where'd she meet him anyhow?"

"She was in Louisville and he came up to her in a shop and introduced himself, said he had known you in the war."

Had he known Shelby Merson? "I met so many people over the past several years. I reckon I just don't remember him."

"Well, for pity's sake, you should! He got that

80

limp from a wound at Shiloh and he's got a bunch of medals." She looked at Rand's gray uniform, devoid of decorations.

"He wasn't in uniform when I met him the other night."

"Well, of course not, silly boy." She fanned herself vigorously. "Because of that leg wound, he's been discharged and gone back into the business world. You know he's from a rich family of cotton brokers in Baltimore."

Rand frowned. "Has anyone met any of his family?"

"No, but you can tell by the elegant cut of his clothes and that big diamond stick pin in his tie, that he's very substantial. He's bought the plantation between yours and Carstairs Oaks."

"Isn't that convenient? Now all three pieces of property will be connected by marriage," Rand said.

"Do you think we all haven't talked about that?" Her golden eyes gleamed with greed. "There's bound to be a big boom after the war ends, no matter which side wins. We'll have the biggest land holdings in the county. Just one great big happy family."

Rand grunted noncommittally. In truth, he didn't like Shelby Merson from the one meeting. The dandy was several years older than he was, shorter, but a little heavier. Maybe it was only that when the man smiled, his hazel eyes didn't. Or maybe it was that he used a strongly perfumed macassar hair tonic that made his dark hair gleam. Shelby was just a little too well-dressed for a country gentleman, and he didn't care much about horses. Fine thoroughbreds were the lifeblood of this area, and Rand loved good horses.

". . . and what do you think, Rand?"

"Beg your pardon?" Startled, he stared at the pretty golden-eyed girl on the bench.

"You're getting just like your father, Rand Erikson. You weren't even listening to me!" Lenore snapped her fan shut and stood up, her hoops rustling under the pale emerald dress.

"Yes, I was listening," he lied. Was he getting just like his father? The thought scared him because he seldom remembered seeing his father smile. Jon Erikson drank too much and seemed to pay little attention to what went on around him, living the same aimless life as the other wealthy plantation owners.

"For pity's sake, Rand, let's not argue, not with you due back tonight at your post." She gave him a pouting smile and leaned forward for a prim, ladylike kiss. "We'll work all this out later."

She planned to do just as she pleased, Rand thought, as his mother and sister had always done. No wonder Father drank. Well, maybe that was the way of women, at least, most of the women he knew. Maybe he was crazy to hope for something more than an empty-headed, pretty wife. He pulled her close and kissed her with passion, knowing he'd regret it.

She jerked away from him, petticoats rustling. "Now, Rand, I'm not some slave girl you can paw over."

Her breasts swelled over the bodice of emerald silk and he needed a woman. He wanted to put his hands on her breasts and kiss her with wild abandon. He wanted to throw her down in the dirt under the camelia bush and rip her lace drawers off. He wanted to—

Was he losing his mind? Lenore was prim and

82

very proper, and only twenty-one years old. If he even tried to kiss her passionately, she would promptly hit him across the face with her damned fan. His fiancee was every inch a lady.

He pulled back. "I don't know what came over me, my dear, I apologize." He took her free hand, kissed it.

"You naughty boy!" Lenore stepped away from him with her mincing walk, smiled teasingly. "Men are such animals, aren't they? I'll allow you to do that to me a few times after we're married."

"A few times?"

"Well, for pity's sake, every time we want a child," she blushed and drew herself up. "It's not even proper to talk about things like this, Rand."

Proper. Yes, Lenore was oh, so proper. She would be just like his mother and his sister, Vanessa. But weren't all women of quality like that?

Lenore whirled about the conservatory, laughing and humming the tune that drifted from the music room—an ancient Christmas carol: "What Child Is This?"

No, it had another name. He had heard Elizabeth Carstairs sing it. "Greensleeves," yes, that was it.

"Greensleeves." He shook his head, trying to make sense of his jumbled thoughts. Emerald silk, golden eyes like a cat's. Then why did green eyes haunt him so? Lenore was humming again and slipping away from him, teasing him a little as she faded into the shadows of the conservatory. Why was he so hot and why did his leg hurt so much? Where was Lenore disappearing to? He could still hear her humming her grandmother's music, but he couldn't find her; maybe she was hiding among the flowers, among the camelias and the oleanders in the conservatory. Camelias? No, *Kimimila*. That didn't make any sense to him.

"Lenore? Come back! Where are you?" He reached out to catch her and suddenly he felt her hand gently stroking his brow. Her small fingers felt gentle and cool on his fevered face. He was so hot, so very hot. She hummed the ancient tune and stroked his naked body with a wet, cool cloth.

No, that couldn't be right; Lenore wouldn't perform such a distasteful task, she'd call for a slave. Slave? No, Rand was the slave. Whose?

His mind was a jumble and his leg hurt. He tried to move his hands, but he seemed tied in place. Rand opened his eyes very slowly, wondering where he was. A tent of some kind and a green-eyed, dark-skinned girl who looked vaguely familiar. "Lenore?"

"No, Camelia," she said. At least that's what the word sounded like. "Kimi. Remember?"

He blinked, stared up at her. Her ebony hair hung in braids, but her eyes were green, not golden.

It all came back to him with a rush. He had left Carstairs Oaks only to be captured a few weeks later. He'd spent months in that Yankee prison, then grabbed the chance to save himself by joining the Union army to fight the Indians.

Indians. He moaned aloud, then cursed softly. Everything came back to his memory. The girl who bent over him, stroking his perspiring body with a cool cloth, was beautiful. Rand remembered now who she was and why he was here. He was a Sioux slave, a captive in this camp. Instead of the elegant white lady with skin as pale as the camelia blossom, he was at the mercy of this primitive, half-

84

breed girl who couldn't be more than fifteen or sixteen years old. He was going to have to charm this pretty savage to save his life.

There was just one question he wanted to ask. "Music . . . I thought I heard familiar music."

Kimi shrugged. "It is my song," she stopped humming, "my spirit song. It has always been mine to sing."

Simple enough explanation, Rand thought, for such an ancient, universal song. Perhaps a passing missionary or priest had taught it to her. Yes, that was a reasonable explanation as to why a half-breed Sioux girl out in the middle of the wilderness knew the tune to "Greensleeves."

Five

Old Wagnuka lay staring into the darkness of the tipi, listening to Kimi's gentle breathing as the girl slept. Wagnuka wished she could sleep, but her mind was on the hated white soldier tied up in the lodge Mato had meant to share with his bride.

Hinzi had been in this camp over a week now and Wagnuka felt more uneasy every day. At first she had hoped he would die of his injuries, but the more he suffered, the more Kimi worried over him and looked after him. She said it was because he was important as a hostage, and maybe even she believed that. Wagnuka did not. She had seen the looks they gave each other, even as they hurled angry, defiant words. The old Sioux woman was wise in the ways of men and women. She had lived a long, long time. Kimi was not going to be hurt by a white man as she herself had had her heart broken.

Quietly she sat up, trying to decide what to do. If she could get away with it, she would sneak in and kill the soldier. She would have no qualms about driving a dagger deep in his lying heart. She would close her eyes and pretend it was that long ago white fur trapper. However, not only would that be defying the old chiefs' orders, it would upset Kimi and make her hate Wagnuka if she found out who had done it.

She would do anything to protect her beloved daughter—anything. No sacrifice was too great. She sneaked outside into the warm spring night. Her old bones always ached but not as badly with the warmer weather This year, the warmer weather brought little relief. How many winters had she seen? Sixty? Seventy?

Time had a way of running faster and faster as one season blended into the next. How many more years she had left, Wagnuka didn't know or even care. She had had her share of love, and heartache, too. Her husband Ptan was no doubt waiting on the Spirit Road for her. All that kept her here now was that she worried lest she die leaving her daughter without the protection of a good husband. Right now, the two women were living off the generosity of good hunters such as One Eye and Gopher, Ptan's friends. This couldn't last. Kimi needed her own man to see that she and her old mother were well-fed in the coming months.

Somewhere sungmanitu, the coyote, howled and its mate answered back. The prairie breeze carried the scent of wild flowers and camp fire smoke. Wagnuka listened a long moment to the sound of the horse herd grazing near the camp. She knew all the sentries on duty since they were young boys. The camp and its herds were safe from surprise as long as mighty braves like those watched for enemies.

What to do about the white soldier? Had he guessed the secret about Kimimila? If he were ransomed by the white soldiers, would he tell the Great White Father about the girl with green eyes? All these years, Wagnuka and her husband had made sure no white men got a good look at Kimi. If they did, they would take her away. She knew how white men lusted after pretty girls and took them with no more thought than a mustang stallion would top a stray mare. She had lost one child to the whites. She did not intend to lose another.

With a mutilated hand, she stroked her wrinkled arm, still marred with knife cuts of mourning for her son-in-law and scars of mourning for her dead husband. What to do about the Hinzi? If she dare not kill him, what else could she do? If he escaped, he might bring the soldiers back with him to take the pretty Kimi away. On the other hand, if he stayed, his smiles might turn the innocent girl's head until she believed his avowals of love. The soldier would treat her like white men always treated Indian women. Not many warriors would take a girl who carried a white man's child in her belly.

If she dare not kill him nor set him free to return with soldiers to take Kimi away, what could she do? Kimi was dear to her She had lost so many children to this harsh life.

Several of the grazing horses whinnied again. Wagnuka looked around the sleeping camp and stared at the tipi where the soldier slept. He was already attempting to make friends with the small children of the camp, learning the Lakota language. It was only a matter of time until some naive girl such as Kimi either trusted him enough to let him escape or ended up in his blankets. Wagnuka had no such illusions about the whites; she had lived too long, seen too much. A trapper had taught Wagnuka more than just the white man's language. Whatever it took to stop this same threat to her daughter, Wagnuka was going to do.

Tomorrow night. Yes, that was the right time. Tomorrow she would make plans. This decision made, she hobbled back to her tipi. Kimi had not stirred. With any luck and some prayers to Wakan Tanka, the girl need never know what had really happened or that Wagnuka had any part in his escape attempt.

At dawn, after feeding the white slave and seeing that he was much improved, Kimi made her decision. "You are not hurt as badly as you pretend," she declared, "and other members of the tribe have already been more than generous in providing food."

He looked at her, curiosity in his blue eyes. "What is it you want of me?"

"I am going to trade your labor to others for the things my mother and I need."

He drew himself up indignantly, cursed under his breath. "You can't treat me like a damned slave! Do you know who I am? My father is one of the richest men in all Kentucky and my mother is a Randolph, the most aristocratic family in the old South."

"You *are* a lowly slave," Kimi said coldly, "and don't forget it. You will do as I order."

"Suppose I won't?" He had just a touch of arrogant defiance in his drawl.

Kimi shrugged. "Then I will beat you, just as you might do a black slave."

"I don't beat my slaves," he snapped.

"Do as you are told, and I won't beat you either," Kimi said. Although she didn't want to admit it, even to herself, she had been more than a little annoyed with him over his whispering the name of that white girl in his delirium. No doubt she herself must look like some primitive, ugly savage beside this elegant Lenore. "You need to learn better manners and a little humility."

For a long moment, she expected an outburst, but instead he took a deep breath, as if struggling to control himself, and gave her a charming smile. "Of course. Forgive me for thinking my life is my own. I forget my life depends on your good will."

She wasn't to be fooled by his attempts to charm her. Kimi called in an old warrior who owned a pair of leg-irons and chains from the time he had spent in the white man's stockade for stealing a little food when hungry. With the heavy irons on his ankles and his hands chained behind him, the big white soldier could be used as a beast of burden around the camp without fear that he might get his hands on a weapon or be of any danger.

His ragged blue pants had been torn away. All he wore now as he stood there awaiting her orders was a small breechcloth Kimi had found for him and the pair of moccasins she had made for Mato.

The brief bit of leather barely hid his prominent maleness. It angered her that she couldn't keep her emotions in check when she looked at the man's body. She remembered again the taste of his mouth, the feel of his yellow hair so much like the silk of the corn the Sioux's hated enemies grew. His hair was getting a bit long for a white man. She stared at the light-colored hair on his massive chest and wondered how it would feel brushing ever so gently against the swollen tips of her nipples.

When she looked up, he almost seemed to be smiling as if he had read her erotic thoughts. An angry, hot flush rushed to her burning cheeks. "That leg needs exercise to strengthen it anyway." She picked up a small quirt. "All right, yellow-haired slave, your work as a beast of burden awaits you."

She heard him swear softly under his breath.

"Hinzi, what is it you say?"

"Nothing, mistress," he ducked his head humbly. "I await your orders."

The soldier was stronger than even Kimi had thought. With a harness around his big chest, he dragged wood from the creek to the camp on a travois and carried sacks of dried meat on his back while small children trailed along behind him curiously.

Others in the camp nodded approval. "The white slave is strong and it is only just that he labor to provide meat for the widow of the slain warrior the soldiers killed."

Kimi felt a little uneasy working him like a beast of burden, but it seemed to still his arrogant attitude, and her mother smiled for the first time in days. More than that, Kimi wanted to do favors for those in the camp who had been giving the three food, and Hinzi did eat a lot.

What she didn't want to admit even to herself was that she was getting a bit of satisfaction out of his humiliation. She would teach him to look at her and think of some beautiful white girl.

At noon, she let him rest a moment by the creek and brought him a bowl of stew. He looked from it to her. "Are you going to unchain me so I can eat?"

"Beasts of burden don't need to use their hands," Kimi said coldly, "and you aren't dangerous with your hands behind you. Eat with your hands chained or starve."

The look on his face told her that if he could, he would grab her, rub her face in the stew, but he took a deep breath. "Yes, mistress. Whatever you say." He went down on his knees, ate out of the bowl like a dog. With his hands chained behind him, he could do nothing else. Then he hobbled to the creek, chains jangling and put his face down to the water, lapped it up. "I'm too tired to work any more," he announced.

"There's a little more to do," Kimi commanded, "and you will work until I say you can stop."

He acted as if he might argue, then kept his silence as she put the harness on him again. When he threw his strength into the load of buffalo hides he dragged on the travois, his muscles rippled, and she saw the tendons of his lean, almost naked hips quiver as he threw his weight against the harness.

He was deliberately working as slowly as possible, Kimi thought; an obstinate show of defiance. Before she thought, she snapped the little quirt at him as she would a lagging horse. She hadn't meant to, but the tip of the lash caught him across the back.

He glared over his shoulder with eyes as cold as blue ice, swearing softly. The anger on his face was frightening. "If I could get out of these chains, I'd show you—"

"What is it you say?" She demanded, wincing at the red weal she had put across his skin. She hadn't really meant to hit him. There was something about his whispering that other woman's name, defying Kimi that infuriated her. She would break this stallion's spirit. Maybe when he seemed more like a mild beast of burden than a man, she could free herself of this terrible attraction she felt and get on with finding herself a new husband among the braves.

That night she fed him, left him chained in his lodge. "You did well today," she said. "Other women have asked that you haul things for them tomorrow. No wonder whites keep slaves. It is useful to have one around to do heavy work."

"Go to hell."

"What did you say?"

He seemed to struggle with himself, gritting his teeth. "I said I would be happy to work as a horse tomorrow for my owner, if only she won't whip me with her quirt again."

Kimi retired for the night to her own tipi. She lay listening to her mother snore and thinking about the soldier. She had meant to break his spirit, humiliate him for his obvious attempts in trying to charm her into letting down her guard so he could escape. More than that, she was a bit jealous of this privileged girl so far away that the Hinzi lusted after.

After a long time, Kimi finally dropped off to sleep, and her dreams were full of images of the soldier's lean hips straining with power as he pulled the travois, of the muscles in his back cording as he threw himself against the harness. In her mind, she saw the two of them in a solitary area near the creek. He would break his chains and turn on her, wrench the quirt from her hand, grab her. She would try to scream for help, but his tongue would be in her mouth so that she could only moan. They would go down together on the soft grass in a tangle of warm skin, cold, steel chains and his hot mouth all over her bare body. His lean, hard hips quivered with power as he rammed into her, holding onto her breasts with his big hands.

Old Wagnuka lay very still, listening. Kimi's gentle breathing told her the girl finally slept after hours of restless turning. Now was the time to put her plan in action. She had sensed the sexual ten-

93

sion between the two; it crackled like summer lightning waiting to explode violently into fire. If Wagnuka didn't do something about Hinzi soon, he would end up mating with Kimi if he had to take her by force. The way Kimi had been looking at the lean, almost naked man, Wagnuka was afraid he wouldn't have to use force. Kimi was a ripe young woman, probably eighteen winters old, and the mating urge was strong in her loins. If she didn't take a husband soon, she might succumb to the charm of this white soldier whose manhood hung as big and heavy as some herd stallion's.

She got up and sneaked from the tipi into the night.

Rand came awake suddenly, listening. He'd thought he'd heard someone's step. He lay there a long time, holding his breath. No sound. Maybe he had only imagined it. While he had been pretending to be more injured than he was the last few days as his leg healed quickly, he still hadn't figured out a way to escape, and he knew that there were Sioux in this camp who would like to see him dead.

For instance, Kimi's mother. He'd seen the way she looked at him. Well, maybe the old woman had good reason. If Kimi were a half-breed as Rand suspected, obviously the old woman had been seduced and betrayed by a white man many years ago and feared Rand would do the same to Kimi.

Not that he hadn't thought about it. In fact he'd thought about it a lot. Kimi might be his only hope of escaping this Indian camp. If he could charm her into falling in love with him, she might help him escape. It would help to have his hands free. Before he'd become engaged to Lenore, he had been a rake among wenches and street sluts. He planned to stay true to Lenore after they were married, but it would be a difficult thing to do when he was a virile man and she was as cold as she was chaste. Rand was skilled with women. If he could ever stroke Kimi, caress her breasts, kiss her mouth, he was certain he could make her fall in love with him, and she could be cajoled into helping him escape.

Rand cursed under his breath. How in the hell could he do that when he was kept chained up like some runaway black slave? Rand pulled at his bonds, hoping he could work them down over his hands, but he had big hands. Like a beast of burden, he thought bitterly, Rand Erikson, the dashing only son of one of the richest families in the county. Only the Carstairs had more wealth.

What if he couldn't escape and the army never found out the Indians had him? No doubt they had already given him up for dead. He might spend the rest of his life as a Sioux slave, used for heavy labor, chained up at night like a workhorse. At least he hadn't been gelded, but if he didn't stop looking at Kimi the way he'd been doing, her mother might take care of that. He couldn't help it. Part of it was her arrogance in the way she treated him and refused to succumb to his charm. The other? Surely an aristocrat who was engaged to an elegant belle like Lenore shouldn't be so drawn to an Indian savage. Would she be so different than with other women he'd had? One thing was certain, it wouldn't be like it would with the prim, ladylike Lenore. The weal across his back still stung. Or was it the humiliation of being whipped like a cart pony?

He'd had some troubled dreams the last couple of nights in which the half-breed girl was the one in chains, begging him not to use his quirt. He'd teach her humiliation if he ever got the chance. More than that, he wanted to teach her about white man's passion. As young as she was, he ought to be ashamed of himself, thinking like that, but it wasn't as if she was an innocent school girl.

The step again. He saw only a shadow, but he tensed into readiness, his heart pounding as he realized someone was sneaking into the tipi. He pulled at his cuffs again, cursing silently. If someone had come to kill him, he was helpless to do much about it.

"Soldier, are you awake?"

The old woman, Kimi's mother. Now just what was she doing sneaking into his lodge? Suppose she had come to kill him?

"Yes, I'm awake," Rand said cautiously, his muscles tensed to fight as best he could should she have a knife. "What is it you want?"

"I want you out of this camp."

He laughed without mirth. "Well, I reckon at least we agree on something. Believe me, there's nothing I'd rather do than leave this camp."

"If I help you escape, will you go away and never come back?"

Immediately Rand sensed a trick. "You hate me," he said. "That's apparent. Why should you want to help me?"

"Help you?" she scoffed, "Not for you; for my own selfish reasons. I have seen the way you look at my daughter, the way she is beginning to look at you."

"You're mistaken," Rand flexed his shoulders, trying to find a comfortable position, "She hates me. I think she would kill me without a second thought."

The old woman made a skeptical grunt. "I must protect my daughter. I know how a white man might desire her, use her with no more thought than satisfying his needs."

I'll bet you do, Rand thought, but he said nothing, thinking only about Kimi's green eyes. Now he knew why the old woman spoke a little English. Maybe a long time ago, Wagnuka had been a pretty young maiden and a soldier or white trader had whispered honeyed promises in her ear, got her with child and abandoned her. Instead, he said, "You would risk defying the Shirt Wearers to free me, help me escape?"

The old woman hesitated. "It is a risk I take to get you away from my daughter. I love her. No sacrifice is too great. Kimimila is young, innocent in the ways of the white world. It is much better that she marry some good warrior and stay among the Sioux rather than be taken to some fort or town to be thrown away after you tire of her."

Would he tire of her? He imagined the hot-blooded little half-breed in his bed at night, clawing his back and moaning for more like the little primitive savage she was. Of course he had forgotten about the elegant Lenore. And Kimi would hardly fit into upper class Kentucky society. No, of course any long term commitment was out of the question. "Wagnuka, what are your plans?"

"I have stolen the key to your chains," she whispered, "and I have tied a horse over the rise near that wild plum bush thicket. By morning, you can

97

be far away and no one will ever know how you escaped."

His heart began to beat hard with hope. "It's a long way, I'll need a weapon, some food and water."

"No, no weapon." She shook her head. "I don't intend to take the chance on your killing any of my people, but here's a small bag of food and a water skin."

"All right, that will have to do." He turned, offering his wrists and she hesitated a long moment as if not sure she was doing the right thing. "Come on, come on!"

She unlocked his wrist and ankle chains, handed him the food and water. "Go now. You know where the horse waits."

For just a moment, it occurred to him that he could use a hostage, then decided against it. For one thing, the old woman would be a lot of trouble and would slow him down. Besides, it didn't seem honorable to trick her that way after she had freed him. He was still a Southern gentleman to the core, he thought wryly.

He stood up, flexed his cramped muscles. "What about you?"

Wagnuka shrugged as she turned to slip from the tipi. "I will return to my bed. In the morning, there will be a big outcry over your disappearance, but no one will suspect me. After all, everyone knows I hate you for the death of my son-in-law."

"Wagnuka, believe me, I didn't kill that warrior."

In the moonlight, her face was grim. "Mato is dead because white soldiers have come into our country as invaders. You are guilty because you ride with those soldiers."

He had never thought of it that way before.

Rand was only trying to survive and that's what the Sioux were trying to do, too. He saw the Indians in a little different light at that moment.

"Maybe," he said softly, "with my wound, the army will let me go back to my people who live far, far from here."

"You have the same soft, drawling voice he had," Wagnuka said, "I wonder if he came from your country?"

"Who?"

"Kimi's father."

"What?"

"Nothing. I said nothing," she answered, "and he is dead anyway." The old woman made a hurrying gesture just before she turned and fled in the darkness. "Go while you still have plenty of night and before the storms come."

As they stepped outside, a rush of cool air blew past them. In the distance, thunder rolled.

Cautiously, Rand looked around as Wagnuka disappeared into the darkness. The camp was asleep. Only an occasional dog barked in the stillness.

Over the rise and behind the wild plum thicket, she had said. Rand crept along between the tipis, fearful less he alert some dog or run into a stray sentinel.

He thought about Kimi and her mysterious father as he slipped through the shadows. Some bluecoat from the South before the war, he thought. He wondered how the old woman knew the man was dead? She must be a lot younger than she looked, but then this hard life was enough to age a woman. He would have guessed Wagnuka was almost as old as Lenore's grandmother, too old to be Kimi's mother. The pretty half-breed surely wasn't any older than fifteen or sixteen.

Kimi. In spite of everything, he wanted her body as he had never lusted after another woman. Too bad he couldn't take her with him. What would happen to her after he had sated his lust? He hadn't thought about that, no more than her errant father had probably thought about what would happen to the Indian girl he took.

Rand found he was holding his breath as he crept along. Any moment, he expected some brave to come out of a tipi or return from guarding the big pony herd and see him, raise the alarm. They would probably kill him without giving him a chance to surrender.

He shook his head, No, he'd rather be killed quickly than surrender and return to being a Sioux slave. He wished he had a weapon. Even a small knife would be better than nothing, but unless he tried to sneak into a tipi and steal one, there was no way. The risk wasn't worth it. Far better to get to that horse and ride away as fast as he could. With any luck, Rand could be almost to the fort before anyone in the Indian camp realized he was gone.

Up ahead, he saw the horse staked out right where she said it would be. Rand paused, breathing hard, feeling perspiration run down his skin. Yet his mouth was so dry, he had a hard time swallowing.

The wind blew cool and he smelled rain on the breeze. Off in the distance, lightning crackled all orange and green against a black sky. There was going to be a storm later tonight all right, and when it came, the thunder might disturb horses and dogs and get the whole camp roused. Someone might discover the captive was missing a lot sooner than they would otherwise. Rand cursed silently at the thought.

Now why would she tie the horse in such an obvious spot? Rand paused even as he was about to run across the prairie toward it. The horse was a gray, its coat shining in the pale light. It hadn't been a good choice, Rand thought with a frown: too visible. Or had she planned it that way?

The natural caution that had kept him alive in the Yankee prison and on the hostile Dakota plains took over and he thought for a long moment. Instead of running across the ground to the horse, he crept around behind the plum thicket, listening.

He heard a man step on a twig, break it. A man's voice said in Lakota, "Be careful about making noise. He should be here any moment."

"Are we ready for him?"

The other grunted in the affirmative.

An ambush. Rand's heart almost stopped. That old woman had set a trap to kill him. She hadn't planned to help him escape at all, but to ambush him as he tried.

Rand cursed under his breath, trying to decide what to do. There was no way he could overpower or deal with those several armed warriors in the plum bushes. He was going to have to do something different. But what?

Rand turned and sneaked back through the camp. He needed a weapon. Was there anything in his lodge he could use? The chains. What could he do with the chains? No, the rattle of them would hinder their limited use as a weapon. He was unarmed. In the shadows of his tipi, he paused, trying to decide what to do next.

Suppose he did the unexpected and went the other direction, through the scattering of cottonwoods over by the little creek? If he had a horse, he might sneak away and let his ambushers wait vainly in the plum thicket all night or at least until the coming storm drove them to shelter.

Maybe he could take a hostage. No, he shook his head. There was no one out and about except the warriors waiting in ambush and the lone guards off in the distance over the next rise guarding the big pony herd. Rand paused in the shadows, looking around the camp.

There were a few of the very best horses right here in camp. Many of the warriors, fearful of having their best war pony stolen, kept it tied right outside their lodge. To steal a man's best pony right from under his nose was a triumph all the tribes enjoyed and delighted in retelling around the camp fire

Tonweya. Scout. He recognized the big buckskin stallion belonging to One Eye tied out before his lodge. Rand would be taking a double risk to creep into the center of the big camp, take One Eye's favorite horse and try to escape without alerting anyone. But if he could, he had a much better chance of getting away. While One Eye owned several good war ponies, Scout was clearly the best and fastest mount in the whole camp. Besides it would be a good joke on the brave.

He had to sneak past Kimi's tipi to reach that horse. Taking a deep breath, Rand crept through the shadows. By her lodge, he paused, listening. Old Wagnuka's snoring drifted on the night air.

He might after all have use for a hostage, and it would serve the old woman right if he took Kimi to pay her back for her deceit. He paused by the tipi and shook his head. No, it wasn't worth the risk. He had to admit that there had been something in his mind besides just needing a hostage.

102

He would forget about revenge and the satisfaction of humbling that arrogant little savage. He needed to concentrate on just escaping alive and returning to civilization.

Abruptly, Kimi crept out of her lodge and looked toward Rand's as if trying to decide whether to go there. Rand stood close enough in the shadows to reach out and touch her. He studied her expression in the next flash of lightning, wondering suddenly if she had been in on her mother's plot. The thought made angry bile rise in his throat.

Rand made his decision in a heartbeat. He did need a hostage. And here she stood.

Six

Rand watched the girl pause in the darkness. The distant lightning outlined the soft curves of her silhouette and he recalled the taste of her lips, the feel of her soothing fingertips on his fevered face. Frowning, he also remembered the leather harness, the chains, and the welt on his back. Sneaking up behind her, he reached out, clasped one hand over her mouth, while the other arm went around her small waist to jerk her up against his big frame.

She fought him, making muffled cries. Then her sharp teeth came down hard on his fingers. He dared not let go. All he could do was curse under his breath and hang on. How had he ever got mixed up with this vixen? If he ever got her away from this camp, he owed the little half-breed a real comeuppance.

Easily he overwhelmed her with sheer strength as she struggled. He had forgotten how small she really was until he held her against his almost naked frame. She looked back over her shoulder, eyes wide as a frightened doe, except these wide eyes were green.

In spite of the danger around him, he couldn't resist giving her a sardonic smile. The captive had become the captor and her eyes mirrored that realization. *Just you wait, little butterfly,* he thought.

If he managed to escape with his prize, he had plans for this savage chit. She had teased him with her ripe body, taunted him with his powerless slavery. Now the tables were turned. He was looking forward to teaching her a little humility.

First he had to get out of this camp alive without her sounding the alarm. There was no way with him having to concentrate on hanging onto his wriggling, biting captive.

Rand had never raised a hand to a woman in his life, but he didn't have any alternative now. He didn't want to hurt her, but he had to render her temporarily helpless.

Sorry to have to do this, Kimi, he thought, even as he clipped her lightly across the jaw. She crumpled, limp and unconscious. How fragile and light she was. He felt like the worst kind of blackguard for striking her, and even the remembrance of her whip didn't make him feel right about it. Rand threw her across his wide shoulder, hanging onto her trim ankles as he crept toward the horse tied before One Eye's tipi.

The big stallion looked up as Rand approached. He could only hope the horse didn't nicker or stamp its hooves, possibly waking those in the tipi.

At any moment, Rand expected to hear a cry of alarm as someone spotted him. The silence hung as heavy as the warm spring night. He seemed to hear his own breathing, the sound of his own moccasins as he moved toward the horse.

The girl felt as light as dandelion fluff to him, but he was keenly aware of the warmth of her body against his naked skin. Stealthily, he draped her across the back of the big horse, picked up a rawhide lariat hanging on a post as he untied the horse. He would need something to tie Kimi up once he got her away from here.

Checking to make sure he had the little bag of food and water the old woman had given him, he held the buckskin's muzzle so it could not whinny. Rand led the stallion out of the camp. His heart thudded as he crept away, expecting to feel the steel of an arrow tip plunge into his back or the pain of a lance driven deep between his shoulders. In the brush, a night bird called and a baby somewhere in the camp cried fretfully. Suppose Kimi awakened and screamed an alarm before he got out of camp? Rand glanced at her. She hung limp and unconscious across the broad back of the buckskin.

On the edge of camp, Rand swung up on the barebacked horse with Kimi in front of him. He had to resist an urge to put his heels to the stallion, urge it away at a clattering gallop that might awaken someone. He forced himself to ride out at a walk, knowing that at any second, the men who waited in ambush on the opposite side of the sprawling encampment might wonder and investigate why their prey had never shown up. His heart pounded so hard, he was certain it could be heard for a hundred yards around.

Finally he was far enough away and lifted the girl to cradle her against him as Scout broke into an easy lope across the prairie. Off in the distance, orange lightning cut across the black sky again. Rain could be both a hindrance and a blessing, he thought. It might wash away his tracks but it might also slow him down.

What to do now? With no stars to guide him on this stormy night, Rand wasn't sure where he was. Anyway he dared not head directly toward the fort; that was what the braves would expect and that's the way they would pursue. When the girl came to, maybe he could force her to guide him. Who was he kidding? She wasn't going to do anything but hinder him every chance she got. He was already beginning to regret taking her along—or was he? She was warm and helpless in his arms and he was already thinking about his revenge.

Rand decided to take a meandering course along the edge of an old series of rolling hills and ravines. It would take longer, but the shadows of the low-lying rises would not silhouette him against sky lit by flashes of lightning as riding across the flat, treeless prairie would.

The girl lay curled soft against his chest. Rand cursed softly. What was he to do with her? Maybe when he was within sight of the fort, he'd give her the horse and turn her loose to return to her people.

On the other hand . . . He felt her velvet skin against his, the feel of her small waist under his hand, her full breasts brushing against his fingers. That hand held the rope on Scout's bridle. The other he put on her thigh to steady the unconscious girl. Her doeskin shift had edged up. Her bare flesh seemed to burn against his fingers. Even the danger of pursuit could not block out the thought of how the half-breed girl would feel lying naked and defenseless under him.

For a moment, he was ashamed of his ungallant desire. Then he remembered how she had humiliated and worked him as a chained slave, and his mouth became a hard line. If he decided to enjoy her, she deserved it for everything she had done to him, didn't she? It wasn't as if she were a virgin. After all, Kimi was a widow even if she was very young. Besides she had taunted him with her body. He felt his manhood go hard and throb against her

107

soft hips and was keenly aware of the soft curve of her breast against his hand.

Generations of gallantry warred inside him against primitive desires. Well, that wasn't a decision to deal with yet, Rand thought ruefully. It was a long way to safety and he might not make it before the warriors tracked him down. Their anger would be terrible at his audacity in stealing both the fine stallion and the girl. But then, they would kill him anyway for escaping. It was only a question of how badly they would torture him before he died.

He paused now and then as the hours passed to rest his horse, looking behind him, expecting to see galloping braves coming over the horizon at any moment. Here and there the brown coal called lignite jutted from timeless, wind-ravaged rises. The wind had picked up and thunder rumbled. In the distance, rain already poured in torrents; he smelled it fresh and sweet on the cool wind as it touched the dry prairie grass and soaked into the rich soil. Even the scent of wild roses came on the breeze.

The girl stirred in his arms and moaned softly. He held her against the warmth of his bare chest protectively, ashamed that he had hit her, but there had been no other way to silence her and carry her out of the camp. He still had one arm around her, her breasts resting against his forearm. His other hand stayed on her thigh and he stroked there, ever so gently.

Her skin felt satin smooth and he couldn't stop his mind from wondering how those thighs would feel lying between them, her long, slim legs locked around his lean hips as she urged him to plunge into her deep and deeper still. *Wishful thinking,*

Rand thought, and he cursed softly. When she finally regained consciousness, she would be a spitting, clawing wildcat. This fiery half-breed hated him. Only in his mind would she reach for him, want him as his body wanted her.

She shivered a little in the cool wind, stirred and moaned again. He had never felt so protective, nor so angry at any female before. Small as she was, she had spunk. Given half a chance, she gave as good as she got—a far cry from the simpering, demure Southern belles Rand had known.

Common sense told him riding double was tiring his horse and slowing his escape. If he had any brains, he'd dump her right now. Maybe she'd finally find her way back to the encampment or the warriors might find her before a wolf or an enemy brave got her.

His mind agreed it was only common sense to drop her off on the grass in the darkness before she ever awakened and he had to deal with the little wildcat's teeth and nails.

And yet she felt too good nestled in his arms for him to even consider it. Up ahead lay a low eroded bluff. Rand rode toward it. The wind came up suddenly, blowing cold, and lightning cracked across the black sky, causing the stallion to snort and shake its head.

"Easy, boy," he muttered as the first drops of rain splattered against Rand's dusty, sweating face. He could ride through the rain without any trouble, but lightning on the plains was a real danger. And if hail began to fall like musket balls, it could easily kill or stun any living thing it hit. In his months in the Dakotas, Rand had seen dead animals after a hailstorm. He might have to seek shelter after all. The rain began in earnest now, big, cold drops that drove like nails against his bare flesh.

The girl shivered again and he held her close, trying to shield her against the rain and icy wind with his own big body. "It's all right," he murmured without thinking, "You're all right, little butterfly. No one's going to hurt you; not as long as I'm around."

He was surprised to realize that he meant it. No, he told himself, he didn't feel protective, it was only possessive, like any male animal with a nubile female. He lusted after her. Maybe it was because of the way she had treated him, but for days, he had been plagued with fantasies of finally possessing her body. After he got her back to the fort and into his bunk a few times, his lust would be slaked and he wouldn't care what happened to her. Any man who wanted the vixen would be welcome to her then. It was all she deserved.

Rand looked down at her ebony hair, now wet with rain, the shape of her profile, and thought of the elegant Miss Lenore Carstairs. What had caused that? Certainly the only thing they had in common was the black hair. He wondered what the aristocratic Kentucky belle was doing at this moment while Rand was fleeing for his life across the Dakota plains with a voluptuous, unconscious girl in his arms? He had never hungered for chaste and virginal Lenore's body the way he wanted Kimi's.

Kimi came awake gradually, wondering where she was. Her face and shift seemed wet with rain and she thought she might be on a horse. What was she doing on a horse?

Her head hurt as she stirred and moaned, trying to remember where she was, what had happened.

Immediately, she felt an arm pull her close against a big, warm body. She stiffened, pretended to be unconscious while she tried to figure out her strange surroundings. She searched her memory. The last thing she remembered was coming out of her tipi in the darkness. She had awakened as her mother had gone outside. She had lain there wondering what Wagnuka was up to.

She had feared for Hinzi, thinking her mother hated the whites enough that she might be capable of something devious to get him out of the camp—or murder him in his sleep.

Hinzi. The last thing Kimi remembered was the sudden sight of his face and then she had been struggling to break free while he held her against his naked, hairy chest. After that, she remembered nothing more.

She said a little prayer to Wakan Tanka as the terrible truth dawned on her. Hinzi had escaped from the Lakota and taken her with him as a hostage. What should she do now? More important, what did he intend to do? At this moment, there was no point in putting up a fight. The soldier was too big for her to win it. She would have to pretend unconsciousness as long as possible, then wait for her chance to take the horse and escape. No bigger than she was, trickery was the only defense she could count on.

The rain pelted down on them and her shift was soaked so that she shivered in the chill night. The only part of her that was warm was her back, up against the heat of his big, almost completely naked body. One muscular arm was around her waist just under her breasts and she felt his aroused manhood against her hips. His hot hand on her bare thigh stroked her skin. She had no doubt what he was thinking or what he intended to do with her first chance he got.

In spite of her fears, his fingers stroking her bare thigh, moving ever higher, made her think of things she shouldn't, just as his hard maleness pushing against her back made her think how warm he would feel between her thighs on this wet, cool night.

The horse stumbled as they rode through the rain, and it occurred to Kimi that the mount was tired, too. If it didn't get some rest soon, it would drop dead in its tracks and they would be afoot out here on the desolate prairie.

The thought came that the big soldier could easily abandon her to make it easier on the horse and maybe thereby get all the way back to the fort safely. She couldn't believe that thought hadn't occurred to him, too.

She half-opened one eye. He cuddled her protectively from the weather up against his blond furred chest and she instinctively pressed closer, letting him protect her from the hard driving rain. The lightning cracked orange against a dark purple sky. Just ahead lay a low bluff.

Abruptly it began to hail, small missiles of ice at first, and then they grew as big as a man's fist, beating against both man and horse. She burrowed deeper into his arms, letting him take the bruising blows, knowing hailstones could kill or injure them. If he didn't do something fast, they were in a very vulnerable position.

He must have realized it, too. At that moment, he urged the tired horse into a gallop and headed toward the bluff. For a long minute they raced through the driving rain and hail clattering down around them, and then they were safely under an outcrop of rock.

She heard him sigh with relief and relax. Even the horse whinnied and looked out at the continuing storm, obviously relieved to be in out of the downpour.

Kimi sneaked a look. There was a small cave beyond the outcrop. She pretended to be unconscious while he slid from the horse, taking her with him. He picked her up with no more effort than he would a knapsack and carried her inside. The horse began to graze on the grass growing under the outcrop.

What should she do? If she fought him and managed to escape, it would be futile to run back out into that hailstorm, and the horse needed rest before it could go any farther. Kimi suddenly recognized the horse. Tonweya. Scout. One Eye would be hot on their trail at dawn and there was no telling what he would do when he caught up with this brazen white man. Kimi needn't do anything, she decided, except wait. When One Eye and the warriors showed up, they'd rescue her and make the foolhardy soldier wish he'd never been born.

He bent to lay her down on some soft dry grass that had accumulated in the small cave over the years. Her shift was soaked through and she was cold, shivering.

"Kimi?"

She decided to pretend she was still unconscious.

"You're cold," he murmured, "I'm going to have to get you out of that wet shift."

Even as his hands reached to touch her, she came awake, sat up. "Don't touch me."

He laughed harshly. "I thought you were playing possum. Take it off and hang it up to dry."

"I won't!"

"Then I'll take it off for you. I intend to use your body heat as you might pull a puppy close to warm you. In this darkness, I can't see anything anyway."

She was freezing. Kimi hesitated, trying to keep her teeth from chattering. "Why don't you just build a fire?"

"Great idea! I suppose you just happen to have matches or a flint on you? There's only a little food and one canteen, nothing else. Now take that wet shift off."

"Suppose I refuse?"

His tone was cold, sneering. "I'm the captor now and you're the captive. You'll do as I say, little butterfly."

She paused, staring out at the rain. The hail still fell with a clatter, making the dark landscape look as if new snow had fallen. But the horse was protected and munching grass and they were safely out of the weather here. No doubt what he intended to do to her was inevitable. With a resigned sigh, she pulled the shift off and draped it over a rock.

"Come here." He sat on the ground.

She clasped her medicine object still hanging from the thong around her neck. "I'd rather stay where I am."

"You're my captive now," he said coldly. "I don't care what you'd rather do. You'll do as I order."

She couldn't win against the big soldier; she knew that. She sat down next to him. He handed her the canteen and she took a long drink. "You can have this little dried meat."

Kimi laughed without mirth. "One Eye and the braves are probably already on our trail. You won't live long enough to get hungry!"

"You are the sassiest thing!" He swore under his

114

breath. "Lenore would be so terrified in the same spot, she'd be in screaming hysterics; having a hissy fit."

It annoyed her that even alone with her and her naked, his mind was on the civilized white girl.

He reached out, grabbed her wrists, and pulled them together.

"Hinzi, what are you doing?"

"What does it seem to you I'm doing? I'm tying you up so I can sleep until this storm is over."

Her indignation knew no bounds, "You're just going to tie me up like you would a dog?"

She sensed him shrug. "You have the nerve to be indignant after you've chained me and used me as a beast of burden? The tables are turned. This is how it feels to be a slave. Humiliating, isn't it?" He finished tying her hands, pushed her onto her back, and looped her bonds over an outcrop of rock so she lay with her hands above her head. "Now try to get some rest." He lay back with a tired sigh.

At least he hadn't tied her ankles. Maybe if she humored him and he dropped off to sleep, even with her wrists tied, she might manage to lift the rope over the rock, mount the horse and ride back to the camp, leaving him stranded at the bluff. She might as well get some rest and wait for her chance. Very cautiously, she settled back on the soft, dry grass, too.

Immediately he crawled closer, reached out and pulled her naked body against him. "I'm cold," he said, "I don't have a blanket or a furry dog to curl up to, so I'll take advantage of your body heat."

She tried to pull away, but he was strong. She was naked and he wore only a breechcloth. Heat radiated from his big, muscular body. It was like curling up against a wolf . . . except that she remembered the fur on his chest was pale gold and soft. He threw his arm across her breasts, and her nipples felt on fire when she breathed and they brushed repeatedly against his arm. "What's that around your neck? Feels like a rock."

"My spirit object." For a moment, she was afraid he would take it away, but his tired sigh told her he hadn't been interested enough to investigate. "If — if you rape me, One Eye and the warriors will make you wish for death."

"They will anyway, since I've taken his favorite horse," he sounded resigned to the fact. "Besides, you flatter yourself. As tired as I am, all I'm interested in is your body heat."

She didn't believe him; not the way he had been looking at her for days. With her hands tied above her head, she was helpless to stop him from doing anything he wanted, she knew that. Even as she struggled, he pulled her closer, half covering her with his body. Immediately the heat from him began to heat her wet, naked flesh and she stopped struggling and let him warm her. She who had never had a man still knew the searing passion of desiring one.

All the way down both their bodies, his skin burned against her's like flame, her breasts crushed against his arm. Between them, she felt his hard maleness pulsating, and her breasts swelled at the image of him rolling over on top of her. With her hands tied, she would be helpless to do anything but submit.

Now that arm caressed down her belly. There was no use fighting him, Kimi thought, when he decided to take her; she was too small to stop him.

Instead, his hand gradually stopped stroking and

in a minute or two, his gentle breathing told her the weary man slept.

For a moment, her only emotion was disbelief; then she felt insulted. Here she was trussed naked and helpless and expecting to be raped most savagely. But the yellow-haired soldier had dropped off to sleep.

Kimi settled down in his arms, finding a more comfortable spot in the soft dry grass. With her hands tied, she couldn't move away from him. She felt his manhood against her. The thought brought all sorts of erotic images to her mind.

What to do? She lay still a long time, watching the rain and hail pour outside. At least the heat his muscular body radiated had warmed her. Finally, she tried to shift positions to be more comfortable. He half roused, pulling her closer, moved his hand back up her belly to her breast. His fingers felt as hot as a firebrand there. Then his other arm slipped under her head and he pulled her still closer against him. Without even realizing she did so, she arched herself against him, made a soft noise in her throat.

At that point, his mouth nuzzled her cheek sleepily and then he kissed her.

She stiffened and opened her mouth to protest. His tongue slipped inside. She couldn't cry out; not with his tongue like velvet between her lips, caressing the inside of her mouth. She must remember he was an enemy. But all she could think of was the hot, sweet taste of his mouth and the heat of his body as she pressed her breasts against him.

In answer, his mouth kissed down her throat and covered one of her nipples. She was powerless to stop him from putting his mouth on her naked body if he chose to. That was the only reason she wasn't protesting or fighting him, she told herself. Her body had a mind of its own, pushing her nipple up so that he might run his tongue across it, suck it deep into his throat. Kimi writhed under him as he tasted her breasts. She was breathing hard through her mouth.

He reached up, unlooped her hands from around the rock, but didn't untie them. Instead, he brought her bound hands down between them and rolled her on her side. "You know what I want," he gasped. "Touch me."

She wasn't sure what he wanted, but as his captive, she dare not argue. Now he was pressing his throbbing manhood against her hands.

"Caress me," he murmured, and his mouth covered hers again even as his arms went around her and his big hands cupped her small bottom, pulling her to him.

The heat and the feel and the male scent of him dazzled her senses. She took his maleness in her two hands, and he was big and hard and throbbing. She began to stroke him there and he pushed against her hands. "More!" he commanded, "More!"

She still wasn't sure what it was he expected, but his hands were caressing her bare hips as his mouth sucked her tongue deep in his throat, his body rubbing against hers. She cupped her bound hands around his rod, stroking him. He cursed almost helplessly, hesitated a long moment and then she felt the hot rush of his male seed on her hands. The scent and the heat of it excited her.

Now he reached down, brought her hands up slowly, and rubbed them across her face. "Mine," he whispered, "You're mine now; I've marked you with my seed the same as if I'd put a brand on

118

you, my half-breed slave."

The scent of it excited her and she wanted something more, but she wasn't certain what it was. He reached to take her bound wrists, lift them over his head so that now she embraced him.

"Sweet butterfly," he murmured, "Even if stopping at this bluff signs my death warrant, I'll say it's been worth it." He ground his hard chest against her nipples, exciting her as he stroked and teased her back and hips with his hands. Then she felt him begin to harden again.

Without leaving the circle of her arms, he pushed her thighs apart. Kimi started to protest, but now he was rubbing himself against the soft V of her womanhood. She forgot that she should protest or fight him. All she could remember were the troubled feelings she had had since that very first time Hinzi had been staked out and had managed to work an arm free to grab and pull her down for a kiss.

She felt him probing against the opening of her womanhood with his fingers and she was overpowered with the urge to spread out and let him tease and tantalize her body with his skillful hands. Her bound wrists were around his neck. She should be pushing him away, not pulling him toward her, and yet. . . .

He rolled her over flat on her back. "This is why you should tie a captive's hand in front," he murmured.

Outside, the lightning crashed again, briefly illuminating the cave, outlining him poised above her. With both big hands grasping her breasts, he paused between her thighs. Even as she arched her back, pushing up against his hands, his thumbs stroked her nipples into two hard points.

119

She couldn't remember anything except that if she spread her thighs as wide as possible, he would fill the aching void there. She felt him hesitate, probing for her opening with his seed-wet manhood. Then he made a grunt of pleasure, almost like a stallion as he rammed into her, hard and deep.

He was big. She felt pain as he impaled her against the cave floor but then his mouth covered hers and she couldn't cry out even if she wanted to, and she was not sure she did.

She tried to remember that she'd been kidnapped and that this was an enemy male. There might be a rock lying close enough to reach that she could use to hit him in the head, knock him unconscious. Certainly, the way he was breathing hard with his mouth on hers, his attention was on nothing else but mating.

He began to ride her, sure and hard and urgent. It seemed to Kimi that her body clutched at his, urging him to go deeper still, wanting, no, demanding that he give her what her velvet vessel hungered for. She dug her nails in his muscular back, urging him into her even as he pulled back and came down again in a rhythmic ride, grinding himself against her each time he went deep into her velvet softness. His hands went under her, holding her in a close embrace even as hers clawed at his muscular neck and shoulders while he rode her. Instinctively, she locked her long, slim legs around him, to hold him prisoner in her depths.

"Kimi, sweet butterfly," he gasped, "if there was ever a girl to drive a man crazy with desire, it's you. I've dreamed of doing nothing else since the first time I saw you."

She was no better than the Pawnee sluts who

hung around the forts and let the soldiers use them, and yet, knowing that he was interested only in his own lust, she couldn't stop herself from wanting him. If nothing else, she told herself, he's dallying here with me when the rain has stopped outside and he could be escaping. Like the male black widow spider, his primitive urge to mate might cost him his life if the warriors found them here. It was her duty to keep his mind off escaping, keep his mind on her body until One Eye and the others could pick up their trail and overtake them.

Then he was pausing, stiffening as he plunged into her one more time, giving up his seed in a surrender to her female vessel. Kimi felt him deep and pulsating inside her, pouring his seed into her. She wanted still more, even though it was hurting her to take his dagger to the hilt in her torn virginity. Then her body reacted on its own, clasping his manhood, squeezing hard, wanting every drop he had to give. She felt herself shuddering in his embrace and then there was nothing but darkness for a long moment.

She tried to remember she must stay awake, must watch for a chance to escape. Instead she lay here in the darkness, her naked body smeared with his seed and her own virgin blood, and this enemy sprawled across her, his body still in hers.

The rain continued to drip outside, but his even breathing told her Hinzi was already drifting off to sleep. Now was her chance to escape, if she could bring herself to withdraw from his body, but she couldn't. With the rain dripping a soft, steady rhythm outside on the rocks, Kimi drifted off to sleep in his embrace.

Rand came awake with a start, knowing some-how that he'd been asleep for hours. Where was he? His eyes blinked open and he saw the mouth of the cave in dawn's light, the horse patiently cropping grass near the entrance. It had stopped raining and was clearing.

Last night came back to him with a rush and he realized he lay with a woman curled in his protect-ive embrace. He pulled away from her, blinked and stared in puzzlement. She was a beauty, completely naked except for some trinket hanging on a thong between full breasts. Her nipples looked swollen, and he remembered how he had sucked them as if he could never get enough of their taste.

His glance went to her thighs, smeared with the slightest trace of crimson blood. A virgin? No, Kimi couldn't be a virgin; she was a widow. He stared at the naked skin in the daylight. Puzzled and confused, he studied her skin, darker by far where the sun had tanned it. But underneath, where the sun never touched . . .

Rand swore softly under his breath. Now he un-derstood why the old woman wanted nothing to do with whites, was afraid for Kimi. She had a valid reason, Rand realized. If the whites ever saw Kimi, they would take her away from the Indians. No doubt she had been captured on a raid.

Her skin in the daylight reminded him of the blossoms in the Carstairs conservatory. Kimi was no Sioux; not even a half-breed. The daylight on her pale, naked skin revealed that Kimi was a white girl.

Seven

Kimi opened her eyes slowly. The soldier leaned on one elbow staring down at her in the early dawn. She managed a weak smile. "Hello, Hinzi."

"We've got to get out of here." He sat up, untied her. "We should have ridden on hours ago. When we've more time, there's some questions I want to ask—"

"You were my first man, if that's what you want to know." She bristled a little, thinking what a fool she had been to succumb to the attraction she had been fighting since the first moment she had seen him. Kimi rubbed her numb wrists, reached for her doeskin shift.

"That's not it." He looked a little chagrined as he shook his head, stood up, pulled her to her feet. "When we get to the fort—"

"The fort?" She paused in putting on the shift. "You are still taking me to the fort?"

Her fear must have shown in her eyes, because he made a soothing gesture. "Don't worry, when they realize you're a white girl, you won't be in any danger."

"White girl?" Kimi stared at him. "I am a woman of the Lakota—"

"Kimi, haven't you ever wondered why your skin

is so much lighter than the other members of your tribe?"

In fact, she had. "My mother grew angry whenever I asked when I was little, so gradually I stopped asking and forgot about it."

He nodded. "And just what did she tell you?"

Kimi shrugged. "That I was kin to the White Buffalo Woman, sacred to the Sioux."

Hinzi snorted with disdain. "That's only an old Sioux legend; even I've heard it. What about your bright green eyes?"

She didn't have a good answer. Maybe she hadn't delved too deeply because she didn't really want to know. If she weren't Lakota, who was she? What was she? "Again, Wagnuka grew impatient with my questions and I stopped asking."

Hinzi reached out to grasp the medicine object that hung between her breasts. "What is this?"

"My sacred medicine."

He turned it over in his hand, face puzzled. "It looks almost like a gold acorn. Where did you get this?"

Kimi shrugged, pulled away from him. "I don't know. I've always had it."

He caught her shoulders in both hands. "Do you remember anything of your past? Perhaps you were stolen from some ranch in a long ago massacre."

The past was a blur to Kimi. When she reached back into her mind, all she remembered was her spirit song, being very thirsty, a big man carrying her. It suddenly dawned on her that the man was white and had eyes the color of her own. *Kimimila.* The Lakota word for butterfly was the only other memory that surfaced. She didn't want to think about it. As devastating as Hinzi's questions were, she wanted to cling to the familiar life of her people, the only life she knew.

"Hinzi, the warriors will be trailing us soon." She went to the mouth of the cave and peered out. The big buckskin stallion still grazed nearby, the first beams of sunlight glistened on rain drops that clung to the grass. How did she feel about this man? Did she want him to escape? Certainly she didn't want to be taken as a prisoner to the fort.

She took a deep breath, thinking. "Hinzi, riding double will slow your horse. Leave me here and go on. One Eye will find me when he comes and by then, you'll be safely back at the fort."

He swore under his breath in that soft drawl. "Don't be a silly little fool! I can't leave you here. You're white, Kimi, somewhere a family is looking for you."

"Are they?" she challenged him. "Even if that is so, I have been among the Sioux so long, I don't even remember any other life, and more than that, I want no other. My white family may all be dead so that I have no place to go."

His face furrowed in thought and he brushed his blond hair out of his sky-colored eyes. "We'll figure all this out when we get back to civilization."

She listened to him gathering up his things as she turned and stared out across the landscape. What she waited to hear was that after last night, he wanted her as his woman and that was why she must go with him. If given the choice, what would her answer be? Everything seemed so different in the harsh light of day.

However, he said nothing, and she remembered that there was a white girl waiting for him. Kimi had only been a night's entertainment for him. The realization both hurt and annoyed her, but then she had known about the other girl from the first. It couldn't be jealousy, she told herself, it was only that she had been used as casually as most white men used an Indian girl with no thought of her feelings. Wagnuka had been right.

On the ridge to the east, outlined against the coming sun, Kimi saw something move. She stiffened, watching . . . riders. A line of riders strung out along the rim of the world. "Soldiers," she whispered.

Hinzi peered over his shoulder, his hairy chest brushing her bare arm. "No, those aren't soldiers." He sounded disappointed. "Paint ponies and I don't see any reflection off brass buttons. It's One Eye and his men."

Kimi shook her head, her heart sinking as she suddenly realized who the riders might be. "Enemy Crow." She watched them ride closer for a long moment, then they disappeared into a ravine. "I can tell by their hair."

He acted as if he weren't sure whether to run out and yell after them. "Are they hostile?"

"To any Sioux, yes; to a soldier, maybe; depending on whether they're renegades or not. Look like they're on a war raid."

Hinzi shrugged as he came around her, caught the horse. "That's not our problem. They're headed west, away from the fort."

She caught his arm. "Hinzi, I'd say they may be headed for my people's camp."

"Well, that's the first good news I've had in a while," the soldier quipped. "Maybe they'll keep One Eye and the others busy long enough for us to escape."

"Hinzi, don't you understand?" she implored, "those are my people they are going to attack —"

126

"Kimi, those are not *your* people. You're as white as I am."

"Not in my heart," she said stubbornly. "Why don't you let me take the horse? Scout is fast, and I know a shortcut through the ravines. I can get there before the Crow surprise the camp."

"And what am I supposed to do? Walk all the way back to the fort?" He raised one sardonic eyebrow. "You'd leave me out here afoot? I reckon you know what my answer is to that!" He swung up on the horse, held out his hand to her. "Let's get out of here."

Instead she turned and started running back toward the Sioux camp. "Go on then, white soldier. I am a swift runner, perhaps I can still get there before them."

Behind her, he called, "and what if the Crow find you out there alone before you reach the village?"

She looked over her shoulder, shrugged, although her soul flinched at the thought. "They will do what men always do to an enemy girl, no matter her color."

"Kimi, don't!"

"Go on, white soldier; forget about me. What is it to you if a bunch of old people and Lakota babies are massacred? You'll be safe back at the fort and they can all laugh when you tell them about making love to a little savage." She turned and began to run.

She heard the sound of Scout's hooves and then Hinzi was beside her, reaching down to lift her, kicking and struggling to the horse before him as he swore under his breath. "Stop kicking me! I'll be damned if I'll let some Crow buck have you!"

"You had me first, so what do you care what

127

man has me next? I hate you! Let me go!" She struggled to get away, but he held her firmly against his hairy, muscled chest.

He didn't say anything for a long moment as he reined in the horse uncertainly. "If I turn this horse and ride to the fort, you'll never forgive me, will you?"

"Forgive you?" she spat it at him, "I'll try to kill you first chance I get!"

"And if we go back to the Lakota, they'll kill me; not much of a choice, I'd say. What a mess!" He nudged the horse and they started toward the Sioux camp at a gallop.

Kimi looked up at him with horror. "What are you doing?"

"Taking you to warn the village." His expression was stoic and he didn't look at her.

"You can't do that; they'll torture you to death!"

"Then do you want to go to the fort?"

So that was his game; putting her in a position to beg him to take her to the fort, thinking maybe she cared enough about him that she didn't want anything to happen to him. "You're not really going to do that," she scoffed.

"Watch me." His arrogant face looked set, determined.

She didn't say anything as they rode. She still didn't believe he would return to the Sioux camp. He would have to be crazy—or care about her very much—to do such a thing, knowing what fate awaited him there. No doubt he would drop her near the camp and take off at a gallop.

Kimi watched the prairie ahead, thinking about One Eye and his warriors that were somewhere in between the pair and the Lakota encampment. She wondered if Hinzi had forgotten about them? If

128

the big Crow war party continued in the direction they were headed, there was a good chance they might cross the trail of One Eye's patrol and wipe them out.

He said nothing more to her as they traveled. Hours passed and the sun climbed in the sky. Now and then they dismounted and walked to cool the lathered horse, then rode on.

Abruptly they topped a rise and saw the Lakota war party riding toward them.

Kimi gasped. "Hinzi, free me here and you can get away with the horse. Once I tell them about the Crow war party, they will lose interest in chasing you."

"Too late. They've spotted us," Hinzi sounded resigned to his fate. "I might as well die facing them as to be ridden down like a cringing dog. I can at least die like a Randolph would be expected to. Besides I've heard Indians won't harm a crazy man and I must qualify." He nudged the horse forward.

One Eye and the others reined in, sat their horses staring in disbelief as Scout loped up. Even as several of the braves put an arrow to their bows, Kimi held up her hand, shouted a protest. "Wait! Hear what we have to say! Hinzi has ridden back to warn you of a Crow war party!"

The Sioux warriors paused. Perhaps they suddenly realized they couldn't get a clear shot at the white soldier with Kimi sitting the horse in front of him.

One Eye frowned as they drew up a few yards away. "Kimi, do you lie to save this white dog?"

"I will bite the knife to show I tell the truth, if need be," Kimi said. Biting the knife was a sacred ceremony throughout the whole Sioux nation. To go through the ceremony swearing words were true when one lied would bring great misfortune, even death to the liar.

Hinzi said in broken Lakota: "Kimi speaks true. We saw almost double the number of warriors who ride with you crossing the rim rock." He gestured toward the horizon. "Kimi thinks they come to ambush your camp tonight."

One Eye looked at him thoughtfully, slowly lowered his bow. "And you, soldier, riding my stolen horse; you return, knowing it means certain death?"

"The Crow warriors will hit your camp hard, perhaps tonight as it sleeps," Hinzi said. "Many will die. I do not intend that Kimi be one of them."

"You are a fool!" One of the other warriors spat out. "The Crow are often allies of the white soldiers and sometimes scout for them. If you had gone to them, they would have helped you escape."

She felt him shrug. "She refused to go with me and I could not be sure she would be safe with them."

"You are either a crazy man, very brave or a fool for a woman's soft body," One Eye said, "and I don't have time to decide that now." He gestured to one of the others. "Tie him up."

She felt Hinzi tense as if he might try to turn his horse and gallop away, then seemed to realize he didn't have a chance. The brave reached to tie Hinzi's hands behind him while another warrior kept an old musket trained on the soldier.

One Eye nodded to Kimi. "Now tell us about the war party you saw."

Torn between her concern for Hinzi and the safety of her people, Kimi told the braves all the details she could remember. "I think we could take a short cut and ambush them at that little spring where the willows grow."

A murmur of approval of her idea ran through the war party.

One Eye said, "Yes, this is what we will do. If we can take the Crow by surprise, their superior numbers won't matter. Here, Kimi," he gestured. "Take one of the spare horses for yourself."

She didn't really want to leave Hinzi. It had felt so comforting to have the heat of his big body against her. Looking at One Eye's stern face, she decided this was not the time to argue. She slid from the horse and took another. Perhaps in the heat of the fight, she might be able to free Hinzi, give him a fresh horse and a head start. The choice between his safety and her people had been a hard one, but she didn't intend that her first lover should die.

"You, soldier, ride next to me so I can watch you." One Eye gestured and Hinzi nudged the buckskin up next to him. His expression showed that he admired Hinzi's reckless defiance. "You have good taste in horses."

Hinzi laughed. "If a man must steal a mount, he should take the best that the most valiant man owns!"

The warriors laughed in spite of themselves. The Sioux liked arrogant courage, even in an enemy. All wheeled and set off at a lope for the spring. She saw grudging admiration on the warriors' faces. Hinzi might be white and he might be a reckless fool, but he had courage and the Sioux respected bravery above all else. They paused once to eat a bite of dried pemmican and cool the horses.

One Eye rubbed his red eye patch. "*Wasicu*, you ride well—for a soldier."

131

The white man smiled, cold disdain in his blue eyes. "I shoot well, too, as you would find out if I had a gun."

"You will die quickly as befits a brave man when we get you back to camp."

The stout Gopher, protested. "No, he should die slowly for taking the woman and your best horse."

"I went with him willingly," Kimi lied, and then wondered why she did so. Maybe because she thought it would be a bad omen for her first lover to be killed.

"So even though you are raised a Sioux, the white blood calls to you." One Eye frowned.

Hinzi snorted with haughtiness. "The girl lies. I wanted her; I took her. Do not the Sioux sometimes carry off women and make them their own in a raid?"

The warrior nodded. "You would protect this girl at risk to yourself? I have never known a white man like you, Hinzi. When we finish with the Crows, I will almost be sorry to see you die."

"You will see I die as bravely as I speak," the soldier said coldly. "The girl had no part in my escape; she is blameless."

Kimi started to protest, realized no one would listen to her.

One Eye directed that the *wasicu* be gagged to keep him from shouting a warning to the Crow, should he decide to. Kimi kept her mind busy as they mounted up and rode out, still scheming ways to save the yellow-haired man. She didn't want to wonder why or think about the fact that when he left, she would never see him again. Last night had been worth it. The memories of his kiss and his embrace would last her the rest of her lifetime even if she ended up married to some Lakota warrior

132

and bearing brown children.

One of the warriors had ridden several miles ahead, scouting the terrain. Now he returned at a gallop to tell them the spring where the willows grew was not far and that the Crow were coming toward the spring from another angle.

"To water their horses, no doubt," One Eye muttered, and rubbed at the scrap of red patch over his right eye. "We will be there waiting when they arrive."

She had never been in a battle before, and she was nervous about it, knowing that the Sioux were outnumbered. If they lost, she would be raped by the victorious Crows.

They dismounted in the little grove of trees and a warrior tied the soldier to a stump, making sure his gag was in place so he could not cry out and warn the enemy. Then each man put a strip of buckskin around his mount's muzzle so it could not whinny and alert the coming riders.

At last the warriors took their places behind stumps and rocks. "Give me a bow," she begged, "I'm a fair shot."

One Eye shook his head. "Stay back in the brush with the horses. At the first sign that we might be overrun, you ride out as fast as you can and warn the camp."

Kimi ran her tongue over her dry lips, listening to the approaching riders. "What about the soldier?"

"What about him?" One Eye shrugged. "If the Crow win, they will free him. If we win, we will bring him back to the camp so all may see his death."

She started to protest, but another warrior motioned her to silence. The enemy was very close now.

Kimi retreated to where Hinzi was tied up near the horses. He gave her a long look and she glanced away, unsure what to do. The warriors crouched down behind brush and small trees, waiting. It occurred to her that in the ensuing fight and confusion, she might be able to get a knife and cut the soldier free. While the two sides fought, he could probably grab a horse and escape. She tried to explain to him with silent gestures what she intended to do.

He looked puzzled a long moment, then troubled as he seemed to understand. His blue eyes asked an unspoken question: *what about you?*

Kimi shook her head. It really didn't matter what happened to her if she could save Hinzi and her people. She hadn't had time yet to think about her white blood, and anyway, what did it matter now? Maybe she had really known it all along and closed her mind to it. Her skin might be white, but inside, she was as much a Sioux as Wagnuka. And she would never think of the old woman as anything but her mother. The time before that was lost to her. Besides she could never fit into his civilization, and Hinzi had a white girl waiting for him when he went back to his people. There was no place for her in his world.

Rand watched the girl, understanding now that in the confusion, she intended to free him so he could escape. He pulled at his bonds, cautious of the warriors who crouched only a few feet away. If he could get the gag out of his mouth, what he should do was yell out and warn the approaching Crow. They might be a friendly bunch who would reward him by helping him return to the fort.

And yet . . . He looked at Kimi, not sure how he felt about her. He had never experienced such ecstasy in a woman's arms, and he was both drawn to her and ashamed. She was not much more than a child, although she had a woman's body. He had taken this ignorant little savage's virginity, so he owed her something, but what? He was pledged to marry aristocratic Lenore Carstairs. Kimi would not fit into his life; in fact, his mother and sister would be appalled and horrified by this primitive girl raised by Indians.

He shifted his cramped muscles, listening to the sounds of horses moving closer. Somewhere a quail called and a grasshopper jumped across the brush near him. His wrists were rubbed raw and his tongue felt parched with the gag. If she managed to free him, should he force Kimi to go with him? No, better he should leave her with the people she loved.

But suppose he did that and the Sioux lost this coming fight? Rand winced, knowing what Kimi's fate would be. In his mind, he saw her spread-eagled naked and staked down for the animal pleasure of the Crow braves.

The thought sickened him, even though he hadn't forgotten her hatred, the way she had treated him like a slave. He studied her shiny black hair and the shape of her small face and thought about Lenore, wondering what she was doing at this very moment. It was the middle of the afternoon back home. Perhaps Lenore was visiting Randolph Hall, sitting out on the veranda, maybe with his sister, Vanessa, having a cool drink and talking of the latest fashions and society gossip. Or maybe she would be sitting doing needlework at Carstairs

Oaks while her grandmother played the piano in the music room.

He wondered what they would say or think if they all knew that on this spring afternoon, Rand was hovering between life and death? He hadn't heard anything all the time he was in that Yankee prison, so maybe they thought him dead. Or had someone finally told them he had gone to fight Indians and was missing in action?

The tension of waiting caused his muscles to ache as he listened to the sound of the riders coming ever closer. Noise exploded around him as the crouching Sioux loosed a barrage of arrows and gunfire at the approaching enemy. Crow horses reared and whinnied, dumping riders. Acrid smoke drifted as guns fired. Somewhere a man screamed. In the choking clouds of gun smoke, it was difficult to know what was happening, who was hit. The sickly sweet scent of fresh blood came to him as he took a deep breath. Who was winning, who was losing? Kimi's face told him she couldn't be sure, either.

Then the Crow seemed to recover from their initial surprise and returned the attack, riding down Lakota warriors, fighting hand to hand. Now was the time if ever he was to escape, Rand thought.

Kimi picked up a small knife, cut the ropes that bound him. "Here's your chance to get away!"

He jerked the gag from his mouth. "Now's *our* chance," he answered. He took the knife from her, caught her hand, dragging her to the tied horses. He didn't know what he would do with her when he got her back to the fort, but he couldn't leave her behind. Maybe it was because she was white, maybe it was nothing more than guilt for having taken her virginity.

She fought and scratched, broke away from him. "My people need me!" She turned and ran back toward the fighting, grabbing up a forgotten bow.

Rand hesitated, cursing. The stubborn little chit! Well, he had tried to help her and she wouldn't let him. He'd better look out for himself. As he paused, he saw a big Crow warrior attack One Eye. Over and over they rolled as they fought and struggled, each holding the other's knife hand. It was clear now that the superior numbers of the Crow were gradually overwhelming One Eye's braves. As Rand hesitated in momentary indecision, Kimi charged that Crow, hitting him across the back with the bow.

The Indian managed to knock her down as he fought with One Eye. His expression revealed what he planned for her later. Kimi's head snapped back and blood ran from her mouth as she collapsed.

Rand forgot everything except that the Crow brave had struck a woman, and maybe hurt her badly. In a red rage, he dropped the horse's reins and ran into the fray. The Crow had One Eye down, taking advantage of his blind side. Rand grabbed up the knife Kimi had dropped. He brought the blade down with all his strength, the steel reflecting the light as he buried it to the hilt in the Crow leader's back. Scarlet blood pumped out and ran down the brown skin.

Rand had never killed a man before in hand-to-hand combat. Instinctively, he threw his head back and shouted a victory song that startled the invading Crow. With their leader dead, they began to retreat, chased by the Lakota warriors.

In the confusion, this was the time to escape if he was going to; to stay meant certain death. He was three kinds of a fool to stay. Yet Rand had thoughts only for Kimi as he ran to her, knelt by her side. "Kimi, Butterfly; are you all right?"

In answer her eyes flickered open and she sat up slowly. "I—I think so. Hinzi, you must leave! You must—"

Then One Eye towered over them. Rand looked up at him. "She's all right, that's all that matters."

Slowly One Eye held out the scalp of the dead Crow. "Take this, Hinzi. You have earned the honor." Grudging respect shown on his face. "You are as brave as any of my warriors."

The others finished picking up the spoils and weapons. "What about the *wasicu?*" someone grumbled.

One Eye shrugged. "Hinzi saved my life and maybe yours, too. If he had not killed the Crow leader, the others might not have fled in terror. We will take him back to camp and call a meeting of the Shirt Wearers. I do not feel it is good medicine to kill a man who has acted so bravely. I give Yellow Hair my best horse, Scout, to show my gratitude."

Most of the others nodded.

"Pilamaya," Rand thanked him. "I am honored to accept this fine gift." He, who owned a pasture full of the finest thoroughbreds in the bluegrass country, had never been as touched as he was now by this Sioux gift of gratitude. He would not think about anything else, but that his life seemed to have been spared for today. There would be other chances to escape, maybe, Rand thought.

Kimi reached up to touch his face. "If the elders permit it, would you live among us as a Sioux and be my man?"

He wasn't going to stay forever, but until he left,

138

he could have this passionate little vixen whenever he felt the urge. That was all it was; lust, not love that he felt for this pretty young savage. Rand didn't answer as he swung her up in his arms, thinking again of another black-haired girl hundreds of miles away and the life that waited for him there as the master of Carstairs Oaks.

Kimi reached to kiss him and the taste of her mouth brought back the passion of last night. He didn't know whether he would tire of her eventually. He didn't want to think past today. Rand knew only one thing; that if he stayed with the Sioux, tonight he could have this soft female in his blankets. Her body would be his to enjoy.

That alone made his decision for him. He had fought for her and won her in a primitive fashion that would shock his aristocratic family and friends. She was little more than a child, and a girl waited for him in Kentucky. He was three kinds of a fool and a lecher besides.

That didn't matter. She was his; that was all he could think of. Carrying Kimi, he turned his back on his life as a bluecoat soldier and swung up on the buckskin stallion, holding her possessively against his big chest. For the time being, at least, he was going to return to the Sioux. Possessing the girl in his arms was all that mattered at this moment!

Eight

Lenore Carstairs cantered her bay mare down the lane toward the manicured lawns of Randolph Hall. It was an unusually warm afternoon for late spring, she thought peevishly, wishing she had worn the lighter pale peach riding habit instead of the dark green one. Maybe now that this silly war had just ended, Kentucky could get its attention back on more important things like fox hunting and cotillions. Instead of a glorious adventure, the war had been a bore and a real inconvenience.

As she drew closer, she saw people sitting out on the side veranda of the old manor house, Randolph Hall, elegant with its red brick and white pillars. On the third story was a magnificent ballroom with French doors leading out onto a balcony. She'd love to attend a ball, but the Eriksons probably wouldn't give one until something was heard from Rand. Of course, with everyone having to free their slaves, maybe there wasn't much to celebrate. Someday, if things went the way she planned, Lenore would be mistress of three magnificent plantations.

She wondered idly where Rand was at this very moment or if he were even alive? Vanessa's beau, Shelby Merson, had been investigating because he said he knew people in high places. Shelby said so far he had been unable to trace Rand. It was possi-

140

ble he had been a prisoner of war or he might even be missing in action. Lenore hoped nothing had happened to her fiancee; black was not her best color.

She cantered up to the entrance and a little black boy with crooked teeth came out to take her horse. "Afternoon, Miz Carstairs. The folks is all around on the side veranda."

"I'm not blind, you idiot!" Lenore dismounted her sidesaddle with a swirl of skirts, and didn't bother to give him a second glance as she went around the shrubbery. It was so hard to get good help these days, so many had fled north. Lenore's feet hurt and she took mincing steps.

Vanessa and Shelby, and Mr. and Mrs. Erikson sat fanning themselves and sipping drinks on the flagstone veranda as Lenore rounded the corner of the house. Shelby Merson and Jon Erikson came to their feet with gallant bows, Rand's father wobbling a little.

Drunk as usual, Lenore thought, but managed to replace her frown with a smile. "Afternoon, y'all." She adjusted her perky hat on her ebony curls. "Hot, isn't it?"

"As hot as where I hope Abe Lincoln is at this moment," Mrs. Erikson snapped, fanning herself vigorously.

"Now, Rose . . ." Jon Erikson seemed to decide it wasn't worth the argument and returned to his bourbon.

"It's just as well my grandmother isn't here to hear you say that, although I couldn't agree with you more." Lenore cooed, taking a seat in the creaking swing. "Her Nigras have always been uppity and she thought Lincoln was a wonderful man."

141

Rose Randolph Erikson fanned herself with nervous gestures and wheezed. She, too, had been a reigning belle, like Lenore's mother, but now Rose was getting plump and wore her corsets too tight in a vain attempt to hide that fact. "Elizabeth Carstairs is from a fine old family, elsewise, she's a bit liberal for my taste. To think anyone could defend that black-loving Republican, even if he was born in Kentucky!"

"Mercy me. She's also the richest woman in the county," Vanessa said a bit vapidly. Vanessa was a younger, more blonde version of her mother—and every bit as stupid, Lenore thought. She considered how kind and generous it was of herself to be Vanessa's best friend.

"Just white trash, that's all he was," Mrs. Erikson said irritably, "not quality folk at all. Have some lemonade, Lenore."

"For pity's sake, I reckon it doesn't matter now that he's dead and the war's over. At least our little area didn't have fighting right close by." Lenore accepted the glass as the plump matron poured it.

"My cousin's big place, farther south, was hit hard," Rose Erikson complained, "but then, he freed his slaves and went off to Arizona just before the war started, so it doesn't matter."

Lenore sipped her lemonade, thinking her riding boots were killing her. She should stop having them made two sizes too small since it didn't help make her feet look tiny anyway. "Is that Quint Randolph, the one who supplied horses for the Pony Express?"

Her hostess nodded and started a dull conversation about her illustrious family and the war. Lenore only half listened, since the conversation wasn't about herself; the most interesting topic of all. Lenore had long ago tired of the war once it began to cause shortages of cloth and luxuries. Since her rather independent grandmother had already freed her slaves, Lenore hadn't thought about how others were managing now that they had to pay the Nigras.

She studied Jon Erikson. He was the saddest looking man she had ever seen. She wondered idly if there was anything to that gossip about his youth? Rand looked just like his once handsome father must have looked at that age; before liquor and time took its toll.

Rose Erikson fanned herself vigorously and wheezed. "For a true Southerner, the war will never be over! I hear the Yankees have been burying their dead soldiers right on the lawn of General Lee's estate out of sheer meanness."

Even from here, Lenore could smell the strong, cloying scent of the perfumed hair oil Shelby wore. She wished he wouldn't do that, but then, it wasn't her place to tell him. Shelby played with the diamond stickpin in his gaudy cravat. "I presume they're trying to keep him from ever living there again?"

"Reckon so," Mrs. Erikson snapped. "Who'd ever want to live at Arlington again with hundreds of dead Yankees buried in the rose gardens?"

Jon Erikson gulped his whiskey. "With everything that's happened and with our son still unaccounted for, only you could worry about something so trivial, my dear." He didn't smile.

Lenore tried not to look at her best friend's fiancee. "For pity's sake, do we have to be so gloomy? Has there been any news?"

"I think," the older man hiccoughed, "we could do without any news for a while. Who would have believed so many things could have happened in one month? First Lee surrenders, then the President assassinated, and finally, the *Sultana* exploding on the Mississippi with fifteen hundred killed."

When Lenore looked up, Shelby was studying her. "Sweet Jesus! It'll be a long time before there's another ship disaster to match that one."

"Mercy me, I doubt there were any quality people on board," Vanessa said with a stifled yawn, "just soldiers going home."

"Yes, just soldiers," Jon Erikson said, "only 'quality' to their wives and mothers. And daughter, you're beginning to sound just like yours." He set his glass down unsteadily.

"Jon, don't be rude," his wife ordered. "You've had too much to drink."

"On the contrary," he said, "I haven't had nearly enough."

Lenore saw Rose Erikson and her daughter exchange annoyed frowns and decided to change the subject. Most of the money in that family had been brought into the marriage by Rose Randolph, and this property was the old Randolph homestead. Rose controlled it and she never let Jon forget it.

Lenore took a sip of lemonade, ran her tongue around the edge of the glass to get the sugar when she thought no one was looking. "By news, I meant about Rand, of course."

Rose Erikson brushed a graying strand of light hair away from her plump face with nervous fingers. "Nothing since that rumor that he might be among the Galvanized Yankees and off fighting Indians."

Shelby reached out to pat her pudgy arm solicitously. "Mother Erikson, I think now that the war's ended, if we don't hear something soon, we should

144

be prepared for the worst."

Lenore thought again about how dreadful she would look in black. "I hope not," she said with conviction.

Rose Erikson glared at her husband. "You'd think with *my* money and the Randolph name, the army would rush to do something—"

"My dear," her husband cut her off coldly, "believe it or not, the War Department has had weightier things on its mind than reassigning one soldier. Rand was always quite spoiled and arrogant. It might make a man of him to leave him up in the Dakotas a while."

"Don't talk nonsense." Rose wheezed. "He's a Randolph, on his mother's side, so he shouldn't expect to be treated like everyone else. The Randolphs have always been quality folk; not like some whose families are only second generation with questions as to where their money came from."

"Excuse me," Jon retorted, "I never have quite understood why it's socially correct to own slaves but not acceptable to fill that demand."

Rose took a deep breath and let it out like a steam engine. "I do declare! Quality folk don't need it explained; it's just different; that's all."

The tension was heavy in the silence, but Jon Erikson only looked a little sadder, reached for the decanter, and poured himself another drink. Even Lenore had heard that rumor about Jon's father having built his fortune on the profits of 'blackbirding,' illegally importing black slaves once Congress had passed a law against bringing in any more from Africa. But then, the Norwegians did have great skill with seagoing clippers. She'd heard the Eriksons had once been partners with the Van Schuylers, the wealthy shipping family in Boston.

145

Vanessa frowned. "Mercy me, Father, you've really had enough, don't you think?"

"Actually, I try not to think at all," the older man leaned back in his chair. He was beginning to get red veins across his nose and his once-handsome face looked puffy.

Mrs. Erikson appeared a bit embarrassed. She shrugged helplessly at Shelby. "Do overlook my husband's lack of manners." Her nervous fingers made helpless motions.

"No one need apologize for me; I'm sick of it." Jon Erikson took another drink.

"Someone has to," his wife wheezed. "Those who have neither breeding nor much money—"

"Marry it, that's what you're about to say, isn't it?" Jon Erikson looked more than a little drunk.

His wife rolled her eyes and looked around for sympathy.

Lenore sighed loudly to bring the attention back to herself. "Poor Rand! I think about him all the time. I wonder where he is on this very afternoon?"

Shelby gave her a sympathetic look. "Miss Lenore, I want you to know Vanessa and I will be here whenever you need us. I just hope the news is finally good."

Vanessa favored him with a vapid smile. "Spoken like a true gentleman. Oh, Shelby, dear, do you suppose you could wear your uniform and all your medals when we marry?"

Shelby ran his finger around his collar as if it were choking him. "I don't know. There's such sad memories attached to the service, with your brother missing and all."

Lenore glanced at Shelby but he looked away. "Oh, for pity's sake, Vanessa, Rand'll come home

146

eventually, and we'll have the grandest double wedding this county ever saw. All the girls we know will be just green with envy."

Jon Erikson sipped his drink. "I didn't know the object of a wedding was to make everyone else green with envy."

"Oh, Jon," Mrs. Erikson gave him a withering look. "What other reason is there to put on a big wedding but to show off wealth and family connections?" She turned to Shelby with a smile. "Shelby, dear boy, your family won't be attending?"

"No," he shook his head, "although the Mersons are quite influential in Memphis, my parents are dead and both my brothers were killed in the war; one on each side."

"Memphis?" Jon Erikson said. "I thought you were from Baltimore?"

Shelby played with the big diamond stickpin, and looked away. "Did I say Memphis? Of course I have connections in both towns because of our vast holdings."

Rose Erikson's pale eyes gleamed with greed. "So tragic that you're the only one left, but that makes you the heir, and how nice that you had enough to purchase the lovely estate between ours and Carstairs Oaks."

Jon Erikson laughed and took a long drink of bourbon. "Is this a marriage or a merger?"

"Father!" Vanessa snapped, "I wish you wouldn't drink so much."

When he spoke, his words came so low that perhaps, Lenore thought, she was the only one to hear him. "That's all that gets me through each day."

"Who's that coming?" Shelby craned his head and looked down the lane.

"That's Pierce Hamilton's buggy, isn't it?" Mrs.

Erikson fanned herself, wheezing heavily. "He doesn't come to call often; wonder what he wants?"

Lenore watched the buggy moving at a fast clip toward the house. She didn't really like her grandmother's longtime beau and lawyer. Lenore sometimes had a feeling that he saw right through her.

No one said anything as the buggy pulled up in front of the house and the black boy came out to take the reins from the old man with the gray mustache and goatee. His distressed expression told Lenore immediately that this was not a social call.

He spoke kindly to the servant, then came around the house, crossed the flagstones. "Afternoon y'all."

"Afternoon, Judge." Mr. Erikson waved him to a wicker chair, "Care for a bourbon?"

The judge shook his head. "A little early in the day for me." He hesitated. "I'm afraid I'm the bearer of bad news."

Shelby leaned forward. "The price of cotton has fallen?"

"Lincoln's not dead after all?" Mrs. Erikson wheezed.

"My grandmother's lost all her money?" Lenore asked.

"Be quiet," Jon Erikson snapped, "and let the man say what he's come to say."

"Thank you, Jon." The judge looked at him gratefully. "I'm glad to find you here, Lenore, I was headed to your place next."

She had a sudden sense of foreboding. "Judge Hamilton, what is it?"

He paused. "On second thought, I believe I will have that drink, Jon."

The silence seemed as heavy as the hot, humid

afternoon. They sat and watched the old man gulp the whiskey. Lenore exchanged puzzled looks with Vanessa, then Shelby.

Pierce Hamilton sighed and looked around sympathetically. "I don't know how to begin, although it's been my sad duty to call on families all during the war—"

"Rand!" Mrs. Erikson gasped and put her hand to her mouth. "My boy; you've finally had news of my poor, dear boy?"

"He's missing in action against the Indians," Judge Hamilton said. "They may find him safe and sound—"

Mrs. Erikson collapsed in a faint and Vanessa began to shriek at the top of her lungs. Servants came running from everywhere in the ensuing confusion.

Missing. Lenore could only blink. Missing. She wasn't sure what she felt. Rand was probably dead. There wouldn't be any elaborate double wedding for all the other girls to envy. Now she'd be wearing black. Would etiquette allow her to substitute a dark gray?

It dawned on her suddenly that through the confusion and wailing, all three men were looking at her. With pity? Curiosity? She should be weeping, they all would expect that. She thought of the beautiful wedding she wouldn't have; how awful she would look in mourning clothes. She would never end up with both Carstairs Oaks and Randolph Hall. Missing. Big tears welled up in her eyes and ran down her face. Lenore buried her face in her hands and sobbed.

"Oh, my poor dear friend," Vanessa clung to her, shedding sloppy tears all over her neck and face, knocking Lenore's perky hat askew.

149

She heard Judge Hamilton's voice trying to bring order to the confusion. "Great Caesar's ghost. I didn't say 'dead.' There's always hope."

Lenore dabbed at her golden eyes. If she wept too much, they would be red and swollen; not attractive at all. She looked appealingly at the judge in a way that would tug at his heart and cooed, "For pity's sake, tell us! Tell us everything."

The judge pulled at his mustache. "He's evidently been missing several weeks in a skirmish against the Sioux—"

"Several weeks?" Mrs. Erikson began to wail again and a maid came running with smelling salts. "He's dead! I just know my dear boy must be dead!"

Rand's father looked pale but sober for a change. "For God's sake, Rose, hush and let the man talk!"

"Yes," Shelby urged, "Sweet Jesus! Do tell us what you know. After all, he was going to be my brother-in-law."

"Was?" Vanessa wept, "you're already thinking of him as dead."

"Please, everyone, be calm," the judge implored. "It took a while to get the message from that isolated fort. Rand may turn up after all; maybe he's just wounded."

Lenore had a sudden vision of herself mincing her way down the aisle on Rand's arm. The wounded hero. He would look wan but elegant in a snappy new uniform. His chest would be covered by glistening medals, far more than Shelby owned. All the other girls would be so envious . . .

"Lenore, dear," Mrs. Erikson said, "are you all right?"

"It—it's been such a shock and I'm tired,"

Lenore gasped. "I think I'd like to go home now."

Judge Hamilton came to his feet. "Great Caesar's ghost, but I'm sorry to bring such bad news. Maybe I should drive you home, Lenore."

"No." She stood up and dabbed at her eyes. Perhaps she would look brave and admirable in black after all. Everyone would comment on her impressive dignity. She had seen a bolt of the finest black silk just a few days ago in a shop.

Shelby stood up, limped over to take her arm. "Sweet Jesus! You're in no condition to leave here alone, Miss Carstairs."

Vanessa clasped her hands together. "Oh, Shelby, you're so gallant! Would you see Lenore home?"

He looked around uncertainly. "But Vanessa, dear, you need me here."

"Yes, he's right," Lenore said, her chin coming up bravely. She recalled a riverboat melodrama which featured a particularly courageous heroine, and Lenore relived that part now, relishing being the center of attention. "You need Shelby with you, dear friend. I'll be all right."

"Oh, but I insist." Vanessa said, "after all, we are very best friends and we were going to be related."

Were. All three women began to weep again.

Lenore took Mrs. Erikson's hand. "I have no words right now, I—I can't even think."

The other woman patted her hand with her own plump one. "I understand, my dear. We'll let you know the minute there's more news."

Shelby took her elbow solicitously. While the judge murmured condolences and hopeful comments, Lenore turned with a swirl of dark green skirts and minced her way around the house to the horses, the limping war hero by her side. Too bad she hadn't had a bigger audience, but she knew Vanessa would retell the scene of pathos and bravery over and over in the coming weeks. Without further words, Shelby helped her to her saddle, mounted his own sorrel gelding and they left Randolph Hall at a slow canter.

She would be the center of attention, Lenore thought, at least for a while. But what did this do to all her other plans? She had worked things out so carefully. Marriage would let her have her cake and eat it, too. Now it appeared Rand might have ruined everything by getting himself killed by Indians. For pity's sake, how inconvenient and thoughtless. No real Southern gentleman would do such a thing. This war had been such a mess; no one could make any plans and know for certain they wouldn't be spoiled.

Neither she nor Shelby said anything as they rode back across Shelby's newly purchased, imposing estate that had formerly belonged to a family financially wiped out by the war. Lost in her own thoughts, Lenore stared at the road ahead of her until she cantered up the oak-lined lane to the imposing house that Grandfather Carstairs had built for his bride just before his death.

She motioned that they would ride around to the glass conservatory on the east side of the house. She wasn't quite up to telling her grandmother that Rand was missing, although it occurred to her that the bad news might throw Elizabeth Carstairs into heart failure. Maybe she should tell her and see . . .

For a moment, she almost smiled, then frowned and shook her head as she reined in. The old girl was as tough as boot leather; otherwise she might never have survived as a young, pregnant widow.

Not only survived, but had made Carstairs Oaks prosper. Elizabeth Carstairs was a strong personality in spite of her age and all the adversities she had dealt with since her only son had taken his family and gone West sixteen years ago. Surely Daddy had meant for Lenore to have everything, but sometimes she despaired of Grandmother ever turning over control of the plantation and the wealth.

Shelby helped her from her horse. "Lenore! Are you all right?"

"Yes. Kind of you to bring me home. Do come in and have a drink."

He limped over to tie both their horses up and they entered the conservatory through a side door. The steamy room was full of green plants and scented with flowers that even overwhelmed his macassar hair tonic. She headed to her favorite place, the wicker settee under the big camelia bush.

Faintly through the conservatory drifted the soft sound of grandmother's piano:

Alas, my love, you do me wrong to cast me off discourteously, and I have loved you so long, delighting in your company. Greensleeves was all my joy, Greensleeves was my delight, Greensleeves was my heart of gold and who but my lady Greensleeves.

Lenore sat down on the settee and Shelby knelt by her side. "Perhaps I should call for some smelling salts."

She shook her head. "For pity's sake, Shelby, I—I'll be all right."

"Shouldn't you tell your grandmother what's happened?"

"Later; it will be such a blow for her. She doted on Rand, although she said he was spoiled rotten. She said eventually he had the makings of a real man. Let her play her stupid piano and be happy a few more minutes."

He took her hand. "Suppose she saw us ride up and comes out here?"

"For pity's sake, stop worrying." She withdrew her hand. "The old woman's getting deaf, half blind and crippled up with arthritis. Sometimes I think she runs on sheer willpower. If it weren't for Judge Hamilton, I'd slap her in an old folks home or an asylum so I could control her money before I'm too old to enjoy it."

He frowned. "Don't talk so loud. Nero might be hanging around."

"That big tattooed nigger? I'm not worried about him." The black butler had been here forever and his allegiance was for her grandmother only.

"You appear to be back to your sweet disposition," Shelby said a little caustically. "I take it you're now over the shock of your great loss?"

"How could Rand do this to me?" She reached out, pulled a green leaf off the camelia bush, and twiddled with it. "Such great plans and he's messed everything up."

"How inconsiderate of him." Shelby leaned back on the settee with a sigh. The light gleamed on his slicked down hair and the big diamond stickpin. Besides the strongly perfumed hair oil, he had the most atrocious taste in neckties, she thought.

"Don't be sarcastic, Shelby." She tucked her large feet under her skirt. Even having her shoes made too small didn't help them look more petite, they just ached. "I had such plans."

"Okay, so you won't get the Erikson money, but

I'll have that, so between us, we'll control it all if something should happen to Vanessa and your grandmother. You are the only heir, aren't you?"

Lenore nodded. "You ask too many questions, Shelby. A few months ago, you were asking all sorts of things about the Eriksons. Surely you know quality folk don't do that."

"I forgot myself," he said.

"For pity's sake, we don't have any other secrets. Yes, I'm the only heir."

Shelby cocked his head, listening. "Grandma's stopped playing. Is she liable to come out here?"

"Probably gone upstairs to take a nap." Lenore unbuttoned the top button of her green riding coat.

"Don't sell the old lady short," Shelby said. "She looks a hellava lot smarter than you may think." He put his hand on her shoulder, fumbled with her collar.

"She's a stern old dragon, despite that patrician demeanor," Lenore complained. "I don't think Grandmother and my mother got on well." she thought a minute, simpered. "Mother. It sounds strange to call her that, even now. She was beautiful and quite vain. Even I had to call her by her first name."

"No one ever heard from your folks after they left?"

"Is that so surprising? Lots of women don't get on well with their mothers-in-law and I think those two disliked each other very much. Maybe Mother never wrote out of sheer spite, or something tragic happened later, or maybe they just decided to close the door on the past and make a clean break. Look on the bright side," Lenore cooed. "After sixteen years, I'm not too worried about having anyone claiming a share of the inheritance."

He fiddled with the lace on her collar. "Honey, you're all heart."

Lenore nodded absently, struggling to remember the hazy details of that long ago stormy night. She knew it had stormed because the faint thunder had awakened her.

The next morning, Lenore had been delighted to discover her family had already left before she awakened. Now she had everything at Carstairs Oaks all to herself and didn't have to share anything with that baby.

After six months of no news, Grandmother began to make inquiries. But there were thousands of people going West and she couldn't find anyone who had seen the Carstairs in any wagon train on the Oregon Trail. After a year Elizabeth Carstairs stopped running to the door when a rider would appear, and no letters arrived. Lenore didn't miss them much; especially her little sister, Laurel. It meant more of everything for herself.

"Lenore?"

"What?" She jerked, startled, and realized Shelby Merson was staring at her.

"Sweet Jesus! Are you all right? Has the shock of the news about Rand been too much for you? Perhaps I should get you a big drink of whiskey—"

"For pity's sake, don't take on so. I'll be fine." She took off her perky hat slowly and stared at it. Her mother had been a reigning beauty who loved fine clothes, parties and excitement. It pleased her that Grandmother always said Lenore was the spitting image of her daughter-in-law.

Shelby leaned over and kissed her. "You think anyone suspects we're lovers?"

Lenore snickered and took a breath of his perfumed hair tonic. She did wish he'd stop wearing that, even though he was handsome. "Certainly not my best and stupid friend, Vanessa. It was going to be so convenient, Shelby, with us married to brother and sister. I'm the only heir now to Carstairs Oaks and the Eriksons can't live forever. Something might eventually happen to Vanessa. Maybe it's better this way; everyone will think it's so sweet that the two of us finally end up together."

He unbuttoned the top buttons of her jacket, put his hand inside, and cupped her breast. "Honey, you think of everything."

She lay her head in his lap.

"Sweet Jesus," he whispered, "not here! Suppose someone should see us?"

"There's no one around and besides, who would think a couple would be brazen enough to make love in a glass conservatory?" She reached to unbutton his pants. The trouble with Rand was that he insisted on treating her like a lady when she wanted a man to do forbidden, undescribable things to her; make her do daring things to him; the kind of things she'd been doing to her friend's fiancee since a few weeks after she met Shelby.

He groaned aloud at what she was doing with her lips. "You little tramp! The paid whores could learn from you."

She arched herself against his hand on her breast. "Then treat me like I want to be treated," she cooed.

Shelby needed no further urging after what she'd been doing to him with her teasing little mouth. They slid off the wicker settee in a tumble of green fabric and snowy lace petticoats into the soft dirt. She liked her rutting hot and frenzied. Rand would have been so surprised to realize he didn't really

157

know her at all. But then he'd been such a gallant gentleman.

In the shadows of late afternoon, Elizabeth watched the pair coupling and panting. How ironic Lenore should choose that place, she thought in disgust before she turned and moved quietly up the stairs to her room. Illicit love. The thought brought back images that she didn't want to remember.

Elizabeth's chest pained her and she took a deep breath, determined to ignore it. Maybe if she ignored it, the problem would go away in spite of what the doctors said. It was her secret. Pierce Hamilton was urging her to make some changes in her will, even though he didn't know about the trip to the doctor in Louisville.

What should she do with all the Carstairs wealth? It had been many years since she had written her will. She still clung to that small hope that they were alive, but of course, even if they were, they might be afraid to contact her.

She paused before the small, faded miniature of her beloved husband that she kept on her dressing table. He looked exactly like the son who carried his name, the child he had not lived to see, with his black hair and emerald eyes. How long had her husband been dead? Almost fifty years. Sometimes it seemed like fifty centuries. She knew she had a reputation as a strong woman, but she still sorrowed for the only man she had ever loved.

She took the small picture and sat down on her bed. "Oh, my darling, I still miss you so!" she whispered, and her chest pained her suddenly. Even Judge Hamilton, her faithful suitor, did not know how little time she had left. She had sworn the doctor to secrecy. She looked at the small picture again, smiled, remembering their brief, happy marriage. He had died saving his pregnant wife from a bad bull loose in the pasture. Pierce Hamilton arrived just in time to shoot the bull. Elizabeth had gathered her young husband's broken body into her arms, begging him not to leave her.

He had pressed his gold watch into her hands. There was blood on the fancy fob, bright red blood. "Give this to my son and tell him how much I loved his mother."

"Don't leave me, dear one, I can't go on without you."

"You're strong, Elizabeth, stronger than you think. You'll survive to raise our child."

"No! I can't bear to lose you." She held him close, wishing it had been her, not him dying on the pasture grass.

"I love you, Elizabeth, always remember that. No sacrifice is too great to make for love."

She had wanted to die, too, and be buried next to him out in the family plot near the old church. Instead she had forced herself to live to give birth to his son, given young James the watch, saw him grow to a man and be swept into a whirlwind marriage by a faithless beauty.

Elizabeth suddenly felt very old and frail, remembering that spring night sixteen years ago. Had it been the right decision? She had done what she had to do to protect her beloved husband's name. The Carstairs had a proud, Scottish heritage that would never be sullied as long as Elizabeth Carstairs was alive to protect it.

It had grown almost dark outside. Elizabeth went to the window, watched Shelby Merson limp out of the conservatory, adjusting his pants as he mounted his horse, and ride away. Illicit love never changes, selfish lust with no thought of those who would be hurt. On the other hand, true love is willing to sacrifice everything.

For sixteen years Elizabeth had waited for a letter that never came. Were they dead or afraid of being found? The secret was still safe; Elizabeth had seen to that.

So what was she going to do about the will? *The apple doesn't fall far from the tree,* Elizabeth thought and brushed back a wisp of white hair with a blue-veined hand. She had tried to love the girl, but knowing what Elizabeth knew . . . Lenore was a beautiful but shameless slut. The spitting image of her mother.

Nine

It was dark now as Kimi, Hinzi and the war party neared the camp. They were returning in triumph with Crow scalps and captured ponies. Having gone out after one escaped white slave, thanks to his help, they had averted tragedy for their people and killed many enemies.

Kimi glanced over at Hinzi riding beside her on Scout, the buckskin stallion. "We can't be sure what the old chiefs will decide. Why did you not escape when you had the chance?"

He shrugged and raised one sardonic eyebrow. "If I had escaped because you freed me, you would have had to answer to the old chiefs for doing so."

"But that is why I cut the ropes," she insisted, fingering her medicine charm.

"I couldn't let you make that sacrifice. And besides, I didn't want to leave you behind."

Was he saying sweet things because he knew she wanted to hear them? Was this white man loco that he would stay when his life might hang in the balance?

She closed her eyes, remembering the intensity of their passion last night, the taste and the heat of his body as they meshed and strained together. Her nipples seemed to swell against her doeskin shift as if they felt again his wet, demanding mouth.

She dare not admit how much last night had

161

stirred her. Suppose she had just been an available female and he had hesitated in escaping only because he knew it was impossible? Perhaps he had thought it better to take a chance on saving a grateful war chief's life.

"Kimi," he said, "about last night . . ."

She waited, but his voice trailed off, leaving her wondering what he had started to say. Had last night meant anything to him? She remembered then that an elegant, civilized white girl waited for Hinzi in a far away place. Maybe he would run away next chance he got and return to that girl. Maybe he would laugh with other white men about the easy virtue of Indian girls. Indian girl? Hinzi said she was white. Perhaps her skin was, but her soul was Sioux.

She blurted without thinking, "If you had made good your escape, using me as a hostage, would you have given me to some of the soldiers for their pleasure?"

Even in the darkness, she saw the anger in his eyes, the grim set of his jaw. "You don't think much of me, do you?"

"I have no way of knowing what white men truly think," Kimi said honestly, watching his yellow hair gleam in the moonlight as the war party rode across the prairie. How often had old Wagnuka warned her to avoid *wasicu;* that their tongues were as crooked as a dog's hind leg and they did not know the meaning of truth? Many times her mother had told her they would carry off Sioux maidens, use them for their pleasure, and trade them off to others.

She had thought she hated him, but last night had been pleasurable for her, too. Did it make her a whore that she had spread her thighs wide, wanting him to thrust deeper still and leave his seed within her?

Could she trust him? Now that she thought about

162

it, it would have been clever of him not to try to escape at that point, knowing he had no chance. If he could get the warriors to trust him and let down their guard, he might have a better chance next time.

She urged her pony forward, riding up beside One Eye. "What do you intend to do with the soldier?"

He turned his head so he could see her with his one good eye. "He saved my life. I am bound to beg mercy for him from the council. I think it bad luck to kill a man who saved me."

Gopher gave her a thoughtful look. "What the old chiefs might want to know is how this soldier happened to escape in the first place, seeing as how he was securely chained?"

"Are you accusing me of turning him loose?"

The plain, squat brave didn't say anything for a long moment. "Women can be foolish over a man, if he is a handsome man."

Kimi didn't answer. She wasn't sure herself how Hinzi had come to be freed. There was no way he could have broken those chains. Then how did he get the key from her tipi to unlock them? Old Wagnuka was the only other person who knew where it was, as far as Kimi knew. However, her mother hated the soldier. She wouldn't try to help him . . . or had she been plotting against him?

Kimi was still thinking about her mother as she answered. "If the Long Knives hear that our braves repaid good with evil, they will think our tongues are forked and that we cannot be trusted. Then we will never be able to live at peace with the whites."

Gopher snorted. "There will never be peace with the whites as long as we have anything they want, which is everything. Already they lust after the land around us and drive their wagons deep into our country, searching for the yellow metal. They would deny us even the Mako Shika, the Badlands to the

163

west, should they find yellow metal there."

Kimi looked at One Eye. "As war leader, do you plan to speak for the soldier?"

"Perhaps his heart can change," One Eye said grudgingly, glancing back over his shoulder at the Yellow Hair flexing his wide shoulders. "Perhaps we might welcome him as a brother and yet keep an eye on him."

"You'll find him as full of tricks as a coyote," Gopher grumbled.

One Eye gave Kimi a long, knowing look. "Yes, I will speak to the old chiefs in his favor. Sometimes a woman can make the difference. For the right woman, a man can throw it all away, turn his back on everything that is precious to him to go with her,"

"I think you see more than there is to see," Kimi said modestly. "Perhaps he is tired of his civilization and just wants to live free as the wind for a while, as other white men have sometimes come among the tribes."

"Only time will tell," One Eye said. "Kimi, I will ask that Hinzi be given some of the captured ponies and a chance to be one of us. In the end, you will be the one who will know whether his heart is good and whether he is fit to be a Lakota warrior. If you want him for your man, Kimi, take him. May Wakan Tanka guide you."

She hated the Hinzi—didn't she? Could she hate him and still find ecstasy in his arms? She didn't know how she felt. With Gopher still grumbling, Kimi turned her pony and rode back to Hinzi. "I think your life will be spared because of what you did for One Eye."

He looked at her. "Is that the only reason?"

She was almost too embarrassed to look at him. "I asked for you. If the council agrees, you are to be my man."

164

"Don't I get anything to say about this?" He raised one eyebrow at her.

"You don't want me?"

"In my civilization, the man does the choosing."

"I thought that's what you were doing when you carried me off. Shall I tell the warriors that you didn't want me, that you only raped me as they would an enemy girl?"

He looked ashamed and regretful. She wondered if his mind was on the white girl waiting for him far away? Kimi felt her heart twist with jealousy. Perhaps he meant more to her than she would even admit to herself.

Or was it only that she wanted to feel again what she had felt in his arms last night? No, it couldn't be love, but she could save his life, make Hinzi happy. No woman would cook and work for him as she would. Every year, her belly would swell with a new son for him. She would make him forget that other girl, forget his own civilization, forget everything but meshing with Kimi's ripe body, pouring his seed into her, kissing her full breasts.

Her thoughts were troubled, wishing she could read his mind. Did he really care about her, or would he flee the first chance he got?

The war party stopped in a small grove of brush several miles from the camp to paint their faces and put on their best war robes as befitted victors. The others willingly shared their finery with the soldier, and Kimi helped him paint his face, combing his golden hair and putting a decorated band around his head.

She looked at his hair shining in the moonlight. "Hinzi: Yellow Hair, a good name for you. Do you have a spirit animal as mine is the butterfly?"

He nodded. "The wolf. My name, Randolph, is an old name. It means protected and guided by wolves."

"It is a good spirit animal." She remembered the lobo howling in the distance when she knelt below Mato's burial platform. Had it been trying to tell her she was to be the bride of the wolf? "Wolves mate for life," she blurted without thinking.

He looked down into her eyes, standing so close, she felt the heat of his big body. "And how long do butterflies mate?"

"I don't know." She felt the blood rise to her face, remembering what had happened in the cave.

"Can the butterfly bear the wolf a son?"

She looked him straight in the eye. "If it will bind the wolf to her, she will give him one every year. Her breasts will stay swollen with milk for the wolf's cubs."

She saw his gaze sweep across her breasts and imagined his mouth there, sucking the rich sweetness from them.

He smiled then, almost grudgingly. "What more could a man ask for than that?"

Nothing more. He didn't say he loved her or that he needed her. In silence she finished applying his war paint, the red and the blue across his rippling muscles. Then she helped paint the buckskin horse, putting lightning symbols on its legs to give it speed, red hand prints on its shoulders to show its rider had killed an enemy in hand-to-hand combat.

The warriors mounted up and rode into camp at a gallop, shouting their victory cries. The women ran out, greeting them with trilling sounds. Old men shot off ancient guns, dogs barked, children shouted and danced about.

Hinzi looked as brave as any Sioux warrior on the spirited stallion, Kimi thought. He was all but naked, the war paint gleaming on his muscular white body. She saw other young women giving him admiring glances as the people gathered close to hear what had happened.

One Eye motioned with his lance for silence. "We have much to tell! This day we have won against a great Crow war party and brought back many scalps and ponies!"

A cheer and victory chants began among the people, but her mother crowded close, glaring first at Kimi, then at Hinzi. "What about this white soldier who escaped? He has no doubt shamed my daughter. I demand he pay with his life!"

Kimi's heart almost stopped beating and she saw the nodding of heads in agreement. A Lakota maiden's virtue was not to be taken lightly.

"I went with him of my own free will," Kimi said.

Her mother glared at her. "Would you dare bite the knife and say that?"

She felt perspiration break out on her skin. If she swore by the knife and lied, something terrible would surely happen to her. Yet in her heart, she realized suddenly that to save Hinzi, she would do anything. "I—I—"

"Woman," Hinzi boomed suddenly in his drawling voice to her mother, "If your people will accept me as one of them, I want your daughter for my own. As a marriage gift, I offer my share of the captured ponies."

A murmur of approval went through the crowd. The white warrior was attempting to do what was right and just among their people. Moreover, it was obvious to all that his share of the milling herd of ponies would be many.

Kimi lowered her eyes modestly as befitted a proper woman, knowing other girls looked at the yellow-haired warrior with admiration and at her with envy.

167

Old Wagnuka seemed almost speechless. "I will talk with my daughter."

One Eye dismounted, joined them. "Do not take too long, old woman, else he will choose another to warm his blankets." He grinned. "Come, Hinzi, we will smoke and eat with the men. Time enough later for women."

Kimi went to her mother's side as the men strode away. "We must get food ready for the braves."

"No. We talk first." Wagnuka looked troubled as she motioned Kimi to follow her.

Kimi dreaded what she knew must come, but she went into the tipi, sat down on a buffalo robe. "Before you ask: yes, he took me. Even now I may be making a child for him."

The old woman scowled. "I feared as much. You are very young and innocent, my daughter. I have warned you how the *wasicu* use Indian girls and then throw them away when they return to their own kind."

She wanted to ask about her own white blood, but hesitated. "I think he would not do that."

"But you have no way of knowing!" Her mother pressed her advantage, and Kimi knew her own uncertainty must be reflected in her face.

Kimi ducked her head. "I have no way of knowing."

"Men say anything they think a young girl wants to hear when the mating urge is upon them. And girls, giddy with love, believe them."

Kimi looked the old woman in the eye, suddenly knowing the truth. "Mother," she whispered, "were you a thrown-away girl?"

For a long moment, Wagnuka's shoulders shook, and when she tried, she could not speak. Her grief was terrible to see. "Yes," she whispered. "No one but Otter, my husband ever knew. A French fur trap-

168

per from the Grandmother Land to the north. I loved him much, but when he tired of me, he swapped me for a new rifle from a trader's store. The trader let many *wasicu* use me before Otter traded for me."

Kimi closed her eyes, wishing now she had not asked. So what Hinzi had said was true; Kimi did have white blood. Now she could understand her mother's bitterness and distrust, yet her heart overruled her reason despite everything. Minutes passed in silence.

Finally her mother threw up her hands in defeat. "Is the white soldier a good hunter?"

Kimi nodded. "There will always be meat in your tipi as the mother-in-law of Hinzi."

"I worry that he will try to take you away to the white civilization."

Kimi put a gentle hand on her arm. "Mother, I promise that as long as you draw breath, we will always be in this camp."

"That is all I can hope for," she sighed, and abruptly Kimi saw how old and sick she looked. "I do not have very long. It was my fondest wish that you be married to a good warrior who would care for you when I am gone."

"Hinzi will care for me, and for you, too, Mother."

"Will he? Or will he only use you and then abandon you when he moves on? Think, daughter!" She shook a wrinkled finger in Kimi's face. "If this soldier returns to his people, will he take you with him? Will you fit in with his kind? You cannot read or write. You have never even sat in a chair. How will you compare to the fine white women he knows? Will he be ashamed to call you his woman there?"

She did not even want to think about it, but already the image of the girl he had spoken of came to her mind. "I will think no further than now," she said firmly, fingering her medicine object. "Remember only that you are about to be a rich woman of many ponies and there will be food in your lodge."

"I remember that an enemy soldier, a killer of my people, a despoiler of our women, is mating with my daughter. That indeed is a bitter thing."

"I love him." Kimi realized that now. She hesitated, wondering if her mother had freed the soldier from his chains. Kimi didn't want to know. No doubt Wagnuka had hoped he would escape and never come near her daughter again. She must have been desperate to risk the old chiefs' wrath that way.

"Love!" The wrinkled face twisted bitterly. "When he puts a baby in your belly and deserts you, you will know how crooked the white man's tongue can be. But if you are bound to do this thing and he has already taken you, I will accept defeat." She made a gesture of surrender and her thin shoulders slumped.

"Mother, I think you will live to know that Hinzi's heart is good and that he truly cares about me."

"A white man like him would have to worship a woman to turn his back on everything he holds dear and live among us forever. Are you sure he is willing to make such a great sacrifice for your sake?"

Kimi could only shrug helplessly. "I have no answers. I listen to my heart."

"Better you should listen to your wise mother. Leave me now," the old woman gestured, "and send in your soldier."

Knowing her mother's heart would hear no reason, Kimi went outside, her thoughts confused. Was she troubled because her mother was so set against Hinzi, or because secretly she feared that her mother spoke the truth? She would not think of that now.

She found Hinzi just coming from council, where One Eye had spoken for him and the old chiefs had decided the soldier might stay until they made a final decision. It was not often, Kimi knew, that an enemy turned his back on his own kind and came to spend his life among them. Perhaps they doubted his intent and had decided to wait and see.

She thought about her Mother's French trapper. A white man. So old Otter was not really her father. She had wanted to press Wagnuka for more information, but dared not. It had hurt her mother enough to tell what little she had revealed.

One Eye rubbed his scarlet eye patch as he quickly told her the details of how he had spoken words of praise and defense for the white soldier.

Humming her spirit song for comfort, Kimi approached the white. "My mother would speak with you."

Hinzi looked questioningly at One Eye, who grinned at him. "It is really not proper for you to meet with Wagnuka. Usually a friend or relative meets with the girl's male relative."

"She wants to meet with Hinzi," Kimi insisted stubbornly.

One Eye nodded and strode away.

Kimi bit her lip. "I know now why Mother distrusts *wasicu* so. I am fathered by a white trapper, a Frenchman from the Grandmother's Land." She gestured toward the north—Canada, the whites called it.

He started to say something, shrugged. "I will be at the big council fire for the feasting and dancing soon. Now I will meet with Wagnuka."

Wagnuka looked up as he entered and sat down cross-legged. He was indeed handsome, she thought, even more handsome than the brown-eyed Frenchman she herself had loved so many, many years ago.

171

"I do not give my approval that you take my daughter as your woman."

"I come to offer gifts," he said and his face was stubborn. "I will have her whether you wish it or not."

"You are forward and not respectful," she snapped.

He peered at her across the fire as if trying to see her soul. "You set me up, woman, tried to lead me into a trap and get me killed. Do you hate me so much?"

"It is not that I hate you but that I love Kimimila," she said without guilt. "I knew as long as you drew breath, you would be a danger to her."

"My intentions are honorable. To show you I speak with a straight tongue, I offer a major gift; ten ponies." He paused. "I give all I have captured."

She was impressed. "There are many girls in this camp whose parents would be pleased with a gift of three."

He smiled and she saw the wanting in his pale eyes. "But they are not the parents of Kimimila."

"Well spoken." She softened a little in spite of herself. "It is not right that you make arrangements through her mother."

He shrugged. "You have no male relatives to do this thing for you?"

She shook her head, feeling very old and ill. "You will take her in your blankets whether I say yea or no."

"I will take her, yes." His jaw looked firm, his mouth a grim line. "The little butterfly is a fever in my blood that can only be quenched by putting my body into hers, feeling her naked against my skin."

"A white man once said something like that to me," she said and her voice sounded bitter as gall in her own ears. "Once I was young and pretty, too, but he threw me away."

"Why do you lie to Kimi?" he whispered.

She felt the blood rush to her face. "I do not know what it is you speak."

"You make her think she is a half-breed, fruit of your own," he insisted, "but I see that she is white as I am. Kimi is trusting and believes you. I say she has not one drop of Sioux blood."

If at that moment she had had a knife, she would have driven it into his heart to make sure he did not reveal what he knew. "I had a half-breed child," she began uncertainly.

"Not Kimi," he insisted, "Besides, you are too old to be her mother."

Wagnuka glared at him across the fire. "You see too much, soldier. Yes, you are right on both counts. Long before Kimi's time, I had a son by a white trapper. When the son was weaned, he took the boy and traded me for a new rifle to another *wasicu* at a trading post. He wanted a son; squaws he could get anywhere."

The soldier's eyes softened in sympathy. "I might have guessed. What happened to the boy?"

Wagnuka shrugged. "I never knew; I never saw him or his father again. Somewhere he is a grown man, this handsome, half-breed son, if he yet lives. I do not even know that." The tears came to her eyes unbidden but she blinked them back. She would not be shamed before this white man.

"How came you by Kimi then?"

He would not stop until he knew; she could tell that by the stubborn glint in his eyes. "All who know are long dead. You are right, soldier, I am too old to be her mother, but innocent and trusting as she is, she has never questioned anything I tell her. If I tell you, will you promise not to take her from this camp or tell my secrets until I am gone?"

He hesitated. "Yes, old woman, I promise, but for myself, I must know. Somewhere a white family looks for her."

Wagnuka shook her gray braids. "I think not. I think her family is long dead out on the plains south of here."

"A raid?"

"No. This is a very strange story I will tell, but if I must, I will bite the knife to prove that what I speak is true."

He sat silently, waiting.

"After the white man threw me away, I was a whore for a white trader until a warrior named Otter rescued me. My son was gone and Otter and I never had any of our own who lived."

"And?" he prompted.

She listened to the chanting and the drums drifting faintly from outside. There would be feasting and dancing tonight to celebrate the victory. And then Hinzi would take her daughter as his own into his lodge, no matter what an old woman said.

"I was past the age to produce children for Ptan and had long ago given up hope. Then one night I dreamed a butterfly lit upon my hand out on the prairie and whispered to me that Wakan Tanka was sending me a girl child to be my very own."

In the silence, the fire crackled and the white warrior waited, patient as any Lakota brave.

"I dreamed I said to the butterfly, 'how will I know this is a child for me'? 'Because she will be different than other children; she will have eyes the same color as those of the sacred White Buffalo Woman of Sioux legends. When the girl speaks, you will know Wakan Tanka sent her to you.' "

"Kimi," Hinzi murmured.

Wagnuka nodded. "Our people were on a buffalo hunt far from here. The next day, Otter and a hunting party ranged a long way off. He told me they found white people scattered over a very far distance as if they had tried to walk from somewhere and gradually, as their strength failed them and their water ran out, they fell one by one and died."

The soldier looked puzzled. "Where did they come from?"

"We never knew. There weren't that many, and no one was sure where they came from. The oxen and a few horses they had were not enough to take them very far and those, too, had died."

"It was not near a white town?"

"No," she shook her head. "The area is very desolate and short of food and water. No doubt somehow they had strayed there and finally realizing they were lost, they made one last desperate attempt to walk out."

"And Kimi was the only one alive?"

"The man who carried the child in his arms was barely alive and yet he protected her with his body. His eyes were green as new grass and he whispered a word, 'kimimila,' before he died.

"But how would a white man speak Lakota?" His handsome face grew puzzled.

"I only tell you about spirit medicine, I don't explain it," Wagnuka said simply. "In his pocket, the man carried a round, gold thing. Its heart beat when Otter held it to his ear. Otter was afraid of its magic and he hit it with a stick until it was crushed and its heart stopped ticking."

"A watch," Hinzi said.

She didn't know what that was. "The medicine object that Kimi wears around her neck was attached to it."

"A watch fob," he muttered. "White gentlemen let it hang from their vest pocket. When did this take place?"

Wagnuka wrinkled her face thoughtfully. "The year my people name the Time the Crow Held the Sioux at Bay."

She could tell by his expression that he did not understand winter counts. The Lakotas kept a calendar on a buffalo hide and each winter was noted by something outstanding that had happened that year.

"Tell me about the child," Hinzi insisted.

"Nothing more to tell. She was so young, maybe not more than two or three winters. The only word the child said was the same one the dying man used, *'kimimila.'* Otter took this as a sign from Wakan Tanka that this was the child the butterfly had promised me. The war party buried the scattered white people where they lay, afraid that the Lakota would be accused of killing them. We never knew any more than that."

"But one of the women must have been the child's mother."

She nodded. "Probably. There was no way to know which of the several dead women scattered down the miles of trail was the mother."

"And you kept Kimi as your own, hiding her whenever whites came near?"

"I knew they would take her from me." Wagnuka swallowed hard. "They would not understand that Wakan Tanka had given her to me; otherwise, why would she know a Lakota word?"

He looked puzzled, too. "It is indeed a mystery. Perhaps you are right; perhaps her people are all dead. Maybe no family searches for her."

She wished she could read the white man's thoughts and know whether his heart was good. "You will not tell Kimi of this talk?"

He hesitated. "Not as long as you live, old woman, you have my word." He stood up slowly.

"One more thing," she said. "Now that I am to be

176

your mother-in-law, it is not a custom to speak to your mother-in-law among our people. This is the last conversation we will ever have."

"You will not try to stop me from taking Kimi as my own then?"

She shook her head, wishing her ambush had worked and that the soldier had been killed. That way she would not have to worry about him taking Kimi away. "Easier to stop a river at spring flood than hot blood pulsing on a warm spring night. Go to her now."

He nodded and stooping his tall frame, left the tipi. Wagnuka looked after him, feeling very old and sick, thinking of the white man she herself had loved so many years ago and wondering what had ever happened to her half-breed son. Perhaps she would never know. Tonight she missed old Otter very much and she wrapped her withered arms around herself and rocked back and forth, keening a grief song. She did not trust this Hinzi, but she was helpless to stop him. Sooner or later he would return to his people, to a place where Kimi would not fit in even if he took her with him. Wagnuka saw nothing but trouble and heartache on the horizon for the white child she had raised as her own. She said a prayer to Wakan Tanka to protect Kimi from the soldier's lust.

Ten

Kimi served the men as they sat around the big fire, modestly keeping her eyes downcast. Hinzi sat in a place of honor next to One Eye, watching the scalp dancing as celebrations went on around the hair of the Crow enemies he had helped slay.

She wanted very much to know what he and old Wagnuka had discussed. Certainly he had looked both annoyed and relieved as he swaggered from the old woman's lodge and strode to join the crowd gathering around the big camp fire.

Now as she served him meat into a gourd, he said softly, "She has agreed. I gave her a gift of ten ponies."

Next to him One Eye laughed good-naturedly. "Ten ponies? Tomorrow everyone in camp will know. There are many pretty girls among the Lakota you might have had for two or three ponies."

Hinzi caught her eye and looked at her solemnly. "I would have given twenty to claim Kimimila."

She felt the blood rush to her face, knowing some of those around him had heard and tomorrow it would be told through the camp that the white warrior was so smitten with Mato's widow that he had given a great bride gift to get her. For a white man to think so highly of a Lakota girl complimented her and raised Hinzi in the tribe's opinion.

White man's whiskey had been passed around the warriors and One Eye frowned. "This drink brings us only trouble."

She watched Hinzi take a big drink, the whiskey running from the corners of his mouth, dripping on his bare, brawny chest. "Kentucky bourbon," he drawled, "it brings back a lot of memories."

She wondered then if he thought of the other girl, but said nothing as she sat down on the ground near him.

The dancing grew more lively, the people writhing to the rhythm of the drums, throwing grotesque shadows in the firelight. The drums beat a rhythm that felt like the beating of her heart. Finally, after a few more sips of whiskey, Hinzi, at the urging of some of the other braves, moved to dance in the circle.

He was as graceful as a cougar, Kimi thought admiringly, despite his size. He danced with a natural ease and rhythm that any warrior might envy. When he looked across the big fire at her, his eyes sent her a message as primitive as time itself. Without realizing she did so, Kimi moved to dance about the circle with him, chanting and twisting to the beat. She took a deep breath and was aware of the scent of the fire and his warm skin. Her own body felt warm beneath her doeskin sheath—or maybe it was only the way Hinzi's pale blue eyes swept over her. There was no doubt in her mind what he wanted.

They danced around the fire, moving gradually to the shadows. Already couples were drifting away to their tipis or to lie on soft buffalo robes out under the stars.

Hinzi reached out and caught her arm. "My body has need of you."

When she hesitated, he swung her up in his

arms. "You are mine now and I will have you. I have thought of nothing else since last night."

She opened her mouth to say that she was not yet ready to leave the dancing, but his hot mouth covered hers, thrusting with an insistent blade of tongue, making her breathe faster.

He smiled ever so slightly. "You want me too." With that, he carried her through the camp and into his lodge. He stood her on her feet.

She hesitated, looking at him across the fire. "Oh, Hinzi, are you sure? Sure you want to stay among the Lakota?"

He stripped off his buckskins and stood there naked as some primitive savage in the firelight. His erect manhood would have done justice to a stallion, and the pale light gleamed on his rippling magnificent body. "I must be three kinds of a fool to lust after one so young," he muttered. "I only know that I want you under me; I can think no further than that. Tomorrow must take care of itself. Still I have never known such freedom," he whispered. "To live as a warrior without the restraints of civilization, wild and free. This is what every white man secretly dreams of."

She looked at him, big and virile and all male. He was what every woman dreamed of, she thought. To be carried off by him and pleasured without thought of anything but the ecstasy and the passion. She would not think past this moment or worry about what would happen in the future.

Very slowly, she took off the doeskin shift and stood there naked.

"Take down your hair," he commanded.

She did as she was bid, letting the waist-length, ebony locks cascade down over her breasts and back.

"Sweet butterfly, you are the most desirable

woman I have ever seen," he whispered. "Turn around slowly; let me look at you."

Kimi took a deep breath, knowing it caused her proud breasts to thrust forward as she slowly turned for his inspection. His look almost seemed like a caress against her bare belly and thighs as he stared at her.

"Now come here."

She obeyed and without realizing she did so, she knelt submissively before him. He reached out, stroked her long black hair. She wrapped her arms about his hips, pressing her breasts against his powerful thighs, and then she kissed his manhood in complete surrender to the symbol of domination it represented.

She felt him draw in his breath sharply, and she knew the touch of her mouth gave him pleasure. She pressed her breasts against his thighs harder, took him deep in her mouth, running her tongue along the pulsating steel of his rod.

He groaned and held her face against him, urging—no, demanding—still more. The taste and scent of his seed excited her as she had not realized she could be thrilled. "Sweet butterfly," he whispered, "I am still your slave."

He reached to swing her up in his arms, kissing her face, her eyes, her lips. "Let me show you how much I desire you!" He lay her down on a soft buffalo robe and began to caress her with his mouth, tasting and kissing her bare skin. His tongue laved her breasts and the hollow of her belly. She felt the heat of his breath on the inside of her thigh.

Surely he wasn't going to . . . ? And then he did. She tried to protest, tried to pull away, but he was insistent and very strong. Who was the slave? All she could do was gasp and arch her back, spreading herself in complete surrender to his dominance as he tasted and caressed where he would. She had not known the forbidden thrust of a man's tongue could send such shivers of passion from where he kissed all up through her body.

When he kissed her mouth, she tasted herself on his lips as his hands sought her breasts, pulling her astride him. After that, she forgot everything except the feel of him throbbing deep inside as she used him for her pleasure . . . and his. In that moment when they reached the zenith of passion together, she forgot that he hadn't said he loved her or that this was an impossible alliance. Kimi remembered only that he was made to fit her sheath and she could not stop herself from urging him to plunge his great dagger deep.

When she lay spent in his arms, listening to his gentle breathing as he slept, she remembered again her mother and wondered if this was how it had been with Wagnuka and her white trapper. Yet knowing that this could not last, that there was a white girl waiting for Hinzi and that someday he would surely leave, Kimi could not force herself not to love him, not to desire him. She would live one day at a time, savoring each moment as long as the white warrior was among the Sioux. Tonight she was the white warrior's woman. She would face the reality of his leaving on the day that it happened and not borrow tomorrow's worries. Promising herself that, despite grave misgivings, Kimi curled up in his strong, protective arms and dropped off to sleep.

The next morning a brave galloped through camp, shouting that a big herd of buffalo had been sighted grazing only a few miles away. Kimi looked from her fire, where she had just fed Hinzi, to the warrior himself. "Do you hear that? Are you a good hunter?"

He smiled at her, paused in repairing the bow One Eye had given him. "A very good hunter, however, I haven't done much buffalo hunting. I don't suppose it can be very different from fox hunting."

Kimi blinked. "The civilized whites eat foxes as the Lakota do dogs?"

Hinzi laughed, his even white teeth gleaming in his tanned face. "No. We merely get a large group of people together on horseback, a bunch of dogs and hunt them. It's a sport; lots of fence jumping and exciting because it's a little dangerous."

She tried to understand. "Then the fox fur must have great value for everyone to go on this hunt."

Hinzi scratched his head. "No, no one really wants the fox hide; although being awarded the brush is quite an honor."

"The ways of the white people are very mysterious," Kimi said and shook her head, "to go on a long, dangerous ride to hunt something that no one plans to eat and no one needs the fur?"

Hinzi looked a little embarrassed. "Now that I think of it," he drawled, "it does sound a little silly, even to me."

"Do women go on these hunts?"

"Sometimes," Hinzi said as he stood up, "but only the very best riders. And they ride sidesaddle."

Kimi didn't say anything. She was an excellent rider herself and wasn't ever sure what a "sidesaddle" was. She was glad that she didn't have to live among silly, wasteful whites who killed a small animal for no good reason. It didn't even sound like it would be very exciting.

The whole camp was awake and full of excitement as the hunters made plans and the women talked of the feast they would have tonight. One Eye had given his favorite horse, Scout, to Hinzi as a gift for saving his life. There were many ceremonies to perform to insure good medicine and a rewarding hunt. Wagnuka joined Kimi as she gathered up her skinning knife and helped with a travois to carry the meat back to camp.

Hinzi looked magnificent astride his spirited horse, Kimi thought, her heart swelling with pride as she watched him join the warriors. He was dressed like any Lakota brave. Except for the moccasins and a brief loincloth, his big, muscular body was naked and tanning fast in the prairie sun. His yellow hair was getting a little shaggy, but still not long enough to braid as the other warriors wore theirs.

Her mother frowned. "Now we will see if your white warrior can provide meat for a lodge. If he is not a good hunter and unable to feed his woman, it does not matter if he was an important person in his own life."

Kimi smiled, looking after him as he joined the men. "I do not worry. Hinzi seems to be fitting in well with the Indian life. Tonight we will all feast."

Old Wagnuka shook her head. "There are still many among our people who are suspicious of him and trust him not. They think the first chance he gets he will run away and return to the whites."

Deep in her heart, Kimi was afraid to admit that that suspicion had crossed her own mind, but she didn't want to think about it. "Come," she motioned, "we are wasting time. We will join the women who make ready to cut up the meat once the braves bring the buffalo down."

Rand's heart quickened as he reined the dancing buckskin stallion in and looked around at the other hunters. Maybe at heart he was just a primitive savage himself. He had not realized until the last few days what a soft, boring life he had led as a rich son of a big plantation owner. Was it this simple, primitive life that seemed so exciting or was it the girl, Kimimila?

Rand glanced back over his shoulder at her, remembering last night. He hadn't realized living as an Indian with no clock and close to nature would appeal to him so much. He imagined Lenore Carstairs in an expensive dress with all its hoops, a whalebone corset, and her mincing, ladylike gait. She always looked as if she might trip and fall. He couldn't even picture her naked on a buffalo robe, reacting with wild, abandoned passion the way Kimi had done last night.

Kimi. He couldn't seem to get enough of the girl's ripe body. Was that love or just lust? At this point he wasn't prepared to say, and didn't even want to think about it. Someday he must go home to the life that he had always led. It wasn't realistic to think he could spend the rest of his life as a white warrior, and yet . . .

One Eye interrupted his thoughts. "Come, brother, hunt beside me. The two of us and Gopher and his young son ride together. Here's a rifle for you, since you are new to the bow."

Rand took the old gun from One Eye, thinking about the many fine rifles he owned back at Randolph Hall. However this wasn't hunting some silly fox for thrills, this was the greatest excitement of all—survival. If a man wasn't a good hunter, his family might go hungry this winter when the snow was deep. Rand had never been hungry except the time he'd spent at Point Lookout prison.

The war. He had lost track of time and all that turmoil seemed so distant and unimportant. Was it over? It didn't even matter any more who had won. What was important was to bring in more than his share of meat, and gain status in the eyes of the Lakota people. This was something he could not buy with family money. Gaining the respect of these primitive people was abruptly more important than any honor he had ever wanted as a Confederate lieutenant or as a wealthy Southern landowner.

The Lakota men rode out to look over the herd, the women with their travois and small children following along. Rand and One Eye joined up with Gopher, and his son, a sturdy, handsome boy who looked about eleven or twelve years old.

The riders scattered out cautiously, watching the huge herd from a distance, careful not to spook them. One Eye explained softly to Rand that buffalo were stupid animals, but they could be dangerous and unpredictable. He frowned. "I hope Gopher's son doesn't do anything foolish. This is his first big hunt and he will be eager to prove himself."

"No more than I," Rand said, looking at his friend.

One Eye smiled. "You have already proven yourself, my friend. I think maybe someday you will be invited to share many of our most secret rites as the others gain confidence in you; maybe even the sun dance."

Rand suddenly realized what those scars on One Eye's bronzed chest were. He imagined himself hanging from rawhide strips strung through his chest muscles to prove his bravery as One Eye had done sometime in the past. Once Rand would have thought that ceremony savage and ridiculous; now it occurred to him that the scars denoted a very brave man with status in the tribe. For a long moment, he imagined himself striding into the camp circle with sun dance scars visible on his brawny chest. Even old Wagnuka would be impressed and Kimi would be proud to belong to such a warrior.

Rand blinked in disbelief. Was he losing his mind? Of course he couldn't go through such a barbaric ceremony. What would his parents say when he returned? Worse yet, what would the very civilized Lenore say when they were married and she saw the scars? Somehow she didn't seem as pretty or as desirable any more. In fact, she would look silly and ridiculous with her elaborate clothes and mincing walk out here. On the other hand, how would Kimi fit in back in a white civilization? Rand didn't want to think about that. For the time being, the little white savage was his to enjoy. He would live for the moment and not face the future until he was actually on his way back South.

He and One Eye joined Gopher and his son on a low rise overlooking the great herd. Rand had never seen anything so impressive as the sight of that moving brown ocean of fur. The beasts grazed or rolled in the dust. Here and there a pair of bulls fought, churning up big swirls of dust with their pawing feet.

The stink of the giant herd of beasts, the sound of their hooves as they drifted and grazed almost overwhelmed his senses. Here and there a lost calf bawled for its dam.

One Eye said softly, "Your horse has been in these hunts before, Hinzi, so he will know what to do. Just be careful about riding too close. If you get surrounded and your horse should stumble, you'll never have a chance. The only way we'll recognize what's left of you is the yellow hair."

"I'll remember." Rand wiped the sweat from his

forehead, touched his beaded headband, looked down at himself, and realized he was all but naked. Mother and sister Vanessa would be shocked. Lenore would probably faint if she could see him out like this. It seemed as if he had been away from white civilization a long, long time. Did he miss it? He wasn't sure.

The morning had turned hot. Summer was coming on, Rand realized, thinking calendars and clocks were becoming less and less important to him. He was beginning to think like the Indians already.

Yes, he would rely on the experience of his horse. Rand wasn't sure what he was supposed to do, but Scout seemed to sense the excitement. It was difficult to keep the spirited horse in check while he waited. Some of the braves were creeping closer and closer, picking off an animal here and there.

Rand looked over his shoulder, searching for Kimi's face in the distance. He saw her now with the other women, awaiting the time to come out on the field and cut up the meat. She gave him a nod of recognition. His woman. He would make her proud of him, bring in more meat than she or the old lady could dry for their needs. There would be plenty left over for the elderly and sick who could not hunt. For the first time in a long time, Rand felt that his life counted for something.

Abruptly the wind shifted and the big brown beasts seemed to scent the men for the first time. They began to bellow and move uneasily, some of the bulls pawing the ground in challenge. Most of them seemed oblivious to the dead animals lying on the ground around them—until they smelled the blood.

With snorts and bellowing, the herd began to

move; slowly at first, a softly undulating wave of brown fur as far as the eye could see.

Now the braves urged their swift ponies forward, racing along both sides of the dark river of beasts, shooting arrows faster than most whites could handle a rifle.

His heart pounding hard with danger and excitement, Rand galloped along beside the herd. Dust swirled in choking clouds and clung to his sweating, naked skin. Pounding hooves vibrated the prairie under his running pony until the sound seemed to boom like thunder.

He looked around for One Eye and saw him far ahead, thrusting a lance into a big bull that stumbled and went down. Here and there, barely visible in the swirling dust, Rand could make out yelping warriors riding along the edges of the herd, firing arrows as rapidly as mighty arms could pull a bow. Rand brought his old rifle up, aimed, fired. A fat cow went down. Reloading as he galloped along, he brought down another prime buffalo.

Without even realizing he did so, Rand threw back his head and yelled to the heavens, glorying in the thrill of the hunt and just being alive. Around him, gunshots echoed and bowstrings sang as warriors picked their animals.

Ahead of him suddenly, he saw Gopher's young son, riding a little too close to the herd, determined to make his own kill. Rand started to shout a warning, but just then the boy pulled his bow and a half-grown, prime animal took the shaft deep in the shoulder, stumbled and crashed down. Too late, the youth seemed to realize he had ridden too close to the herd that now parted to surround him.

In a heartbeat, Rand took in the scene, the boy's tense, brown face as his pony galloped, swept along by the crazed buffalo. For only an instant, Rand hesitated, knowing the dangers that he faced if he made any attempt to ride closer himself. As aristocrat Randolph Erikson, his first priority had always been himself. However even as he hesitated, he saw the boy's frightened face, saw he was prepared to die bravely under the thundering hooves if he couldn't maneuver his paint pony to the edge of the stampede.

Lenore would think him three kinds of a fool, Rand thought, urging Scout closer. Even his horse seemed to question Rand's judgement. The big buckskin stallion seemed to hesitate an instant as Rand urged him forward, pressing into the tightly knit pack of brown, furry bodies.

He heard a shout, saw the boy's father trying to move closer to save his son, but he was too far away to help, and his horrified expression revealed that he, too, realized that.

Instinctively, Rand pushed closer. Around him, big brown bodies pressed and jostled as the beasts ran. Scout threw his head up, struggling to keep his balance. Just ahead of them, the small boy's pony was tiring, that was plain to see. Despite the boy's skill, he couldn't seem to work his way to the outside of the deadly torrent of brown bodies. Rand didn't want to think about what he was doing or why or what would happen if his horse stepped in a hole. He had to clear a path for the boy's horse.

But even as Rand reached the boy's side, the paint pony stumbled and went down. Could Scout do it? He'd have to or they were all going to die. Even as the boy fell, Rand reached for him. His arm seemed to be almost pulled from its socket, but he had the boy in his grasp. Rand felt determined not to turn loose even if he were pulled off balance and they both perished. No matter what color his skin, this was a child and any man worthy of the name must try to save him.

Sweat seemed to bead on Rand's forehead as he lifted the boy clear of the falling pony. For a heartbeat, he was not sure he was strong enough. It seemed Rand would lose him to the pounding hooves or be pulled off balance and they would both die.

Without even realizing he did so, Rand breathed a prayer to Wakan Tanka and put almost superhuman strength into his effort. He had him! The grateful look on the boy's face as he clung to Rand was reward enough. His arm still ached as he pulled the child up onto his horse and now Scout was fighting to reach the outside of the thundering herd. Rand hung onto the trembling boy and didn't look back. If he saw what the stampede had done to the boy's pony, he was afraid his nerve would give out, and Rand didn't intend to die here. More than that, he didn't intend to let the boy die.

Valiantly, the stallion struggled toward the outside of the running herd, lathered and blowing, fighting to stay on his feet as the great beasts bellowed and pushed in around him. Out of the corner of his eye, Rand saw One Eye and Gopher helping clear a path for him, shouting and firing at the buffalo.

Abruptly Scout was clear of the herd, and it thundered on past while the horse stumbled to a halt, lathered and blowing.

Rand's arm was aching as it had never ached before. Very slowly, he set the boy safely on the ground even as One Eye and Gopher galloped up, full of praise for Rand's bravery.

As befitted any great warrior, he accepted the thanks modestly, knowing that Kimi must be watching from the rise.

The buffalo herd galloped over the horizon, but there were many fat beasts lying dead on the prairie.

One Eye looked at Rand. "Hinzi, are you all right?"

Rand nodded, too shaken to speak.

"That was a very brave thing you did."

The stout Gopher said gravely. "My family is forever in your debt."

Rand shrugged and dismounted, reached for his skinning knife. "It was nothing any man wouldn't have done."

"Lakota warrior, yes." One Eye grinned, dismounting. "I didn't think a white soldier could be so brave."

"I am not a white soldier," Rand reminded him, and he swaggered a little as they strode toward the fallen buffalo, "I am Hinzi, Yellow Hair." He knelt and began to skin the fat cow he had killed.

"Then here, white warrior." One Eye cut into the carcass, handed Rand a piece of warm, raw liver. "This is a treat we all savor."

Rand hesitated only an instant, and then he took a big bite, was surprised to find he liked it. Maybe he was no longer Rand Erikson, the civilized Southerner. He looked at the blood on his hand, the raw meat in his fist. Maybe he really was becoming a primitive savage. Kimi came up about them with her travois and the proud look on her face made it all worthwhile.

Later that night there was great feasting in the camp. Big fires were built and meat roasted. Rand washed in the creek and put on the fine buckskin and beadwork the grateful boy's family had given him. He ate more meat than he had ever eaten in his life. Kimi, busy with women's chores kept sneaking glances at him, smiling, promising with her eyes. Rand watched her, more than aware what her emerald glance promised later tonight after the camp was quiet. But for now, it was pleasant to sit in the camp circle, listening to the drums, watching the dancing. He ducked his head modestly as Gopher told of the white warrior's brave deed and promised that they would always be friends.

The child's mother said, "What is the white warrior's name?"

"Randolph," Rand said, "it means protected and advised by the wolf."

A murmur of approval with much head nodding went around the camp circle. "It is a good name," the boy's old grandfather said. "In your honor, we are giving our boy a new name, a man's name to wear the rest of his life."

Everyone waited quietly as he paused for emphasis and the boy smiled proudly. "Henceforth, he shall be called 'Saved By The Wolf.' "

Rand nodded, equally stoic. "That is a good name. I am much honored. I think Wakan Tanka had me there for a reason. I think someday Saved By The Wolf will do some great, brave deed that will bring honor to his family."

One Eye, sitting next to him, leaned close. "Well spoken," he whispered. "You are beginning to think like the Teton Sioux."

Rand could not remember when he had felt such contentment, such a feeling of being in charge of his own destiny, his life reduced to the most basic of needs and wants. He suddenly felt like Adam in a primitive Eden.

Rand should have known there was always a snake or maybe more than one ready to invade Eden. Late in the evening, there was a sudden hush as three men leading pack horses rode into the camp; white men. And they were accompanied by an Indian girl.

Rand's first thought was he and Kimi should hide before they were seen. Too late he saw the bearded traders looking at Kimi with hungry eyes. The rough men had seen his delicate butterfly and lusted for her. He didn't intend to give her up without a fight. She belonged to him and he shared his woman with no man.

Eleven

Kimi felt apprehension run up her spine and half rose from her place next to Hinzi. Always before, she had hidden when traders came into the camp. However, she realized it was already too late. The sudden widening of their eyes warned her they had seen her. She sat back down, moving a little closer to the big blond man as the three dismounted, left their horses and pack mules in charge of the Indian girl, and walked to the fire.

All three of them were dirty, clad in stained buckskin. Only one, the tall one who looked almost as big as Hinzi, was even slightly handsome. The one with the dirty, tangled beard held his hand up to show it was empty of weapons, spoke to the chiefs in a mixture of Lakota and English. "Hau! It has been long since I was here to trade."

The old chiefs nodded. "You have brought many things?"

"Yes. Buck and his friends, Lucky and Tech, have brought many things to trade for good furs and buffalo robes."

One of the warriors looked at him with greedy eyes. "You bring whiskey?"

Buck ran his fingers through his beard, nodded. "Anything you want, I have, including a pretty Pawnee captive that Lucky owns." He nodded toward the tall trader.

195

Kimi looked at the girl holding the horses. Pawnee. That tribe was a legendary enemy of all the Sioux because they often scouted for the white soldiers. She glared at the girl when she realized suddenly that the Pawnee was smiling archly at Hinzi. Uneasily Kimi saw that Hinzi was returning the girl's curious gaze.

The old chiefs gestured the three traders to a spot near the fire where they sat down cross-legged and looked around. Buck took a deep breath. "We ain't et since this morning. My belly thinks my throat's been cut. Do I smell fresh meat?"

One Eye gestured to Kimi and several of the other younger women. "We made a big kill today. Our women will bring you some."

Kimi assisted in serving the three. The tall one reached out and caught her arm. "This here one a breed? Tech, I don't remember seein' this here green-eyed gal before."

His friend guffawed and wiped his greasy face on his dirty sleeve. He had bad smallpox scars on his long face. "Shucks, Lucky, we'll trade her man something for usin' her later."

A sudden silence fell over the circle. Kimi tried to pull away from the man's hand, but he held her fast.

"Get your hands off her. That is my woman." Hinzi's voice boomed across the firelit circle. There was no mistaking the threat in his voice.

The trader hesitated. "A white man? What's a white man doin' ridin' with the Sioux?"

Kimi waited, seeing the cold blue fire in Hinzi's eyes. "I am Hinzi," he said in Lakota, "a warrior of these people. Now get your hand off my woman before I cut it off!"

"No problem." Immediately Lucky let go of Kimi, smiling in a fawning way. "I meant no

196

harm."

Buck ran his fingers through his beard. "Lucky's just got an eye for women, can't leave 'em alone. We come to trade, that's all. Some camps offer hospitality by giving a guest a pretty girl to warm his bed while he's there; maybe he thought—"

"No." Hinzi gestured Kimi to return to her place beside him. He put his hand on the big knife in his waistband. "Don't even think about it."

Buck and the other two rushed to explain to the stony-faced circle that they had meant no offense. With a sigh of relief, Kimi sank back down next to Hinzi, feeling very safe and protected. She looked over at her mother and saw the frown and uncertainty on old Wagnuka's wrinkled face. She must be worried about what might happen now that the three traders had seen her daughter.

Hinzi reached out and put his hand on Kimi's knee in a possessive movement. She saw the three dirty white men looking her over curiously, and she watched their questioning gazes go to Hinzi.

They gestured to the Pawnee girl, who brought whiskey bottles to set before Lucky. She swayed her hips and took a deep breath so that her firm breasts jutted out as she passed Hinzi. There was no mistaking that inviting smile on her lips as she looked the big blond man up and down. In fact, the Pawnee girl looked a little drunk herself. The handsome trader began to share the whiskey around while a murmur ran through the warriors at the enemy's girl's ripe body.

Lucky took out a cigar. "Any man here have a hankerin' for a woman? For a little tradin', the Pawnee chit will take on any man who wants her for a few minutes. In fact, she's for sale if a man wants to pay enough. Show them yourself, Sugar," he ordered.

The Pawnee girl sat down near the fire not far from Kimi. She hesitated, sighed. Then she hiked her buckskin dress so that slim, brown legs showed. Looking around the circle, she smiled at all the men, but her eyes kept coming back to Hinzi. She leaned on one elbow so that the front of her shift showed a generous expanse of perfect big breasts.

Kimi felt a twinge of jealousy as she glanced up and saw Hinzi looking the Pawnee girl over. He asked, "What do you want for her?"

Lucky grinned. "I don't know; make me an offer. I'm ready to trade her off. In the meantime, you're welcome to try her out. Wouldn't expect a man to buy a mare he ain't rode and got the feel of."

The girl was sitting close to Kimi. As the men returned to their eating, whiskey drinking and talking, Kimi whispered to her through clenched teeth. "And which of these dirty white dogs is your man?"

The girl hesitated, looking a bit chagrined. "I ran away with Lucky, but he makes me service all of them."

Kimi was incredulous. "All three of them?"

The Pawnee bristled a little. "I have no choice. They take turns with me and I am also used by any man who has the price."

Kimi might have almost felt sorry for her if she hadn't been a Pawnee and if she hadn't been looking at Hinzi as if she would like to spread her thighs for him.

In the next several hours, the women did a little trading for beads and small mirrors, iron kettles and trinkets. Then gradually the women and children drifted away as the warriors and the traders continued to swap, drink, and share gossip. Even

Wagnuka finally went to her tipi. Kimi was almost afraid to leave, afraid that, the way the Pawnee girl kept issuing invitations with her dark eyes, Hinzi might decide he wanted her.

Hinzi seemed to notice Kimi's jealous looks. "Go to bed, woman," he drawled. "I would stay and trade with these white men."

"Be careful what you trade for," Kimi said jealously.

"I know what I'm doing," he snapped. "I have already bought you a few pretty beads, that is all that concerns you. A warrior will not be told what to do by his woman."

Kimi left the camp fire in a huff. She pretended to go to her tipi, but instead, she circled back around where she could watch what went on in the circle without anyone realizing she hid in the shadows. Nervously she fingered her spirit charm and watched. There was some drinking, although Hinzi didn't seem to be drinking much. He kept staring at the pretty Pawnee girl who looked back at him with frank interest.

The trading continued. Kimi watched one of the young, unmarried warriors gesture toward the Pawnee girl. "How much?" he asked in pidgin English.

"You want buy her?" Lucky grinned.

The young man shook his head. "No, I only want to mount her a few minutes like the white men at the fort do a woman."

He made a deal, caught the girl's arm, and pulled her to her feet. She hesitated only a moment before she led him to a blanket spread out under the trees near the pack mules. As Kimi watched from her hiding place, the Pawnee girl stripped off her buckskin shift, standing in the moonlight so that all present could get a good look at her ripe body. She smiled at Hinzi again, taking a deep breath so that her perfect breasts moved.

The Sioux warrior who had paid to use her looked a little drunk, too. Kimi did not know him very well. She watched as he grabbed the Pawnee girl by the arm. Now that the young warrior had made the first offer, others began to bargain to use the girl.

"Wait!" Hinzi said.

Kimi, from her hiding place, glanced at Hinzi. It was the expression on his face that bothered her. Obviously he didn't like the image of all those warriors gathered around the girl. He frowned at the trader. "I will give two good ponies for the girl."

Lucky ran his hand through his hair, grinned. "Tell you what I'll do; why don't I give *you* five ponies and trade her for your woman?"

Hinzi bristled. "No. My woman is not to be traded, but I will buy the Pawnee captive."

Kimi felt heartsick and jealous as she listened. Many warriors had two wives. Most often they were sisters. But if Hinzi thought Kimi would share her man with an enemy slut, he was going to be very mistaken. She wished the traders had never come.

There was a long silence with only the sound of the crackling fire.

The warrior holding onto the Pawnee girl paused, listening to the bargaining. Hinzi looked over toward the girl. "I will give three ponies," he said.

Kimi took a deep, angry breath. He was offering too much for the pretty Pawnee. He must want her badly. Kimi was both hurt and furious.

Lucky spat into the fire. "Five and we close the deal."

There was a sharp intake of breath among the men. Five for an enemy girl? The Yellow Hair

200

must desire her greatly. Kimi counted up in her mind. Not counting Scout, Hinzi had no horses left as his share of the raid after he had given her mother her gift.

Even the Pawnee girl had pushed the waiting warrior away, sat up on the blanket, looking appealingly at the soldier. "If the yellow hair buys me," she said in broken English, "I will do things to please him that no woman has ever done."

Lucky laughed and lit a cigar. "Damn me if she don't speak truth! Brown Sugar is a skilled whore; the three of us have used her for many months now. Think of her as an investment; if you invest five ponies, her ripe body will earn that much back in a few weeks and you'll have her warmin' your own robes 'tween times."

Some of the warriors smiled. They had lost too many good men at the hands of Pawnee braves to feel any sympathy for the girl. Hinzi did not laugh. Even as Kimi watched, he looked with mute appeal at One Eye.

One Eye shrugged and sighed. "What you want with this one when you have Kimi, I do not know, but I will give you the ponies from my share, friend."

"Done, then!" Hinzi leaped up, strode to the blanket. The girl wrapped her arms around his thighs, murmuring her thanks while she pressed her naked breasts against his legs.

Kimi could bear to watch no more. Tears blinding her, she turned and fled to her mother's tipi. Old Wagnuka sat up with a start. "Daughter? What are you doing here? Why aren't you with your man?"

She sat down on a buffalo robe, angry tears running down her face. "You were right about the white man," she gulped. "Already he has taken a

201

liking to that Pawnee whore who came with those traders and has bought her!"

Her mother sighed. "Some men take more than one wife, although it is usually a sister. How can you deal with sharing with an enemy?"

What was she to do? She couldn't bear to lie in that tipi tonight, pretending to be asleep while Hinzi enjoyed his new prize only a few feet away. "I don't know. It is insulting to have him take an enemy whore as a second wife."

Wagnuka didn't say anything for a long minute. "He has turned out to be a good hunter and is already gaining respect in the camp. For the first time, there is more than enough meat in my lodge. He is a very virile man; perhaps he needs two women to satisfy him."

Kimi chewed her lip in anguish. She had thought their lovemaking was good. Had she not been enough for him?

She heard the step of a big man outside. "Kimi? Are you in there?"

Kimi hesitated, looking at her mother, "What am I to do?"

"Daughter, that is for you to decide. I tried to warn you to choose a Lakota brave."

"Kimi, come out!" Hinzi commanded.

"No!" she shouted, "go back to your Pawnee slut!"

"Enough of this foolishness!" He strode into the tipi, bending his tall frame as he came through the door. "We will talk," He picked her up easily, carrying her outside as she struggled.

"There's nothing to talk about. You shame me before all by paying so much for the enemy girl. I will not abide a Pawnee as your other woman."

He stood her on her feet, smiling. "So that's what this is all about? Let me explain—"

She slapped him then, a ringing sound. She saw the sudden fury in his blue eyes. His hands trembled as he reached out and grabbed her shoulders. She was abruptly very aware of the strength and size of the man.

"Don't you ever do that again, Butterfly. No doubt even the Lakota would not fault me if I beat you for striking your man across the face."

"So hit me!" she challenged, sticking her chin out defiantly, but inside, she was quaking. Hinzi was a big, powerful man. No doubt he could kill her with his bare hands. If he beat her, the warriors might not say anything when they heard she had paid him the supreme insult by hitting him in the face.

"You sassy little chit. You're the only one I know with more arrogance than me," Even as she struggled, he pulled her close, kissed her, forced her lips apart, plunged his tongue inside. She tried to pull away from him, but his superior strength molded her small body against him all the way down both their lengths. His strong fingers burned into her shoulders as she tried to twist away from him, but his mouth and hands were relentless in their stroking and caressing.

With a moan of surrender, Kimi clung to him. She was his, body and soul, every quaking nerve fiber in her body was wanting him. Her pride meant nothing to her as she stopped fighting and let him ravage her mouth with his tongue, his hands stroking and caressing her.

Kimi could feel his hard arousal against her belly. By sheer determination, she pulled away from him. "No, take your passion to the girl you just bought."

"I will not take orders from my woman," he thundered. "Trust me. I don't intend to keep her.

I—"

"You expect me to believe that?" She faced him in a fury. "Every woman in the camp knows you bought her. They are snickering at me behind their hands."

"Kimi, you're behaving like a jealous schoolgirl. However, that's what I did for getting involved with such a young—"

"I don't want to hear your forked tongue lies. I return to my mother's lodge." She backed away from him.

He looked so angry, it scared her. "All right. When you come to your senses, return to our tipi, otherwise, you can sleep in your mother's lodge. What will the Lakotas say to that?" He turned and strode away.

Kimi started to call after him, stopped herself. Although it hurt her, she knew that enemy girls were sometimes passed around by their captors. Should she listen to what he had to say? Obviously he was going to use the Pawnee girl for his pleasure whether Kimi liked it or not. Kimi would have to decide whether she was going to accept this or leave Hinzi.

A Sioux woman was allowed to divorce her husband. But she had seen the looks in other girls' eyes when they looked the big white man over. There would be many willing to take Kimi's place, even if he kept the captive as a second wife until he traded her off to some man who wanted her ripe body.

She fled, headed as far away as she could get. Near the creek, she paused and leaned against a tree. What was going on back in Hinzi's lodge with that Pawnee girl? Kimi didn't even want to think about it.

Rand's cheek still stung as he turned his back on Kimi and walked to his tipi. He swore under his breath. Damn the jealous little chit anyway! She hadn't even been willing to listen to reason and probably wouldn't have believed him anyway. Well, he owed her no explanation. He'd give it more thought tomorrow when she had cooled down. In the meantime, let her sulk in her mother's lodge all night and think the worst of him.

He flexed his wide shoulders, then stooped and entered his lodge. The Pawnee girl sat there before the small, flickering fire, and she was naked, the light playing on her soft curves. She rose up from the fur robe and smiled at him. "I have been waiting for you, master. I can't thank you enough for buying me."

She was beautiful. Rand tried to avert his eyes. "I didn't buy you for the reason you think."

Her shoulders slumped and her face saddened. "You don't find me pretty?" She stood up, turned around slowly, displaying her lush charms.

"I find you *very* pretty," he admitted, and his body reacted at the sight of her nakedness. "But I didn't buy you for that."

She paused, looking sad. "You will make me whore for you? Very well, even that will be better than being used by those three filthy traders every night. I will earn you much and maybe once in a while, you, too, will make love to me,"

He didn't answer, looking at her ripe curves as she moved toward him. As much as his pride hated to admit it, his mind desired Kimi, but his body didn't know one female body from another. This girl belonged to him and was willing. He was aroused, his breath coming deeper as the girl crossed to him. The Pawnee girl had a fine body.

If he closed his eyes, he could pretend she was Kimi. He might as well be guilty of what Kimi had suspicioned.

The girl slipped her arms around his neck, a little unsteady on her feet. She kissed him and he tasted whiskey on her tongue. "The white traders force it down my throat," she murmured, "otherwise I could not bear to go through what they do to me every night. With you, it would be different."

He started to tell her he didn't want her, but she kissed him again and rubbed her bare breasts against his naked chest. Rand took a deep, agonized breath. His whole groin felt on fire. It took all the resolve in him to pull away from her. "No, I have a woman already."

The girl laughed softly, looking up at him. "Your body makes a liar out of you!"

Indeed his traitor manhood was rigid, throbbing with desire. "I have a woman," he said again.

"Then where is she?" The girl challenged. "I am here and willing to do things to you no woman has ever done before, teach you ways of love I have learned from many men."

She lowered her head and ran her hot, pink tongue across his nipples until he gasped and held her wet mouth hard against his chest, fighting for control. He was shaking all over, struggling with himself. He could have this girl, she was more than willing, and Kimi would never know. This lustful rutting could be over in a couple of minutes.

The girl laughed softly and kissed her way down his chest to his belly as she sank to his knees. He wore only moccasins and a brief loincloth. Surely she wasn't going to . . . ?

With almost superhuman effort, he pulled away from her. "No." Why was he denying himself this

206

pleasure? He must be three kinds of a fool.

The girl sighed, stepped back. "You are a fool, white Lakota, to be loyal to the jealous, stubborn chit."

He didn't even want to think about her words. They might make too much sense. "I bought you to set you free. Can you get back to your people?"

She blinked, her pretty face puzzled. "You ride with the Lakota and you set an enemy Pawnee girl free? It is too much to expect."

"Nonetheless, that's what I intend." Rand nodded, "It made me sick to imagine what those traders had put you through."

At that point the girl lost her composure and began to sob. "I was lured away from my people. Lucky promised me I would be his woman. I did not know until it was too late that he would lend me to his partners and make me earn money with my body from any man who had the price."

Rand frowned, feeling desperately sorry for her. He reached out and gently stroked her hair. "How are you called?"

"They call me 'Brown Sugar,' but my Pawnee name is Kirit."

"Kirit, if I help you get out of this camp tonight, do you have a place to go?"

She looked up at him, tears on her face. "My brother has a friend riding with the soldiers' Pawnee scouts. He might be at Fort Berthold. Even Lucky does not know this. Maybe I can find my brother through him."

Such a lovely body; such a waste, Rand thought, but he only picked up her shift and tossed it to her. "If I give you a horse and send you out of this camp, can you find your way to that fort?"

The girl nodded. "I think so." She slipped the shift over her head, put on her moccasins. "I'll ride out the opposite side, away from the creek so Lucky won't follow and recapture me."

Rand took her hand and led her outside into the darkness. The whole camp was asleep. Even the traders' campsite across the creek was quiet. He was three kinds of a fool, Rand thought, not to enjoy both Indian girls until he figured out a way to return to civilization and his elegant fiancée. Sometimes he was too noble even for a Southern gentleman. Chivalry could be the only reason he was spurning this girl's amorous offer, he told himself.

Carrying a small canteen and a little pack of pemmican, Rand led the girl quietly across the camp in the opposite direction of the creek. He led her to Kimi's pony. "Here, Kirit, let me help you up."

For a split second, she was in his arms and she reached to kiss him. "Good-bye, yellow-haired warrior. I wish I could stay with you forever."

She clung to him, molding herself against him. With great difficulty, he forced himself to pull away from her. He put her on the pony's back and handed her the food and water. "Go now and find your people," he said. "Forget about the nightmare you have endured and find yourself a good man."

She gave him a long look. "I *found* a good man. But he does not want me." She looked off toward the creek. "I only regret that I do not get to take revenge on Lucky."

"Sooner or later, justice will be done," Rand assured her. "Go now and remember that all things are in the hands of Wakan Tanka."

She nodded and rode away at a walk. Rand watched her silhouette growing smaller in the moonlight. Wakan Tanka, indeed. He cursed softly, slapping a quirt against his leg. He was even beginning to think like an Indian.

Kimi. What was he going to do about her? He turned and walked back to his tipi. He had humiliated himself enough by going to her mother's lodge once this evening. He should throw away this little white savage who made him forget who he was, forget his cold, respectable fiancee, forget everything but coupling with her like an animal. If she were going to be angry with him, let her. Since when did Rand Erikson have to beg a woman for her forgiveness or favors? This luscious womanchild had made him lose his pride. She had made a fool of the heir of one of Kentucky's wealthiest families.

She was a fever in his blood, but eventually men either recover or die from fever. He must begin to think about recovering, putting this whole impossible adventure behind him, returning to Kentucky to pick up the pieces of his former life. He flexed his broad shoulders, trying to reduce the tension he felt. Rand went into his tipi and lay down on a buffalo robe. For a long time, he couldn't sleep, angry with Kimi, knowing she was over at her mother's lodge sulking when she could be here in his arms. Finally he dropped off to sleep.

Kimi leaned against the cottonwood tree, staring at the shallow water of the creek. She had been here for only a few minutes, but it seemed like hours. What was going on in Hinzi's tipi? She didn't even want to think about that oh-so-grateful enemy girl making love to him. Should Kimi swallow her pride? Could she bear to lie in that tipi at night after he had made love to her and watch him mount that other girl? Her mother was right; Hinzi was a virile stallion of a man. No doubt he could keep two women serviced and satisfied.

She heard a twig snap and looked up, startled. In the moonlight, she realized it was the tall trader, Lucky.

"Ah," he smiled at her, "I scared you? Didn't mean no harm."

She took two steps back, a little uneasy.

He made a soothing gesture with his hands "I was out havin' myself a smoke. What are you doing out alone, sweet stuff? You should be safely asleep in the arms of your man."

"My man is the one you sold the Pawnee girl to."

He laughed softly. "A little jealous then, are you?" He scratched his chin and looked out across the camp. "No doubt at this very moment, he is enjoying the taste of Brown Sugar. She is very skilled at pleasing men—not the innocent she was when I took her from her people."

Kimi didn't want to hear about it. She turned away from the trader, imagining Hinzi lying between that girl's thighs, kissing her, running his hands over her.

Behind her, Lucky said, "I tried to trade for you, sweet stuff. Maybe now you wished you had not objected?"

"I must get back," Kimi said, uneasy at the turn his conversation was taking.

He caught her arm. "Don't run away, pretty thing; I won't hurt you. While your man is busy with that Pawnee girl, why don't you earn a few pretties for yourself? He'll never know the difference."

She turned and glared at him. "I don't know what you mean."

He grinned. "Sure you do. Come back to my camp. For a few minutes of your time, my friends and I will give you many beads and ribbons. Now do you know what I mean?"

Kimi grimaced as the images he hinted at came to her mind. For the first time, she had a little sympathy for the enemy girl and thought of her as an unfortunate woman instead of a nameless enemy. "No," she shook her head, "Hinzi would kill you for it."

He laughed easily. "I think the white warrior is too busy with Brown Sugar's charms to even know or care what you do for the next hour. How did a pretty half-breed like you get into this camp, and what's a white man doing living among the Sioux?"

Kimi didn't answer. If he reported having seen Hinzi, would the soldiers come and take him away? "You must not tell that he is here," she said urgently.

He ran his fingers up and down her arm "And what will you give me, sweet stuff, if I promise I won't tell?"

The hair seemed to rise up on the back of her neck as she realized what he was demanding. She didn't even like the feel of his dirty hand on her arm.

"Maybe I can give you some ponies." Perhaps her mother might be persuaded to part with the ones Hinzi had given her.

Lucky laughed. "Don't need any ponies. Just a kiss," he wheedled, moving closer, "just one."

A kiss. Maybe she could stand that. Could she trust him to keep his word? She should go tell Hinzi what the trader threatened. Then she paused as she realized the Pawnee girl was no doubt keeping Hinzi too busy to interrupt him at this moment.

"Just one little kiss," Lucky murmured. Even as she hesitated, he reached out and pulled her into his embrace. She opened her mouth to protest, but his own covered hers, his wet tongue slipping between her lips.

Sickened, Kimi struggled to pull away. Lucky was strong from years of surviving on the frontier. He held her more tightly, crushing her against him all the way down both their bodies. His sweaty hands ran over her, his mouth on hers so hard that he cut her lip and she tasted her own blood. She managed to bite his mouth and he hit her across the face, cursing. "I'll teach you, you little slut!"

Half-dazed, Kimi tried to cry out, but now he had his hand over her mouth. She fought to get away from him, knowing she was no match for his strength.

He laughed softly. "I ain't called 'Lucky' for nothin'. Pretty Injun slut, you will now take Brown Sugar's place. By the time anyone realizes you're gone, you'll be many miles from here. Your man will think you've run away in a fit of jealous rage. What he won't know is that besides me and my two friends, you'll earn much money for me as a whore among the tribes and around the forts!"

Twelve

This had been the longest, most terrifying night of Kimi's life, she thought as she rode in front of Lucky on his horse, her hands tied behind her.

How foolish she had been to go down near the creek alone where he could grab her. He had tied and gagged her, then carried her to his camp. Quickly he and his partners had loaded up and left the sleeping Sioux village. She had struggled for hours to slip from the rawhide thongs that bound her, but they held firm.

If only she could have gotten her mouth free to scream, but Lucky had double-checked the rag that gagged her. All she could do was utter soft moans, none loud enough for the sleeping Indians to hear as the three traders rode quietly out of camp and off into the darkness.

All night they had ridden at a gallop, fearing pursuit. They stopped only now and then for a moment to cool the lathered horses then remounted and rode on. Now Lucky held her close against him on the horse and laughed against her hair. "So little Injun gal, you think now you wish you'd stayed in your man's tipi, even while he made love to the Pawnee gal, eh? Your jealousy has gotten you into a whole heap a trouble."

Kimi flinched, remembering. It would probably

be morning before the tribe realized she was missing. Would Hinzi come? Too late, she remembered her fury, slapping his face. He might not bother to look for her. He might think she had gone with the traders willingly.

Buck looked behind him. "Damn it, Lucky, this time you went too far. Didn't you see that white Injun's face? He'll cut your gizzard open for this, and maybe ours, too."

"Aw, quit worryin'. Brown Sugar's keepin' him occupied. Nobody will know she's missing for hours."

"Shucks," Tech said, "we been riding for hours. How long do you figure we'll have to ride before we're safe from them redskins?"

"Goddamn it! We don't dare relax yet," Buck warned.

Lucky kissed up and down the back of her neck. She struggled to pull away, but he only laughed and pulled her up against his lean body. "Don't fight me, sweet stuff. You're helpless and dependent on my good will. I expect you to be very, very good to me when you get the chance."

The other two laughed.

Tech said, "And to your old partners, too, Lucky, don't forget that."

"She'll be very good to all of us — or else." Lucky promised and ran his hands over Kimi's breasts. Even through the doeskin she felt the heat of them.

Kimi pulled away from his stroking hands and sat up stiff and straight in the saddle, letting him know she had no intention of cooperating.

He laughed again and nuzzled the back of her neck. "Sweet stuff, by the time we get finished, you'll be like that Pawnee: eager to please us so we won't beat you. Maybe sometimes we'll even give you a little whiskey."

Too late Kimi felt pity for the Pawnee girl and what she must have survived the last few months in the ownership of this ruthless trio.

Buck said, "She's gonna be a little gold mine, ain't she? We'll make a pile of money off her from soldiers: They like half-breed gals."

"Shucks, we gonna let Injuns use her, too?" Tech looked over at her. The lust in his hard eyes made her shudder.

"If they got some good furs and ponies to trade," Lucky said and ran his hand over her body again.

Her doeskin shift had worked its way up so that he now had his dirty hand on her thigh. She tried to concentrate on her anger, what she would like to do to this trio if she had a knife or a gun and could work her hands free. It kept her from thinking about the inevitable time when the traders felt that they were far enough from the Lakotas to make camp.

He stroked her bare thigh. "Yes, sweet stuff," he whispered against her hair, "when we finally make camp, *you* are going to entertain us. We'll see if you are as talented with your ripe body as Brown Sugar was."

She protested against the gag, letting him know she would fight him when he tried to take her.

He only snickered. "Oh, but you will, Injun. The three of us are bigger than you are, so we will take your sweetness as a bee takes honey whenever and however often we want. Even if you tell the soldiers at some of the forts, none of them will pay any attention to the protests of a half-breed gal. They will be too eager to sample your charms themselves. All white men think of Indian girls as sluts to be used for their pleasure."

Was that true? Kimi thought of Hinzi, asleep even now back at the Lakota camp with the voluptuous enemy girl in his arms. Had he enjoyed that girl as he had enjoyed Kimi? More importantly, had that Pawnee pleasured him more than Kimi had? He might not even be interested in getting Kimi back this morning. Well, her mother and some of the others would start a search.

They rode all night long, stopping now and then to rest the horses. Kimi was so tired from sitting on the horse that she kept nodding off, only to be jerked awake by Lucky's dirty hands fondling her. If only she could sleep. She knew that when they finally stopped to take a long rest, the three traders had plans for her. In her mind, she saw herself spread-eagled on a blanket under a scrubby tree, maybe two of them holding her down while another raped her. Then they would change places until all had been satisfied several times. After that, they would sleep and leave her tied up and smeared with their sweat and seed until they were ready to ride again.

They didn't stop at dawn, but kept riding, pausing now and then to rest the horses which were becoming noticeably weary. They rested only a few minutes at a time, eating in the saddle. While Tech and Lucky looked at her with increasingly lustful glances, Buck said, "Hold off. We don't have time to really enjoy her now; wait 'til sundown. By then we will be at our favorite camping spot."

She had never been so thirsty in her whole life. No, that wasn't true. A memory came to her, bobbed in and out of her mind like a leaf on a stream. She had been thirsty then, too. Maybe it was only a hazy dream of a lifetime ago. Her

216

tongue had seemed swollen so that she couldn't swallow. How old was she then? Kimi tried to grab hold of the allusive memory, but all she could remember was crying softly for water and a big man, a white man, patiently explaining that there was none. Water. They had to walk to water. Kimi was too small to walk. The man seemed so weak he could hardly stand up, yet he carried her. Hinzi? No, the image from the long ago memory had eyes as green as new grass. She tried to remember more but everything was lost in a blur of time and forgetfulness. *Kimimila, my love . . . Oh, Kimimila . . .* Now why was the memory of a butterfly important? The handsome man muttered it over and over as he carried her, fell, got up, and stumbled on and on. . . .

The images that came and faded like mirages in her mind had to do with another life. Kimi groped through mental shadows and cobwebs to put it all together. Thirsty, so thirsty . . .

She was miserable, not knowing if she was asleep or half delirious as the troubled images came and went. Maybe she had only dreamed it all.

Kimi started, realizing she had dozed off from sheer exhaustion. All three of the dirty men were leering at her. Buck took the gag out of her mouth and offered her the canteen. Her mouth was so dry, she seemed to have no feeling in her tongue. Her hands were still tied behind her back, and he didn't untie her. He held the canteen to her mouth. The water sloshed down her face, dripped into the neck of her shift.

Lucky wiped his mouth. "I reckon I'll take a drink off what's drippin' down her neck."

"No, you won't," Buck frowned. "Later, when we got more time."

Tech scratched his crotch slowly. "Shucks, for

that one, I could make time."

"Later," Buck promised, "and she'll be very cooperative, won't you, sweet?"

"No, you son of a tick-bitten coyote!" Kimi snarled.

He reached to grab her bound hands, lifted them high behind her until it stressed her shoulders and caused her to flinch in pain. "Now you better learn to behave yourself, gal, so we won't hurt you. Right, Sioux slut?"

She was determined, but the pain was more than she could bear. "Yes, anything," she gasped.

"See? Obedience is rewarded." He let go of her wrists and she sighed with relief that the pain had stopped. "There will come a time, gal, when you will do anything we want—*anything,* because you know what will happen if you don't. Here, eat." He spread some meat on a rock before her.

She looked up at him, waiting for him to untie her hands, but he only laughed and shook his head. "No, you will do the best you can or starve. Pride and dignity are not for a half-breed bitch who is to be used for men's enjoyment."

She had never hated anyone as much as she hated the bearded, dirty man at this moment. Kimi hesitated, knowing he was expecting her to spit and curse so he could slap her around, deny her any food. It was tempting, so tempting. Now she knew how Hinzi had felt when she had chained and treated him the same way. He was so proud, and she had shamed and humiliated him, She felt her face burn with guilt. However, Kimi forced herself to contain her temper, knowing that if she did not eat she would gradually lose strength and be too weak to escape if she finally did get the chance. She must eat.

With a deep sigh, she knelt and began to eat the

meat off the rocks. Her dress had pushed up high on her thighs and she wore nothing underneath, affording them a look at her thighs and the soft curves of her hips. As she leaned over to eat, she knew they also got a good view of her breasts in the low-cut front of her shift. It couldn't be helped. Her medicine object dangled out of the neck of her shift as she bent over the food. She would have to contain her anger, pretend to be docile, and watch for her chance.

She ate the food while the men smoked and watched her, laughing at her clumsy attempts to eat with her hands tied behind her.

"Shucks," Tech breathed, "she's just in the position I like best—just like a mare, waitin' to be mounted—"

"Not yet," Buck took a deep drag on his cigar. "Just keep thinkin' about how good it will be this evening when we finally camp. Then we've got all night long to share her around."

All night long. Kimi tried not to shudder visibly at the images that brought to mind.

Lucky noticed the spirit object dangling from its rawhide thong. "What's this?"

He bent and took it in his hand, grinned. "Still warm from resting against your tits, sweet stuff, where I intend to sleep tonight. What is this?"

"It's my medicine charm. I've had it always."

Lucky's face furrowed as he turned it over in his hand. "Wonder if it's gold? Lucky ain't my name for nothin'—"

"Gold? Naw!" Tech snorted and spat. "No Injun tart would have real gold around her neck; it must be just a cheap brass geegaw from some trader's store."

"Yes, that's what it is," Kimi hastened to say. She had never thought of it as possibly valuable. If it were, the men would take it away from her. She wasn't sure herself how she had come by the medicine object. Maybe old Otter had found it on a raid.

"See, slut?" Buck combed his tangled beard with his dirty fingers, "We do you a favor, let you keep this piece of junk for now." He grabbed the thong that held the object and dragged her to her feet. The leather cut into her neck as he lifted her. "You don't seem near as full of fight as you was before, gal. Maybe you're already learnin' what is expected." He reached for the gag again.

"Please," Kimi blurted, "please don't gag me. I promise I won't scream."

Lucky grinned. "Wouldn't do you no good no how, sweet stuff. We're miles now from anyone who would help you."

The men chuckled knowingly. Abruptly, Lucky reached out, dragged her to him, and kissed her brutally. He shoved his tongue deep in her throat, bending her almost backward. She knew better than fight or bite him. She let him ravage her mouth for a long moment before he pulled back, breathing heavily, aroused desire in his hard eyes. "You taste good, all right. Bet you can be taught to do much more excitin' things with that hot little mouth."

What he hinted at sickened her, but she managed to keep her face immobile.

"Shucks, I wanna kiss her, too," Tech whined.

"Naw, no time for that now," Buck shook his head as he took her away from Lucky, lifting her up to his horse and mounting up behind her. "It's my turn to handle her a little. Anything else has to wait 'til tonight," he promised, putting his hand on her bare thigh. Kimi felt the heat of his dirty fingers on her skin and forced herself not to struggle.

She must save her strength and cunning to try to escape later.

" 'Tain't fair," Tech said, "I ain't had no turn at holdin' her. You two are gettin' all the fun."

"Remember I'm the one who brought both these sweet things in and shared them with my friends," Lucky said, "so I should get to hold this one."

Tech sided with him. "Yeah, that's true, Buck."

"God damn, you act like kids with a toy," Buck grumbled. "All right, Lucky."

Lucky smiled as he reached for her. There was no use fighting him, she thought wearily. He held her tightly against him, his eager hand roaming her frame. He twisted her head around to kiss her. He smelled of stale whiskey. Kimi lost her temper and bit him, tasting his blood, hot and warm as he cursed and struck her. "Damned squaw! Can't be trusted no how!"

Half conscious, she slumped against him and felt his hot hands stroking her body as they rode on. Kimi's head hurt and her wrists were raw from being tied. She thought of the punishment her body would take when they finally camped tonight. She would either have to submit or be beaten half to death.

The next time they stopped to rest she would attempt to leave a clue for the pursuers. If she left the medicine charm hanging on a bush or rock, would Hinzi find it?

She closed her eyes and thought of Hinzi back in the camp, recalling his gentle, sensitive lovemaking. She would have given anything to be safely asleep in his big, protective embrace, as the Pawnee girl had been all night. Had she been missed when dawn broke? Did Hinzi care enough to come looking for her? Kimi had delayed the trio as much as possible so the Lakota warriors could catch up

221

with them. Suppose her people thought she had run away with the traders in a fit of jealous anger? Suppose no one was in pursuit at all?

Hinzi, she thought desperately, where are you? I need your help so badly!

Rand had slept fitfully all night, his arms reaching for the soft body of his delicate butterfly. Then when his embrace closed on an empty spot on the blanket, he would awaken, feel around in the darkness, and realize Kimi was not beside him. He would lie back, angry with her for her petulance. He swore under his breath. He should have kept the Pawnee girl. At least when he awakened in the middle of the night wanting a woman to caress, a soft pair of breasts on which to lay his face, he would have them. What difference did it make as long as the girl was eager and willing?

He sighed heavily and closed his eyes, angry with Kimi. Was she even now lying sleepless, too, in her mother's lodge? He half rose on one elbow, thinking he would slip through the darkened camp, lift her bodily, and take her back to where she belonged — in his arms and in his blankets. Rand was a virile man who needed a woman often. More than that, he hungered for the feel and scent of Kimi's softness, the taste of her mouth and nipples.

Was he in love with her? Of course not. He only lusted after her and remembered how good she felt, wet and hot beneath him, as he thrust his body into hers. Someday he must return to his other life hundreds of miles away, a civilized life with a civilized girl who could waltz and do needlepoint and make idle chitchat about fashion with his mother and sister. Kimi would never fit in or be accepted even if he took her back to his world. The only thing that made sense was enjoying her while he was among the Sioux, then forgetting about her when he finally returned to his life. Wasn't that what soldiers had always done with the enemy's women?

He dozed off again, sleeping fitfully, remembering the nightmare of events that had brought him to this point. *Lenore.* He dreamed of saying goodbye to his fiance in the glass conservatory of her grandmother's estate. Rand had changed some. Lenore complained about it. It was hard to think of gala balls and fine mansions with all the death and hell he'd seen. He'd been a dispatch carrier for the gallant John Hunt Morgan.

What had happened to all those daring Rebels who had ridden with Morgan's Raiders? He didn't know. Rand had been captured by a young general named George Armstrong Custer. He remembered the brash upstart because like himself, Custer had such pale eyes and light hair. That ended the war for Rand. He was sent to Point Lookout prison and then volunteered for Fort Rice.

Fort Rice. A miserable outpost on the edge of the world. Rand didn't think he had much choice but join up when the Yankees came through the prison stockade recruiting. Like Cherokee Evans, who'd been at Point Lookout since his capture at Shiloh, Rand felt he was staring death in the face every day as men starved or sickened and died around him.

The volunteers were put on a ship called the *Continental* and sent to New York. From there, the Galvanized Yankees were loaded on a train West. At the Missouri River, they were put aboard an overloaded stern-wheeler named the *Effie Deans*.

Even in his sleep, Rand shuddered, remembering the execution. Rand had thought young Colonel

Dimon was bluffing when he decided to make an example of a man, *any man,* to reinforce discipline. It was against all military rules to try and execute a soldier without proper board review. In the end, the President himself had the power to commute a death sentence, and Lincoln was notoriously softhearted and lenient.

That didn't faze young Colonel Dimon. He chose a man out of the hundreds on board, claiming the red-haired blacksmith from Tennessee, William Dowdy, had plotted to take over the boat.

Only Cherokee Evans had had the guts to argue with the colonel as the river boat inched its way up the Missouri toward Dakota Territory.

Rand didn't even know the scared, condemned boy personally. After all, Dowdy wasn't even an officer, much less from the same social strata. Besides Rand didn't think Colonel Dimon would take the responsibility for not going through proper channels.

Rand would never forget that day in 1864. As the overloaded boat moved up the muddy river in the September heat, Dowdy sat chained while a couple of soldiers built a wooden coffin. The sounds of the hammers and saws were louder than the stern wheel churning up the water. There is something about a man marked for death that scares other men away. Only Cherokee had sat and talked with the red-headed blacksmith.

It was past noon and the day was hellishly hot when Dimon had the *Effie Deans* anchor just above the village of Omaha. With the soldiers standing mutely as witnesses, young Dowdy was marched ashore. From the boat deck, Rand had watched in disbelief. Dimon was certainly carrying this bluff a long way. Damned Yankee officer. Rand cursed softly under his breath. Young Dowdy

MORE PASSION AND ADVENTURE AWAIT... YOUR TRIP TO A BIG ADVENTUROUS WORLD BEGINS WHEN YOU ACCEPT YOUR FIRST 4 NOVELS ABSOLUTELY *FREE* (AN $18.00 VALUE)

Accept your Free gift and start to experience more of the passion and adventure you like in a historical romance novel. Each Zebra novel is filled with proud men, spirited women and tempestuous love that you'll remember long after you turn the last page.

Zebra Historical Romances are the finest novels of their kind. They are written by authors who really know how to weave tales of romance and adventure in the historical settings you love. You'll feel like you've actually gone back in time with the thrilling stories that each Zebra novel offers.

GET YOUR FREE GIFT WITH THE START OF YOUR HOME SUBSCRIPTION

Our readers tell us that these books sell out very fast in book stores and often they miss the newest titles. So Zebra has made arrangements for you to receive the four newest novels published each month.

You'll be guaranteed that you'll never miss a title, and home delivery is so convenient. And to show you just how easy it is to get Zebra Historical Romances, we'll send you your first 4 books absolutely FREE! Our gift to you just for trying our home subscription service.

BIG SAVINGS AND FREE HOME DELIVERY

Each month, you'll receive the four newest titles as soon as they are published. You'll probably receive them even before the bookstores do. What's more, you may preview these exciting novels free for 10 days. If you like them as much as we think you will, just pay the low preferred subscriber's price of just $3.75 each. *You'll save $3.00 each month off the publisher's price.* AND, your savings are even greater because there are never any shipping, handling or other hidden charges—FREE Home Delivery. Of course you can return any shipment within 10 days for full credit, no questions asked. There is no minimum number of books you must buy.

TO GET YOUR 4 FREE BOOKS WORTH $18.00 —MAIL IN THE FREE BOOK CERTIFICATE T O D A Y

Fill in the Free Book Certificate below, and we'll send your FREE BOOKS to you as soon as we receive it.

If the certificate is missing below, write to: Zebra Home Subscription Service, Inc., P.O. Box 5214, 120 Brighton Road, Clifton, New Jersey 07015-5214.

4 FREE BOOKS

4 FREE BOOK CERTIFICATE

ZEBRA HOME SUBSCRIPTION SERVICE, INC.

YES! Please start my subscription to Zebra Historical Romances and send me my first 4 books absolutely FREE. I understand that each month I may preview four new Zebra Historical Romances free for 10 days. If I'm not satisfied with them, I may return the four books within 10 days and owe nothing. Otherwise, I will pay the low preferred subscriber's price of just $3.75 each; a total of $15.00, *a savings off the publisher's price of $3.00.* I may return any shipment and I may cancel this subscription at any time. There is no obligation to buy any shipment and there are no shipping, handling or other hidden charges. Regardless of what I decide, the four free books are mine to keep.

NAME

ADDRESS _____ APT _____

CITY _____ STATE _____ ZIP _____

(   )
TELEPHONE

SIGNATURE _____
(if under 18, parent or guardian must sign)

Terms, offer and prices subject to change without notice. Subscription subject to acceptance by Zebra Books. Zebra Books reserves the right to reject any order or cancel any subscription.

slumped down on the wooden box while soldiers dug a hole. *Dimon can't do this,* Rand thought.

He remembered mostly how hot it was, the feel of sweat running down the neck of his blue wool jacket, and the way the slight breeze moved the prairie grass. Of course the colonel could do it; they were hundreds of miles from authority. The firing squad lined up.

Bob white. Bob, bob white. It seemed strange that quail whistled and a rabbit jumped out of the grass and scampered away as though executing a man didn't change the world at all.

The sound of the rifles cracked through his mind, sending frightened quail exploding up out of the grass. What had been a man crumpled and fell. Now it was only a pile of blue cloth on a body. Rand blinked, staring in disbelief, listening to the mutter from the men. He had seen a lot of death in the past several years, but nothing that affected him like watching this execution on the flimsiest of charges. And he hadn't protested, hadn't done a thing to stop it.

Young Dowdy was hastily put in the wooden box, buried by the river. In minutes the *Effie Deans* continued on her way upstream as if nothing important had happened. Rand stared at the fresh mound of dirt as the boat pulled away. He spent the next few hours looking into the darkness, contemplating his own life and the world around him. He was ashamed that he had done nothing—not raised a hand, not uttered a word of protest. Only the half-breed Cherokee had tried to stop the killing.

Abruptly it seemed very important to Rand that he do something to ease his guilty conscience. Evans didn't like him, Rand knew that. The former officer with the Tennessee troops made it clear he thought Rand self-centered, spoiled, and worthless. It was abruptly important to Rand that Cherokee Evans think well of him, so when Rand heard a rumor that Dimon had marked Evans as a trouble-maker and the next candidate for his firing squad, Rand took action.

Late at night, disguising his voice, Rand crept to Cherokee and warned him. Cherokee went over the side of the boat and escaped. What had happened to the man? Did he drown in the muddy Missouri that warm September night? Rand had often won-dered. After that night, he began to change a little, knowing the world didn't revolve around him any more. It could have just as easily been him left back there in a shallow grave on the riverbank as the unfortunate blacksmith.

He awakened suddenly, breathing hard. Bright sunlight streamed across his face. Where was he? Oh, yes, in a Lakota camp. He swore under his breath with sheer relief, flexed his shoulders. It was good to be alive. He remembered his dream. Well, none of that mattered anymore. Kimi. Would she come to him this morning and tell him how sorry she was? He'd had enough! She was his as long as he stayed with the Sioux, and he didn't intend to be made a fool of by a woman's jealousy.

He got up, stretched, went outside. The camp was busy. Women were cooking and carrying water, children were playing. He looked out toward where the traders had been camped. They were gone. Just as well. If that filthy trio had tried to trade for Kimi one more time, Rand would not be able to control his anger. At least the Pawnee girl had no doubt made it back to her kin by now. In a small way, maybe Rand had repaid the debt his guilty conscience owed for not doing anything to help poor Dowdy.

Rand strode toward old Wagnuka's tipi, slapping his quirt against his leg. His feelings at this moment were that he might turn Kimi across his knee and spank her until she promised to mend her ways. He thought about it a minute and shook his head. He couldn't do anything to hurt her, not even a spanking, although the little chit deserved it for what she'd put him through. Lenore was so bland by comparison. He hadn't known a relationship with a female could have so much crackle and conflict. He wasn't used to it and he didn't know what he thought about it.

He wasn't sorry he had bought the captive Pawnee girl with borrowed ponies that must still be repaid. It was beneath his dignity to explain it to the fiery white savage. Yes, that's what she was. Could she ever be turned into a genteel lady? Would she have the same fascination for him if that happened?

He stuck his head through the tipi flap. "Wagnuka, I know it's taboo for me to speak to you, but I need to talk to Kimi. Where is she?"

The old woman frowned at his breech of etiquette. "You make a joke. She is with you."

He got a funny feeling deep in the pit of his stomach. "She hasn't been in this lodge all night?"

She stood up. He saw the alarm in her wrinkled face. "She is not with you? I haven't seen her since last night."

Slowly Rand shook his head even as he looked toward the empty camp of the traders and began to curse under his breath. "Search the village quickly," he said, even though in his heart, he knew it would do no good.

He stared out across the creek where the traders'

camp had been. With a sinking feeling, he remembered the way those three had looked at her. Had she gone on her own or been kidnapped? It didn't matter, she belonged to him and he would not share her. "Get One Eye and the other braves," he ordered as he turned to run back to his lodge for his weapons. "I think I know where she's gone and I'm going after her!"

Thirteen

Still not quite willing to believe Kimi might be gone, Rand did a quick search in the dawn's light. Wagnuka checked among the girl's friends. Word spread quickly. As Rand gathered up his weapons, Gopher and One Eye joined him. "Kimimila is gone?"

Rand nodded, and they followed him over to look around the traders' deserted campsite for a clue. All he saw was one very small moccasin track. While that might have been Kimi's, it also might have been left earlier by one of the children who had walked in the area. "I'm going after her. Will some of the warriors go with me?"

"Yes." One Eye rubbed the red patch, his handsome face furrowed. "You think she might go willingly with the traders?"

"Do you?" Rand looked at him squarely.

Gopher said, "She was upset about the Pawnee girl."

"Women!" Rand snorted. "There's no figuring them. I sent the enemy girl on her way. She's probably back with her family by now."

One Eye drew breath sharply, no doubt thinking the same as Rand. "If the traders have Kimi, they'll use her as they did the Pawnee girl."

The thought sickened Rand. He swung his quirt against his leg so hard, he felt the sting. If they dared touch her . . . He put his hand on the hilt of the big knife in his waistband. "Friends, will you ride with me? I want my woman back and I want those three scalps to hang from the dance pole."

One Eye nodded. "You have gained much respect among the Akicita society, Hinzi, and the traders weren't well-liked anyway. We will ride!"

They rode out as soon as possible. Rand had wanted to leave immediately, but there were proper ceremonies to be done, One Eye insisted, including prayers to Wakan Tanka and painting themselves and their horses for a proper war party. It was the Indian way, and there was no changing it. The only thing that comforted Rand was that, with pack mules and a captive, the traders couldn't move as fast as a war party.

Hinzi. Yellow Hair of the Lakota warriors. Rand, when he looked in a reflective disk of copper, was amazed at how fierce he looked with red and blue paint streaking his face and body, his buckskin horse painted with symbols and its tail tied up for war.

The late spring sun beat down on his naked skin as the war party rode out, the women encouraging them with trilling cries. Although Rand was fast becoming a good tracker, Gopher was an expert, and only too happy to follow the traders' trail for the man who had saved his son's life.

Rand glanced up at the sun as they rode out, wondering how long ago the traders had left and trying not to think about what Kimi might be going through at this very moment.

One Eye must have seen his worried expression, because he reined his horse so that he rode alongside, resplendent in his shirt decorated with the hair of enemies. "They will not touch her yet," he said. "They will be intent on putting much distance between us and them, knowing we will follow."

Rand glanced up at the sun, cursed under his breath. "They've got a long head start, but you're probably right. No doubt they won't feel safe until they get closer to a fort where they think the Sioux fear to ride."

As if to reaffirm his words, Gopher galloped back from scouting ahead. "I think they may be headed to the fort."

Rand said, "Fort Rice?"

Gopher shook his head, "No, not that one; the one farther up the Wakpa Rehanka."

Rand glanced questioningly at One Eye.

"You whites call it the Missouri River," the respected Shirt Wearer explained. "They may be headed for Fort Berthold. They are smart; no doubt they wouldn't head south for fear of running across Sitting Bull's Hunkpapas or a war party of Sans Arcs. They may expect to lose us somewhere between the Heart and the Knife Rivers."

"Pilamaya, Gopher," Rand said. His sturdy friend nodded and galloped back up to scout ahead.

"Gopher is the best of trackers," One Eye comforted. "He could track a mouse from here to our sacred hills. He is in your debt, so he will try very hard."

He only hoped it was enough, Rand sighed, thinking about the day moving slowly into afternoon. Kimi was safe for now, maybe. They

231

wouldn't stop to enjoy her probably until dark, knowing the Sioux might be following.

After a couple of hours of hard riding, they lost the trail in an area of rocky ground.

Gopher frowned. "These *wasicu* are smart as coyotes. It would be hard to track a grasshopper across here. The only thing we can do is fan out, search to see where they might have come off the rocks. There are a dozen different trails they might have taken out. I think the traders are smart enough to wrap their ponies feet in buckskin, so there'll be no tracks. No doubt they made a cold camp at noon, so there would be no smoke scent in the air."

Rand's anxiety built as more precious time was lost searching the area to pick up the trail again. How many hours was it to nightfall? He glanced up at the sun. Past high noon. In six or eight hours, Kimi might be spread out and raped by the trio. He tried not to picture the scene because it added fury to an anger that was already blazing hot. He told himself it was only because she was his as his horse and rifle were his. No man took anything that belonged to Rand Erikson.

He reminded himself that he was engaged to be married to an elegant beauty back in Kentucky and that, sooner or later, he'd be leaving the Dakota territory. The thought crossed his mind that if the war party passed near the fort, it would be easy to ride in, give himself up, tell the army he was no deserter, but that he'd been held captive.

Even as the thought came to him, squat Gopher called out in triumph. He had picked up the trail again and the war party was once more on the move.

When they crossed a little creek and he saw his own reflection in the water, he was stunned at how much like a warrior he looked with his naked, tanned body and painted face. True enough his hair was light and getting shaggy, but otherwise . . . *Hinzi. Yellow Hair.* Except for that, he looked as much like a savage as any of the men who rode with him. Underneath the thin veneer of civilization, there lurks a primitive savage in the most sophisticated of men, Rand thought grimly. His old life didn't seem as appealing as it once had. Sometimes civilization had stifling restraints and restrictions. In contrast, the Sioux lived without clocks and drifted across thousands of miles, following the great herds of buffalo.

Time passed. Again they lost the trail in a rocky place. They spent precious time searching for some sign. Just as Rand thought they had lost the trail completely, he saw something glittering in a small bush.

His heart beating hard, he galloped over and retrieved it. Kimi's medicine object hanging from its thong and reflecting the light. "Hohay!" he exclaimed, "she knows we will be on the trail. She left this to point the way!"

He put it around his own neck, feeling the heat of the sun-warmed gold against his brawny bare chest. It was almost like having her small, warm body against his. There was something familiar about the object, as if he'd seen it before, he thought, then dismissed the idea. The little acorn was surely not even gold—just a cheap brass trinket.

Nudging his big stallion into a gallop, he led the war party following the trail again. Rand glanced up at the sun. Only a few more hours and the trio would be camping. There, maybe feeling secure from pursuit, they would take the time to enjoy Kimi. The thought made Rand both sick and grim; wondering if he would get there in time. He put his hand on his big knife. One thing was certain, if and when he caught up with those three, he would take more than their scalps.

Kimi looked up at the sun as she and the three traders continued their journey. Relentlessly the sun moved toward the western horizon. Hoping that Hinzi and the Lakota warriors might be in pursuit, she delayed the traders as much as she dared every time they stopped to rest the horses or eat a bite. Buck noticed and slapped her around for it. "You think your man follows, huh?" the trader laughed. "He has the Pawnee girl to play with now, so he might not have even noticed you're gone."

Lucky stood up in his stirrups and looked behind him, peering at the horizon. "Maybe if they think she left on her own with us, they may not even bother to come lookin.' "

Tech agreed. "Shucks, we shore ain't seen no sign of them, and I been watchin'."

Kimi didn't say anything. Maybe they were right; maybe Hinzi wouldn't come or the warriors had lost the trail. In that case . . . no, she didn't even want to think about her fate.

All too soon the sun sank low over the hot, hostile country and Lucky reined in. "I know where there's a little protected grove of bushes ahead. We'll camp there." He ran his hands up and down Kimi's arm, holding her close in the saddle. "And you, sweet stuff, you know what's coming tonight, don't you?"

The three men guffawed and Kimi shuddered visibly.

Tech laughed and winked at Lucky, a grin on

his hard face. "Shucks! She's so eager, she's tremblin'. Ain't that right, Lucky?"

"Damned right! Why she's almost as eager as we are, ain't you, sweet stuff?" He nuzzled the back of her neck, and ran his hot hands over her body while she struggled to pull away from him. He nudged his horse and, in the deepening purple twilight, they rode on until they reached the cluster of straggly bushes.

The three men dismounted. Lucky reached up to lift Kimi down while the other two hobbled the horses. He held her by the shoulders, looking into her face. "Okay, sweet stuff. First we eat. Later we'll see how much you know about pleasing a man—and how much we can teach you."

He pushed her to Buck, who nuzzled her with his dirty beard while she struggled to get away from him.

Lucky began to unsaddle his mount. "Wonder if her name is Mae? Did anyone ask her?"

"Shucks! Are we gonna havta hear that story again?" Tech complained as he spat tobacco juice, began to build a fire.

"Mae is the one I'm waitin' for," Lucky began as if he hadn't heard Tech. "A fortune teller tole me once that the keys to my future was four words, 'Mae,' 'fire,' 'whiskey,' and 'cricket.' "

"Shucks," Tech snorted as he gathered buffalo chips for fuel, "that ain't much of a fortune teller. I wouldn't have paid her. She tell you how the words fit together?"

Lucky finished unsaddling, carried his gear over by the fire. "The way I figure it, Mae is a special gal; one worth waitin' for. I'll spend my old age sitting by a fireplace with a big bottle of whiskey and this gorgeous, naked gal in my lap, and maybe a cricket chirpin' on the hearth."

"Sounds good to me," Buck said. "I knew a gal named Mae once; she was real talented. Wonder if it's the same one?"

Tech reached for a skillet. "They do say the Chinee think crickets is good luck." He looked at Kimi. "Reckon that little half-breed gal can cook?"

"We can find out." Buck untied Kimi. "Don't go too far, you hear, sweet? Ain't no place out on the prairie to hide no way."

Kimi didn't answer as she rubbed her wrists. Her arms ached from being tied all this time, and her mouth was sore from the gag. Even in the darkness, there wouldn't be any place to run in this desolate stretch.

"Well, we got whiskey and a woman," Lucky grinned.

"Shucks," the scar-faced one complained, "you're lucky some woman's husband ain't kilt you yet."

"How do you think I got my name?" He flopped down on the ground, leaned against his saddle.

"Quit jawin," Buck complained. He motioned to Kimi. "You, gal, get some grub out of the supplies, cook us up a little dinner. Tech, don't built that fire so big."

"Shucks, you don't really think those Sioux are still on our trail? Why, we're within five or ten miles of the fort."

"You can't never tell about Injuns." Buck spread his blanket by the fire. "They're most dangerous when you least expect them; like snakes when you step on one in the dark."

The other two grunted agreement, and Kimi looked around, deciding that with all the horses hobbled and the weapons where the trio could watch them, she didn't have a chance of escaping at the moment. She needed time. Food would occupy their minds for a while. She got a small skillet and a slab of bacon from the supplies, moving as slowly as possible.

It was dusk now, a pale lavender-and-gray twilight. Quail called somewhere, cicadas chirped in the stillness.

Lucky got out a bottle of whiskey and some tobacco. "Yep, no man could want a better life than this; I'm a lucky man, all right."

Buck grinned and reached for the bottle. "After supper, that's when we all get lucky."

Tech took a big drink as Buck handed him the bottle, "Hey, Injun, your name Mae?"

Kimi shook her head, and didn't look up, although she felt all three of the men watching her as she cooked. She pretended not to notice, but her skin crawled at what she knew they were imagining. Maybe if they drank enough, she might have a chance of escaping.

"Shucks, she's the prettiest I've seen in a long time."

Buck took a big drink, wiped his bearded face on his dirty sleeve. "Hell, Tech, any woman is purty once a man's had a few drinks."

"That's a fact," Lucky grinned and leaned back against his saddle. "I ain't never gone to bed with an ugly woman, but I've woke up with a few."

Tech scratched his pox-scarred face. "If they ain't, I jest close my eyes. Then you can't tell what color they is, how old, or if they're purty or not. All cats look gray in the dark."

The three guffawed and passed the bottle around again.

Kimi watched them out of the corner of her eye while she fixed food as slowly as possible. It was

237

dark now, and the fire she cooked over wasn't much bigger than her hand. She thought about gradually adding fuel to it, maybe turn it into a roaring blaze that might be seen a long distance, then decided against it. The traders weren't that stupid. Better she should delay getting the food ready, hoping they would drink enough on empty bellies to render themselves either unconscious or too impotent to be interested in her later. It was a dim chance, Kimi knew, but it was all she could cling to at the moment. She'd almost given up the idea that Hinzi and a war party would catch up to them soon enough to help. In a few minutes, it would be as black as these men's hearts. It appeared nothing would help her tonight.

Rand looked up at the sun now low on the horizon. At least it would be cooler with the sun down, he thought, it's been hot for early May. Then he wished he could turn the time back a dozen hours, no matter the heat, because he knew all too well the ordeal Kimi would endure after dark when her kidnappers finally camped. He wasn't sorry he had helped the Pawnee girl, though. He'd do it again.

He looked over at One Eye as they rode. "Friend, do you speak any Pawnee?"

"A little. It helps when you're trying to get information from captives. Why?"

"What does the name Kirit mean?"

"Cricket. Why?"

Rand shrugged. "Just wondering."

Gopher returned just then, interrupting Rand's thoughts. "Hinzi, I think I smelled just a trace of smoke carried on the wind."

Rand's heart quickened and he looked at One

Eye. "Can it be—?"

"Don't get your hopes up," One Eye cautioned. "It could be a prairie fire or the brown coal, the whites call lignite, that lightning's set on fire. Some of the areas of the Bad Lands have burned for years. Many think *Inyan,* the ancestor of all things, dwells in the rocks."

"Let's hope it's a camp fire." Rand nudged Scout forward.

"Easy, my friend," One Eye cautioned. "If they even suspect we're out here, they may kill her or use her as a hostage."

That was true enough. "All right," Rand said, "we'll be as sneaky as the coyote. We'll fan out, surround the camp, if it's them. Pass the word her safety comes before the counting of coups or revenge, even though I can hardly wait to dip my own blade in their blood."

One Eye nodded. "We'd better use knives or lances. A gunshot carries a long way. There might be an army or Pawnee scout patrol in the area. More and more whites seem to be coming into our country, and the Great White Father sends more and more soldiers."

An army patrol, Rand thought almost with disinterest as they dismounted, tied their ponies muzzles' with strips of rawhide to keep them from whinnying and giving away the ambush when they scented the traders' horses. Only a couple of weeks ago, he would have been pleased to run across an army patrol that might rescue him. Now all he could think of was the safety of a young green-eyed girl.

They rode forward. It was dark now; a moonless night as dark as the bottom of a well. Rand signaled the others to step silently as they crept toward the camp. He could smell the scent of smoke, too. With hand signals, he, One Eye and Gopher placed their men. Leaving their horses back with a waiting brave, the three crawled on their bellies through the dry, sparse grass toward the campsite.

It was them, all right. He had to force himself to lie in the grass quietly watching the scene. His first impulse had been to rush in, take Kimi in his arms, and kill the traders who lounged on blankets by the fire, drinking whiskey.

They had obviously just finished eating, judging from the dirty tin plates that Kimi was cleaning up. He watched her, sighing with relief. She didn't appear to be much the worse for wear, except for a bad bruise on her face. When Rand imagined how she had come by that injury, rage boiled up in him, sour as bile, and he trembled.

One Eye must have realized his mood because his friend reached out, caught his arm, shook his head. *Wait,* he mouthed silently in Lakota.

One Eye was right. When Kimi was safe, Rand could enjoy a slow revenge. As a Lakota warrior, Kimi was his, and woe to the man who touched his woman.

He waited, watching the men drink and Kimi moving about quietly. The weary strain on her lovely face betrayed that she was almost to the breaking point. No doubt this had been a horrifying ordeal for the petite girl. He would see that the three were paid in their own coin. When he closed the trap, he didn't want Kimi hurt, or any of the culprits to escape his vengeance. For now, he forced himself to watch and wait.

Kimi picked up the dirty tin plate with a shaking hand. She had delayed the three as long as possible so they might drink enough to pass out, but it hadn't worked. Now that they had finished eating and were back lounging on their blankets and guzzling the cheap, potent whiskey, it was only a matter of time until their interest turned to her.

What could she do? The night was hot and moonless, so that if she managed to slip away from the fire, maybe she stood a slight chance of not being found until daylight. By then they might give up and go on without her. In fact, if she could walk back toward the Sioux camp, she might run into Hinzi and the warriors if they were trailing. The traders were smart as hunted coyotes. They had done every trick in the book to throw a tracker off their trail.

Automatically she reached up for the comforting feel of her medicine charm; then she remembered it wasn't there.

Lucky seemed to notice her gesture, stumbled to his feet and swayed toward her. "Hey, sweet stuff, what'd you do with that little fetish?"

Had Hinzi found it? She dare not let the trader know she had left it hanging on a bush to show the way. "I—the thong broke and I lost it along the trail somewhere."

"Too bad," he swayed over her, "it looked like it was real gold." He reached out, caught her by the throat. "I envy the thing, know why?"

"Why?" She tried to pull away, but he held her.

He pulled her to her feet, grinning. "Because it's been against your pretty tits all this time, that's why. I'm getting ready to do something about that."

The other two laughed.

"Yeah," Buck said, "bring her over here. I been lookin' forward to tryin' her out."

"I'm about to find out how good Sweet Stuff is." Lucky pulled her to her feet.

"Wouldn't you like another drink?" she said, trying to pull away from the feel of his dirty, sweaty hands. He reeked of sour whiskey.

"Yeah, I'll have another drink," he laughed, dragging her toward the blanket. "You know where I'm gonna drink it from? The hollow of your pretty belly!"

She looked around frantically for a weapon, some way of escape. She saw none.

He had both hands on her shoulders, pulling at her shift as he bent his head to kiss her.

She might submit and live or fight them and be killed. Either way, she didn't stand a chance against three big, drunken men. But she would take some of their blood with her. A big steel fork lay by the flickering fire. It was almost as good as a knife if she could reach it. Even as she broke away, diving for it, Buck grabbed her arm and twisted it cruelly. "You little bitch!"

She was determined not to give him the satisfaction of a scream as the pain ran through her body, but she had to bite her lip to hold it back. Even as she fell, half fainting, she heard sudden shrieks in the darkness and painted faces and half-naked bodies rose up around the circle in the night, shouting and screaming as they rushed in.

Maybe in her terror, she was only imagining she was saved. She managed to raise her head, saw Hinzi in the middle of the firelit circle and the anger of his painted face was terrifying.

"Stay down, Kimi!" he shouted as he turned toward the wide-eyed Buck. "Stay down till it's over!"

All around her, warriors were leaping into the circle, attacking the three traders.

Kimi struggled to raise up on one elbow, but she was dizzy and in pain. A blur of action and bodies seemed to swirl around her. Hinzi and the bearded one were locked in mortal combat near the small fire. She saw the sudden gleam in Buck's eyes and realized what he was about to do even as he rolled Hinzi over and over toward the fire. "Look out, Hinzi!"

But Buck's momentum carried them to the edge of the fire. By sheer strength, he tried to force the white warrior's almost naked body into the scarlet and yellow flames. Even as he did so, Hinzi, reflexes quick as a cougar's, threw Buck off balance and into the fire. Buck screamed as his beard flamed. Dropping his knife, he clawed at his face. Even as Buck dropped his knife, Hinzi raised his own blade and brought it down in one swift stroke, light from the fiery blaze reflecting off the steel. It caught Buck in the heart and went all the way to the hilt. He was dead even before his body hit the ground.

Cursing under his breath, Hinzi knelt and in two swift strokes took Buck's scalp and then his manhood. He held both up triumphantly, shrieking a victory chant that sent shivers up Kimi's back. Civilized he might be, but at this moment, he was a primitive savage, extracting vengeance against another for daring to take his mate.

She looked around. Lucky had disappeared, but One Eye threw his lance, pinned Tech against the ground, wiggling like a speared rabbit. The other warriors ransacked the camp, helping themselves to weapons and supplies.

"Kimi, are you all right?" Hinzi tossed his grisly trophies away, turned toward her, his magnificent body gleaming with perspiration and blood.

She suddenly realized she had been holding her

243

breath. Exhaling abruptly, Kimi stumbled to her feet, ran toward him; hesitated at the sight of blood. "Oh, Hinzi, you're hurt!"

He swung her up in his powerful arms, held her against him like a small doll. "It's his blood. I've only a scratch or two. Did they—?"

"No." She collapsed against his wide chest, safe now in his embrace and shaking with relief. "I'm all right. They were just getting ready to—"

"I saw. By Wakan Tanka, I'm sorry I killed him so quickly. I meant to make him beg for death!"

"Oh, Hinzi, I've been so scared!" She pressed her face against him, shaking as he smoothed her hair.

"Didn't you know I'd come?" He looked down into her face. "What belongs to me, no man takes."

Was that all she was to him, a possession like his horse or his gun? Like a mare in a stallion's harem, she thought, along with the Pawnee girl.

One Eye strode over in the firelight, waving Tech's bloody scalp. "He didn't last very long. I meant to make him die slowly."

Hinzi, still holding Kimi, looked around. "What happened to the third one?"

Gopher paused in going through a saddle bag, scratched his head. "I stabbed him myself and left him lying there." He pointed to a blood smear on the edge of the darkness. "I was sure he was dead."

Hinzi cursed under his breath. "Scatter out, see if you can find him and finish him off. We need to clear out of here and be far away by dawn; don't want to run into an army patrol."

Kimi slipped her arms around his neck, sighing with relief that her ordeal was over. "Hinzi, about the Pawnee girl; if you intend to keep her for a second wife—"

"You are mine and what a warrior does is not the concern of women." Then he smiled gently, kissed her bruised cheek. "My jealous little butterfly. I never meant to keep the girl, I turned her loose last night. By now she should be back safe among her own people."

"I've been such a fool!" She hid her face against him and wept. "I'll be yours forever."

He held her close and stroked her. "Nothing is forever, Kimi," he murmured against her hair, "we will cherish whatever time Wakan Tanka gives us because who knows when it will end?"

Was he telling her something? Preparing her for what was bound to happen sooner or later when he went away? She didn't even want to think about that now. It was enough to be safe in his arms, held tightly against his heart as he strode over to Scout and swung up onto the horse's back. "Did anyone find the missing trader?"

A murmur of denials came from the men still walking around out in the darkness.

"Then hear me, warriors! Gather your spoils and ride out. We must not be seen close to a fort by dawn's light."

Gopher protested. "What about the missing man? He should not be allowed to escape."

"Didn't you say he was wounded?"

"Yes. I found blood."

Hinzi shrugged. "Then he won't last long out here in the heat of this trackless, barren prairie. He'll die a more agonizing death than the other two; that is enough for me. We go now!"

As Hinzi turned his big stallion back toward the Sioux camp, Kimi nestled herself against his powerful chest, safe in his embrace. She thought about the missing man. There was a slight chance that an army patrol might find him if he were fortunate. Lucky. Maybe he would be. If the elements didn't get him, maybe his fortune-teller would be right in her prediction. Maybe Lucky would finally meet his fate by a roaring fire with a chirping cricket, a pretty girl named Mae and a bottle of whiskey after all.

Fourteen

Lucky lay hidden in the brush, watching the Sioux war party kill his partners and loot the camp. Oh, God! They'd be looking for him next!

He burrowed into the dry buffalo grass as deep as possible, holding his breath, watching and waiting. He had a bad cut on his arm and across his foot where that squat-looking Injun had caught him with a tomahawk. He knew he'd left a blood trail. However, his wounds had stopped bleeding as he crawled off into the brush and for a few minutes the savages were too busy killing and scalping his partners and looting the supplies to even notice he was gone.

At least he was alive, even though his wounds throbbed with pain. He bit his lip to hold back a moan as he watched the Indians in the firelight. Was there the slightest chance he was going to live up to his name?

It was moonless and warm, Lucky noted, as dark as the inside of a buffalo's gut tonight. That would discourage and hinder the braves if they began to search for him. He lay very still, his wounds aching. He tasted his own blood from his bitten lip, wished he had a bottle of whiskey from his packs. Only a few feet away, the rampaging savages were guzzling some of the whiskey and breaking the other bottles.

Both Buck and Tech had died fighting, knowing

what the vengeful braves would do to them if they took them alive.

What was that the white warrior was holding aloft in the fire light and singing a victory chant over? Oh, God, it was Buck's . . .

Lucky managed to keep from gagging as he looked away. Buck wasn't gonna need it any more anyhow. He'd topped his last female. All because of a half-breed gal who belonged to a yellow-haired white man who spoke Lakota and acted like a Sioux warrior.

He lay watching that one-eyed brave scalp Tech and heard enough of the Sioux words to know they were wondering what had happened to the third man.

If they took him alive, they'd make him beg for death. Maybe he wasn't so lucky after all, he thought, flattening himself out on the ground as they began to search the area for him. If he had a knife, he'd kill himself rather than be taken alive. Even a broken whiskey bottle would do; a scrap of metal, anything. The Sioux were searching the area while others wrecked the camp, took or destroyed supplies.

The shorter, heavier brave walked slowly out toward him through the grass. Lucky lay very still. It almost seemed to him that the man might hear the scared pounding of his heart. He felt sweat break out on his face, run down in his eyes. All over a woman, a damned woman, Lucky thought, as the brave walked close enough to touch his moccasin. Lucky should have kept the Pawnee girl and left the green-eyed one alone. Women were his weakness, had always been. He resolved as he lay there, that if he survived this, he'd change his ways. He'd spend his energy at gambling and drinking.

He must have fainted for a long moment from the agony, because when he came to, the Sioux had evidently given up the search. They were burning the camp, taking what they wanted. Lucky watched the white warrior embrace the small half-breed beauty and swing her up into his powerful arms. The way she clung to him left no doubt about her feelings for the man.

A yellow haired, blue-eyed Sioux, that's what he was; spoke pretty good Lakota. Probably a boy carried off by them a long time ago after some raid on a ranch or wagon train. Lucky had heard stories like that.

Lucky watched the pale savage carry her to his buckskin horse. The others, under the orders of that one-eyed brave in the shirt decorated with enemy hair, finished ransacking the camp, taking what they needed and burning the rest. Would they see him in the firelight? Lucky lay as still as he could, pressed against the rough dirt, the stiff buffalo grass. They acted as if they were in a big hurry to get moving, no doubt afraid an army patrol might be in the area.

The fort. That thought gave Lucky hope. He didn't know how far it was; maybe five or ten miles. There was always a chance an army patrol might be around close. Probably that had occurred to the Indians too. They acted as if they were in an all-fired hurry to leave. He drew a breath of relief. Lucky had been afraid they might stay until dawn to search him out in the daylight. The savages finished mutilating his partners' bodies and gathered up most of the supplies, even taking the pack mules. Then they mounted up and rode out, headed back the direction they had come. The girl clung to the white warrior as he swung her up on his horse, nudged it, and started out of the camp. The others followed.

Lucky lay still, the moments ticking with each beat of his heart. The loss of blood had made him thirsty. He ran his tongue over his dry, crackled lips, thinking about whiskey.

The dying fire reflected off some object in the ravaged camp. A glass bottle. One bottle of whiskey that had escaped the Indians' notice lay near the small fire. But when he crawled to it, his hopes were dashed. The cork was gone, the liquor soaked into the dirt.

The fort. That's where he needed to go. It might be a long way, but that was his only chance. Hell! His name wasn't Lucky for nothing. The scudding clouds drifted some, and dim stars came out.

Lucky began to crawl on his belly across the endless prairie. With that injured foot, he wasn't sure he could walk and anyway, he was leery of being outlined against the black sky should the moon suddenly show itself. Those Sioux had eyes like eagles.

He crawled maybe a half mile or even a mile on his belly, the rocks cutting into his hands, the dry buffalo grass scratching his face. He heard small things scurrying in the darkness as he disturbed them, and he didn't even want to think about what they might be—rattlesnakes, big spiders, maybe scorpions.

Before he could stand, he needed a crutch. All he found searching around in the darkness was a gleaming white bone. When he found the skull, he realized it was what was left of a man: white or Indian, he couldn't tell. A man's leg bone. He could use it as a cane. Lucky wasn't superstitious. He finally mustered the strength and courage to pull himself to his feet and stagger on across the endless prairie, using the bone to help him. His flesh was a mass of pain, but that was nothing compared to his terror. Suppose the warriors decided to come back? Suppose he ran into one of their other bands or some of their allies, the Cheyenne or Arapaho?

"Remember your name is Lucky," he reminded

himself as he swayed on his feet. "You aren't going to be killed by Indians or you'd have died that way long ago. Remember the fortune teller. Somewhere, there's a gal named Mae and a cheery fireplace with a cricket chirping away." He saw himself as an old man in a rocking chair by that fire. He'd be old, but Mae would be young and full-figured, sitting on his lap naked. The thought cheered him.

Thus encouraged, he stumbled on toward the fort. The night had gradually turned cool as the hours passed and he shivered from the cold, wishing he'd dug through the wreckage for a blanket or a jacket. Probably the avenging warriors hadn't left anything like that behind. All they had left was two dead men and one who was certain to die out on the trackless prairie.

He didn't waste any regrets or sympathy on his two partners. He was only pleased they were the dead ones and not himself.

Once he tripped and fell. He lay there a long minute, shivering and breathing hard. It would be so easy just to close his eyes and lie here forever. But no, he hadn't escaped the Sioux only to die of exhaustion and exposure out here in the wilderness. There were still a lot of hot women he hadn't mounted.

He had to grit his teeth against the pain to force himself to his feet and stagger on through the chill darkness. Thirst began to plague him and he wished he had a canteen. Right now, he'd almost rather have water than whiskey. He had neither As the hours passed and the night deepened, the cold became almost unbearable and his teeth chattered. Even though he'd be easy to spot walking across the prairie in the daylight, he began to wish for dawn. At least with the sun out, he wouldn't be so damned cold.

Don't think about it, he told himself and kept walking. Think about something else. *Think about being warm. Think about something you really like. Women.* In his mind, he saw the little Pawnee girl the night he had taken her virginity. Brown Sugar. Such a little, trusting fool. What white man in his right mind would want an Injun girl permanently? Yet she had been stupid enough to believe him. He remembered how warm and smooth her naked body had felt against him, how her breasts had tasted and the scent of her hot skin. Yep, that was the way to keep warm, all right.

Finally the sun came up after a forever of cold blackness. Lucky stumbled on, not knowing or caring anymore how much time had passed or how far he had come. He wasn't moving very fast and he had to keep stopping to rest. All that mattered was that he could finally see where he was going so he wouldn't keep tripping and falling, and that he was finally going to be warm again.

Within hours he was cursing the sun and praying for darkness. The sun beat on him, making sweat run down his body, stinging where it ran into a scratch or wound. His tongue had begun to swell so that it was difficult to swallow.

Water. That was what he thought about now: not whiskey, not women. Before this was over, he might wish he were dead. Lucky paused, swaying on his feet, and looked around. He felt like the only living thing on this trackless, treeless prairie. The sun hung like a fried egg in a faded blue denim sky; the heat so intense that little waves seemed to rise up off the ground and blur his vision. In his suffering, he pulled off his shirt and threw it away.

Lucky kept walking. His lips were so dry and cracked they bled, and he found himself sucking the moisture of his own blood. The salt of it only made

252

him thirstier. Too late, he regretted having thrown away his shirt. He felt the sun cooking his bare back and he had no defense against its relentless rays. He thought of nothing now but water. He imagined plunging his face into a cold spring and drinking deep, the drops running down his face and onto the shaggy hair of his chest. He imagined that half-breed Sioux girl naked, her body covered with droplets of cold water that he licked off slowly while she writhed at the touch of his tongue.

Snow. As his back cooked from the sun and his feet began to swell in his boots, Lucky thought about Michigan snow where he grew up. He was running naked through the swirling storm with a faceless whore named Mae. Together they rolled in the icy white flakes and it felt good, oh, so good. Mae broke off an icicle that hung from a tree branch and licked it slowly, provocatively. He kissed her and her mouth was cold on his, and he relished the cold on his tongue. Mae laughed and lay down in his lap and her mouth found something else to run her tongue over, slowly, teasing.

They made torrid love, the snow melting under her beautiful, naked body as he rode her. Yeah, first cold water, then a woman, then a big steak and a bottle of whiskey. Yeah, that's what he'd have when he finally made it to the fort. Lucky kept the image dangling in front of his mind like a carrot before a pack mule to force his swollen, bloody feet to keep moving forward.

By late afternoon, he couldn't always remember who he was or why he was out here. He only knew that to stop moving forward was to die and he wasn't meant to die out here alone. The fort, oh, yes, the fort. He looked at the sun, slanting like a fireball not far above the horizon. If he didn't get help soon, he wasn't sure he could last through another night without water. His feet were so badly swollen, he took off his boots. Then couldn't get them back on so he abandoned them and kept walking. Within a hundred yards his feet began to bleed and he regretted leaving his boots, but couldn't seem to produce the necessary energy to go back to get them. No, he must keep moving forward. His tongue had long ago swollen to the point that he could no longer swallow.

He should be dead, he thought without much emotion. He was almost past caring. What kept him walking now was fury and a lust for vengeance. That damned white Indian—he was responsible for Lucky's plight! He pictured the yellow-haired man lying naked between both the Pawnee and the Sioux girls. They were doing all sorts of forbidden things to the Yellow Hair while he lolled on a buffalo robe, a big gourd of cold water in one hand, a bottle of whiskey from Lucky's own pack in the other. Damn him. Damn him!

They'd left Lucky to die, but he would fool them. He was moving now on sheer hatred and anger. He had to live long enough to tell the soldiers about that white Sioux.

It was almost sundown when Lucky happened to look over his shoulder He thought he spotted a movement on the horizon. What was that? He hesitated, not sure he'd seen anything. Could it be Sioux? Not from that direction. Big wolves running in a pack? Wolves could smell blood for a long way on the wind. For a moment, he shook, imagining them pulling him down like they would an old, injured buffalo bull, ripping the flesh from his bones before he was really dead. Even as he paused, the animals moving toward him got bigger, bigger than wolves. He strained his weary eyes. Buffalo? He didn't have any weapon to kill one with.

Men. There were men on the animals' backs. For a

heart-stopping minute, he stared in terror. Then he saw the blue of their coats, the reflection of brass buttons.

He was saved! Lucky tried to shout but his voice was a mere croak in his throat. They were riding to the east of him, probably headed to the fort. They might not see him at all. The thought of being so close and yet so far from rescue sent him into hysteria. With the last of his remaining strength, Lucky waved frantically with the bone.

For another heart-stopping moment he thought they hadn't seen him. Then the horses reined in and the patrol turned and galloped toward him.

A dead man's leg bone had saved him. Why had he ever doubted that fortune teller? The small patrol galloped up to him as he collapsed in the dirt. One young, pink-faced lieutenant, his patrol, and a half-dozen Indian scouts. Pawnee? 'Ree? Crow?

What difference did it make? Even if they were Pawnees, they wouldn't know about Brown Sugar. He pitched over on his face as they galloped up. The lieutenant and one of the scouts knelt by him, propping him up, putting a canteen to his lips. "My God." The pink-faced officer looked horrified. "My God, man, what happened to you?"

Lucky didn't answer. He was too busy gulping the tepid water. Oh, it tasted so good! It wasn't his time to die after all.

The handsome Indian scout pulled it from his hands. "Not too much," he cautioned gently. "Wait a minute, then drink a little more." He wore a blue army cap at a rakish angle over one eye, and white teeth flashed in his dark face when he grinned.

Lucky tried to talk, couldn't. He reached for the canteen again; guzzled the water. The prissy officer took his own canteen, poured a little water on his snowy white handkerchief, wiped Lucky's face. "You look like a piece of raw meat. What happened?"

Lucky didn't answer for a full five minutes. He just kept drinking water. He looked up into the two faces, sighed. "Whiskey. I'd love some whiskey."

The scout said to the officer, "Sir, I've got some snake bite remedy in my saddlebags."

The pink-faced officer frowned. "Terry, I'm not sure that's by the book."

"Believe it or not, sir, this isn't West Point." The handsome Indian grinned. "We don't always follow regulations."

"Then get it, Terry." The officer gestured.

"Terry? Hellava name for an Injun scout." Lucky grinned with expectation. Whatever tribe he was, most of the ones who scouted for the army were enemies of the Sioux. When he could get his breath, he'd tell about the massacre of his partners and the white warrior riding with the Sioux.

The officer took off his gloves. He had fine, well-manicured hands. A greenhorn. He'd been found by some wet-nosed, "by-the-book" greenhorn, Lucky thought, but anyway, he was safe. The Indian held out a bottle. Lucky accepted it gratefully and took a long drink. Then the scout stuck a cigar between Lucky's cracked lips, and lit it. "I am *Ter-ra-re-cox:* Warcry. The soldiers call me 'Terry.' "

"Thanks, Terry, much obliged." Lucky took a deep puff, sighed loudly. The smoke tasted good. He was feeling better by the minute. A little food, some rest, a woman, and he'd be as good as new.

The lieutenant peered at him. "Mister, you look like you died and forgot to lie down. How long you been out here, anyway?"

Lucky took the cigar out of his mouth, reached for the whiskey again, and struggled to find his voice. "Damned if I remember. Don't even know what month it is."

"May," the officer volunteered.

It was hard to speak, but he had to tell him. "White man riding with the Sioux," Lucky said. "Yellow hair . . . blue eyes . . . you'd swear he was Injun, speaks good Lakota."

"A *white* man?" The young greenhorn looked thunderstruck.

"Sioux?" The scout's expression changed. The buck was thinking about scalp-taking, all right.

There was so much more to tell, but his strength deserted him. *Tomorrow,* Lucky thought with grim satisfaction, *tomorrow I'll tell them enough to have every soldier in the Dakotas looking for that white Injun.*

The lieutenant started to wipe the sweat from his pink face with his handkerchief, looked as the grime Lucky had left smeared on it, frowned, and used his manicured fingers instead. "What's your name and what are you doing out here?"

"Trader," Lucky gasped. "They call me Lucky."

Something about the scout's expression changed. "You alone?"

Lucky nodded. "Two partners dead; Sioux got 'em."

The young officer scratched a cheek covered with almost peach fuzz. "Well, you're lucky, all right, Mister. You could have died out here."

"Ain't my time yet." He took a puff on the cigar.

The officer stood up, looked at the scout. "We've got to get this man back to the fort; he's in a bad way."

The scout nodded. "Tell you what, lieutenant, why don't you take your patrol, ride back to the fort and tell them we're coming. I'll keep my scouts, we'll rig a travois and bring him in."

"Good idea!" The pink-faced man turned and looked longingly off in the direction of the fort. "I'll tell the colonel what's happened so we can map strategy."

Map strategy. The high-toned boy sounded like a West Point cadet, all right. Lucky saw the scorn in the scout's dark eyes, quickly hidden. "Sir, dragging a travois, we'll be moving slow. Tell the colonel I'll report as soon as I get in; probably after dawn."

"A *written* report," the lieutenant reminded him primly; "Everything by the book."

"Yes sir."

The rest was a vague blur to Lucky. Dimly he remembered the patrol riding away in the dusk. The handful of Indian scouts began to make a travois from lances and blankets and carried Lucky to it. They gave him a hunk of crispy fried rabbit, a canteen of water, a full bottle of whiskey, and a fistful of cigars.

"For an Injun, you're all right," he told the chief scout. "I'll see the colonel knows how well you've treated me; it'll look good on your record."

The rakish brave tipped his cavalry cap over one eye, looked pleased, and motioned for his men to mount up. He rode beside Lucky as the travois moved along.

Lucky took a deep puff of his cigar. He was feeling a lot better. "The only other things I want are a big steak, more whiskey, and a pretty woman. No, I'd like the whiskey and the woman first." He winked at the scout.

The scout nodded, his handsome dark face immobile. "Our village is just a little out of the way. You'd be more comfortable there. I have a good friend with a pretty sister." He winked back.

Lucky thought about the grim infirmary of the fort. The sawbones would put him on soup, most likely, no whiskey, and no women. "Sounds good to me. Is the girl pretty?"

The scout pushed his hat back. "Only if you like a small girl with big breasts. We call her Kirit."

Lucky snickered. "Maybe I don't care if we ever reach the fort."

Terry motioned to one of the other scouts. "Ride and tell Kirit that we bring an injured white man named Lucky. He'll need her care."

The man mounted up, rode out.

Dusk had fallen, but the Indians had given Lucky a blanket, and he was content, even though his wounds hurt some. They traveled for hours. He would have sworn they turned west, but Lucky couldn't be sure. He thought he remembered some of those eternally burning lignite hills to the west — or was he confusing the terrain with the Badlands, that hostile environment General Sully called "Hell with the fires out?" In the distant pale lavender glow of moonlight, the smoldering brown coal outcrops that had been set afire by long ago lightning sent wisps of smoke into the sky.

Lucky looked around. "This don't look like the way to the fort."

The handsome Indian scout made a soothing gesture. "Wouldn't you rather go with us to our camp? That fort infirmary won't have anything but quinine and bitters."

Lucky thought about the girl he had been promised, Kirit. A pretty Indian girl, some roast buffalo tongue and a bottle of whiskey while he recuperated; that sounded good to him. He lay back and relaxed while the travois moved.

It must have been almost dawn when the little party finally arrived at the camp. It was a temporary camp, the kind many of the tribes set up when they were on a hunt. Dogs barked and curious Indians came out to see who was coming in. On the ridge, he saw a pale glow of burning lignite. It had turned cool again, and the thought of warming his hands near the lightning-caused fire appealed to him.

The scout grinned. "You comfortable? Pretty cool for a May night."

May night. Mae, naw, couldn't be "Your friend's sister pretty?"

Terry nodded. "Kirit is small and dark. That's why they named her Cricket."

May. Cricket. Lucky tried to make sense of it, recall just exactly what the fortune teller had said.

The travois halted. Terry leaned on his black stallion's neck, smiled at Lucky. "The pretty girl is going to walk with us."

"Where?" Not that he much minded, Lucky thought ruefully. He was plenty drunk from that comforting bottle of whiskey the scout had given him at the beginning. "Terry, you're all right!" He grinned crookedly up at him.

He heard the girl come out of her lodge, turned to see if she was as pretty and young as promised. Although her face was shadowed, her body looked inviting as she stood there in the glow of the slow-burning background fires.

Abruptly, the warriors who carried the litter paused.

"Hey!" he protested. "What the—?"

"You asked for some whiskey and a woman." Terry's voice was abruptly as hard as his dark eyes. "You are about to get both. I think you've met."

He blinked as the girl stepped out of the shadows. Was it? Could it be?

"Hello, Lucky." The girl stepped from the shadows, holding a bottle of whiskey. "I've waited a long time for this moment."

"Brown Sugar?" He could only stare at her, almost in disbelief. "I thought you was in the Sioux camp?"

May. Whiskey. Cricket. All the bits of the prediction fell into place; all but one.

The Indian girl knelt by his side even as the warriors came forward suddenly, pinned his arms and legs. Even as he struggled, they took him off the litter, spread-eagled him, staked him down.

He felt cold sweat beading on his face. "Look, Sugar, there's been some mistake—"

"And you made it," she reminded him. Very slowly, she poured a stream of whiskey all over his body.

He didn't like the cold look on her face. "Look, Sugar or Cricket, or whatever you're called, you can't scare me," he blustered, pulling at his bonds, but they held. "The army knows I'm here."

"Its unfortunate that you were in worse shape than the scouts realized," she said. "You died unexpectedly before they could get you to the fort."

This had to be a joke. She was trying to scare him. He'd call her bluff. "You can't kill a man by soaking his clothes with whiskey."

"Can't I?"

Only then did he see the warrior stepping forward with a iron kettle full of the burning coal from the ridge.

Warcry rode into the fort at midafternoon, dismounted, tied up his horse, entered the lieutenant's office, and saluted.

"Oh, Terry." The lieutenant looked up from the report he was writing in prim, precise strokes. "At ease. The colonel's been eager to interview that trader we found."

261

"Bad news, sir." Terry frowned and leaned on the desk with both hands. "The man took a turn for the worse, so we stopped at our camp because it was closer. He lasted until almost noon."

"Dead?" The young man's eyes widened and he sat up straight behind his desk, tapping his pen against his teeth. "His wounds didn't look that bad to me."

The scout tipped his cavalry cap to the back of his head. "Me neither, sir, but he was a long time dying — badly burned."

"Damn!" The pink-faced young man threw his pen across the room like a spoiled child tossing a toy, "I forget how relentless that sun can be."

"Isn't it, though?" Terry smiled, remembering. Cricket had had her revenge. The trader had begged for death. He had kept mumbling about a fortune teller.

"You should have sent a messenger to the fort," the lieutenant grumbled, "but I don't suppose he would have been any better off in our infirmary. I hate having to report all this to the colonel."

"I'll accept the blame, sir. We went ahead and buried the man. We don't even know what his real name was. He called himself Lucky."

"That's ironic, isn't it?" The lieutenant rubbed his beardless pink face with a well-manicured hand. "You think there's anything to that story about that white warrior?"

The scout paused a long moment. He had promised Cricket he would try to protect the white man who had helped her, although it went against his grain, since the man rode with the enemy. He shook his head. "No, I think the trader was out of his mind from sun. It doesn't make much sense that a white man would be riding with the Sioux, does it?"

The other man tapped his soft, well-manicured fingers on his report. "Nevertheless, I keep thinking about that deserted wagon train me and a friend of mine, Lieutenant Ware, found last year."

"Sir?"

"We were with a detachment last November near Julesburg, trying to keep the lid on the Indian problems. Not that it did any good. Later that month, Chivington started a wholesale war by attacking the Cheyenne camped at Sand Creek."

"Mind if I smoke?" Warcry already had his tobacco out and was rolling a cigarette.

The officer frowned at his impudence, then seemed to remember the Pawnee was going to take the heat from the grumpy colonel and nodded permission. "About forty miles from Julesburg, out in the middle of nowhere, we find this wagon train. It was the spookiest thing you've ever seen; no people, no animals, no sign of life at all."

Even the Pawnee scout was interested now. He puffed his cigarette. "It'd been attacked by Indians?"

The lieutenant shook his head. "If so, there was no sign of it; no arrows or bullets or anything burned or torn up. Damndest thing I'd ever seen. I said no sign of life, and that's what I meant, no bodies, no skeletons, no animal carcasses. It looked like they had just circled their wagons as if they were going to camp for the night and disappeared into thin air."

The big scout paused. "What do you suppose happened to everyone?"

"We never did find out, although there was a lot of publicity over it. Those sixteen wagons had been parked there so long, the canvas had rotted off the frames. The metal on the wheels was rusted away. We couldn't even figure out how long they'd been there; maybe a couple of years, maybe twenty."

"Isn't that kind of far off any known trail?" The scout smoked and thought about it. "Not much water up that way. Maybe when they realized they were hopelessly lost, they tried to abandon the wagons, walk out."

"Poor devils, who knows?" The officer leaned forward, his eyes gleaming. "That's why I'm so intrigued by this trader's story of a white Sioux."

Terry's dark eyes must have mirrored the fact that he didn't see any connection at all.

"Don't you see?" The officer clapped his pink hands together triumphantly. "Think what a news story this would make if this man was a lost white child who came from that wagon train and had been raised all these years as a Sioux."

Terry couldn't hold back a grin as he blew smoke toward the ceiling. "Lieutenant, that's the wildest story I've ever heard."

"Why? It happened with that little Cynthia Ann Parker in Texas. When they found her a couple of years ago, she was just like a savage herself: had to be forced to return to civilization."

Terry shook his head. "Lieutenant, I've got two brothers riding as scouts with other outfits. Between the three of us, we're all over the frontier. If there was a white Sioux warrior out there all these years, one of us would know about it by now."

"Oh, yes," the officer leaned back in his chair. "One of them rides with Frank North's Pawnee Scouts, doesn't he?"

Terry nodded. "The youngest, Asataka."

The pink-faced officer looked impressed. "Asataka. Is that the one everyone calls Johnny Ace?

"Yes." Terry tossed his cigarette into the spittoon. "Our father was killed by a Cheyenne Dog Soldier named Iron Knife; but he had killed Iron Knife's father years before."

"I've heard of Iron Knife, too," the officer frowned. "Is it true what they say about those Dog

Soldiers? I heard in a fight, they tie themselves to a stake driven in the ground so they either have to win or die on that spot."

Terry nodded. "It's true. The Sioux have the same sort of thing, the red sash of the Strong Heart warrior society. One of them's a tough Hunkpapas named Sitting Bull. There's two Oglalas, Red Cloud and Crazy Horse that you'll be hearing more of before these Indian wars end."

The Lieutenant snorted with laughter. "Really, Terry, you can't be serious! They're just primitive savages. What can the Cheyenne and Sioux do against the mighty United States army?"

Terry paused in the doorway. "Lieutenant, a smart man who wants to stay alive knows his enemy, respects his ability. There'll come a day you'll remember my words."

He turned and strode out of the office.

The big Pawnee hadn't even waited to be dismissed. Lieutenant Jackson sniffed in disgust at this breaking of rules as he went to the door and watched the wide-shouldered Pawnee swagger away.

Getting all alarmed over nothing. Those primitive savages had better not stand in the way of civilization. With a smug, self-satisfied smile, he picked up his pen off the floor and returned to his report. By the book. That's how things were supposed to be done. If it were up to him, he wouldn't even hire those uppity Indian scouts.

Too bad that trader had died. Not that the dead man appeared to be anyone of consequence. There'd probably be no big fuss raised over him. But whatever he knew had died with him.

The white Sioux. Lieutenant Jackson leaned back in his chair and put his hands behind his head. The idea intrigued him. Certainly he'd been looking for a way to get a little attention the last few months. He

wanted a promotion and a ticket out of this godfor-
saken spot. If he found this white warrior who'd
been raised by Indians, he'd be the darling of the
newspapers. At least it was worth a try.

Some of the forts were beginning to close now that
the war was over and the "Galvanized Yankees" were
being mustered out. Colonel Dimon was being transferred from Fort Rice, and that was one of those
hellholes that would probably be closed in a few
months, but there were others across the frontier.

After a moment's thought, he reached for a new
pen and dipped it in the inkwell. He'd send a message to the other forts on the frontier, asking them to
be on the lookout for a white warrior riding with the
Sioux. If this yellow-haired savage really existed,
Jackson intended to track him down and capture
him. Maybe an ambitious lieutenant could earn himself some captain's bars and a comfortable post back
East!

Fifteen

Kimi and Hinzi returned to the Lakota camp with the war party. The old chiefs frowned as the men gathered to tell what had happened.

One of them shook his head, staring into the council fire. "That one who might have escaped will go to the soldiers if he lives. Or the bluecoats might find the bodies and begin to hunt us like rabbits. They are looking for any excuse to attack us."

Hinzi nodded. "This is true. From my time at Fort Rice, I can tell you the whites lust after your whole land because they think the area is full of gold. They will push the Army to move or destroy the tribes."

One Eye smoked the pipe and passed it on. "Perhaps we should move our camp."

Gopher accepted the pipe, took a puff. "We cannot avoid the whites by continually moving. Sooner or later, they will have us cornered and there will be no place to go."

The old man sighed. "We will fight only when we have to, knowing that in the long run, we cannot win; we can only buy a little time for ourselves. So we will pack the camp now and move deeper into the hills."

* * *

And so it was done.

Kimi breathed a sigh of relief as they traveled deeper into the wild country away from the forts. "Perhaps," she said to Hinzi as she set up her tipi and helped her mother with hers, "perhaps now we can be left alone and be happy."

Wagnuka looked frail and ill. "We are running on borrowed time, daughter, all of us. No matter how hard we fight, sooner or later the *wasicu* will wash us away like a river sweeping along the brown sand. I do not expect to live long enough to see it, but you will, Kimimila."

Kimi frowned. "You have a long time to live yet, Mother, and now we will have plenty to eat and you will be well-cared for with Hinzi as your son-in-law."

"No." The old woman shook her head. "I have not felt well for many moons, but I hid it from you, knowing there was no one else to look after you."

"Hinzi will look after me." Kimi said confidently as they built a camp fire."

"I truly hope so." Wagnuka looked at her. "Remember his own civilization calls to his heart. Someday he may return to his other life."

"In that case, he will take me with him." She reached for a kettle.

"Will he?" Her mother gave her a piercing look. "And if he does, will you fit in? Will you be happy among the rich white people he comes from?"

"Anywhere Hinzi is, there I will go and be happy," Kimi answered, but she felt slightly troubled. She fingered the medicine charm on the thong around her neck. Would her white love be ashamed of her when he saw how poorly she fitted

268

in among his friends? She would not borrow trouble by thinking about it.

The weeks that followed were like a dream to her, the summer warm and bittersweet. Always Kimi would remember that time, how she and Hinzi rode through the prairies and lazed about beside small creeks. There was plenty of game and the living was easy. In the heat of the afternoon they made love and slept until dusk. In the evening they gathered around the council fires and listened to the ancient tales of the Sioux.

Hinzi was soon accepted better than Kimi could ever have hoped for. He learned to speak Lakota more fluently, learned to handle a bow and lance as well as any warrior, and rode in the front of war parties against the enemy tribes.

Army patrols were seen more often and there was no way of knowing what was happening among the whites as the summer deepened. Some of the camps of the Seven Council Fires clashed with the soldiers periodically, but this band went out of their way to avoid trouble. In the month whites call July, Sitting Bull and some of his followers attacked Fort Rice, with mixed results, or so the messages carried by the criers between the Sioux camps said. This only brought more soldiers into the Dakotas.

When this word came, Hinzi's face grew sad, and he seemed to brood. "Perhaps I bring trouble to your people," he said, staring into their tipi fire late at night. "Perhaps the soldiers are looking for me."

Kimi put her arms around his neck and hugged him to her. "No, it is the gold and land they want.

No doubt they have thought you dead a long time now."

He patted her arm absently. "It bothers me that my family may be grieving for me, sad because they, too, think me dead."

It was the first time he had mentioned his white life in a long time. "Do you miss your other life?" she blurted without thinking and then was sorry she did so, knowing she might not want to know the answer.

"Not like I thought I would. Sometimes my other life seems only a distant dream like a spirit vision."

She thought about her own vague spirit dreams. Sometimes a memory stirred, but even as her mind grabbed for it, like smoke it drifted away and was lost.

"Kimi, I know in my heart the Sioux's days are numbered. They cannot live this way forever. Sooner or later, the army will gather them all up and put them on reservations. Then your people will be neither wild or free."

Your people. He did not say *our* people. She leaned against his shoulder and stared into the fire. "We will fight. The men of the Seven Council Fires are brave."

"Yes." Hinzi nodded. "But in the end, it will do no good."

"If we fight, will you fight with us?"

"Against my own people? I don't know. I don't seem to know where my heart lies anymore."

For a long time he said nothing else, and Kimi waited, wondering if he were thinking about the elegant beauty and whether she was still waiting for him back in civilization. Maybe if Kimi delayed him long enough here, she could give him a son and the other woman would look far less desirable to him. Absently Kimi picked up a stick with her left hand and drew a butterfly in the dirt as she hummed her spirit song.

"You never have told me how you knew that song."

She paused. "What song?"

He put his arm around her shoulders. "Never mind, little butterfly." He kissed her very gently. "I suppose your past doesn't matter any more—least of all to you."

She snuggled against him, feeling safe and loved. "Nothing in my life seemed to matter until I met you, Hinzi." She wondered if he felt the same, but he didn't say anything, only began to make love to her with a slow sweetness that tantalized the senses and made her dizzy with feeling for him.

Late in the summer, old Wagnuka's health grew worse and she took to her blankets, hardly venturing out at all. Kimi sat by her mother's bed near the fire of the tipi, gently wiping her fevered brow.

"My daughter, I will be gone before the first frost comes." Her voice was almost a whisper.

"Don't be foolish." Kimi struggled to keep her voice from breaking. "You seem to be a little better. Besides, what would I do without you?"

"I used to worry about what would happen to you, Kimi, after Otter and I were gone." She put a frail hand on Kimi's arm. "Now I do not worry. I think the white warrior will look after you. I would speak with him."

Kimi hesitated. It was taboo for a son-in-law to speak to his wife's mother.

"I am dying," Wagnuka said. "There is something I need to tell him."

Kimi tried to speak. Her throat seemed to choke up and she could not swallow. Her eyes blinded by hot, stinging tears. All she could do was nod as she went outside to find Hinzi. "My mother would speak with you."

She saw the somber expression of his handsome face. "She is worse?"

Kimi nodded. He put his arm around her and they both stooped to reenter the tipi.

"Mother," Kimi said softly, "Hinzi has come as you asked."

The old woman's eyes flickered open and she smiled. "It is good that a woman have a man," she whispered. "I have missed mine a long time now. Perhaps tonight I will ride the Spirit Road to the stars and see him again."

Hinzi patted her hand. "You will live a long time yet; live to see grandchildren playing around your tipi."

"I wish I could," she whispered, "but I have been sick a long time. Perhaps I only hung on all this time waiting for someone who would take care of my butterfly."

Hinzi assured her. "I will take care of her, Wagnuka, you know that."

"I release you from your promise," she whispered.

"What promise?" Kimi asked.

Hinzi hesitated as if loathe to tell.

Wagnuka said, "I made him promise he wouldn't take you away to the white civilization as long as I lived. Maybe it was selfish on my part."

Kimi felt her heart lurch. Was that what had been keeping Hinzi here? Now at the first chance he got, would he return to civilization and take her with him? She wanted to stay with the Sioux; they were the only family she had ever known. She would do whatever was best for Hinzi, even if it meant letting him leave her behind. True love sacrifices all with no thought of self.

Old Wagnuka died that night. They dressed her in her finest things, placed her on a platform up in the hills and killed a good pony beneath the burial scaffold so she might ride to join her husband. When Kimi tried to cut her arm and legs with a knife to show her grief, Hinzi stopped her. Nor would he let her sit alone out there, keening and grieving. He picked her up and carried her, sobbing, back to their tipi.

"She would not want this, Kimi," he said softly.

"I know; but it's the way of my people. She was all I had in this world."

"No, sweet butterfly, you have me and I will take care of you." He held her while she wept against his chest. She felt safe in his powerful arms, and finally she snuggled down against him and slept, too weary and grieved to think of anything but the comfort of his heart beating against her.

The summer passed and her grief lessened because it is the way of things for death to follow life and she knew Wagnuka was part of that cycle. As the Moon of the Changing Seasons that *wasicu* call October loomed on the horizon, Kimi began to hope for a child.

Hinzi stopped repairing a bow and frowned when she mentioned it. "I am not sure this is the time to have a child, Kimi. Besides to me, you are not much more than a child yourself. I should be ashamed to use you like a woman."

"I have a woman's body and desires," she argued.

"Don't I know that?" He pulled her to him, kissed her deeply. "Sometimes I forget that I was ever an arrogant, rich *wasicu* named Rand Erikson."

"I want a child," she repeated. "When your strong son sucks my milk, you will be proud and never again think of going away."

He shook his head and frowned. "The reports we hear from the other Council Fires is bad; there is more trouble with the whites invading the land."

"Always people have had to face this," Kimi said, kissing him. "There is never a good time to bring a child into the world."

He didn't answer, and Kimi wondered if he were beginning to regret taking her as his woman or if he hungered for a return to the life he had known. She was afraid to ask. Kimi loved him—but she was not sure he truly loved her. If not, she didn't want to know.

Gradually, as the leaves turned gold and red, she stopped grieving for her mother. Hinzi himself seemed happy. In the crisp, cool dawns, they made love, then went for long rides, galloping their horses across the prairie. At night, they feasted on fat buffalo and deer and gathered around the big campfire to dance to the drums and hear the old legends.

Hinzi grew more skilled with a bow and lance. In the weeks that passed, he became known as a great hunter and a killer of their enemies when he went out with war parties against the Crow and 'Ree. There was talk that next year he might take part in the sacred Sun Dance that only the bravest of the warriors experienced, or be invited to join the Akicita warriors' society.

The happiness seemed too good to last, and Kimi sometimes lay awake at night after Hinzi slept beside her, thanking Wakan Tanka for her good fortune. This love, this happiness seemed almost too precious, too fragile, so she savored every minute of it.

It ended sooner than she expected.

One crisp autumn day, Kimi, Hinzi, little Saved By the Wolf and some other children were out picking nuts when Kimi spotted distant riders and pointed. "Look, Hinzi, it might be enemies."

He frowned. "Maybe they haven't seen us. Children, get to your horses."

The children obeyed, looking nervous.

Saved By the Wolf said, "They are dressed in blue. Are they soldiers?"

Hinzi nodded as he helped Kimi up on her horse and swung up on his own buckskin. "Perhaps we can clear out without them seeing us."

Kimi saw the concern in his eyes. The two adults might outrun a pursuing patrol, but the children might not be able to keep up the fast pace.

"Children," Hinzi said, "we will go a roundabout trail back to the camp so we won't lead the patrol there."

Saved by the Wolf nodded. "I know the way, Hinzi. I will help."

"Whatever happens," Hinzi said, to him and Kimi, "keep going and don't look back. The children must escape."

"Oh, Hinzi, come with us!" Kimi cried, "What will they do with you if they capture you?"

He laughed without mirth. "Hang me as a deserter, I reckon."

Kimi's heart began to beat hard. "Then you should get out of here first, Hinzi."

"And desert the children? No real man would do that!"

The soldiers were still a long way off. Perhaps they had not seen the Lakota. Even as that hope crossed her mind, in the distance, she heard the echo of commands—and then a shot echoed past her head.

Hinzi cursed under his breath. "They've seen us! Head back to camp!" They all whipped up their ponies and took off at a gallop. Kimi glanced back over her shoulder. The soldiers were running their mounts, and they rode fine, grain-fed, horses.

Kimi urged on her paint. The children were strung out ahead of her, riding hard. Hinzi rode to one side of her. Behind them, the soldiers fired again. The Indians' only advantage, she realized, was that they knew the terrain and the white soldiers didn't.

Kimi's horse began to lag slightly behind. Hinzi didn't seem to notice; his attention was on the children riding ahead of them. She knew his thinking; he would reach a little rise in the trail about a mile ahead in the hills, turn, and try a delaying action, firing arrows from the rocks.

She could only hope the noise might carry all the way to camp and some of the other warriors would come riding out to even up the numbers.

Her heart pounded in her throat and the dust stung her face. She was too scared to think of anything but saving the children. Who knew what white soldiers would do with children if they captured them? And right now, they were shooting wildly, not caring how old their targets were.

If they could just get near enough camp for One Eye and Gopher to hear the firing! Desperately, she concentrated on that goal, but when she looked back, she saw the patrol was gaining on them. About that time, she felt her paint step in a prairie dog hole, stumble and go down.

She cried out once, felt herself going over the mare's head, and managed to twist her lithe body to avoid being caught under the falling horse as she went down.

At least Hinzi would see to it that the children were safe, Kimi thought as she scrambled to her feet; that was all that mattered.

The soldiers stirred up big clouds of dust in their mad pursuit. She looked around frantically, knowing there was no place to hide. Her mare had broken her neck in the fall. Would all the soldiers rape her?

"Kimi!" She heard Hinzi's frantic yell as he turned in his saddle, seemed to realize what had happened, and wheeled the buckskin to come galloping back.

"No! Go on!" She tried to wave him away. It didn't matter what the soldiers did to her, it only mattered that Hinzi and his small charges escape. In the distance, she saw the ponies growing smaller on the horizon as the children fled.

Hinzi whirled Scout on his hind legs and galloped back to her. She looked toward the soldiers and realized Hinzi wasn't going to be able to reach her before the men in blue did. Once again she tried to wave him off. It meant more to her that her lover escape the white man's justice than that she be rescued from possible rape and death.

The first soldiers surrounded her, churning up dust as their horses danced nervously around her. Hinzi had no chance, but still he came on.

"No, Hinzi! Save yourself!"

His face was a grim mask of determination, his eyes like blue fire as he galloped forward, holding his lance high. Just as he reached her, one of the bluecoats aimed and fired. She saw the sudden red crease across Hinzi's light hair and screamed out in protest.

Scout's momentum carried him forward even as the unconscious man slid from his broad back.

With a scream, Kimi fought her way clear of the soldiers and ran to her love lying in a heap on the ground. "Hinzi, dear one; are you alive?"

His pulse still beat, but there was blood in the blond hair as he lay sprawled in her lap. She held him to her, hugging him, sobbing. She didn't care what the soldiers did to her. She was only frantic about her lover.

A group of soldiers surrounded her. Crisp, autumn sunlight reflected off their brass buttons. She could understand some of the language they spoke.

"Well, I'll be damned!" The fat-faced sergeant took off his hat and scratched his head. "A white Sioux! A white man riding with the savages! Jones, ride ahead to the fort, tell him the dispatches were true. We've captured a pretty half-breed girl and a yellow-haired warrior!"

Rand began to come back to consciousness, his head splitting with pain. Where was he? Kimi.

278

What had happened to Kimi? He struggled to stand up.

"Christ! Hold him! He's coming around." A man's voice, with a strong Yankee accent. New York, maybe.

In Lakota, a woman's voice: "Don't hurt him! Hinzi, are you all right?"

Slowly, Rand opened his eyes. He was in a chair in a room. A lieutenant sat across a desk from him. He had a bad complexion and he picked at his face absently. It was Baker, the rotten officer from the *Effie Deans* and Fort Rice. The two privates grabbed Rand's arms as he struggled to stand up, and they pulled him back down.

Kimi sat in another chair, her pretty face a mask of worry.

Oh, now he remembered. The army patrol. The chase. What had happened then? He relaxed in the chair and the two men released his arms. Gingerly, he reached up, touched his head, and found the dried blood. Someone had creased him with a bullet. He was probably lucky to be alive.

He turned—ever so slightly, so the nervous guards wouldn't pounce on him again. "Kimi," he asked in Lakota, "are you all right?"

She nodded, and the lieutenant behind the desk scowled. "Speak English, man. You do know how to speak English, don't you?" Yes, it was Baker. The man from New York.

"Probably better than you do," Rand said coolly.

"Christ!" The officer made a threatening gesture. "I don't have to take that from you, you savage. If I had my way—"

A plump colonel entered the office just then and Baker jumped up and saluted, all smiles and oily charm now. "Afternoon, sir. I was just about to interrogate the prisoner."

The older officer frowned and gestured. "You're sitting in my chair, Baker."

The lieutenant scrambled away from the desk, evidently annoyed at the reprimand.

"So what have we found out so far?" The colonel addressed Rand as he sank his bulk into the desk chair.

Rand decided not to answer.

The officer leaned on his elbows, staring at Rand. "So this white savage thing is true. I never would have believed it. Do you speak English?"

"Yes." Rand had to think through his words. He had been speaking Lakota so long, his native language didn't come naturally to him anymore.

"There's a story making the rounds of an abandoned wagon train found out on the plains."

"Sir?" Rand looked at him, baffled. He glanced over at Kimi, who appeared to be trying to follow the conversation but was having difficulty.

"A wagon train," the officer repeated. "Said it looked like it had been out there ten or fifteen years or even more." He described the area where a Lieutenant Ware had found it. "Is there any chance you were a child on that ill-fated train and have been raised by the Sioux?"

Rand hesitated, staring at Kimi. Was there the slightest chance that that was where she had come from? "Can you tell me a little more?"

The colonel shook his head, leaned back in his chair, and it creaked under his weight. "That's about all we know. No signs of violence, no bodies, not even any animals. Ware figured they were trying to go up the Oregon Trail and got lost. All sorts of men hiring out as guides these days who couldn't find their way from here to the out-house and back."

He might as well confess. Maybe it would make it easier for Kimi, even if it did get him the firing squad. "Sir, my real name is Randolph Erikson. I've probably been reported missing in action from the First Volunteer Regiment at Fort Rice."

The officer relaxed visibly. "A deserter? You're telling me you're just a common deserter?"

"Not exactly," Rand began. He didn't want to get Kimi and the Sioux in any more trouble. So they thought Kimi was a half-breed. She certainly looked enough of one with that ebony hair, buck-skin dress, and tanned skin.

She stood up suddenly. "Please, officer." Her English was rusty and she seemed to be feeling for words. "It wasn't his fault. Hinzi was wounded and left for dead and my people found him and saved his life."

"Hinzi?" The colonel stared at her with interest, looked back to Rand. "Tell me about it? How long have you been gone?"

He tried to think. "I don't even know for sure because I don't even know what month it is now."

"October," the colonel volunteered.

"How is the war going? What did Lincoln finally do—?"

"Good Lord, man," the colonel's eyes widened, "you have been gone awhile. The war ended last April and Lincoln's been assassinated."

"We lost?" He didn't know whether to believe the man or not, shrugged as he decided there was no reason for him to lie.

"Depends on who 'we' is," the colonel said. "Judging from your accent, you're a Southerner. What are you doing up here in the Dakotas?"

"I was a 'Galvanized Yankee,'" Rand admitted, "one of Colonel Dimon's men."

The older man frowned. Obviously he didn't care much for the brash young Colonel. "Baker," he said, "you were with that bunch before you were transferred to me. Do you remember this man?"

Baker stopped picking at his bad complexion, leaned closer to Rand. "What did you say your name was?"

"Rand Erikson. I was aboard the *Effie Deans*."

"Christ! Of course I remember. How could anybody forget what happened on that trip?"

The colonel chewed the end of his gray mustache. "Is that the one where that young idiot Dimon had a quick trial and executed a man?"

Rand nodded.

The colonel said, "Your old outfit left just a few days ago. They're being mustered out in Kansas."

Baker frowned. "This arrogant Reb's still a deserter, sir."

"I didn't desert!" Rand lost his temper. "I was trying to help cover a withdrawal from an ambush Dimon had led us into. I was hit and abandoned in the confusion. When I woke up, the Sioux had taken me captive."

"A captive?" The plump officer looked at him a long moment. There was no sound save the creak of his chair. "If you were a captive, why didn't you ride toward our patrol and be rescued rather than try to escape?"

He wasn't sure himself. "Even with my blond hair, I'm dressed like an Indian," Rand said, "I was afraid those green troops on that patrol would shoot first and ask questions later."

"Hmm," the older man mused and he turned and stared at Kimi without saying anything. Rand could almost see the wheels of his mind turning. What Rand had said might have seemed reasonable . . . except that for a girl like Kimi, maybe any man would desert. He turned his attention back to Rand. "Where'd you say you were from?"

Rand gave him all the details and the officer said, "I want to check out your story, look into this whole mess. In the meantime, Lieutenant Baker, put him in the guard house."

"What about the girl?" Baker's eyes left no doubt what he had in mind for her.

Kimi jumped up, ran to Rand. Automatically, he put a protective arm over her small shoulders. "She stays with me," he said.

The colonel stood up. "She doesn't look like much more than a child; a schoolgirl. If you go back to Kentucky, do you intend to take this little savage with you?"

She turned on the man like the fiery wildcat she was. "I am not a child! I am Hinzi's woman."

"Well?" The colonel looked at him, "what do you say to that?"

Rand looked down into Kimi's eyes. What would be best for Kimi? What would he do about Lenore? "I don't know," he admitted.

Sixteen

Everything had happened with such dizzying speed. Kimi could hardly follow events, although her English was improving enough to follow the conversations between white people. Neither she nor Hinzi let anyone know she was white. She had asked him not to tell because she had some horrifying picture in her mind of strangers turning up to claim her as a daughter or sister who would want to take her away to some unknown place. From the snide remarks and sly grins, she soon realized that with her green eyes, the soldiers thought she was a half-breed product of some long ago coupling of a soldier or trapper with a squaw. It must be common enough not to raise any eyebrows among the whites on the frontier.

After a couple of days everyone's attitude seemed to change. They freed Hinzi. Outside the colonel's office at dusk, she asked, "What did he say?"

"I think the army either feels I'm not completely sane or that it's liable to embarrass them if it comes out a patrol retreated in panic, leaving a wounded man to die." He paused. "Possibly he's investigated and found out my father is rich and influential."

"Your father is a chief?"

"You might say that."

She sighed with relief. "You think they will not kill you or throw you in jail?"

"Hardly. It seems Colonel Dimon reported that I was lost in action covering the retreat. They thought I was dead. The army calls me a 'hero.' They're shipping me home. I—I don't know what to do about you. You're so very young, Kimi—"

"I am eighteen winters old." She tried to keep the tremor from her voice. *Shipping him home.* Hadn't she always known that some day it would come? It was the way of soldiers, she supposed—making casual liaisons with enemy women and leaving them behind when they left.

The skeptical expression on his handsome face gave her to know he didn't believe her. "Eighteen? Uh huh. I reckon you would bite the knife and say that?"

"Well, I think I'm eighteen. When I was naked in your arms and you were making love to me, you weren't concerned with my age."

"Don't remind me. Fifteen's a better guess. I feel enough of a rotter already, forcing my passion on a girl who ought to be in boarding school. I don't know what to do about you."

Her temper flared. She would at least salvage her pride. "Do? You don't have to *do* anything about me. If you are going back to your home, I will go back to my people."

He caught her arm. "What will happen to you there?"

"I suppose some warrior will marry me eventually. Gopher once told me he might take me as a second wife."

"The thought of another man touching you drives me crazy!" He pulled her small body to him, holding her close, kissing the top of her head.

The thought upset her, too, but she managed to blink back the tears. "Perhaps I could stay here at the fort. Lieutenant Baker said he could find me work here."

"I'll just bet he could!"

Kimi bristled. How dare Hinzi act so possessive when he was about to abandon her? "I made it clear that it had to be something like sewing or cleaning."

He rubbed his jaw. "Don't trust him, Kimi."

"Trust him? I'm through trusting white soldiers." She tried to keep the emotion out of her voice and failed. She started to leave.

He reached out, caught her, pulled her up against him. "This is tearing me apart." He put his hands on her shoulders. "When I met you, I didn't think about anything else, any other commitments or responsibilities. Now if I'm to be honorable, I have to face those."

She couldn't fault him for that. All the tribes admired a man who was honorable and kept his word. "I suppose that other girl has waited a long time for you to return to her."

"Yes. How can a Southern gentleman go back and tell a fiancee who's been waiting faithfully that there's someone else? Lord knows what my family would say. I'd probably be disinherited." He sounded uncertain and unhappy.

"It's all right. I understand." Without thinking, she reached up and patted his hand to comfort him as she remembered all he had told her of his family. Hinzi had always had wealth, a life of ease until he became her slave. It would be expecting too much that he turn his back on all that. Kimi faced reality at that moment. Even if Hinzi weren't an honorable man, Kimi could never fit into his

286

white life. She couldn't read. She didn't even know how to use a fork. A white savage, that's all she was. Civilized people would gawk at her like some strange animal imported for their amusement in a zoo.

"Perhaps I can figure out some way, perhaps enroll you in some nice girls' finishing school. . . ." He sounded uncertain, tortured.

She would give him one final gift of love; a clear conscience. Stepping away from him, she whirled and shrugged her shoulders. "I can't go with you, if that's what you're about to ask. I'm not sure I would even want to. It sounds crowded and dull. I'll be all right, don't worry about me."

He looked both sad and relieved. "I reckon I thought I meant more to you than that."

He meant *everything* to her. "When are you going?"

"Tomorrow morning."

She tried to keep her voice light. "Well then, I'll either find myself a position around the fort or return to my people." When he left in the morning, he would take her heart with him.

"You meant a lot to me, Kimi, if I weren't obligated to Lenore Carstairs, and you weren't so young, I—"

"But you are and I wouldn't be accepted by your people anyway."

He didn't deny that. She saw the truth of her words in his blue eyes. "Will you—will you see me off in the morning?"

"I really don't see any point in it." She managed to sound bored, as if seeing him leave would be the least interesting event she could imagine. In reality, Kimi knew that if she had to stand there and wave good-bye, she might forget her pride, run after

287

him, and beg him to take her with him. She would be his slave, his servant, his mistress, anything to stay by his side.

"Well I certainly wouldn't want to waste your time." He sounded hurt and angry as he turned and strode away into the darkness.

She stood looking after him, thinking it was good that it was dark. If he saw the tears beginning to run down her face, he might realize how she really felt and take her with him. Later he would regret it and that would hurt her even worse.

Kimi returned to the cramped little quarters Lieutenant Baker had found her, and she tried to sleep. As she tossed restlessly, all she could think of was that each passing moment brought her closer to dawn when her love would ride away forever.

Finally in the late hours of the night when the whole post seemed asleep, she went outside and walked around awhile. Without meaning to, she found herself near Hinzi's quarters. Just being close to him seemed almost comforting, yet it was torture for her. She must not do this.

Kimi turned and started back to her quarters.

"Who goes there?" She stopped, startled at the outline of a man crossing her path. "Oh, Christ! It's you."

"You startled me," Kimi breathed a sigh of relief as she recognized Lieutenant Baker. "I didn't think anyone was around but me."

"I was just checking the sentries. It isn't safe for you to be out unescorted on this post."

His concern touched her. "I'm not worried."

"Christ! With your looks, you should be." He moved closer.

Now Kimi felt a little uneasy. He was attracted

288

to her, he had made that clear from the start. She could use a friend in this fort after Hinzi was gone. She would be all alone in the world.

Her silence must have encouraged him. He put his hand on her shoulder. "I could be very helpful to you. All you have to do is be friendly."

She looked up into his pitted face, tried not to shudder. "I don't know what you mean."

At that, he laughed. "Don't give me that! Haven't you been playing the squaw for Rand Erikson?"

She brought up her hand to slap him hard, but he caught her wrist and dragged her to him. His mouth covered hers, forcing his tongue between her lips, bruising her soft breasts as he held her so tightly that she had to struggle to breathe.

Kimi fought to break free. If she could escape from him and return to her quarters, she could lock the door. It wouldn't do her any good to scream, she knew that. The other white soldiers would think she had offered herself to Baker and then changed her mind. What was the rape of one half-breed girl more or less to a bunch of soldiers?

Hinzi. If she could reach Hinzi, he would help her. Already, the officer was dragging her back toward the shadows of some buildings. He had one hand over her mouth, the other around her breasts as he dragged her, kicking and fighting. "Christ! Don't you bite me or I'll break your jaw. I'm gonna have you, squaw, so you might as well submit and make it easy on both of us."

"Let go of her, Baker, or I swear to God I'll kill you!" A big, tall man stepped out of the darkness, swearing under his breath. The moonlight glinted on his yellow hair. "You heard me!"

"I hear you, all right, you crazy white savage!"

Baker threw Kimi to one side and stood feet wide apart.

She saw the sudden reflection of steel. "Hinzi, watch out! He's got a knife!"

"Get out of here, Kimi!" Hinzi ordered and then he dived for the officer's middle.

She didn't answer or obey as she watched the men mesh and roll over and over in the dirt. What should she do? If she called a guard or screamed, things might go badly for her love. There was no telling what Baker would tell everyone. One thing was certain, Hinzi might be in big trouble and no one would believe her word against the officer's if he said she offered herself to him and then demanded more money.

She felt powerless as she watched them fight like two stags clashing over a doe. Hinzi grabbed the other's arm and by sheer power managed to take the knife from him and toss it away into the shadows. They fought silently, probably both mindful of bringing the sentries on the run and having to explain to the colonel.

Baker tripped the bigger man, but Hinzi was as light on his feet as a cougar. As he went down, he twisted out from under Baker, hit him a blow with his fist that sent the other staggering back against a building. Hinzi charged him, hitting him again and again with uncontrolled rage.

Kimi saw the blood on the officer's pale face. She grabbed Hinzi's arm. "Stop it! You'll kill him and get yourself in trouble!"

Her words seemed to get through to the white warrior, although his eyes still looked like cold blue ice in the moonlight. He stepped back, breathing hard, swearing softly under his breath. "She's right, you slimy bastard! Get the hell out of here before I kill you!"

Baker needed no second offer. With blood smearing his pitted complexion, he turned and ran for his quarters.

She and Hinzi faced each other a long moment. "I suppose I was wrong about him."

Hinzi rubbed his bruised knuckles. "Fortunate for you I couldn't sleep, was out for a smoke."

She wanted desperately to run into his powerful, protective arms, but she managed to control herself. *"Pilamaya."* Thank you. She cleared her throat to keep from sobbing. "It's almost dawn. Tomorrow, I'll go back to my people."

"You don't have much waiting for you there without me except maybe as some warrior's second wife."

"I know, but it's better than staying at the fort."

"I feel responsible for you, Kimi." He moved his hands awkwardly as if he wanted to reach out, pull her into his embrace, was forcing himself not to touch her. "Kimi, you're a white girl, I feel I should give you a chance at living among your own kind. You might like it."

He did not say he wanted her, she thought. Perhaps he only felt obligated and guilty toward her. Perhaps he did not want to be one of those "squaw men" who used a pretty girl for his convenience and then deserted her without a backward glance.

"Look," he gestured, "You could stay as my family's houseguest until you decide what to do, or maybe find out if you have any relatives anywhere."

She wanted to throw her arms around him and kiss his dear face. But if she did that, they might end up making frenzied love and it could never work out for them.

"Hinzi, that's a kind offer, but I can't make it in white civilization; I don't know anything about their customs."

"You're smart; you could learn. I could enroll you in some nice school."

"Far away from you?"

"It would make it easier for both of us, Kimi. I have plenty of money to send you to the best female academy."

"What would Lenore think?"

He sighed. "She'd probably think I was doing my Christian duty toward the heathen. She need never know what happened between us. I'm engaged to her. That means I've given my word I'll marry her. That's as sacred to a white man of good heart as it is to an Indian." He ran his hand through his hair. "Lenore has waited faithfully all these years for my return. I would be scorned if I go home and don't marry her."

She could respect his sense of honor. Honor was important to a man, no matter what color. "How could you possibly explain me to her; to your family?"

"I will take you back as a white girl I found living among the Indians. Once you try living as a white, you might like it."

She was determined not to show her anguish. He was going to marry that other girl and was feeling guilty about Kimi, trying to do the "right thing" by her for having taken her virginity. Her pride screamed for her to refuse, but she had no pride where he was concerned. Just to be close to him for a while longer, that's all she could think of now. "Fine," she said, drawing herself up proudly, "I don't want to upset your life. Perhaps I can be a houseguest for a few weeks until I learn the culture. No one need ever know about what happened between us."

"Do you think I could ever forget?" He snarled. "I'm engaged to Lenore and I know this thing between us could never work out, but when I think of the way you return my passion when I make love to you, I want you all over again!" He grabbed her, kissing her hotly, his hands stroking her back and hips.

She tried not to let him mold her against him all the way down both their bodies, but she had no will where he was concerned. He had said he wanted her, he hadn't said he loved her. She loved him with all her heart.

He had her up against the frame building in the shadows, his mouth ravaging hers while he worked her shift up with his hands. She wore nothing underneath it. The doeskin shift had fallen off one shoulder so that her bare breasts were pressed against him. Kimi slipped her arms around his neck, digging her nails into his shoulders in a frenzied passion as she felt him reach to unbutton his pants. "Come to me," he demanded in a hoarse whisper, "come to me!"

She could do nothing but obey his need and her own. Still standing against the building, he rammed up into her and she locked her legs around his waist as he guided her to him. They coupled standing up while his mouth sucked her tongue into his throat. He seemed to be crushing her against the wood in the hot frenzy of their mutual need. This time, there was nothing gentle or tender in their meshing in the darkness like two wild things, and her need was as great as his. For a long moment, they gasped and strained together, and then it was over. She let her slim legs slide down his virile body, and he disengaged from her, but he didn't let her out of his embrace. He leaned against her, breathing hard and she let him, feeling his hot seed running down her thighs.

What had she done? No matter how much she loved him, she must have more pride and honor than this. Kimi took a deep, shuddering breath and straightened her clothes. Then she pulled away from him. "You think to keep me for your pleasure yet marry her. A woman who would settle for that is a fool."

"I never meant what happened just now to ever happen again, Kimi, you've got to believe that. I can't leave you here in this wilderness where you won't be taken care of. Go with me. At least I can send you to a boarding school or something, so you can learn to make your own way in the white world."

"I suppose you feel you owe me that to salve your conscience," she snapped. "All right, I will be your family's houseguest, but not your mistress." She kept her tone icy. "If I get a little education or track down my family, that's all I need from you. I might even meet a man I like better. Then you have no problem with your elegant fiance or your honor. From now on, I will speak English and call you Rand."

"Kimi, I don't want you to think—"

"Don't worry about it." She tossed her head. "Frankly, maybe after I see the way civilized people live, I'll like it so much, I'll thank you for giving me the chance. And I suppose I can't blame you for anything, when you had this other obligation, this other girl chosen before I ever came into your life."

He swore under his breath. "There's no good answer." His voice was ragged, tense. He looked stressed. "Get ready to go. It'll be dawn in an hour. I'll make arrangements for you."

She stood there a long moment, struggling with her heart. How could she go with him, watch him marry that other girl, thinking of him sleeping with her? Yet even though she knew she could only be hurt, she couldn't stop herself from loving him, wanting to be with him if it was only for a few days longer. "I—I—all right."

She forced herself not to think of all the gloomy consequences as she turned and ran to her quarters to gather her few things. She was going with Hinzi. Nothing else mattered but being close to him, even if only for a little while.

"Damn that puppy anyhow!" Lenore kicked at the dog as it dug at the base of the camelia bush. "Shelby, would you put him out of here?"

"Sure," he grinned at Lenore and reached down to grab the clumsy foxhound pup. "Sweet Jesus. We can't have Grandma know we're out here a lot, can we?"

He grabbed the dog roughly, dragged it to the French doors. The piano music drifting softly through the doors as he opened them. Pushing the puppy into the hall, he closed the doors and came back to join the beauty on the wicker settee. "Doesn't the old lady ever play anything else?"

Lenore agreed. "Greensleeves? I get sick of it too. It was my father's favorite. She always wore green silk; it looked beautiful on her."

"Who?"

"My mother." She paused, remembering the regal beauty in the green silk rustling through the halls.

Sometimes at night when it was very dark and late, it almost seemed Lenore heard her full skirts rustling. When she awakened, it was always the big oak trees blowing in the night air. "It seems strange to call her that. She was quite vain and very cold. She didn't like to be called 'Mother.' She made me and my little sister call her by her first name."

"Strange." His tone told her he was dismissing the conversation. "Discussing your family isn't too entertaining, honey." He reached out to stroke her soft skin where it swelled above her low-cut canary yellow bodice. "We're taking a chance meeting here, you know."

She caught his hand and clasped it over her breast. "For pity's sake! Grandmother's so old, I think she's getting hard of hearing, half blind, and senile. She doesn't know what we're up to."

"She seems pretty sharp to me. Where did she get that damned dog, anyway?"

"Tally Ho?" Lenore shrugged. "It's a cull from the Erikson's pack: too timid to hunt. It should have been shot, but Grandmother saved it. Stupid mutt. It's dug up every flower bed around the house. She keeps him shut out of the conservatory. I forgot to close the door."

"If the dog had pooped around her favorite camelia bush, she might figure out we'd been out here."

"For pity's sake, that's no way to talk around a lady." She whacked him hard with her fan.

He acted as if he were about to say something, then changed his mind. His hair, with its perfumed oil, shone in the light. "How come you live with your grandmother? Where's your folks and that little sister?"

"They went West." Lenore leaned forward so his

296

fingers could reach inside her bodice.

Shelby looked puzzled. "With all this, they picked up and went West? Doesn't make sense."

"I think there was some kind of disagreement with my grandmother; I don't know what about. I was in school and they were going to send for me. We never heard from them again."

He looked mystified. "That's all?"

She nodded and yawned to indicate how bored she was with the topic. She never liked to stray from her favorite topic, herself, very long. Shelby didn't seem as entertaining as he once had. She wondered what Vanessa saw in him? Probably the only offer the poor thing had had, with all the men off getting killed in the war. "For pity's sake, Shelby, you know that. Stop talking! You know what I want."

"What I want, too, honey." He ran both hands down the front of her dress.

She took a deep breath, liking the feel of a man's hands on her. She wondered whether Rand was skilled at making love. He was such an honorable, old-fashioned Southerner, naive enough to think Lenore would be offended by anything less than gentlemanly conduct. "Vanessa had you yet?"

He laughed and leaned to kiss the swell of her breasts. "Now is that a question for a lady to ask?" Instead of answering, he kissed her.

She smacked him with her fan. "You silly boy, she's my best friend; I think I have the right to know."

"Some best friend you are to her, honey."

"Why don't you just dump her?" Lenore unbuttoned his pants, liking the feel of him hot and big in her hand.

He groaned with pleasure. "If we play our cards

right, we can end up with both fortunes. Suppose I marry Vanessa? Her parents can't last forever and then if she should meet with an unfortunate accident, I'd be a rich, grieving widower. With Rand dead, there's no reason we couldn't get married then and end up with both fortunes."

Lenore liked a clever, greedy man. She and Shelby were well-matched. "For pity's sake, Shelby, I do admire a man who knows what he wants!"

"I'm taking chances making love to a single woman," he murmured against her neck. "My brother-in-law was a real lady's man and he always told me to choose a married woman or one who was about to be married."

"Why?"

"Because if she comes up with a kid, her husband thinks it's his."

"Don't worry. If I could have a baby, I'd have a flock by now, after what we've been doing all these weeks."

"Don't you worry about Grandma catching you?"

"She's old, and getting senile," Lenore said, enjoying the feel of his hands roaming over her body. "She can't last much longer. If she doesn't die soon, I may try to find her a nice rest home."

He laughed, pulled her to him, and kissed her. "Don't you think the judge would put a fast stop to that?"

"I haven't figured out a way to get around him yet," Lenore complained, "I'll have to think about it some more. Maybe he's the one who should meet with an accident."

Shelby reached to pull off her lace drawers. "You know what I like about you, Lenore?"

"It's rare for a lady to be so good at sex?"

"It is rare, all right, you'd put a whore to shame.

298

My brother-in-law once told me elegant ladies could be deceiving with their appetites. He had one wealthy beauty who couldn't get enough of him while her old man was out of town on business."

"I don't want to hear about your relatives," she gasped as she pulled him to her. "You know what I want."

"You little slut," he whispered as his hand went up under her lace drawers, stroking . . . stroking . . . stroking the most secret, sensitive part of her. "That's all you are under that fine pretense."

"And that's what you like about me."

They made passionate love with no more emotion than two animals rutting, but Lenore liked it that way. Poor Rand, he'd been so naive and gallant. She regretted now she'd never got to enjoy him, but he had such old-fashioned ideas. He would have been shocked if he had known the real Lenore Carstairs. She gave herself up to the enjoyment of Shelby's maleness. She liked to be treated like a whore, not a lady. That was where Rand had made his mistake.

They were just finishing straightening their clothes when she heard a rider galloping up the lane, shouting.

"What's that all about?" Lenore frowned.

"You don't suppose—?"

"For pity's sake, don't be foolish. No one knows you're here. Slip out the side door. If it's important, you'll soon know."

He did as he was bid. Lenore hastily straightened her clothes and crossed the conservatory in her tight shoes, her full skirts rustling as she minced through the plants toward the entry hall. She heard the piano stop playing abruptly and her grand-mother came out of the music room. "Lenore, what is all that shouting about?"

"For pity's sake, I don't know, but I aim to find out."

Elizabeth Carstairs came with her. As they reached the entry, Nero, the big, black butler, rushed to open the door.

The little black boy with the crooked teeth, the Erikson's servant, swung down off the horse and ran inside.

Nero's tattooed face frowned, and he scolded him. "Where's your manners, boy!"

The child ignored him and ran to the two women, breathless with urgency and excitement. "He be found! He comin' home!"

"My family!" Elizabeth clutched her throat, looking pale. "I just knew someday they'd return! Where? When?"

"No, ma'am."

"You little nigger!" Lenore snapped, "stop shouting before I take a strap to you! What are you talking about?"

"It's Marse Rand, ma'am," he said, obviously afraid of her ill-tempered fury. "Word just come to de house. He been found alive and he comin' home!"

Seventeen

Elizabeth sat at her piano. She enjoyed playing, although arthritis had affected her hands. The piano brought back memories of happier times with her beloved husband and later, her son Jim and his family.

Slowly she played Jim's favorite:

Alas, my love you do me wrong—to cast me off discourteously, and I have loved you so long, delighting in your company. Greensleeves was all my joy, Greensleeves was my delight, Greensleeves was my heart of gold and who but my lady Greensleeves. . . .

How prophetic, Elizabeth thought sadly as she played, remembering everything that had happened in the past. After a few minutes, her arthritis began to bother her again and she stopped playing. She rubbed her hands together and looked around the music room. Seventy-five wasn't so old. She had been a widow almost fifty years. Fifty years without her love.

She stood up with a rustle of hoops and Clair-de-Lune-colored silk. Clair de Lune. Moonlight. The pale bluish green lavender color complemented her gray eyes and white hair. Late afternoon sun shone in through the music room windows, illuminating the painting on the far wall. Elizabeth walked across the room to it. The fox hound puppy raised its head from the corner, thumped its tail, and went back to sleep.

It was a beautiful painting, she thought. Her son, Jim, so serious and handsome standing behind the chair, his left hand holding his father's watch with the gold acorn fob that represented Carstairs Oaks. Elizabeth frowned as she studied his elegant, beautiful wife in her expensive green velvet dress seated in the chair. Jim had met and married the beauty in a whirlwind love affair on a trip to Memphis. When Elizabeth had questioned the wisdom of such a hurried union, Jim told her why they had wed posthaste. A baby. Yes, the ebony-haired beauty would make any man forget about waiting until after the vows to consummate the union.

The children. Elizabeth smiled as she reached out with a trembling hand to touch the toddler's face. Laurel. She sat on her mother's lap reaching for Jim's watch with her left hand. Elizabeth had tried to change the toddler's hand preference, but to no avail. Even when the child sat on Elizabeth's lap at the piano and picked out the notes, she played with her left hand. The other little girl, Lenore, leaned against the chair, pretty and remote as her mother. Elizabeth's gaze swept over the painting. One little girl had her father's eyes, the other her mother's. Frowning, Elizabeth turned away from the painting. If she had only known then . . .

Nero, the butler, came to the door, interrupting her thought. The tribal tattoos on his face always scared first-time visitors. "Yes, Nero?"

"Excuse me, Miz Elizabeth, the judge is here."

"Show him in." She stared after Nero's departing back. He had gray in his hair now, too. Strange, it seemed like only yesterday that she as a young widow, had bought him from a slave trader who was whipping the little boy to death.

She felt a pain in her chest, winced, then managed to straighten up and forced her face to smile as Pierce entered the room.

"My dear Elizabeth." He took her hands, kissed them. "Great Caesar's ghost! Are you all right? You don't look well at all."

"Oh, Pierce." She laughed and turned toward the sideboard, pouring him a brandy and herself a sherry. "You worry over me like a mother hen."

"I'd rather worry over you as your husband." He took the brandy and sat down in a big leather chair near the fireplace.

"Thank you for your offer, it makes a lady feel good to know she has a beau." She smiled and sat down on the leather sofa across from him.

"For fifty years now," he reminded her gently and stroked his gray mustache.

"For some women, there is only one man in her lifetime."

"How many times have we had this same conversation?" he smiled a bit sadly and sipped his brandy.

She smiled. He would always be there for her, she knew that. He and Nero had devoted their lives to Elizabeth Carstairs' welfare.

"Elizabeth, you don't look well. You should see a doctor."

"I did and he said I would live to be a hundred," she lied. "Stop being such a fussbudget." She would not worry him about what the doctor in Louisville had told her and she'd sworn the doctor to secrecy. All that had kept her going for the past several years was the hope that they still might be alive somewhere in the West, that she might yet hear from them.

"You've heard of course, that young Rand has been found and is on his way home?"

"Yes. He's to arrive this evening, I hear. Surely you didn't drive out here to tell me that?"

He blushed and fidgeted with his brandy. "Of course not, although I never pass up a chance to come by when I'm near. How has Lenore reacted?"

"Appears to be deliriously happy, but I don't know how it will affect her scandalous carrying on with her best friend's fiancee."

"That hasn't stopped then?"

She frowned, looked toward the painting. "Lenore is just like her mother. I have half a mind to warn young Rand."

"But of course you won't. You would do anything to protect the Carstairs name."

A look passed between them and she remembered. Sixteen long, long years. "You know I would. No scandal shall ever smear the Carstairs reputation. I will protect it at all costs."

"As would I," he reminded her gently.

"I know, Pierce. That night, if you and Nero hadn't helped—"

"You owe me no gratitude." He made a dismissing gesture. "Your husband was an old school friend of mine. I couldn't bear to see the name sullied, although," he sighed, "young Lenore's behavior may create a scandal yet."

"So far, only you and I and Nero know," she acknowledged, a little weary of worrying about it. "Maybe she can't help it, Pierce." She glanced toward the painting. "It's in her blood. I feel I must do something. With young Rand returning, if she keeps on, her behavior will become common gossip. I'm thinking about sending her off to that fancy girls' school, Miss Priddy's, in Boston."

"She's a little old for that, isn't she? And what would people think with her fiancee finally coming home to marry her?"

Her sherry trembled in her frail hand. "I reckon twenty-one is a bit old to be sending her off to school, but frankly, I don't know what to do with her. I will not stand by and have her destroy the Carstairs name."

"Have you had a talk with her?"

Elizabeth shook her head. "I suppose that's the next step, but I hate to acknowledge that I know about her trampy goings on. I once tried to talk to her mother about the same thing to no avail. I think my daughter-in-law was shocked that I knew."

"Too bad she didn't heed your warning; the tragedy might have been averted."

She looked at the painting. "It was bound to happen sooner or later."

He reached for his pipe. "May I?"

"You know you never have to ask, Pierce, I like the smell of a pipe."

He filled his pipe awkwardly. His right arm had taken a mini ball at the First Battle of Bull Run. Elizabeth smiled with a touch of sheer mischief. Rose Randolph Erikson had never quite forgiven Pierce for being on the Union side of the fight.

She looked at the painting, although she knew every inch of it by heart. "I would do what I did all over again, Pierce. I'm sorry I involved you. It could have cost you everything. Perhaps it bothers your conscience, having the sterling character you do."

He looked troubled. "It's been a long time since we spoke of what happened, Elizabeth. I'd rather forget it. What we did was not legal, but it was moral. As long as justice was served, I suppose that's all that counts."

"You didn't do it for justice, you did it for me as did Nero."

"Yes, for you," he admitted and the old warmth shone in his brown eyes. "I'm not sorry. And not just because your husband was my best friend. I loved you from the first moment I saw you when he brought you here as a young bride. To protect you and look after you and your son after he was killed has been my personal honor and privilege."

She blinked back tears, thinking how sad he would be when she was gone. He was younger than she and in good health. "Someday, Pierce, I hope you will go into politics. This country needs men like you to guide it."

He laughed and shrugged. "Great Caesar's ghost. Don't think I haven't considered it, but going to Washington would take me too far from you, my dear."

"Should you outlive me, I hope you will reconsider." She sipped her sherry, wondering again why he had come.

He grunted and shrugged as if he didn't even want to think of a world without her in it. "Elizabeth—" He hesitated as if he had something to discuss that he didn't want to speak of. While he hesitated, she wondered suddenly if the doctor had broken his oath. Pierce Hamilton had a vast network of friends in high places.

"Elizabeth," he said again and cleared his throat,

"I've heard some disturbing news that I need to discuss with you."

He knew about her heart. Oh, Lord, he knew. "Yes?"

"Something Lenore is up to."

She relaxed and tried not to look too relieved. "Oh, what has the scheming little chit done this time? I've tried to love her, I really have, Pierce, but she's so devious and immoral. Besides, knowing what I know—"

"Perhaps she can't help it. She's the spitting image of her mother."

Elizabeth looked toward the painting. "I suppose she's inherited some of it from her. I often wonder what she inherited from her father?"

"That's not important at the moment," he seemed to shrug her off as if to return to the topic he came to discuss. "I have friends in other states and one of them, knowing I'm your lawyer, has contacted me. Lenore has been making inquiries into a place called Rose Haven."

"Rose Haven? Sounds like a cemetery."

"Elizabeth"—his eyes bored into her—"it's a private asylum for the insane."

The idea baffled her. "Lenore thinks she's losing her mind? Oh, the poor girl, I—"

"It's for her grandmother." Now he hurried on as if to tell it all before Elizabeth interrupted him. "It seems her elderly grandmother is getting senile and Lenore hopes to put her away at this expensive, but isolated asylum."

Elizabeth stared back at him, her mouth open. Her frail hand holding the sherry suddenly trembled so much, she reached out and put it on the lamp table to keep from dropping it. She was too astounded to speak.

"It's true, my dear. I've checked it all out."

She finally found her voice. "The conniving little—! Surely she didn't think she could legally do this with you as my lawyer?"

"Apparently she was willing to try. Rose Haven is very secluded and pleasant. Once a patient is in there, there's no contact with the outside world unless the person with power of attorney allows it."

Elizabeth threw back her head and laughed. "Lenore has more gall than I gave her credit for! Why would she bother? I'm an old lady and she surely thinks she'll get everything when I die. If she only knew—"

"Don't laugh, Elizabeth, this is serious business! Perhaps she's impatient to get her hands on your money. I could shock her by telling her now about the terms of your will. It should have been changed before now—"

"No." She shook her head. "The hope that they're still alive somewhere is what keeps me going, Pierce. I keep hoping they haven't contacted me because they're afraid of being traced by the law." She paused, looking toward the painting, remembering that dreadful night.

"Great Caesar's ghost! You know how many inquiries I've made? How many wild goose chases I've checked out?" He stroked his gray mustache again. "No trace. It would be so much easier on you, my dear, if you faced the fact that after almost sixteen years, they surely must be dead—"

"I don't want to hear that!" she snapped, with a spirit that surprised even herself. "I reckon I should make some changes in my will, though. I wouldn't want there to be speculation and idle gossip after I'm gone."

He sighed heavily. "I've been telling you that all

308

along. Are you going to let Lenore know you're on to her about Rose Haven and her affair?"

"Not yet," she mused. "Perhaps she'll end this scandalous thing with Shelby Merson now that Rand Erikson is coming home."

Pierce frowned and puffed his pipe. "Maybe like her mother, she likes living on the edge, playing with danger." He set his glass down and seemed to think it over. "I've got some Baltimore contacts. Think I'll look into the Merson family. Didn't I hear Shelby's supposed to be from old Baltimore money?"

"That's my understanding. He doesn't look like a gentleman, does he?"

"Not to me. I reckon Lenore finds him handsome, but there is something phony about him."

She stared into the fireplace. "In the meantime, with young Rand returning, can I keep silent and allow him to marry the faithless twit?"

"To expose her would bring dishonor and shame on the Carstairs' name. Remember what we have gone through to protect it."

She nodded, sighed. "You're right, of course. Do you suppose young Rand's still as spoiled and arrogant as before? In that case, they deserve each other."

"War changes people," he mused, playing with the stem of his pipe, "and he's been gone a long time. Even more alarming, they say he's been a captive of the Indians for months."

"Then he's bound to have changed for the better . . . or the worse. I always felt he was such a young rotter that he deserved Lenore. Now I'm having second thoughts. She's just too much like her mother."

"If he's in love with the chit, it won't do any

good. Would your son have listened?" He looked toward the beauty in the painting. "Perhaps Lenore will change her ways."

"Leopards don't change their spots. My daughter-in-law didn't and I doubt Lenore will either."

The judge stood up. "I must be going, my dear."

The puppy in the corner seemed to rouse itself, got up, and came over, wagging its tail. He bent to pet it.

"I should give him to you, Pierce. He keeps digging up flower beds. Just look at him, he's got dirt on his nose."

"Good dog, huh, Tally Ho?" Pierce stroked the puppy's ears, frowned up at her. "Suppose he digs—?"

"Don't you think that hasn't crossed my mind?" The possible consequences sent a pain coursing through her chest. "Don't worry, I've given strict orders."

Pierce straightened up, started to leave the music room, turned in the doorway. "I'll keep you posted."

She nodded, not terribly concerned. Elizabeth Carstairs was a strong personality, even if she were fragile and old. Lenore had better not underestimate her.

Kimi looked out the window of the carriage as it neared the palatial estate. Fine, blooded horses grazed in beautiful green pastures surrounded by white wood fences. "Oh, Hinzi, does this all belong to your family?"

He nodded, looking preoccupied. "Kimi, it might be better if you would begin to call me Rand; that's what all my family and friends call me."

She felt even more uneasy as the carriage neared the big house with the pillars and balcony. Everything about it spoke of wealth and power. "I thought everything would be destroyed in this war you spoke of."

"Seems this area was lucky and didn't get hit hard and now everything's on the mend. Besides Kentucky stayed with the Union, so the fighting was mostly farther south, although probably some of the local men were killed or wounded."

She looked down at her clothes. She still wore the deerskin dress and moccasins, although Hinzi— Rand—had been given something a little better by one of the trappers at the fort. Having seen what some of the white women wore while coming all these hundreds of miles, Kimi was a little uneasy. "I shouldn't have come," she said, clutching her medicine object for comfort.

"I could hardly leave you at the fort with Lieutenant Baker still there," he reminded her.

"I should have gone back to my people."

"Kimi, stop saying that; you're white."

"Not in my heart." She shook her head.

"Well, you may learn to like living among the whites." He didn't look too sure.

She thought about everything that had happened the last few days since they had left the fort. On the trip south, white people had stared at her in her strange costume. Rand seemed too occupied to even think about clothes, and besides, he had no money except the little the colonel had given him. He had not touched her since that night he had rescued her from the lustful officer. "Hinzi, Rand, does your family know you're bringing someone with you?"

A startled look crossed his handsome face, and

she had her answer. Had he simply forgotten or didn't know exactly what to wire his parents? "It'll be all right, Kimi."

He sounded almost as uncertain as she felt. "I won't stay long," she assured him. "I'll start looking for my relatives and find myself a job somewhere."

"Kimi, I want you to understand. I don't mean to hurt you. You're very young; too young. There's some fine boarding schools for young ladies and the Randolphs have money."

Kimi didn't answer. She'd heard a white man's saying: "out of sight, out of mind." She hadn't come all this way to be hidden away in some strict boarding school. As a matter of fact, she was no longer sure why she had come at all. "You're worried about what your parents will think, aren't you?"

He looked embarrassed. "I have always had everything that money can buy. I think my mother would see to it that I'm disinherited and I don't know what it is to live without wealth."

She started to remind him he had managed well enough among her people, then decided not to point that out. "I'll be hard to explain," she said, "you should have left me at the fort."

He had dark circles under his eyes as if he'd lost a lot of sleep struggling with this dilemma. "Kimi, I wish . . ."

She waited, but he didn't finish. He was trying to be honorable, she realized that; but his world of money and privilege meant more to him than any woman. Whatever was right for Rand, that's what Kimi would do. She wanted him to be happy. All she had done by accompanying him was create problems for both of them. For the hundredth time

312

she wished she had not come.

Her heart beat faster as she looked out the window at the big house and the people running from all directions. The carriage stopped and the driver got down to open the door, even as two white women and several servants came out of the house, all rushing toward the carriage.

Rand took a deep breath, as if to steel himself, and stepped out. As Kimi watched, the two white women threw their arms around him with glad cries.

"Rand, dear," the older exclaimed, "you're early! We weren't expecting you for hours!"

Kimi watched him embrace the two awkwardly. "Sorry, mother, I was trying to avoid some huge 'Welcome home' gathering. How are you, Vanessa?"

The young, pretty one looked like Rand. Now she pouted. "Mercy me! I declare you've ruined our big greeting! Lenore will be upset that she wasn't here. . . ." Kimi realized that the girl's eyes widened and her voice trailed off as she caught sight of Kimi in the carriage. "Who is that?"

Kimi saw the sudden hostility in his sister's blue eyes, the sheer curiosity in his mother's.

Rand turned. "Oh, this is Kimi." He extended his hand to help her from the carriage.

She felt Mrs. Erikson's cold stare. "We didn't realize anyone would be coming with Rand. How do you do, my dear?"

"Very well, thank you," Kimi tried to remember what little she'd been told about proper white behavior. Both Mrs. Erikson and Rand's sister were looking at her almost open-mouthed. She glanced down, realized they were staring at her doeskin dress and moccasins. She felt suddenly as if she'd just walked into a gathering of enemy Crow or

Pawnee.

"Kimi has spent most of her life among the Sioux," Rand explained, "and when we were both found by that army patrol, she didn't have any place to go, so I invited her to come with me."

"How nice," Vanessa said coolly, but her expression said she didn't think it was so nice.

By now Rand had turned away and was shaking hands and greeting the black servants who were still running from every direction.

She saw Mrs. Erikson and Vanessa exchange looks.

"Kimi," Mother said and while her mouth smiled, her eyes didn't, "I don't believe I caught your last name."

She would not be bullied by this rich woman. She looked her straight in the eye. "Kimi will do."

"Well, Kimi, will you be staying long?" Her tone said she certainly hoped not.

Kimi looked toward Rand, but he was busy shaking hands with the help and didn't seem to hear what was being said. "No, as soon as I make some plans, I'll be going on. Your son was kind enough to offer me the hospitality of Randolph Hall for a few days."

Rose Erikson visibly relaxed, but his sister didn't. "Oh, what a shame you won't be staying. You know my brother and his fiancee will probably be getting married right away, and you'll miss the biggest wedding this county ever saw."

"Yes, I know. He told me." Kimi forced herself to smile, determined not to make trouble for him.

Rand came back from the servants. "Let's not stand out here all day, let's go inside." They went into the entry hall of the mansion.

Kimi stared. Even the hall was big enough for a

family to live in. Evidently Rand's family had much wealth and many ponies. In spite of her brave front, she felt very ill-at-ease in her primitive clothing in comparison with the two richly dressed women.

She was only thankful that Rand had helped her for hours every day to learn the English words and grammar on the trip back to Kentucky. Now she wished there had been more time for him to tutor her in proper manners, dress, and other small things these white women would take for granted.

Rand looked around. "Where's Father?"

"Out in the east fields," Mrs. Erikson said, "we weren't expecting you for hours."

"Rand," his sister said, "of course you'll be wanting to go over to Carstairs Oaks immediately."

"I have a better idea," his mother said brightly, "why don't I send someone to let Lenore know you've arrived? That will give you a chance to rest and clean up and we can all have dinner here."

He looked a little relieved. "That sounds fine; I am tired from the trip. Sister, I hear from the servants that you haven't married Shelby yet."

"Mercy me!" Vanessa said, looking at Kimi, "We decided to wait until you came home. In fact, Lenore and I have sort of planned a double wedding."

Rand looked at Kimi, seemed about to say something, bit his lip instead. "I think I'll go find Father. Vanessa, do you reckon you could find Kimi something to change into?"

"Certainly. I'm sure one of the servants—"

"I meant one of *your* lovely dresses," he said with a slight edge to his voice. "As I remember, you always had wardrobes full of clothes."

"Of course, dear boy." His mother's hands fluttered nervously and she wheezed when she talked as if she wore a tight corset to squeeze her generous flesh. "I'm sure Vanessa has something she's not wearing anymore."

Kimi said, "I don't want to be any trouble. I'm awfully tired. If I could just rest awhile—"

"You're probably exhausted," Rand said. "Vanessa will find you a nice guest room, too."

"And we'll have a chance to get to know each other," Vanessa said with a big smile, but like her mother, her pale eyes didn't smile. "Come along with me, Kimi."

She didn't really want to go with Vanessa, but she didn't want to seem impolite. They went up the big, circular stairway together.

They walked down the upstairs hall. Vanessa glanced at her curiously. "Your name was Kimi? Rather unusual, isn't it?"

Kimi started to explain that it was really Kimimila, decided not to bother. "It's Lakota for butterfly."

"How very quaint!" Vanessa said. "Were you a captive of the savages, too?"

"They aren't savages, they're Sioux," Kimi said, "I was raised by them."

"So what happened to your relatives?"

Kimi tried to remember. "It's been so long. I really don't recall anything about my family."

Vanessa paused with her hand on a doorknob. "Mercy me! How sad. You know, in this part of the country, family is very important. My brother is engaged to my best friend. The Carstairs are an old, *quality* family." Her tone left no doubt what she thought about Kimi's family background.

"Yes, I know about Miss Carstairs." Although she was seething at the implied insult, Kimi decided she must not make trouble for Rand.

"There's to be a family dinner here tonight and you'll get to meet my fiancee and Rand's. When you see her, you'll know why Rand is so madly in love with her. Lenore Carstairs is considered a great beauty and a reigning belle."

"How very nice for her," Kimi said, wondering just what response Vanessa expected. Perhaps she suspected that there was more to the relationship between Rand and Kimi than met the eye and was probing for more information.

Vanessa led her into a bedroom that was large and beautiful by anyone's standards. "You can have this room. I'll see if I can find you a dress and send Millie to help you with your hair and bath."

"I'm perfectly capable of doing that myself," Kimi said.

Vanessa's nose wrinkled in distaste. "Ladies of quality have maids." She smiled sweetly, "but of course, I don't suppose you'd know much about that, would you?"

Kimi smiled back just as sweetly. "I've been told ladies of quality are also polite and well-mannered. But I suppose you don't know much about that, do you?"

Pretty Vanessa's mouth opened and closed a couple of times. Then without saying anything else, she turned and flounced out.

Kimi's pluck abandoned her, and she sat down morosely on the big bed. Any hope she might have had that Rand's family would be warm, wonderful people, who would be kind and friendly to a white waif with no relatives or any place to go, vanished. Where would she go and what would she do? One thing was certain, she wouldn't go whining to Rand about his sister's hostility.

A black girl stuck her head in the door. "I's Millie with clothes and things; bathwater on de way up."

Kimi gestured her in.

The girl entered with her arms full of hoops and lace petticoats. "It be a big dinner, ma'am. Miss Lenore is comin' and Miss Vanessa's intended, Marse Shelby Merson."

She pictured the gaiety and Lenore hanging on Rand's arm. Kimi couldn't bear to see that. "I don't think I feel like going down to dinner. Perhaps I could just have a tray sent up here to my room."

The girl looked at her a long moment. "I's got orders, ma'am, to get you ready for dinner. Miz Vanessa said."

Kimi had a sudden feeling that even though they'd been freed, the blacks here were not treated very well by Rand's sister. "Millie, I—I won't know what to do. I've never been to a fancy dinner before."

"Is dat all?" she shrugged. "Jes' watch and do what everyone else does. If'n you don't know what to say, do what Miss Lenore and Miss Vanessa do, just flutter your eyelashes and fan and giggle."

"Is that what belles do? They must look very shallow and silly!"

"I didn't say dat, ma'am, you did. Wif' your looks, you outshine dem both."

Kimi saw the girl's expression and realized she'd found an ally. She couldn't imagine herself giggling, but she didn't want to get Millie in trouble, either. Kimi stood up slowly. Was Rand really expecting her to attend this intimate family dinner or had it been Vanessa's idea to show him how barbaric Kimi looked next to the elegant Lenore?

318

Was there any possibility that she could compete with the lovely Southern belles? She decided suddenly that she wasn't going to give Rand up without a fight. "Millie, do you think you can make me look like those other two girls?"

"Shore. I been doin' ladies' hair for years and you is got pretty green eyes ma'am."

She might not know how to read or what fork to use, but maybe she could learn, Kimi decided. She looked at the hoops and corset and Florida Water fragrance that Millie carried. "Do your best, Millie, I'm going for a big win."

Millie's white teeth gleamed in her black face. "I don't like those two spoiled white gals, Miss; neither does the rest of the help. It's gonna be my pleasure to make you look better than both of them put together!"

Eighteen

Even as Kimi dressed for dinner, her nerve began
to fail her. Millie assured her she looked "purtier
than a speckled pup" but still Kimi stared at herself in the full-length mirror although she knew
everyone else must be ready.

Even Rand knocked on her door. "Kimi, are you
coming?"

He must have known she was uneasy. The image
staring back at her looked unfamiliar. Millie had
laced her into a tight corset and big hoop skirts.
The dress Vanessa had lent her was willow green
cotton, which Vanessa had said she was about to
give the maid anyway because it wasn't Vanessa's
best color. Kimi's ebony braids had been redone
into an elegant French twist with little ringlets
about her face. While the pointy shoes pinched
and she could scarcely breathe in the tight corset,
she felt as if most of her bosom was bare in the
low-cut bodice. Her medicine object looked rather
out of place on its rawhide thong.

Millie shook her head. "Ma'am, why don't you
let me find a gold chain for your doodad? Until I
do, you can wear some of dese pearls tonight."

She was reluctant to take it off, but she substi-
tuted pearls after Millie promised again to replace
the thong with a gold chain by tomorrow.

She heard a buggy drive up outside in the twilight and ran to the window. A beautiful black-haired girl in an expensive autumn russet-colored velvet dress, and a distinguished older man with a gray mustache and goatee were alighting. The black-haired girl moved with a mincing, ladylike step. Was that the fabled Lenore? She was so beautiful, she took Kimi's breath away. There was also something vaguely familiar about her. Of course Kimi was certain it was because Rand had described Lenore so often, she knew what she would look like. How could Kimi compete with a sophisticated beauty like that? Her nerve failed her.

Rand knocked again. "Kimi, are you coming?"

"I'm not quite ready," Kimi lied. "Go on down. I'll be there in a minute."

"Are you all right?"

"Of course. I'm just not quite ready, that's all."

About that time, Kimi heard Mrs. Erikson's voice floating up the stairs. "Yoo hoo, dear boy, come down. Our guests have arrived."

"Kimi," he said again.

"Go on, I'll be along in a moment."

She listened to him leave, heaved a sigh of relief. How could she go down and face the girl who was going to marry Rand? Having seen Lenore out the window, Kimi thought her more beautiful than any girl she had ever seen. No wonder Rand was attracted to me, Kimi thought miserably. I must have reminded him of her—about the same height with ebony hair.

Millie handed her a small, lace object. "Here's your fan, Miss. Just flutter it and flirts with de gentlemen."

"I'll feel silly. It seems so stupid."

"Fancy white ladies wouldn't be caught dead

321

without a fan, ma'am. You be prettier than her, miss. Don't let her outdo you none now. 'Course, we got to try to soak you down wif' buttermilk, get that tan off your skin."

That gave Kimi one more thing to worry about. Very pale white skin denoted beauty among these people. "I don't know where—"

"Dey be in de library first."

"What's a library?"

The girl started to laugh, then seemed to realize Kimi wasn't joking and her expression warmed with sympathy. "Look for de room full of books."

Kimi opened her door a crack. Below her, she heard the front door open, then the sounds of laughter and greetings as Lenore Carstairs and the old family friend arrived. Maybe Kimi could suddenly be taken sick and have a tray sent up. But that was a cowardly way out, and she wasn't a very good liar.

Kimi hesitated, finally built up her courage and went downstairs, walking carefully in the miserable, tight shoes. Kimi had very small feet, but evidently all ladies' shoes were made to hurt. Dealing with the hoops was awkward. She began to feel a little sorry for white women. So this was what it felt like to be civilized. She followed the conversation and found everyone sitting or standing around in a big room filled with books. She paused in the doorway and all heads turned toward her.

Rand's eyes widened and his mouth dropped open. Kimi waited uneasily. *I must look ridiculous,* she thought, *from the expression on all the men's faces.*

Rand stared at Kimi a long moment, startled into complete silence. Dressed as a Southern lady, Kimi was more than pretty; she was a vision of

322

beauty in pale green, a swan among awkward ducks. He tried to find words, but could only gape at her. By comparison, she made Lenore and his sister Vanessa look like dumpy servant girls. The other men apparently shared his assessment; they were both staring at Kimi as if a goddess had suddenly floated into the library.

Rand managed to pull himself together, cleared his throat, and smiled at Kimi reassuringly. "Everyone, this is my friend, Kimi, who returned with me from the Sioux camp. Kimi, this is Lenore Carstairs. You know my mother and sister."

Lenore looked her up and down. "How do you do?" She said coldly as if she really hoped not very well.

"Fine and you?" Kimi could only be thankful Millie had coaxed her a little.

"Very well now that *my* fiancee is home again."

Rand looked ill at ease, hurried on with the introductions. "May I present my father and Judge Hamilton?"

Jon Erikson had the saddest expression on his handsome face. He also appeared to be a bit drunk. This is exactly what Rand would look like in twenty-five years, Kimi thought, if he stayed in civilization; a bit paunchy, red veins in his nose from too much bourbon and rich food. Mr. Erikson staggered a little as he crossed the carpet, took her hand, and kissed it. "So pleased to have you here, Miss Kimi."

Judge Hamilton smiled and stroked his gray mustache. "Great Caesar's ghost, Rand, you didn't tell us she was so lovely. Young lady, will you honor an old man by being his dinner partner?"

She liked him immediately. "Why, judge, I'd be delighted."

She heard someone in the hall and turned as another man entered. He was handsome, older than Rand, but shorter and heavier. He walked with a slight limp. "Evenin', y'all, sorry I'm a bit late."

"Shelby, I was wondering where you were." Vanessa took his arm possessively.

Introductions were made and Shelby bent over Kimi's hand. "Well, I can see why anyone would want to run away to the Indians."

He hung onto her fingers a long moment and his felt clammy, his kiss wet on the back of her hand. The lamp light reflected off his oiled hair.

Kimi took a deep breath and smelled perfumed hair tonic. "You are too kind, sir." She managed to pull her fingers from his.

Vanessa pouted at her. "Shelby is my fiancee. We are planning a double wedding with Rand and Lenore."

What did she expect Kimi to say? Kimi smiled. "So you've told me before. I hope you'll all be very happy."

There was an awkward pause. All three women were glaring at her, Rand looked discomforted, Shelby Merson leered and the judge gallantly offered her his arm. "Remember, my dear, you promised to be my dinner partner."

She took his arm after seeing Lenore take Rand's. "Certainly." She wished she felt as confident as she forced herself to sound. Already she sensed that the three women saw her as an adversary. The judge seemed genuinely friendly.

The dining room had Victorian scarlet wallpaper and heavy velvet drapes. A chandelier glittered over the long ornate walnut table. She paused as they reached the table, not quite sure what to do next, even as the judge pulled her chair out. What was she supposed to do now? She watched Rand, Shelby and Mr. Erikson seat the other women. So that was the way it was done. Kimi lifted the yards of green skirt and smiled at the judge as he pulled her chair out, seated her.

Kimi looked up from the gold-rimmed dinner service she was contemplating to find the judge was staring at her. His face grew puzzled. "Miss Kimi, is there any possibility we've ever met before?"

Rand laughed. "Judge, if you weren't a respected senior citizen of this county, we might all think you were flirting with the young lady."

"And if I weren't such a senior, I might," the judge retorted, a twinkle in his eyes.

Everyone laughed and Kimi felt herself blush. "I think I would be honored if the judge were so inclined."

Mister Erikson, at the end of the table, said, "For a girl who hasn't been raised like a Southern belle, ma'am, you certainly know instinctively the repartee."

"Seriously," the judge said, "she just looked familiar, that's all. Miss Kimi, green is certainly your color; it goes with your eyes."

Vanessa, sitting next to Kimi said, "Isn't it lucky I had an old dress I could lend her? I had intended to give it to a servant."

Rand gave his sister a cold look from his place on his mother's right. "You never looked so good in it, sister."

A sudden chill seemed to descend on the room. Kimi licked her dry lower lip. "It was very nice of her to lend me the dress. I really didn't have anything nice enough to wear."

Lenore said, "We're about the same size. Perhaps before you leave the area, I could give you a few things. I'd consider it my Christian duty."

In the library, Kimi had noticed the one flaw in Lenore's beauty; her large feet. Kimi certainly couldn't wear her shoes. She forced herself to smile. "You're too kind, Miss Carstairs."

"You should have seen her when she arrived," Vanessa said smugly to the other guests, "she was in moccasins and a leather shift when she stepped out of the carriage."

Kimi felt all eyes upon her. A savage, that's what they think of me; an uncivilized savage, a curiosity.

"Well," said the judge, "she certainly is lovely. I'll wager she made that buckskin look as good as she does Miss Vanessa's dress."

"Pierce," Mrs. Erikson said from the end of the table, "Elizabeth wasn't up to coming?"

He shook his head and looked worried as he spread his napkin over his lap. "She does invite all of you to dinner tomorrow night." He looked at Kimi, "and of course, your guest is invited, too."

Kimi, watching him, spread her napkin on her lap, also. The chair wasn't all that comfortable, and the tight corset made it hard to breathe. She thought wistfully of sitting before a camp fire on the ground, cooking a piece of meat.

Rand's father had already finished his wine, was gesturing to the black servant to fill his glass again.

Mrs. Erikson pursed her lips in disapproval. "Really, Jon, that's your fourth glass."

"I don't have to count, not with my dear wife keeping score." With an almost defiant gesture, he took a long drink.

The air seemed tense. Kimi glanced at Rand. He looked a little embarrassed and unhappy as he began to ask about how the war had affected the

326

area and gossip about people they all knew. Kimi knew none of the people being discussed, so she concentrated on the food in her plate. She looked at all the silver on each side of the gold-rimmed china. What to use?

The judge caught her eye, made an elaborate gesture of picking up a fork. His expression gave her to know he would try to help her. Immediately, Kimi felt a little better. She had an ally. Rand was too far down the table to give her any hints. Kimi did exactly as the judge did.

Mrs. Erikson said, "Oh, by the way, Rand, about the Harvest Moon Ball I've planned for this Saturday night—"

"Mother!" Vanessa pouted, "you've spoiled the surprise."

"Oh, for pity's sake, Vanessa, it's not that big a thing," Lenore said with an airy wave of her hand. "It's just to announce our engagements, that's all."

Kimi managed to keep her face immobile as she struggled with her knife and fork. Everything seemed fried and too rich or salty for her taste, but then she was used to simple stews and buffalo steaks roasted on a slow spit over a fire.

She looked up to find Shelby Merson staring at her low bodice as if he were mentally taking her clothes off. "Do you waltz, Miss Kimi?"

She started to shake her head, but Rand said, "I was just in the process of teaching her." He locked his gaze on hers. "I wouldn't want you to miss the ball, Kimi."

Lenore bristled and paused with her delicate crystal wine glass half way to her lips. "I understand Miss Kimi is only a temporary houseguest. She might be gone by then."

"On the other hand"—Kimi looked her straight

in the eye—"I might not."

Jon Erikson seemed to come out of his stupor and grinned at her sassiness. "Of course you're invited to the ball, my dear. I'll look forward to your saving a dance for me."

Rand and Kimi exchanged looks. "Mother," he said, "I wish you'd ask me before you start making big plans."

"Mercy me, brother," Vanessa sipped her wine, "we thought it might be a wonderful time to set a double wedding."

Rand appeared a bit testy. "I had forgotten how all you women manage my life for me."

"Why should you be any different?" Jon Erikson muttered. "They've always interfered in mine."

Rand's mother frowned the length of the table at him. "Did you say something, Jon?"

"No, my dear."

Kimi watched Rand's father. He had retreated to his fried chicken and his wine.

Judge Hamilton immediately changed the subject, talking about how the war had affected Kentucky, cotton prices, almost any less volatile subject.

Kimi picked at her food. She wasn't very good with a fork and she was more than a little afraid of embarrassing herself. She could scarcely breath in the tight corset, and the yards and yards of skirt seemed to smother her while the shoes pinched her feet. She thought longingly of her soft doeskin dress and moccasins. Could she ever fit into white society? Did she want to? She felt someone's eyes on her, glanced up suddenly, and caught Rand watching her. When their eyes met he looked away. For a moment his face seemed almost as sad as Jon Erikson's. Rand's happiness was all that mattered to her. What would make him happiest?

They got through the dinner somehow and Kimi managed to keep herself from yawning at the dullness of it all. So this was how privileged white ladies lived. She hoped this harvest ball would not be so dull. As she stifled a yawn, the judge smiled at her. Evidently he had read her thoughts, maybe some of these people were not the old man's favorites, either.

They lingered over coffee for a long time. Mrs. Erikson suggested several times that the ladies retire to the drawing room for sherry and leave the gentlemen to their cigars and brandy, but Rand shook his head. "I hate to disappoint everyone on my first night back, but I'm exhausted, as is Kimi, I'm sure. We ought to call it a night early."

Lenore took a deep breath and her nostrils seemed to flare. "Why, Rand, for pity's sake, I thought you might want to drive me home."

"Well, I—"

"Now, Lenore," the judge broke in with a long look at Kimi, "you heard Rand say how weary he is. I drove you over, I can certainly drive you home."

"Of course." Lenore bit off her words and glared daggers at Kimi. "How thoughtless of me not to remember that."

Vanessa threw down her napkin. "Is the hunt still planned for tomorrow?"

"Oh, yes," Mrs. Erikson wheezed, "I had forgotten to mention it to Rand. The club has planned a fox hunt to welcome you home."

"Hmm," Rand said without much enthusiasm.

"Why, Rand," Lenore said, "you used to love it."

He looked at Kimi. "Someone pointed out to me that chasing and killing something just for the joy of it is not a very sporting thing to do."

"Why, for pity's sake," Lenore said, "it's part of our civilized tradition."

"Until I was away, I hadn't realized how many questionable traditions we have. Maybe fox hunting needs to go the way of slavery," Rand said.

Mrs. Erikson's mouth fell open. "Why, I do believe that serving in that Yankee army has affected the poor boy's mind. You never used to talk like this, dear."

"I've also been doing a lot of thinking. I never used to do that," Rand shrugged. He was looking at Kimi.

Shelby Merson played with the diamond stickpin in his gaudy tie. "Everyone who is anybody will be there; all the fashionable people."

Rand seemed to grit his teeth. "People are still reeling from the war and our crowd is back to its mindless, idle way of life, destroying crops galloping after one damned fox!"

Lenore's mouth fell open. "Swearing in the presence of ladies! I declare, you've been among the savages too long!"

Rand muttered an apology, but he didn't look as if he meant it.

His mother looked bewildered. "Rand, dear, you used to love our way of life. I merely planned—"

"I'm a little weary of people always making plans for me." He threw down his napkin. "It is, after all, my life."

Mrs. Erikson's pale eyes blinked. "Why, dear, things are as they always were. Perhaps you've forgotten."

"You're right, I had," Rand said.

His father shrugged and signaled for the servant to pour him another glass of wine. "Well, never forget, son, the hand that holds the money rules the world."

Mrs. Erikson pursed her lips. "Did you say something, Jon?"

"No, my dear." He gulped his drink.

Kimi suddenly felt quite sorry for Jon Erikson. If this was the way rich white families lived, why would anyone want to be part of one of them? She caught Judge Hamilton's eye and realized from his expression that he was suffering, too.

He stood up. "It has been a lovely dinner, Rose. I really think it's getting late and I should drive Lenore home before I go on."

He and Rand helped the ladies from their chairs. Mister Erikson seemed a little unsteady on his feet.

Vanessa glared at Kimi. "I have an extra riding habit if you care to go on the hunt."

"Well, I don't know." Kimi didn't feel very welcome.

"Oh, yes, you must come along." Lenore's golden eyes gleamed. "I have a wonderful new horse I'll lend you."

Rand looked puzzled at the pair's sudden generosity. "I doubt Kimi has ever participated in something like this."

While she couldn't waltz or do needlepoint, or a thousand things that seemed so important to these prissy white women, Kimi was an expert rider. Abruptly it occurred to her that here was a chance to show that she wasn't completely without skills. "Of course I'd love to."

Jon Erikson cleared his throat. "I'm the master of the hunt, my dear, and we'll be crossing Randolph Hall's land. Give you a chance to see what we do for fun."

Vanessa smiled. "Oh, yes, this will be so much

331

fun, won't it, Lenore?"

Kimi was puzzled at the looks the two other girls were exchanging. Perhaps they thought she couldn't ride and intended to make her look like a fool.

"Then if we're all going in the morning," Rand said, "we really do need to end this evening early."

They all said their good-nights and Kimi went upstairs while Rand saw the judge and Lenore Carstairs off. She locked her door, pulled off the tight shoes and rubbed her aching feet. It was even more difficult to get herself out of the boned corset, even with Millie's help. No wonder Rose Erikson wheezed. Kimi threw herself across the bed. What had she gotten herself into? She didn't belong among these petty, sarcastic women. Yet she had no money and nowhere to go. She had never spent a more miserable evening in her whole life.

She pictured the dark, cold beauty of Lenore Carstairs. She was about the same general size and coloring as Kimi herself, ebony hair, small frame. She had been breathtaking in her russet gown. Maybe it was those strange, almost golden eyes. There was something hauntingly familiar about them—sort of like looking at a cat's, she thought.

She lay back on her bed, thinking about the beauty Rand was engaged to marry. For comfort, she reached for her spirit object on the bedside table, began to hum her spirit song very softly. She dozed off into a troubled sleep. Kimimila . . . Kimimila . . . a voice called in her dreams. Was it a memory? Was it . . . ?

"Kimimila. Kimi, are you asleep?"

The soft knock at her door brought her awake with a start.

"Kimi?"

Rand's voice. She got up, tiptoed to the door,

and opened it just a crack. "Go away. Suppose your mother or sister hear you?"

"I wanted to tell you I'm sorry about tonight. When I get a chance, I want to talk to Mother about breaking the engagement."

"No, you can't do that." She opened the door, faced him in her sheer nightdress. He was barefooted and bare-chested. She had forgotten how much golden hair he had on his chest. "You might live to regret it. Rand, I'm not sure I can ever fit into your—"

He cut off her words with his kiss and she lost all control and clung to him. For a long moment as they embraced, nothing else mattered but being in his arms, having his lips warm on hers. Through the sheer lace of her nightgown she felt the hair of his chest brush against her nipples. For a split second, she was transported back to the wild Dakota territory where things were so much more simple, where he was the white warrior and she was his woman.

She managed to push both hands flat against his naked chest, took a deep breath for control. "Rand, I don't think it will ever work. Your mother and sister will never accept me. Your friends would laugh at me behind my back, pity you."

He kissed along her cheek. "The judge didn't laugh."

"He's different." There was something special about Pierce Hamilton, she decided. In her dreams she had imagined a kindly old uncle like the judge and a white-haired grandmother with gray eyes and a pale lavender gray dress. Both images puzzled her.

"Let me stay the night," Rand whispered along

her neck, his hand caressing her breast, "Damn me for a cradle-robbing cad, I want to make love to you!"

She steeled her resolve, managed to pull away from him. "We can't do that, not right here in your parents' home."

"But Kimi—"

"No!" She managed to pull away from him, slam the door in his face, and lock it. She leaned against it, shaking.

"Kimi?"

She didn't answer. He was like a lot of white men. He would end up marrying the society girl, but wanted to sneak into another woman's bed at night. She got back in bed, burrowed in under her pillows so that she couldn't hear his voice begging her to open the door. Finally he went away.

She thought of the snug tipi she had shared with Hinzi among the Sioux. The wind blew around the big house, rattling the windows. Soon it would be the Moon of the Falling Leaves that whites called November. The first snow of the season might already be falling in the northern country of her people. She imagined herself curled up naked in a buffalo fur robe with Hinzi, making love before the campfire; trying to conceive a baby who would be born in the summer. She would not cry. She must not cry. Outside, the wind seemed to be doing it for her. Finally, she dropped off into a troubled sleep. The Eriksons didn't seem to be a very happy family. But if this was the life Rand wanted, Kimi would try to be glad for him.

Kimi stared at herself in the morning light reflecting on the mirror. "Surely I'm not supposed to ride a horse in this outfit?"

"Of course," Vanessa seemed amused by her astonishment. Then Kimi realized Rand's sister was dressed in the same manner. Vanessa said, "It is a lovely outfit; one of my finest. I wouldn't want my brother to think I wasn't doing my very best to make his guest feel welcome."

Kimi looked at her reflection again. She was dressed just like Vanessa in a dark hunting coat and long skirt, a jaunty top hat with a veil. Vanessa had lent her a pair of black boots; they were a bit too big since Kimi had such small feet, but she had stuffed some cotton in the toes.

Yes, even Rand would think she was pretty in this. Perhaps she had misjudged his sister. "I want to thank you, Vanessa, for your kindness. I had thought you plotted to make me look bad."

Vanessa fidgeted uneasily, and didn't meet her gaze. "Come on. Lenore has already sent the horse over for you."

From down in the front hall, she heard Rand call: "Come on you two! That whole hunt club is gathering out front."

They went down the stairs. Dogs baying outside. Rand wore a scarlet coat and slapped a whip against his leg.

"Oh," Kimi said with admiration, "I'd like a red coat, too."

Vanessa laughed. "Mercy me, don't be silly! Ladies aren't allowed to wear pinks."

"I didn't say 'pink,' " Kimi said, "I said 'red.' "

"Kimi," Rand said, "the coats are called 'pinks,' and Vanessa's right; ladies don't wear them."

It dawned on Kimi abruptly that it must be like the scarlet sash of the Strongheart Society.

Rand paused and stared at Kimi.

"Your sister was kind enough to lend me an outfit," Kimi said, pleased and happy at the admiration in his eyes.

Vanessa seemed to catch the electricity between the pair. "Too bad you won't be staying long, Kimi. Someday you must come back for a visit. By then, Shelby and I will have Randolph Hall, and Rand will be master of Carstairs Oaks. It's such a lovely place."

"Vanessa," he began, "about this double wedding, I —"

"Our guests are waiting," Vanessa interrupted.

"You're right," Rand said, "perhaps this is not the proper time to discuss this." He looked troubled and uncertain as he opened the door.

A large group of riders had gathered out past the flagstone veranda. Sure enough, the other women were similarly attired. Most of the men wore dark coats, but several, including Jon Erikson, wore scarlet. The trio went down the steps where black grooms stood holding the horses. A pack of spotted hounds yelped and ran around the yard, causing the horses to snort nervously and stamp their hooves. The huntsman in charge snapped his whip, trying to bring order to the confusion.

People descended on Rand, shaking his hand, telling him how glad they were he had returned. They stared at Kimi with unbridled curiosity as Rand introduced her. Evidently, the gossip had already started.

"Are we ready to go?" Jon Erikson looked a little drunk on a big chestnut thoroughbred, as he shouted over the baying hounds.

"No, Lenore isn't here yet. Wouldn't you know she'd want to make an entrance?"

336

"Mercy me, here she comes." Vanessa strained her eyes toward the horizon. "Looks like she stopped to get Shelby."

The two cantered up together, Lenore leading a tall, ebony mare that snorted and swung its head. The two riders were dressed in dark coats. Kimi admitted to herself that Lenore looked very fashionable in hunt clothes.

"Good morning, y'all." Lenore gave the assembled crowd of riders a dazzling smile and cooed, "Rand, dear, do ride beside me. I brought Onyx for Kimi."

Kimi looked at the black horse. There was something about the way it laid its ears back and stamped its hooves that warned her.

Rand studied the mare and shook his head. "Lenore, this looks like a lot of horse for a small woman who hasn't done any riding to the hounds. Why don't I exchange horses with her?"

Lenore frowned. "You'd have to change the saddles and there isn't time. Onyx is a perfectly safe horse—if Kimi can ride."

It seemed a belligerent challenge. Kimi looked her in the eye. "I can ride," she said, "Rand, give me a hand."

He appeared as if he would protest as he stood there slapping his whip against his thigh. Then he seemed to realize the silent war that was raging between the two women. Even as he offered his hands to boost her onto the big horse, Kimi realized with a sudden shock that the saddle was unlike anything she'd ever seen.

Vanessa must have seen her dismayed expression. "Mercy me, haven't you ever seen a sidesaddle?" She laughed, and a ripple of laughter went through the mounted ladies. "This is the way civilized ladies always ride."

Kimi looked around at the other women riders. Sure enough, they all sat with both legs on the same side of the horse, long skirt trailing almost to the ground.

Rand must have seen the uncertainty on her face. "Kimi, you don't have to do this. You can wait for me to change saddles out and give you my reliable—"

"No, on the contrary," Kimi fixed Vanessa and Lenore with an icy glare through the veil of her jaunty hat. "Miss Lenore has chosen this horse and I think she and your sister intend to have a little fun at my expense. I wouldn't disappoint them for the world!"

She swung up on the tall horse and settled herself in the sidesaddle. She couldn't imagine how anyone rode with the thing. It put a twist in her back that she knew would be aching before she had ridden very far. First pointy shoes, corsets and yards of skirt, now a sidesaddle. At least she had her medicine charm back, safely hanging from a gold chain under her riding jacket.

All these dozens of people and baying dogs gathering to go after one small fox? They must not have much to keep them busy. If it had been a herd of fat buffalo or some tasty deer, it would be worth the trouble. She was fast losing her envy and awe of white civilization. The servants circulated among the riders, offering a final stirrup cup to brace them against the crisp autumn air.

The black horse moved restlessly under her, ears laid back. Kimi was an expert rider, but she'd usually ridden bareback and astride. Defiantly, she nudged Onyx and moved up next to Lenore, Shelby, Vanessa and Rand.

Lenore frowned at her. "Since you're a novice, you really should ride in the back with the 'hill-toppers' so you won't have to try to keep up with us."

Kimi looked at her. "Where will the best riders be?"

"Why, for pity's sake, in front, where the action is, of course."

Kimi set her mouth stubbornly. "Then that's where I'll be, too."

Rand scowled with worry. "Have you ever done any jumping before, Kimi?"

"Only a few creeks and logs." She saw Lenore and Vanessa exchange satisfied smirks. Kimi had been too trusting. Of course they hoped to make her look like a fool in front of Rand and all the Erikson's friends. She made a silent vow that she wouldn't allow that to happen.

The huntsman blew his horn and the dogs trotted across the field, sniffing for a scent. The group of riders followed behind at a slow trot.

Kimi looked over at Lenore. "I don't see any weapons except whips."

Rand said, "those are for the dogs, Kimi, we won't need any weapons."

"Why not?"

Vanessa and Lenore giggled with delight at her ignorance. "Because, silly, the pack of hounds tears the fox to pieces if they catch it. If we're to have any of it at all, someone has to whip the dogs back."

Kimi frowned. "There won't be much of the meat or fur left after the dogs get through, will there?"

Lenore looked at her as if she were too stupid to be believed. "All we get out of this is the ride, although someone may be awarded the fox's tail or mask."

Kimi looked around at all the riders trotting across the field after the big pack of hounds. "It seems like a lot of work for nothing."

Vanessa said loftily, "It's a ritual. Of course, we wouldn't expect an uncivilized girl to understand—"

"Stop it, Vanessa," Rand snapped.

Lenore smiled. "Now, Rand," she cooed, "just to show our heart's in the right place, we'll see your little friend gets blooded—"

"What?" Kimi asked.

Rand looked ill at ease. "When they take a novice on a first hunt, they smear some of the dead fox's blood on that rider."

Kimi looked at him incredulously as they rode. "Rich people are smearing blood on white ladies? And you call the Sioux 'savages'?"

"For pity's sake, it's not the same," Lenore snapped.

At this point, Kimi decided to say no more. Actually, she was enjoying the ride. Onyx was an excellent mount, but a little spirited.

Abruptly the pack of spotted hounds began an excited baying, took off across the field toward a split rail fence. The huntsman blew his horn to alert the riders and the riders urged their horses into a gallop, following the pack.

Kimi was an excellent rider, but unused to riding sidesaddle with a swirl of skirts. She urged Onyx forward, gritting her teeth as the spirited mare loped toward the fence. The satisfied smirks on the two girls' faces let her know they expected her to get dumped and they hoped to be there to lead the crowd in laughing. Her pride had gotten in the way. If she had had any sense, she would have let

340

Rand change mounts with her. His bay looked steady and reliable.

The black mare cleared the fence and came down hard on the other side, its hooves throwing up bits of turf as it landed and galloped on. If it hadn't been for the sidesaddle, Kimi would have loved the ride.

Onyx obviously didn't intend to be left in the back of the pack of riders. Kimi had a hard time slowing her down as she picked up speed and pace. She glanced around. Somewhere over the past half mile of meadow she had lost track of Rand in the crowd of riders. Up ahead the baying of the hounds echoed over the crisp October morning.

Kimi leaned into the jump, willing herself to feel lighter as the big horse took a low stone wall and kept going. When she glanced back, she saw a chestnut with a blaze face refuse the jump and the lady rider went over the wall in a tumble of skirts with her hat askew. A rolling meadow lay ahead, and the speed of Kimi's mount put her near the front of the pack of riders. Onyx jumped a brook that caused two horses to refuse, and their riders went tumbling over their heads into the water. Up ahead was a solid brick wall that looked as tall as a man's head. Her heart pounded uncertainly as she galloped toward it. She could turn her horse aside, not attempt it. Then she looked behind her and saw Rand coming in the distance, shaking his head and signaling with one hand to go around, not to chance it. On each side of him rode Vanessa and Lenore, pleased smirks on their faces.

Kimi knew it was a big jump. Many of those ahead of her were reining in, going down to the gate through the fence several hundred yards away. In the distance, the excited yelping of the hounds

341

increased as they picked up the pace. She would show Lenore! No doubt the white girl was an excellent rider who had ridden this course many times. She intended to best Kimi here, make Rand admire her, show him he really belonged with a Kentucky lady of wealth.

For a split-second, she almost turned aside, then stubborn pride took over and she urged Onyx toward the wall. The mare hesitated, then sailed off the ground. Kimi's heart seemed to stop beating for a split second, then Onyx hit the wall and fell back on the same side, throwing Kimi in the dirt. Her jaunty top hat was crushed, the veil torn.

Behind her, she heard Lenore and Vanessa's delighted laughter and Rand's shout. "I'm coming, Kimi. Are you hurt?"

Gritting her teeth against the pain of her bruises, Kimi stumbled to her feet, quickly checked the horse to make sure it was all right. All around her, horses were refusing the jump. If it weren't for the damned riding skirt and the sidesaddle, she would have made it.

Rand and the majority of the riders would reach here any second. Kimi intended to clear this wall and she didn't intend that anyone should stop her. Quickly, she stripped the saddle off, hiked up her skirts and swung up astride on the mare's bare back.

"Look at that girl, she's riding astride!" A chorus of voices expressed shock and dismay at the sight of Kimi with her white lace drawers showing as she backed her horse up, skirts flying.

"Kimi, what are you doing?" Rand shouted behind her, "You aren't going to try it again? Kimi?"

She would not be stopped. Even as he galloped toward her, Kimi spurred the big horse and raced again toward the wall. For a long, heart-stopping moment, they hung in midair, Kimi leaning into the jump, urging the horse, giving her plenty of rein. Onyx hit the ground on the other side, bits of turf flying, and kept running. Behind her, she heard a cheer going up from some of the men and gasps and murmurs of shock from most of the women.

"Did you see that? Riding astride like a man!"

"The lace on her drawers is showing! Has she no shame?"

Kimi ignored them, and kept galloping. Up ahead the huntsman and Jon Erikson, master of the hunt, had dismounted, while the hounds ran about in confusion, sniffing the air and yelping.

Mr. Erikson smiled at her. "Well, young lady, you beat Lenore and Vanessa here. Too bad the hounds have lost the trail."

Kimi heaved a sigh of relief. "Then we won't kill the fox?"

"No," Jon took off his hat, wiped his face. "We'll go back to Randolph Hall and have a big hunt breakfast and some good Kentucky bourbon."

Kimi shook her head as she dismounted. "The breakfast sounds good."

Behind her came the rest of the hunters, their horses lathered and tired. The men seemed to be looking at her with veiled admiration, but the women appeared shocked and hostile.

Rand swung down. "Kimi, are you all right?"

She nodded, patting Onyx. "Good girl."

Vanessa and Lenore reined in, glared at Kimi. "It's not proper for a lady to ride astride."

Kimi glared back. "Is it proper for ladies to try to set a guest up for a deliberate nasty spill?"

Rand smiled, slapped his whip against his leg as

343

if he'd like to use it on the pair of conspirators. "Sister, Kimi only gave you two tit for tat, even if it was a little unorthodox." There was admiration in his eyes and his voice.

Shelby leaned on his horse's neck and grinned. "Sweet Jesus, what a sight! My congratulations, Miss Kimi, on a great ride."

She felt triumphant and justified. However, when Kimi looked around, she saw the hostility on the faces of most of the women and some of the men. "Isn't that the young savage who's been raised by the Indians? She behaves like poor white trash."

Judge Hamilton had driven his buggy out to see the end of the hunt and now he chuckled as he stepped down. "Young lady, you're not only a good rider, you've got spunk! Allow me to drive you back to Randolph Hall." He lowered his voice to a whisper. "I do hope you're coming to Carstairs Oaks tonight for the little dinner party; Elizabeth told me to extend an invitation. She admires spunk."

Kimi looked around at the closed, hostile faces and the frown in Vanessa and Lenore's eyes. She did not belong in this group of elegant people, and she could not earn her way into it. She would have to be landed gentry, born to wealth and privilege to ever become part of them, part of Rand's life. She couldn't win, but she was too valiant to give Rand up without a fight.

She smiled at the Judge. "Why, of course I'll consider that a personal invitation, sir." Kimi tried to appear confident, but her heart was aching as the judge helped her into the buggy and tied Onyx on behind.

Nineteen

Kimi never got a chance to speak to Rand when they got back to Randolph Hall because of the crowd that gathered for the hunt breakfast and stayed to drink and visit. No one seemed to have any work to do except the blacks. While a few of the men complimented her on her morning's performance, the majority of those present, particularly the women, seemed chilly and distant. Snobs, Kimi thought, or friends of Lenore Carstairs. Rand's parents had evidently heard about it, because Mr. Erikson seemed to be almost smiling for a change, but his mother glared at her. More and more, Kimi realized the vast chasm between her and these rich people.

On the other hand, Rand seemed to fit in easily, although he didn't look as if he were having all that much fun. In fact, he didn't look much happier than his father, who appeared to have already been drinking at this early hour. For a man with wealth, land and a socially prominent wife, Jon looked almost tragic. Yet he belonged to this local wealthy gentry, a closed group that seemingly did not accept outsiders into their midst.

She stood there talking to the judge, feeling awkward and out of place. Every time she looked up, Rand was watching her. She had a distinct feeling that he wanted to talk, but Lenore hung onto his arm as if she never intended to let go. Shelby Merson seemed to be watching her, too, but Vanessa kept him occupied. Kimi could hear the silly banter and giggles from the women. They seemed insipid and shallow.

Later that afternoon, when everyone was gone, Kimi hoped to be able to speak to Rand. However, the next thing she knew, Lenore and Jon Erikson had taken Rand out to inspect the year's crop of colts, and Kimi found herself alone in her room.

A knock at the door. Who could that be? "Come in."

Mrs. Erikson entered, smiling and self-satisfied, wheezing a little in her tight corset. "Kimi, I thought while everyone else was gone, we might have a little talk."

"Yes?" Kimi offered her a chair, sat down on her bed.

"I don't quite know how to put this delicately, my dear." Her stern expression said the lady didn't intend to be delicate at all. "And your background or whatever relationship you might have had with my son is really none of my business."

Kimi steeled herself and looked her in the eye. "When people say something is none of their business, why do they always follow that with questions that are none of their business?"

"My! You are quite blunt, aren't you?" Mrs. Erikson's nervous hands fluttered. Her eyes were as cold as pale blue ice. "Very well, then, we'll get right to it. I had my son's attention diverted this afternoon just so you and I could have a little chat. Naturally you won't tell him we had it."

"Naturally. I suspect you think it would anger him. Hinzi is a little more independent than you might think."

"Hinzi?"

"It was his name among the Sioux. It means 'Yellow Hair.' "

"How quaint." She fanned herself even though the room was not warm. "Kimi, Randolph is not a savage; he's from some of the bluest blood in Kentucky and along with his background comes money and position, and responsibility."

She knew what was coming. "Mrs. Erikson, let me assure you I have no interest in your son's money or position."

"But you are interested in my son?" She leaned closer, her frame tense.

Kimi started to deny it, realized it must show in her face. She said nothing.

"My side of the family, the Randolphs, have always bred thoroughbred horses. To us, background and breeding are of utmost importance."

"And I come without a pedigree, unable to tell you whether I come from a proper dam and sire?"

The lady smoothed a pleat in her full skirt. "Correct. Rand will marry Lenore Carstairs. Everything about her is perfect — family, social position. Since her father, mother, and younger sister are presumed lost on a trip West, Lenore will be the heir to the vast Carstairs fortune. It has always been my dearest wish that we combine the two biggest land holdings in this county by his marrying Lenore."

"What about Rand's wishes?" Kimi said. "Did you even ask him? What about love and his happiness?"

"Love! It is very much overrated."

347

"Is it?" Kimi flared back. "Somehow I doubt that you know very much about it. Your husband is the saddest-looking person I ever met."

Rose Erikson stood up, bristling. "You are not only a nobody, you are impudent besides. Totally unsuitable!" Her nervous hands fluttered. "Very well, I can be forthright, too. Rand could be disinherited if he goes against his family's wishes. I don't know what went on between you and my son before and I really don't care. Men will be men, after all. However, when good sense prevails and parents have a little talk, a young man generally sees the light and marries properly and in his own class."

Suddenly Kimi realized why Jon Erikson looked so unhappy. "And did someone have 'a little talk' with your husband's 'unsuitable' woman?"

"There was no need," Mrs. Erikson snapped as if without thinking. "His mother sold her! She was only a mulatto—" She took a deep breath, paused, as if realizing she had let herself be led into revealing things she didn't want known. "You will not marry my son, you little snip." Her voice was cold with barely held anger.

She could not win, Kimi realized that. Even if she let Rand send her off to school, turn her into a lady, his mother would never accept her. Hadn't she known that all along? "What is it you want me to do?" She was resigned to defeat. All this could only hurt Rand.

Kimi wondered what had happened to that long-ago slave girl? Jon Erikson must regret his bargain. No wonder he drank. But Kimi had seen her future in Rose Erikson's cold eyes. No matter how much she loved Rand, this was never going to work out. She wasn't part of this aristocratic life, and the stubborn set of Rose Erikson's chin let Kimi know the social leader would see to it that Kimi was never accepted. All she could do by staying on was create more problems for Rand. Perhaps his mother was right; perhaps he would be better off with Lenore. Should she tell Rand about this conversation? What good would it do? It wouldn't change anything.

"Tonight we all have an invitation to the Carstairs for refreshments. I understand Judge Hamilton invited you also."

"You want me not to go?"

Mrs. Erikson shrugged. "Of course you will go; it would create too many explanations if you didn't. We intend to announce my son's engagement to Lenore at the Harvest Ball we are giving here Saturday night."

"You want me to be gone by then?"

The woman nodded as she went to the door, turned. "Tell Rand whatever you like; just leave here in the next day or so. I will offer you our hospitality, tell you how welcome you are to stay, but of course you won't accept my offer. Please do not leave any clues as to where he can find you. I want this to be a clear break."

Kimi closed her eyes a long moment, seeing Rand's beloved face in her mind. She could not win. The Eriksons, the Carstairs, and all their family friends would be allied against her. In the end, she could only make Rand unhappy. "I love your son; but that doesn't matter to you, does it?"

"Not one whit!" The woman paused, her hand on the doorknob. "I am doing what I have to do, just as Jon's mother did. If you tell my son about our little conversation, I'll deny it. Rand has always been wealthy. I don't know how he would survive if

349

he were to be disinherited. Do you understand me?"

Unable to speak, Kimi could only nod.

"The carriage will be ready at six," Rose said.

"I don't think I feel like going to the Carstairs," Kimi said.

"Oh, but you must! I want you to see what you've been up against from the start." She left the room with a rustle of hoops and skirts.

Kimi collapsed on her bed and wept.

When Rand knocked on her door later and said, "Kimi? Can we talk?" She pretended to be napping and didn't answer. She didn't want to face him alone. If he took her in his arms and kissed her, her resolve would melt, and she might not be able to leave. Where was she going to go? What did it matter? That was the least of her worries. Perhaps she could find a job in another state as a maid or helping in some small shop.

Tomorrow, she thought. Tonight I will get through this thing at the Carstairs and tomorrow I will tell Rand I really don't care about him and am going away.

The evening came too soon. Millie helped her bathe and dress in the low-cut green dress Vanessa had given her. Kimi put her medicine charm on the slender gold chain and hooked the clasp around her slender neck. It lay in the hollow of her throat just above the swell of her breasts. Rand tried once again to talk to her, but when he knocked at her door, she called that she was busy getting dressed and she'd see him downstairs when it was time to leave.

Finally it was time and Kimi was ready. Millie smiled, showing white teeth in frank admiration. "You looks good, Miz Kimi, much prettier dan de gal his mama chose."

"Pilamaya."

"What you say?"

"It's Lakota. It means 'thanks.' " Kimi felt too heartsick to care how she looked.

She waited until she was sure everyone else was ready and the carriage waiting out front before she came out of her room in a swirl of willow green and hoop skirts. But Rand waylaid her in the upstairs hall. "Why have you been avoiding me?"

She looked away and tried to pull out of his grasp. "We've both been so busy."

He pulled her to him, kissed down her neck and along the swell of her breasts. "You were wonderful this morning and a little outrageous, too."

His mouth covered hers for a long moment and she swayed against him, weakening at the insistent pressure of his hard body against her. She forced herself to pull away. "Really, Rand, someone will see us."

He was breathing hard, his eyes intense with longing. "I'm not sure I care what's proper anymore."

"Your family would. I can just imagine the servants' gossip spreading all over the county that Marse Rand was making love to that no-count white savage girl in the upstairs hall." With that, she forced herself to pull out of his arms and hurried down the stairs and out to the carriage.

They drove over with little conversation except

between Vanessa and her mother about fashions and social events. Kimi wondered resignedly if the two shallow women ever talked about anything else. When she caught Kimi's eye, Mrs. Erikson's gaze was triumphant and self-satisfied. Rand stared out across the beautifully manicured meadows and white-fenced pastures, boredom etched on his handsome face. His pitiful father had already been drinking this evening. Kimi could smell it on him.

It was dusk as they drove down the lane under a long expanse of giant oaks so big their branches met in the middle and provided a canopy. Absently, Kimi clutched her medicine charm and peered at the house as the carriage approached an imposing brick mansion with big white pillars, a large glass conservatory on the east side. Somewhere a cicada began its rhythmic chirping, and a tall black butler waited on the porch to welcome them. Strange tattoos were etched on his stolid, square face. He looked almost menacing.

Kimi was struck with a sense of deja vu as if somewhere in her past, she had experienced a home like this one. *Of course you have, silly,* she reminded herself, *it's a lot like Randolph Hall.* Perhaps all Southern plantation homes seemed much alike. She wasn't looking forward to this evening.

The carriage stopped and the butler opened the carriage door. He didn't speak, he only nodded as he assisted them from the carriage. Had the Carstairs' butler come to Randolph Hall in the last day or two? Yes, that's where she must have seen him. Or maybe the Randolphs had a servant who looked a little like him.

They went in to be met by Judge Hamilton in the front hall with hearty greetings. "Welcome! Welcome! Elizabeth is waiting in the music room."

He took Kimi's hand warmly. "Great Caesar's ghost! Glad you were able to make it, young lady, that was quite a ride this morning."

"Yes," Mrs. Erikson said, "I understand she made quite a spectacle of herself."

"Now, Mother," Rand began.

"What did I say?" Mrs. Erikson feigned hurt astonishment.

The judge seemed to decide to smooth things over. "Let's go on in. Lenore will be down in a moment. Here, young lady, I admire your feisty nature. Let me escort you." He offered Kimi his arm and she took it, noting in the meantime the annoyance on Mrs. Erikson and Vanessa's faces.

About that time, Lenore swept down the stairs in an elegant daffodil yellow gown of rustling silk—a grand entrance that Kimi was sure had been perfectly planned. "For pity's sake! Am I late?" she cooed. "I do apologize."

There was an exchange of greetings, during which Lenore ignored Kimi. Then she took Rand's arm and led the way into the music room. She walked with a mincing, off-balance step, Kimi thought, and it dawned on her that Lenore was attempting to downplay her large feet by wearing shoes that were much too small. No wonder there seemed to be a perpetual frowning expression on her pretty face.

There was something almost hauntingly familiar about this room, Kimi thought as she entered and looked around. She couldn't remember whether Rand's home had a music room or not. Perhaps she had heard one described or dreamed of one like this. It was done in pastels, fine Oriental rugs with a large fireplace and glimmering lamp light, not the gaudy, dark Victorian look that Rand's mother favored.

The others were busy greeting each other. Shelby Merson arrived, bringing with him the aroma of cheap hair oil. Before she could finish looking about, the judge diverted her attention. "Here, my dear, I want to introduce you to Mrs. James Carstairs, mistress of Carstairs Oaks. Elizabeth, this is the young lady I told you about."

"Hello, Kimi. So glad you could come." She held out a frail hand and Kimi took it. The elderly lady peered at her a long moment. "Have we met before?"

"Not if you weren't on the fox hunt this morning."

Mrs. Carstairs laughed easily. "I heard about it. Pierce said he hadn't seen such spunk and spirit since I took a whip away from a slave trader to save a boy's life."

Kimi wondered what had happened to the young boy. Then she looked up and saw the strange, tattooed butler look with adoration at the old lady and knew. She hadn't been prepared to like Lenore's grandmother, but she found herself warming to her in spite of everything. There was something haunting about this majestic lady, Kimi thought as she accepted a glass of sherry. If she could choose a grandmother, Elizabeth Carstairs seemed to fit the image she had pictured.

Then Kimi caught sight of the big grand piano near the fireplace. "Oh, may I?"

"Do you play, my dear?"

"I—I don't think so." Kimi shook her head, fascinated by the instrument. It was as if there was some magic here that pulled at her. Without thinking, she walked over to the piano, put down her glass of sherry, and stroked the keys with her left

354

hand. Rose, Lenore and Vanessa smirked, obviously thinking she was about to make a fool of herself again.

Kimi ran her fingers over the ivory keys, liking the feel of them. She struggled with her thoughts for a long moment, realizing the others were staring in silence. She didn't care; a memory was trying hard to surface. Slowly she picked out a melody, one slow note at a time with her left hand: *Alas, my love, you do me wrong to caste me off discourteously, and I have loved you for so long. . . .*

She heard Mrs. Carstairs gasp, and when she looked up, the elderly lady had gone pale and the others were frowning. "Have I done something wrong?"

Mrs. Carstairs took a deep breath. "I just haven't heard anyone but me play that in many, many years."

"It was his favorite song," Kimi whispered.

Elizabeth Carstairs stared at her. "How do you know that? Who are you speaking of?"

Kimi blinked uncertainly. "I don't know." She had to find that shadowy memory that came and went. *She had to.* She began to pick notes out again: *Greensleeves was all my joy, Greensleeves was my delight. . . .*

Lenore glared at her. "What kind of cruel joke is this?"

Mrs. Erikson took a deep, wheezing breath and her hands fluttered. "I must apologize for my houseguest, Elizabeth, but she doesn't know any better."

Rand shot his mother a black look and said gently, "Kimi, I don't really think you should play Mrs. Carstairs' piano without her permission."

"I'm sorry, I meant no harm," she turned toward the old lady, realizing the others in the room were glaring at her in grim disapproval.

Mrs. Carstairs cleared her throat, touched her lips with a handkerchief. "My little granddaughter was left-handed, too. She used to sit on my lap and pick that out. It was her father's favorite song." She gestured toward the painting on the opposite wall.

For the first time, Kimi saw the painting. Almost in a trance, she moved across the room to stare up at it.

Rand watched her. What on earth did Kimi think she was doing? The judge and Mrs. Carstairs stared at her, the others were glaring in frank disapproval of her rudeness. "Kimi," he said, and went to her side, "I think perhaps . . ."

Kimi seemed entranced by the painting as if she had not heard a word he said. She clasped the gold charm in her hand and turned very pale as her gaze swept over the portrait.

Rand paused, looking up at the painting. He had grown so used to it hanging there, he hadn't really looked at it in years. He just barely remembered that it was a portrait of Lenore's family who had left many years ago. Rand had been a small boy then. He took a good long look at the people in the portrait, the gold fob on the man's watch, the beauty with the white flowers tucked in the low bodice of her dress. Kimi reached up to put her hand on the beauty's face. "She would never let us call her 'mama,' " she whispered. And then she said her own name. "Kimimila."

Rand glanced at the white blossoms in the beauty's low-cut bodice and an impossible idea came to him. "Mrs. Carstairs, what—what was your daughter-in-law's name?"

The old lady was already on her feet, her lovely face pale as the snowy blossoms. She looked from Kimi to the painting. "Camelia."

Kimi nodded, still lost in the painting. "Camelia, and Sister and Daddy and little Laurel."

Rand stared at her. Camelia. Kimimila. Could it possibly be—?

The judge cleared his throat. "This isn't funny, young lady. I'll not have you upsetting Elizabeth—" He paused, took a really good look at Kimi. "Great Caesar's ghost . . ."

The elderly lady looked visibly angry. "What is it, Pierce?" She crossed the room to Kimi's side. "Now, see here young lady, I don't know what kind of prank you're pulling, but it's gone far enough—"

At that point, she seemed to see the spirit object hanging on a chain around Kimi's neck. With a cry, the old lady gasped and fainted dead away.

The next several minutes were a blur of confusion to Kimi, with maids running for smelling salts, Mrs. Erikson and Vanessa's shocked faces, and Lenore screaming that this primitive savage couldn't possibly be her missing baby sister. Rand didn't say anything. He only stared at her with wide eyes as if he'd never really looked at her before.

Kimi felt bewildered as the memories came flooding back and she answered questions. She didn't have very many answers.

Lenore's pretty face screwed into a mask of jealousy and anger. "I think she's a fake! She

357

doesn't remember very much."

The judge looked Kimi over. "A two-year-old wouldn't remember very much, I'm afraid, but she looks like Camelia, except for the eyes. No wonder we all keep thinking we've met her before. I'd say she's a Carstairs: green eyes like Jim's, left-handed, and she's got the gold acorn from his watch fob."

Elizabeth Carstairs lay on the sofa while the judge rubbed her frail hand. Obviously the shock had been almost too much for her. When she recovered somewhat, she plied Kimi with questions. "What—what do you remember besides what you've told us? Do you remember the night you all left here? The trip?" She looked almost afraid that Kimi might.

Lenore stuck her face close to Kimi's. "Yes, tell us about that night. Do you remember the thunder?"

"Thunder?" Kimi asked, bewildered.

"Never mind, Lenore," the judge said hurriedly.

Kimi shook her head. "I—I don't remember much except a man carrying me in his arms. He hummed my spirit song."

Mrs. Carstairs looked questioningly at Rand. "Greensleeves," he explained. "Mrs. Carstairs, how old would your missing granddaughter be?"

Before she could answer, Kimi answered that herself. "Eighteen winter counts."

The white-haired lady blinked. "That's right."

Rand slapped his hand against his thigh. "I've been three kinds of a fool."

Kimi stared at the painting, still dredging up forgotten memories. "Lost. Thirsty, very thirsty."

Rand stepped in at that point and volunteered what little he knew of old Wagnuka's husband finding the child in a dying man's arms out in the wilderness, the bodies scattered along the trail as if a wagon train had gotten lost and the people tried to walk out.

Elizabeth sighed deeply. Tragedy was etched in the wrinkles of her lovely old face. "I suppose I always knew it. Somehow I just kept hoping—"

"But what about the rest of them?" Lenore demanded, pushing her face close to Kimi's. "What about Camelia?"

She tried to remember, then shook her head helplessly. "I don't recall anything else."

Vanessa and Mrs. Erikson still looked skeptical. The older woman fanned herself and wheezed. "Surely, Elizabeth, you aren't going to take the word of this waif that she's your missing granddaughter?"

Mrs. Carstairs glared at her. "Rose, you knew my daughter-in-law and my son. Can you not look Kimi in the face and see she looks like both of them?"

"Now, Mrs. Carstairs," Vanessa soothed, "maybe you're seeing a resemblance that's not really there; I mean, just because this ragtag girl has green eyes. Why, look at Lenore; you *know* she's your granddaughter and while she looks more like her mother than this Kimi does, she doesn't have green eyes and isn't left-handed, so that doesn't mean anything."

Kimi saw Elizabeth Carstairs glance toward Judge Hamilton. A look passed between them that she couldn't quite understand. The old man stroked his gray mustache. "If you want to know what I think, Elizabeth, I would stake my life that this is Laurel."

"What I never understood, Elizabeth," Mrs. Erikson mused, "was why Jim and Camelia left so suddenly in the first place?"

The old lady hesitated and the judge stepped in. "Like she's told everyone many times, they had made plans months before to go West. Jim had a hankering to take the Oregon Trail. They were going to send for Lenore later and then come back and visit when they finally got settled."

"Oh, don't lie, Pierce. Yes, there was a family fuss," Elizabeth admitted grudgingly, looking at Rand's mother. "If you remember my daughter-in-law, we never got on well."

The other lady nodded in sudden understanding. "Well, of course everyone knew she wasn't from as fine a family as the Carstairs. But she was such a great beauty, that none of us were surprised when Jim met and married her so quickly over in Memphis."

"Yes, Camelia was a great beauty," Elizabeth agreed. "She could turn any man's head." There was an infinite sadness in her gray eyes. "At least I finally know what happened and can quit hoping. Pierce, call my butler in."

The judge went to the bell pull, rang it. After several minutes, the big tattooed man came into the room. "Yes, Miz Elizabeth?"

She motioned toward Kimi, still standing by the painting. "Take a good look at that girl."

There was a deathly silence and a question on the big black's face as he turned and took a long look at Kimi. As he stared, his expression grew more and more troubled. He looked from her to the painting, back again. Very slowly, he crossed the room, still staring at her. "Miz Laurel, is it you?"

Part of the memory fell into place. His name; she knew his name. "Yes, Nero, it's really me." She began to cry.

Elizabeth sat up on the sofa. "That does it," she said and held out her arms to Kimi. "Welcome home, dear, we have a lot to make up for."

"Nana," Kimi wept and went into her arms.

"Yes, that's what you called me," Elizabeth said softly, "Oh, Laurel, if you only knew—" She began to weep.

Rand blinked back tears at the touching scene. His father looked as if he couldn't quite deal with this show of raw emotion and the judge pulled out a handkerchief to blow his nose loudly. Shelby appeared to be quite disturbed. He kept looking from Kimi to Lenore, shaking his head and playing absently with his diamond stickpin. Only the other three women looked betrayed and angry.

Rose Erikson seemed dismayed and annoyed as she fanned hard. "If I were you, Elizabeth, I wouldn't take her at face value. She may be a fake, trading on your loss."

"You aren't me, Rose, and I don't remember asking your opinion." The elderly lady had recovered her spunk.

It had been a long time since he had seen his mother at a loss for words. He rather enjoyed watching her mouth open and close like a surprised fish thrown up on a river bank. Then she seemed to remember Elizabeth Carstairs was the richest woman in the county and not one to offend. "Elizabeth," she said gently, "perhaps we should cancel the big harvest ball? I mean, with this news of your son and his wife's deaths, it might not be socially correct—"

"No, don't cancel it," Elizabeth said firmly.

"With all the invitations already out for Saturday night, it would be difficult to cancel at this late date anyway." She sighed and looked at her veined hands. "After all, it must have happened almost sixteen years ago. I reckon I've always known it all along deep in my heart. I just wouldn't face it." She smiled at Kimi. "At least some good has come of this tragedy."

Lenore glared at Kimi. "For pity's sake! So what do we do about her?"

"That's not a charitable attitude toward your sister," Elizabeth said.

"Sister?" Lenore was no longer the cooing flirt. Her voice rose like a fish wife. Are you really going to accept this—this savage as my sister?"

The judge smiled. "Perhaps you didn't understand your grandmother, my dear. Laurel or Kimi, or whatever name she goes by, is a Carstairs." He turned to Kimi. "Of course beginning tonight, your grandmother will expect you to live here."

Kimi was so overcome with emotion that she couldn't speak for a long moment. *"Pilamaya,"* she managed to say finally. She didn't know what to think and she was overwhelmed by all of this.

They got through the rest of the evening and dinner with Kimi almost in a daze. All she could think of was that now she was on an equal footing with Lenore. Did that mean she had a chance with Rand? Not the way his mother was giving Kimi black looks.

Shelby Merson and then the Eriksons departed, Rand whispering softly that they would talk later.

Lenore had flounced off to bed in a huff, saying she still didn't believe this poor white trash could possibly be a Carstairs.

Kimi still felt in a state of shock and disbelief as she looked from the judge to the white-haired lady.

Pierce Hamilton took both her hands in his. "Welcome home, Laurel. Your grandmother has waited so long for this. If you only knew . . ."

She waited for him to go on, but instead he cleared his throat, and fumbled with his pipe.

She was abruptly weary. Her grandmother seemed to notice and motioned for the judge to ring for a servant. A maid escorted Kimi up to a sumptuous room, complete with a delicate lace nightdress and a promise of dozens of lovely dresses as soon as possible. Kimi lay staring at the ceiling a long time, thinking of her father whom she could barely remember. Only one thing more seemed important to her; if she were indeed a Carstairs, would the snooty friends of both families accept her and now would she have a chance of upsetting Mrs. Erikson's plans and marrying Rand?

On the other hand, did she want him if he would only consider marrying her after he found out she was from a wealthy, blue-blooded family and would undoubtedly come into half the Carstairs' estate?

Lenore tiptoed down the dark stairs barefooted. She couldn't sleep after what had happened here this evening, and she wanted a glass of milk and a piece of pecan pie. The house was quiet but a light shone under the closed music room door. Just what was happening? Was that little savage going through Grandmother's things? If she could catch that Kimi up to no good, she might convince Grandmother to toss the twit out. She didn't know

363

and didn't care whether this savage was in reality her baby sister. While she didn't know how she was going to do it just yet, Lenore had no intentions of sharing the Carstairs wealth or Rand Erikson with Kimi.

As for her parents, if they were dead out there somewhere in the wilderness, Lenore had lost interest in that subject long ago. Mostly she was interested in herself and how events affected her own welfare. Why had this Kimi turned up just when Lenore had things going her way? She'd had such great plans to marry Rand, continue sleeping with Shelby, and bide her time until Grandmother died or Lenore figured out how to place her at Rose Haven so Lenore would have a free hand with the estate. As for old Nero, she intended to fire him the moment Grandmother was out of the way. She had never liked the tattooed black servant anyway, and he certainly had no loyalty to her.

When she tiptoed to the music room door and listened, she recognized Grandmother and Judge Hamilton's voices. Lenore had a talent for eavesdropping. She peeked through the keyhole and watched them eating a late supper in front of the cozy fire.

Pierce Hamilton wiped his mustache with his napkin. "So now what do you intend to do about your estate? I suggest you divide it equally between them, so there won't be any gossip later as there would be if it all goes to the one."

Elizabeth Carstairs paused with her tea cup at her lips. "I don't know. I suppose you're right, but my heart's not in it. Dead. Hard to believe." She sighed audibly. "I thought maybe they'd been afraid to contact me, afraid that the secret had come out and the law was looking for him."

The judge filled his pipe and lit it thoughtfully. "How much do you suppose Lenore remembers of that night? After all, she was five years old."

"Not much, I think." Grandmother stared into the fire. "She mentioned the thunder this evening; I think that's all she recalls."

He blew savory smoke toward the ceiling, sipped his coffee. "Maybe we shouldn't have tried to cover it up."

"I have no regrets." She looked at him. "I would do anything, *anything* to protect the Carstairs name from scandal." There was steely resolve in her voice.

"Great Caesar's ghost." He nodded in understanding. "Don't you think I know that? Still and all, it's been a terrible thing for you to deal with all these years."

"No more than you, Pierce. Whether it was an accident or not, if your part in it ever came out, you would be disgraced."

"I would help you all over again, Elizabeth. I love you; I've always loved you. Your husband was my best friend, and I did all I could in helping rear his son. Jim was the son I never had, and the one I might have had if I had met you before your husband did."

She reached out and patted his hand absently. "You're a dear friend, Pierce, but no man ever had a chance after I met him. If something should happen to me, remember that I wanted you to turn Carstairs Oaks into a school or a home for the underprivileged. You should go into politics. This country needs men like you."

"Don't talk that way, my dear," he laughed and puffed his pipe. "You act as if you know something I don't know."

"Do I?"

The fox hound pup got up from before the fire, yawned and stretched, and ambled over to beg off her plate. She fed it a bite. "I suppose I will let you change my will. Give each girl half. That way, my granddaughter will be protected from scandal. As you said, people will whisper if I leave one out. While it upsets me to see my money go to that gambler's offspring, I must protect my family name at any cost. No one, not even the two girls must know that one of them is not really a Carstairs!"

Lenore gasped in surprise. So that was why her Grandmother was so willing to accept that Kimi into the family. Lenore just barely remembered that Daddy was sometimes gone into Louisville on business, and sometimes, when he was gone, another man came to call on Camelia. Once she had seen them kissing in the dark on the east lawn. She searched her memory. He was dark, too, and handsome. What could she remember from that final night? Spring, very warm. Her upstairs bedroom looked out over the east lawn and her window was open. Angry voices. A scream. Thunder. What had happened?

Lenore tried to recall more, but she only remembered putting her pillow over her head and going back to sleep. Had Camelia and her lover done something terrible to Daddy and then fled with their bastard baby?

Would Elizabeth Carstairs help cover up something like the murder of her own son? To protect the Carstairs name, and reputation, the old lady was capable of anything. With a smug smile, Lenore tiptoed back up to her room to think and plan. She wasn't sure how she was going to use this newfound knowledge yet, but one thing she did know for sure—Lenore wasn't about to share her inheritance with her mother's bastard by some white trash gambler. No, she wouldn't share, not even to protect the family name. When it came to a choice, Lenore would rather have the money, *all* of it.

Blackmail. Whatever had happened that long ago night, Grandmother and Judge Hamilton were hiding at least a scandal, and maybe a crime. Lenore lay in bed and smiled with satisfaction. She wanted not only all the inheritance but a chance to get rid of her bastard sister so that Rand would never be tempted by her again. And Saturday night, Lenore would announce her engagement to Rand Erikson at the autumn ball.

Twenty

Kimi awakened at the sound of the door chimes downstairs and looked around. Where was she? Her gaze swept over the elegant spacious bedroom. Then everything came flooding back. Yes, there was something familiar about this room after all these years. While she remembered little else about her past besides what she had told her grandmother, she did recognize the old bedroom. Laurel Carstairs. She was rich and from an acceptable family. Did that mean that now she could become Mrs. Rand Erikson? And yet . . . Kimi had a conscience. Could she wreck her newly found sister's future marriage, no matter how mean Lenore had been to her?

Stretching and yawning, she reached for a delicate velvet robe. Someone knocked on the door.

"Miz Laurel?" One of the young maids.

"Yes?"

"Marse Rand is here."

Kimi hesitated. Did he want her now that she might meet with his mother's approval? Would he have cared enough to defy his family and marry her anyway even if she hadn't? The knowledge that now she might never know annoyed and troubled her as much as the fact that he was her sister's fiancée. "Tell him I'll be down in a minute."

What should she wear? The wardrobe was full of Lenore's old clothes, most of them still lovely. The biggest problem with being a civilized girl was all the miserable tight corsets. Besides that, she was beginning to think they had too many rules to live by and never had any fun. She had been much happier among the Indians. She got dressed but had to wear the old shoes Vanessa had given her. Lenore's were much too large for Kimi's small feet.

She went down to greet Rand, who sat in the conservatory. He looked handsome in his expensive, handmade clothes that fitted his wide shoulders and accentuated his trim body. He'd left the French doors open and the fox hound puppy was sniffing and digging under the camelia bush.

"Hello, Rand, I've asked the maid to have Nero bring some coffee, sweet rolls, and fresh fruit out for us."

He rose, took both her hands in his. "Hello Kimi, or should I call you Laurel?"

She shook her head. "I honestly don't know who I am any more, but I still think of myself as Kimi. None of this seems very real."

"But this is every girl's dream, to wake up rich with a fine house and beautiful clothes," he reminded her.

"Is it?" The stays of the corset seemed to be cutting into her flesh. She noticed the puppy, the dirt flying. "Oh my! Tally Ho, stop that! You'll dig up Nana's flowers and she'll be very upset!" She looked at the bush thoughtfully, remembering. "White camellias were my mother's favorite flower."

The puppy had stopped digging at her reprimand. Just then, Nero came in with a silver tray full of delicacies and saw the fresh dirt. "That dog! Pup, you better stop! Miz Elizabeth goan' be real mad!" He set the tray down on the wicker table and gathered the puppy up in his arms. "Miz Elizabeth don't 'low him in here."

"I can see why." Rand laughed and slapped his quirt against his leg absently as Nero went out the French doors, carrying the dog.

Kimi poured them both some coffee from the ornate silver pot. "Cream?"

He shook his head and accepted the delicate china cup.

She poured fresh cream into her own strong coffee and tasted it. On this crisp autumn morning, it tasted good. They breakfasted in silence, Kimi spreading fresh butter and homemade blackberry jam on her roll. "So how did your mother and sister react on the drive home last night?"

"Need you ask?" He stared down at his cup. "About the way Lenore did, I reckon. They aren't convinced you aren't a fake and even if you aren't, they prefer Lenore because, as my mother says, 'anyone can tell she's really a Carstairs. Class and breeding shows.' "

"I suppose it does. Your sister, Lenore, and most of your social set have been terribly rude and cruel to me ever since I arrived. There are some things money and good finishing schools can't buy." She set her cup on the fine silver tray, debated with herself as to whether to tell him about the conversation with his mother, and decided against it.

"I'm sorry, Kimi, I know everyone's been beastly to you." He set his cup aside, took her hand in his. "I think everyone will be very friendly from now on."

"Because now I have money, and that makes a difference, doesn't it? And they call the Sioux 'savages.' " She tried to keep the bitterness out of her voice, and failed. She pulled her hand from his. "I suppose even your mother might eventually find me acceptable, since she figures the Carstairs estate is sizable and I'll be an heir."

He looked a little sheepish. "Life here doesn't seem as satisfying as I remember it. I don't think things have changed much, but maybe I have." He flexed his shoulders as if his muscles were tense.

She looked around at the beautiful greenery, the flowers, the ornate silver and china on the wicker table. For a long moment, she thought of the simple, satisfying life they had shared in their own tipi. She missed that.

Rand picked up his quirt and slapped it against his leg absently. "I'd forgotten how many rules and regulations we have to live by in white society. Life seemed so much freer and more enjoyable when I was among the Sioux. And I miss One Eye, Gopher, and Saved By the Wolf." He looked at her eagerly. "You know what I'd like to do? Why don't we get a picnic basket and go to the creek for the afternoon?"

For a moment, her mood brightened, then she remembered and shook her head. "I can't. Appointment with the dressmaker and a trip into the village to look at fabrics and calling cards and all the rest of the things white society girls require. I'm supposed to have a dress for the ball that will turn every girl in the county green with envy."

"You don't sound too happy about it."

"I miss our wild, free days among the Lakota, too."

"Mother is insisting on announcing my engagement to Lenore at the ball. She's threatening to disinherit me if I don't fall into line."

"Are you going to be like your father, Rand?"

"What?" He appeared puzzled and she knew he didn't know. She looked at him a long moment, so civilized and dressed like a rich white man's son, sitting there comfortably looking the part of the country squire after a rich breakfast served with the best crystal and china.

Abruptly she realized that she wasn't in love with the oh, so civilized and so impeccably dressed Rand Erikson; she was in love with Hinzi, the white warrior. She had a fleeting vision of his brawny, hairy chest, his painted face as he swept her up and carried her into his tipi. That was the man she loved — decisive, commanding, strong. "Rand, what are you doing sitting here? You're engaged to my sister. There'll be hell to pay if she comes downstairs and finds you with me."

He took both her hands in his. "Kimi, I love you."

She couldn't resist hurting him as he had hurt her. "Now that I'm a Carstairs, you say that. Otherwise, you would have kept me for a mistress."

"That's not true. I'm going to have a talk with my mother about breaking the engagement, then I'll have to tell Lenore. Maybe I won't be disinherited."

It occurred to her that he would expect that Kimi would get a sizable inheritance, so it wouldn't be such a great sacrifice for him. Like his father, he would live off his wife's money. "Breaking the engagement will be embarrassing; everyone's expecting the announcement."

"Would you believe I don't give a damn?" He looked out of sorts.

She shook her head. "Think about it a long time, Rand. Even with the Carstairs money and background, some of your friends and relatives will never accept me. Life could be very miserable for both of us."

"You can learn to be everything Lenore is; you're smarter and prettier. You can show them all."

Now it was her time to sigh pensively. "Would you believe I don't give a damn about showing them all? I think we've maybe got a chasm here we can't cross,

Rand. Maybe you belong with Lenore after all."

"Are you saying you don't love me?" He put his hands on her shoulders, pulled her to him.

"I don't know what I'm saying." She looked up at him and he seemed almost a stranger to her, this impeccably groomed and well-dressed white man. Did he love her as she was or did he want Laurel Carstairs? Could she ever be that girl? Did she want to be?

And then he kissed her and she clung to him, remembering all the nights she had spent in his arms, their passionate lovemaking.

"Kimi," he whispered, "oh, Kimi, you can be Laurel Carstairs if only you'll put your mind to it! We can have a good life together. You'll learn to read and to waltz and all the other things ladies do."

Ladies. White ladies with their corsets and silly hoop skirts, their mincing, prissy gaits and sidesaddles. She pulled away from him, troubled. "Don't do anything yet until we've both had a chance to think some more."

"What's there to think about?" His expression was intense, aroused.

"Such things can't be decided on the spur of the moment. I'm not sure whether this girl you think you love is a Sioux named Kimimila or a wealthy belle named Laurel Carstairs."

"Don't talk in riddles; they're one in the same."

She shook her head sadly. "No, Rand, I'm not sure they are. I have a lot of thinking of my own to do." She stood up. He stood up, too, and for a long moment, she thought he would take her in his arms. She stepped away from him to discourage that. If he embraced her, that would sway her judgement and lose her control in an eddy of passion. To take her sister's fiancée would create terrible problems for

Kimi, and she wasn't sure his family would ever forgive her. She wasn't sure what her grandmother and the judge would say and their opinions mattered very much to her.

"You need to go; we both have thinking to do," she said again.

"All right, I'll go. Let me know when you're ready to talk." He brought her hand to his mouth and kissed it, then turned and left.

Kimi went back to her room, torn with indecision. Should she listen to her heart or her brain? At least she didn't have to decide anything definite today. She needed to get dressed to go to the dressmaker's. Judge Hamilton had offered to drive her and her grandmother there.

Shelby watched the buggy driving away from the house from where he sat his horse in the shade of a tree. The old lady, the judge, and that pretty girl who'd been raised by the Injuns. Word had spread fast that she was the missing Carstairs heiress. God, he'd like a chance to get her clothes off!

Shelby waited until the buggy had disappeared from sight, then rode around to the conservatory. He knew Lenore's room was right over that. He whistled and tossed pebbles against the window until she stuck her head out and motioned for him to join her in the conservatory.

He tilted his hat at a jaunty angle, went in, and flopped down on the wicker settee. Lenore was a nice enough kid, so was Vanessa Erikson. If he could figure out a way to do it, Shelby would like to end up with the money from both estates and sleep with all three of the girls.

Sweet Jesus, he had really struck a gold mine! Here he had come snooping around this area looking for clues to his missing brother-in-law, and had fallen into all this money and eager women.

Rand was a fly in the ointment. When Shelby had said he'd investigate Rand's whereabouts during the months Rand was missing, he'd lied. Shelby knew Jon Erikson had the money to rescue his son if he found him, and Shelby hoped that Rand was either already dead or rotting away in some military prison. Matter of fact, Shelby had managed to intercept what little mail got through. It would have been so much easier if Vanessa's brother were dead. He rode around to the conservatory and went in.

Lenore hurried through the French doors. "Oh, Shelby, you shouldn't have come. I don't know how long they'll be gone to the dressmaker's."

"For you, honey, any risk is worth it!" He knew what women wanted to hear. He caught her hand and pulled her down beside him and nuzzled her neck. "So tell me what the latest gossip is about the Injun being your long-lost sister?"

Lenore frowned. "For pity's sake, I swear servant gossip travels faster than the telegraph. Grandmother believes her. I think the girl's a fake."

"If Grandma believes her, that's what counts. She's the one with the money." He thought about the irony of it all. All he'd been trying to do was track down his brother-in-law who had run out on his sister so long ago. Not that he gave a damn about his now dead sister, he just remembered something Clint had laughed about. . . .

"It was all so mysterious that night my mother and Father went away," Lenore mused.

"Oh?" What did this chit know that might give him a clue?

"I was only five years old," Lenore said, "but I think my mother was seeing another man when my father was away on business."

Shelby laughed and ran his hand through his greasy hair. "When the cat's away . . ."

"For pity's sake, don't be crude," Lenore snapped and played with her fan.

"Tell me about that night," he urged.

"I remember angry words that woke me up," Lenore said, looking at the camelia bush. "It was warm outside and my window was open. Something was happening on the lawn below my room. That was before the conservatory was built."

He tried not to look too interested. "Did you ever see this other man?"

She shook her head. "Only from a distance. I wouldn't recognize him; handsome, black hair."

And big feet, Shelby remembered. He had suspected Rose Erikson might be the woman. Couldn't tell it now, but he'd heard she had been a beauty a long time ago. "Did you recognize the voices?" Again she shook her head, "I don't even know what happened after that. There was thunder and I was scared so I hid under my pillow."

"Thunder?"

"Well, maybe it wasn't," she admitted, twisting her lace fan. "It wasn't that loud. When I got up the next morning, Mother and Daddy and my little sister had gone away. They were going to send for me later because I was just beginning school."

Thunder, Shelby thought. His brother-in-law was a riverboat gambler. Clint carried a two shot derringer belly gun with ivory inlays.

"Now this chit comes back and claims to be my missing sister, Laurel, and Grandmother accepted her wild story."

"Just what did Kimi say? Could she remember much?"

"No. You know what I think?" She leaned closer. "I think there was a killing that night and Grandmother helped keep the secret."

His brother-in-law wouldn't have any qualms about shooting down an irate husband. What Shelby didn't know was whether Clint would care enough about the lady to take her and run away. "Would your Grandmother be a party to something like that? She strikes me as a sweet and very proper lady."

"For pity's sake don't let that fool you," Lenore said smugly. "Elizabeth Carstairs has a backbone of steel; she's not some weak old lady. I think she would do anything, I mean, *anything* to protect the Carstairs reputation and name. She's never been what I would call a loving grandmother, and now I'm beginning to think I never really knew her at all."

Just as you don't know me. War hero. If only this pretty miss knew how he came by his limp. The medals that so enthralled Lenore, Shelby had taken off a dead man's chest near a battle that Shelby was running from.

"For pity's sake, Shelby, are you listening to me?"

"What? Oh, sure, honey." He fingered the diamond stickpin in his tie.

"After all, this concerns you, too, because of the money."

"Money?" Shelby said. *If only you knew how I came by mine.*

Lenore nodded. "I overheard Grandmother and the judge talking last night about her will. From what I understand, this Kimi is a bastard by Mother's lover, but Grandmother feels she must include her in the will or people will talk, and she doesn't want them to guess that."

A kid. Yes, Clint had said the lady had a child by him that her husband thought was his, mentioned the county. A wealthy, beautiful woman with two kids, one of them Clint's. And the lady's name was a flower. That had narrowed it down to two women.

All these months, Shelby had thought it might be Rose Erikson.

"I think the Eriksons are going to announce both engagements at the ball," Lenore said, "you and Vanessa and me and Rand."

"So the new younger sister doesn't change anything?"

"Not as far as I'm concerned. We can still keep meeting, Shelby. Something's bound to work out." She went into his arms, and he kissed her hard and ran his hand down the front of her bodice.

Somewhere were the final pieces of the puzzle. Who around here knew more than they were telling? Had Clint really cared so much for the lady that he had killed her husband and run away with her? And if so, would the old lady really help hide her own son's death to protect her family's name and reputation? Now that he had met Elizabeth Carstairs, he wouldn't put anything past her. She might be elderly and frail, but there was steel to that lady. Anyone who underestimated her was a fool.

"Wait a minute," he thought aloud, "a couple of little sounds that might or might have been thunder—or gunshots. Pretty slim."

"What do you mean?"

"I mean, my sweet, you couldn't convince anyone, not even me, that that adds up to a murder, not without a body." He fiddled with his diamond stickpin, thinking. "In fact, the more I think about it, the sillier it sounds. Anyway, what the hell does it matter? What matters now is who controls the money, and I'm afraid, my sweet, that's Grandma. If she wants to cut that girl into the will, whether this Kimi is really a Carstairs or not, and that's all that counts."

"But if Grandmother *thought* I knew something, I could blackmail her."

378

Shelby threw back his head and laughed. "Sweet Jesus! I'll bet your aristocratic fiancée would be shocked out of his mind if he knew the *real* you."

"Don't laugh, Shelby, I won't have that bit of poor white trash who is no relation to the Carstairs, getting her hands in the Carstairs money."

He started to tell her right then—it was such an ironic joke—but he decided against it. "When you find some real evidence, honey, then you can go head to head with Grandma; otherwise, watch out."

"Oh, you never take me seriously, Shelby."

"Anyone ever tell you you're pretty when you pout?"

"Am I?"

"You know you are." He knew what women liked to hear. Clint had taught him that. Shelby had come looking for Clint, hoping maybe he'd ended up with that rich lady he'd been sleeping with, hoping to find Clint living in the lap of luxury, hoping he'd cut Shelby in.

"Prettier than Vanessa or that Kimi?"

"Of course. Neither of them can hold a candle to you, sweet." Kimi. He'd sure like to get her clothes off. He'd had both the other girls and found them stupid and banal. Kimi was pretty, and seemed smart, too.

"Make love to me, Shelby." She slipped her tongue between his lips and rubbed her breasts up against him.

He ran his hand up under her dress.

"It's exciting to take chances." Lenore smiled. "I can see why my mother did it."

Shelby pulled her off the wicker settee into the soft dirt under the camelia bush and unbuttoned her bodice. "Just a quick one, honey."

She dug her nails into his shoulders, pulling him down on her. "A quick one is all I need—for now."

379

* * *

She was a bitch to satisfy, he thought, as Lenore brushed the dirt off her dress and, with her mincing walk, accompanied him out the side door. He grinned as he limped to his horses and swung up.

"For pity's sake, Shelby, what's so funny?"

If you only knew. No, not funny—ironic. "Nothing. The engagements still going to be announced at the Erikson's ball?"

"Vanessa and I've planned it that way, although I've hardly seen anything of Rand. Instead of the eager lover, he acts as if he's avoiding me."

If I could get between that Kimi's thighs, I wouldn't want you either, Shelby thought. But of course, he only smiled, said his good-byes, and rode away.

Lenore stood there a long moment, watching Shelby ride away, the sunlight reflecting off his slicked down hair. Just when she thought she had everything planned, that Kimi had showed up and threatened to ruin everything. What was she going to do about it?

Lenore turned and went back into the conservatory. The puppy had wandered in through the door she'd left ajar and was digging under the camelia bush. "Stop it, you damned mutt!" She kicked at him. "Grandmother will be mad if you dig up her flowers and wonder how you got in here."

Tally Ho paid no attention to her and kept on digging.

"For pity's sake!" Lenore grabbed him by the scruff of the neck and pulled him away. He had dug quite a hole already. Lenore dragged him over to the outside door, pushed him out, and shut the door.

She surveyed the damage. If that bush died, there was going to be big trouble with her Grandmother.

Maybe if she filled it carefully, Grandmother would never know about it. She dropped to her knees and began to push the dirt back into the shallow hole with her hands. This was nigger work, she thought. She ought to call a servant to do it, but she didn't trust any of them not to tattle to Grandmother; especially that Nero. He had never liked her. Still it galled her. She was a Carstairs and the Carstairs were bluebloods. Lenore was above doing this kind of dirty work.

Sunlight reflected off something in the hole. A button? A coin? No, it was bigger than that. Had Shelby dropped something? Puzzled, she picked the object up, stared at it. Rusty. It had been buried in the dirt a long, long time. Lenore held it up to the light. There was no mistake. It was an ivory-handled derringer.

Twenty-one

Lenore hid the little weapon in her bureau, knowing the three would be home soon from the dressmaker's. Now just why would a derringer be buried in her grandmother's conservatory? Still puzzled, Lenore spent the rest of the day deciding what to do about it. Should she tell Shelby? No, he'd only laugh and tell her some soldier had dropped it during the war. But did soldiers carry derringers?

Two days had passed since the night Elizabeth had found her long-lost granddaughter. These had been both the happiest and the most bittersweet days of the last sixteen years. She had had to face the truth about the wagon train. However, the fact that she had finally found her granddaughter made up for it.

There was something strange going on that Elizabeth couldn't quite figure out. Lenore suddenly looked like a cat who had caught a mouse, smiling secretly to herself. Who knew what the little sneak was up to?

On the other hand, Laurel looked miserable, and young Rand was staying away from the house. When he did come to call on Lenore, he looked ill at ease, as if he were holding back something that he dare not say.

Elizabeth decided to stay out of it, not knowing what she could or should do. She had realized that Rand was in love with Laurel, but Laurel seemed loath to break up her sister's engagement. Well, half-sister . . .

Elizabeth stopped playing the piano and listened. In the dusk darkness, she heard the judge's buggy pull up out front and Nero greeting him. She rose from her piano bench as her old friend entered. "Pierce, so nice of you to escort the girls to the ball tonight! I don't think they're quite ready. You know how women are."

"Not really," he reminded her, "I've lived all my life without one because the widow I wanted wouldn't say yes."

She felt the pain in her chest again, but forced herself to keep smiling. "You're as sweet as ever, Pierce."

He took both her hands in his. "Great Caesar's ghost, Elizabeth, you are as beautiful as ever! Why don't you change your mind and go with us? Afraid you'll outshine all the silly young things?"

She laughed gently as they went to sit in front of the fire. "You really should go into politics. You're more honest and smarter than most of them, and you're charming besides. When they finally give women the vote, they would all vote for you."

"Are you all right, my dear?" He peered at her anxiously. "You haven't looked well lately."

"Don't be such an old fussbudget." She dismissed him with a frail hand. "But if you're pouring yourself a drink, I'll take a little sherry. I'm just a bit under the weather tonight, that's all."

He went over, closed the door, then got them each a drink.

"You've learned something?" she guessed, and took the glass, sipped it, waiting for the bracing effect.

He fingered his mustache, sighed heavily. "Yes. Just as we suspected, Shelby Merson has a fake name and he's not a wealthy merchant from Baltimore."

"I thought not; the accent isn't right. Who is he?"

"Clint Nutter's brother-in-law."

"Oh Lord!" In her dismay, the sherry sloshed over her shaking hand. "After all these years . . ."

"Are you all right, Elizabeth?" He handed her his handkerchief to wipe her hands.

For a long moment, she didn't answer. Her chest hurt so badly, she wondered if tonight was the night she would die. The clock on the wall ticked loudly. "I suppose it was too much to hope that the secret was forever safe."

"I told you at the time we should report it. The three of us are accessories for our part in it."

"I know, I know." She took a sip of sherry. "All I could think of at the time was the scandal and protecting the Carstairs name. And you, Pierce, you helped me, knowing it would ruin your career if your part in it was ever discovered."

"I'm not sorry about that, my dear," he said gently and filled his pipe. "For you, I would do anything."

She stared into the fire. "What do you think he's after?"

"The truth maybe, but money more likely. I don't think you want to know where he got the money he used to buy that plantation between yours and the Erikson's."

"Tell me anyway."

He paused to light his pipe. "It seems Shelby, like his older brother-in-law, preys on wealthy society ladies. He charms or blackmails vulnerable rich women out of their funds. As a matter of fact, he was wounded escaping from a Memphis lady's bedroom when her husband came home unexpectedly."

She groaned aloud. "Worse than I thought. Where do you suppose he got the medals?"

"Great Caesar's ghost, who knows? One thing for certain, he didn't serve in the war. In fact, he's spent five years in jail."

"I don't suppose Lenore knows about him?"

He took a puff of his pipe. "Of course not. She's too snooty to bother with poor white trash. She's as foolish and immoral as her mother. She's probably being used."

"So now he hopes for a permanent income by marrying the Erikson girl. Yet he's dallying on the side with Lenore."

"Why not?" The judge shrugged and drank his brandy. "He's probably trying to figure out how he can end up with both fortunes."

"Over my very dead body!" Elizabeth put her glass down abruptly. "The Carstairs holdings are going to a Carstairs!"

Lenore had heard the judge's buggy arrive outside as she primped. Was this the time to confront the two old people about that derringer to see if they did indeed know something incriminating? She tiptoed out into the hall. There was no one about, although a light shown from under Kimi's door. Her bastard sister was still getting ready for the ball. Kimi had tried to be sisterly, but Lenore would have none of it. She could hardly wait to see Kimi's face when she told her the scandal.

At least she would be the most beautiful one at the ball. Lenore had had the dressmaker secretly copy that elegant emerald silk dress with the big sleeves from Camelia's portrait. She didn't intend to be upstaged by this newly found sister.

The green silk rustled along the hall as Lenore minced her way quietly down the stairs, looking around for the butler. Nero didn't seem to be anywhere around. Her feet were already hurting, and the evening hadn't even started. She put her eye to the keyhole in the music room door. The two old people sat before the fire.

"Does anyone but the two of us know this?" Grandmother asked.

"I doubt it." The judge puffed his pipe. "The question is, what do we do about it?"

Elizabeth Carstairs looked at him. "How do you suppose he knew?"

Judge Hamilton shrugged. "I suppose there's just the slightest chance that it's mere coincidence."

"I doubt that. How much do you suppose he knows?"

"Probably not enough or he'd already be either calling the law or blackmailing you."

Grandmother looked grim. "I thought the secret was safe, but it obviously isn't. I must protect the Carstairs name from scandal at any cost."

"That's why I told you you needed to rewrite your will, Elizabeth, and let me take care of it immediately. Otherwise, there will be questions and rumors."

Outside the door, Lenore bit her lip to keep from throwing the doors open and storming in with an angry tirade. She had no intention of sharing the Carstairs fortune with that Kimi.

The elderly lady sipped her sherry, sighed. "Questions and rumors; yes, you're right, Pierce, I'll have to divide the money and property down the middle, treat both girls as beloved grandchildren, even though it galls me to give anything to a bastard child fathered by that tinhorn gambler. It must never get out that one of them is no blood kin of the Carstairs at all."

Outside the door, Lenore took a deep breath. Now she had the knowledge and the power to get what she wanted. Throwing the door open, she strode into the music room. "For pity's sake, I don't know why you always tell me not to listen at keyholes, Grandmother. One learns so many interesting things that way."

Both of them turned pale. Judge Hamilton reacted first. "How long have you been listening?"

"Long enough." Actually she hadn't heard much at all, but they didn't know that. "So Camelia had begun sneaking around with a lover? Now that I think back, I remember a handsome man turning up sometimes when Daddy was gone on business."

Grandmother looked as if she might have a heart attack. "You were so little," she murmured, "I didn't think you were aware of what was going on." She looked at the dress, then at the portrait.

"Yes, I look like her, don't I?" Lenore smiled with satisfaction. "And you never liked her."

"There was a reason," Grandmother said. "She was just like you are. In fact, if I believed in reincarnation, when I saw you walk in just now—"

"Oh, stop it!" She confronted the old lady. "You would do anything, anything to protect your precious husband's family name. Well, maybe you went too far!"

"Young lady," the judge bristled, "don't talk to Elizabeth that way!"

"I'll talk any way I want because I seem to have the winning hand," Lenore gloated. "One thing I won't do is stand by while you change your will. I demand that you leave it alone. Your *real* granddaughter, not the bastard, should get every last cent! Do you hear me?"

"But Lenore," Grandmother said, "if I do that, as the judge says, people will wonder—"

"I don't care! Leave the will alone, you hear?"

Elizabeth Carstairs opened her mouth as if to protest, but the old man waved her into silence. "You heard what she said, Elizabeth." He looked at Lenore, nodded defeat. "All right, as her lawyer, she'll leave the will exactly as it was written many years ago. We'll just have to worry about the gossip later."

Lenore glowed with triumph. "I don't know why you're both so worried. If you're dead, what do you care what anyone thinks about the family?"

Her grandmother looked up at her with grave dignity. "I know this is hard for you to understand, but I loved James Carstairs enough to do anything to protect the name he gave me and his son."

Lenore snorted with derision. "I'll just bet you would! I remember the thunder that night, only after all these years, I'm not sure it was thunder at all."

She saw them exchange glances.

The judge took the pipe from between his teeth. "Explain yourself, young lady!"

"No, it's you two who need to explain. It occurs to me now the thunder might have been gunshots. Did that damned gambler shoot my father, and run away with my whore of a mother and his bastard brat?"

Elizabeth Carstairs looked as if she were on the verge of a heart attack. "What—whatever made

388

you say such a thing?"

"Because I know you would do anything, even hide the death of your own son to protect the Carstairs name. And by the way, I found a certain ivory-handled derringer."

Grandmother's sherry crashed to the floor with a tinkle of glass. She gasped and tried to get her breath. Immediately, the judge was by her side. "Are you all right, Elizabeth?" He held his brandy to her lips.

Lenore watched without emotion as the color gradually came back to Grandmother's face. If Elizabeth Carstairs dropped dead at this moment, she would be the heir, that was the thought that crossed her mind. That and the satisfying thought that they were both guilty of something terrible. Their faces when she had mentioned the gun told her that.

The color gradually returned to Grandmother's face. "Lenore, I don't know what you're talking about."

"Don't you?" she asked smugly. "Couldn't tell it by the expressions on both your faces."

"Young lady," the judge thundered, "you're making all this up to upset Elizabeth. I don't know where or why you think this supposed weapon has anything to do with Elizabeth, but—"

"It was buried in the conservatory." Lenore nodded to the puppy snoozing in the corner. "Your damned mutt dug it up under the camelia bush. Now tell me the truth. Did Kimi's father shoot and kill my father?"

"It was all an accident," Elizabeth blurted. "Jim came home unexpectedly and found them in an embrace in the shadows on the east lawn—"

"Elizabeth!" the judge thundered. "Say no more! You owe her no explanation!"

"And you're in on it, too, aren't you? You supposed paragon of virtue!" Lenore sneered, "and I'll bet even Nero is part of it. He's big enough to carry the body."

Neither spoke, but she saw the truth of what she had said in their stressed faces. "They killed my father and ran away, taking their bastard brat with them. And you, my dear grandmother, what kind of a woman would do *anything* to protect the family name, even hide a murder?"

The judge glared at her. "The kind you'll never be. You haven't got the guts or the class Elizabeth has."

Lenore backed toward the door, shaking her head. "Don't you talk about principles and class to me, you pompous old windbag! I don't know much about the law, but I'll wager it's a crime to cover up a murder—"

"It wasn't a murder," Elizabeth blurted, "it was an accident—"

"Elizabeth," the judge snapped, "say nothing more."

Lenore smiled. "Ah, so there was a death! When I find out what Nero did with the body, I could humiliate you, ruin your career."

"And disgrace an elderly lady?" Pierce Hamilton looked toward Grandmother.

Lenore laughed. "The family name doesn't mean that much to me as long as I get what I want! Now I'm in the catbird seat. I'll call the shots and do whatever I please. You two won't interfere. If so, I'll keep mine shut about the gun."

"You keep talking about a gun, but we haven't seen it," the judge said.

"I'm not that stupid. Could I describe it if I hadn't seen it, or tell you where I dug it up? I've hidden it. Now if you two behave yourselves, I

390

won't tell the sheriff. In the meantime," she glared at the judge, "you will not change the will; understand?"

The judge nodded, held up his hand. "You have my word I will not change your grandmother's will. Don't you agree, Elizabeth?"

She smiled ever so slightly. "If that's the way Lenore wants it."

"Where does it go in case the heir doesn't get it?" Lenore demanded.

"To fund charities and a hospital for the poor," Elizabeth said, "and the house will become a school."

Lenore snickered. "For pity's sake, what a waste. When we have time, judge, we'll make some changes, all right and I'll dictate them. Damned if I'll give a penny to niggers and white trash!"

The clock on the wall chimed the hour.

"Eight o'clock," Lenore said, "Time to leave for the ball."

Her grandmother looked startled. "After all this, you're going on as if nothing had happened?"

"Why not? Didn't you sixteen years ago? If I don't show up, there'll be gossip and we do need to protect the family name. That's important to you, isn't it?"

Neither answered; only looked at each other.

Lenore said, "Judge, I don't think I want to ride with you and my bastard half-sister. I'll take your buggy and drive myself. You two can come later in Grandmother's carriage."

He looked alarmed. "What are you going to do?"

She felt confident, almost cocky with the power of the knowledge she possessed. "I'm not intending to announce the scandal at the party, if that's what you're worried about. If the secret's out, I don't have any power over you two anymore. No, I'll keep quiet, and from now on I run things around here."

Elizabeth looked into Lenore's golden eyes that seemed as hard as metal. Just like her mother — always was. There was no point in further discussion. Elizabeth would have to do a lot of thinking.

"No answer? Good. Then we're agreed." Lenore smiled with satisfaction, whirled with a rustle of green silk and left the room. Elizabeth leaned back in her chair with a sigh, and in silence they listened to the buggy drive away. "Pull the bell cord for Nero, Pierce. It looks like you'll have to do as she says."

He reached over, took her hand, patted it. "Are you all right, my dear?"

"Yes," she lied. Her chest was hurting again. All the stressful years of hiding the secret had taken its toll worse than anything the law might have done to her. Pierce's drawn face said the same. They had both paid for their part in it. In a strange way, maybe justice had been done all around. Elizabeth had made her choices and she didn't regret them.

The puppy raised its head and yawned, making her think of immediate problems. "Pierce, when you go home after the ball, I think you'd better take Tally Ho with you before he does any more digging."

At the sound of his name, the dog's tail thumped lazily.

"Elizabeth, why didn't you tell Lenore the whole truth?"

She shrugged. "To what purpose? It would be even a bigger mess than if she doesn't know. Do as she ordered, Pierce, don't change the will."

He sighed, and put his face in his hand for a long moment. "It's ironic, isn't it?"

"Maybe. But it's what she demanded." There was another long pause and the puppy scratched a flea. "If only she didn't have the gun, she wouldn't have any proof."

His face wrinkled a long moment. "While we're gone, put Nero to looking. She's not that smart. It's bound to be someplace in the house."

Another pause. "Do you suppose the Eriksons will announce the double engagement tonight?"

"Great Caesar's ghost. What do you want me to do? This is a Pandora's box I've been trying to keep the lid closed on for sixteen years now."

"You did it for me, Pierce, I know that. It could cost you everything, including your professional reputation."

He went to the fireplace and knocked the ashes from his pipe against the andiron. "I have always loved you, you know that. I'd do it again."

"Thank you for that. I loved my son and his child more than anything else in this world. I don't regret my part in it. I did what I had to do to protect them and my dear husband's family name."

"Somehow I have a feeling Shelby doesn't know about the gun. He would have handled everything a little smarter than this. If you find it, hide it again."

"The sheriff is bound to be one of those invited tonight. Suppose Lenore or Shelby hunts him up, tells him—"

"Tells what, my dear? If Shelby tells who he is, he'll be arrested for past crimes. If Lenore talks, she has no secret left to blackmail us with."

"What on earth are we going to do, Pierce? I don't want to hurt Laurel by all this."

He took her hands in his. "What she doesn't

know won't hurt her. Maybe we can keep it that way."

More than anything, she must protect her granddaughter against pain. "I feel so sorry for her, Pierce. She's madly in love with young Rand."

The judge shrugged and sat down. "That's something that's out of our hands; his decision and hers. Maybe he'll decide on his own not to marry Lenore. Maybe he'll turn out to be more of a man than we think, defy his mother and marry Kimi, I mean Laurel."

"And be cut out of her will?" Elizabeth frowned. "I wish I could believe he was that much of a real man. I'm afraid he'll be more like his father."

"You know about Jon Erikson then?" The judge turned toward her.

Elizabeth nodded. "In a choice between love and money, Jon wasn't willing to give up everything for love. I'm afraid his son is too much like him."

Elizabeth stared into the fire, remembering her own love. She wanted Laurel to find that kind of happiness. "Laurel isn't fitting in, Pierce, and she seems miserable."

He stuck his thumbs in his vest. "Give her time. She's a fighter; she'll make this county eat crow. One day, when she's learned all the proper manners, she'll be the reigning queen of local society just as you have always been."

She leaned back in her chair, troubled. "I don't doubt that. What worries me is that I'm not sure she'll be happy doing it. Our civilization seems petty, cruel and confining to her. I suspect she misses the unfettered life among the Indians. Then there's hateful Lenore to contend with."

"Don't worry, Elizabeth, I'll figure out something."

They heard footsteps in the hall.

"Grandmother? Where is everyone?"

The judge went to the door, opened it. "Come in, Laurel, dear. Lenore went on early. Ask Nero to get the carriage ready and we'll go together."

She stepped through the door. She was so beautiful, Elizabeth thought, dressed in a pale peach dress that complemented her ebony hair and emerald eyes. "Nana, are you feeling well? Why don't you go with us? We'll wait for you to dress."

Elizabeth managed a smile, shook her head. "No, you two run along. Tell me about it when you get back."

Laurel nodded, looking troubled.

Elizabeth wondered suddenly if Rand would have the guts to marry this one instead. Tonight at the ball it would all come to a showdown and no one could make those choices for the two of them. Some of it depended on what Lenore knew; or thought she knew. Anyway, Elizabeth was a tired old lady, it was all out of her hands.

She said her good-byes and watched Pierce and Laurel drive away in the carriage. Quickly, she gave instructions to Nero. He frowned, nodded, went up the stairs.

She really should help him search, but she was so very weary from everything that had happened tonight. She went back into the music room. The big painting seemed to draw her like a magnet. She went over and stood before it.

Her son's green eyes seemed to speak to her. "Jim," she whispered, "in spite of everything I tried to do, it all came to naught."

Her son lay in some lonely grave a thousand miles from here, instead of the family plot at the church. Camelia's golden eyes seemed to mock her. Elizabeth stared at the beautiful but faithless wife and the two little girls in the painting, one with her father's eyes, the other with eyes like her mother's. Elizabeth had kept silent even though the moment she had first seen the baby she had known why Camelia had rushed Jim into marriage. Her son had seemed blind to the obvious because he loved the beauty so. But Elizabeth had known her husband's father and grandfather. It was in the bloodlines; a heritage that had been passed down through generation after generation; all the Carstairs had green eyes.

Twenty-two

Kimi thought the judge seemed unusually preoccupied and quiet on the drive to Randolph Hall. "Is there something wrong, sir?"

"Uh, no, of course not; just tired, that's all. I must say you look beautiful tonight, my dear. In fact, I was just thinking how much you remind me of your lovely grandmother, although you have your father's eyes."

"Thank you," she responded warmly, trying to get her mind off the party. This was going to be a miserable evening. She should have stayed home. "Did you know him well?"

He nodded. "He was like the son I never had. I looked after him and his mother. You know your grandfather was killed before Jim Junior was born."

She reached to touch her medicine charm. Now she knew where it came from. That made it even more special to her. "I'm surprised Grandmother never married you. She's been a widow most of her life, hasn't she?"

"Why do you think I never married? I kept thinking I could wear her down; change her mind. Elizabeth's heart belonged to only one man. She could never love another."

Like me, Kimi thought and blinked back a tear. She had refused to see Rand the last time he had called. Tonight, she supposed, his mother would announce his coming wedding. Could Kimi behave like a lady and congratulate them both, even though her heart was breaking? She must, no matter how much it hurt to do so. She would not bring dishonor on a proud family name. She was suddenly aware, as the carriage clopped along, that the judge was studying her.

"This is going to be a real ordeal for you tonight, isn't it? Most girls would have been suddenly taken sick and stayed home."

Kimi swallowed hard. "I won't disgrace my grandmother or cause gossip by not attending when the Eriksons might be making a surprise double announcement."

"Spoken like a true Carstairs," the judge said with evident satisfaction. He patted her hand and cleared his throat several times. She had a feeling he was trying to get up the nerve to talk to her about something he found distasteful. "Laurel, dear, I'm the nearest thing to a grandfather you've got, so I'm going to take the liberty of discussing something personal with you. You'll probably think this old goat should mind his own business."

"If it's about Rand Erikson, I'd rather not—"

"No," he shook his head, "that I feel is out of my hands. I want to talk about your father—the past." He hesitated again. "Someday you may hear things. . . ."

Baffled, she waited for him to go on but he seemed to be fumbling for words. "Gossip, cruel gossip. Lenore may even say something to you."

She was even more mystified. "I don't understand."

She heard him swallow hard. "I—there are some

398

things I can't tell you. . . ."

She waited, wondering what it was he was trying to say. The sound of the horses' hooves and the squeak of the carriage seemed loud in the silence.

He cleared his throat. "After your grandmother is finally gone, there may be some big surprises in her will—"

"I'm not after her money," Kimi said quickly.

"I know that, my sweet dear; I'm sorry I can't say the same for Lenore. A lot of things may come out then, and I won't be able to stop it, although I'll do the best I can to protect the Carstairs. In fact, it seems I've spent my whole life doing that."

She had no idea what he was talking about. Perhaps the old man was getting a little senile. "If you're telling me you or Nero or Lenore are getting everything, that wouldn't bother me."

He chuckled. "I wish I could say the same for your sister." He hesitated a long time and she listened to the carriage creak as they drove along. "Laurel," he hesitated. "If you were to end up with all your grandmother's wealth, what would you do with it?"

Her mouth fell open. "What about Lenore?"

"Answer my question," he ordered sternly.

"I'd probably give it away. Money and possessions don't mean much to me. I suppose it has to do with being reared by the Sioux." She thought of them with nostalgia. "Indians give away much of their wealth when a relative dies."

"Then you'd approve of turning Carstairs Oaks into a school or hospital, giving the money to worthwhile charities?"

"I certainly would. Is old Nero taken care of?"

"Yes. Your grandmother has provided well for all her employees, but especially for Nero. He's been with her since he was a boy."

"But what about Lenore? I don't understand—"

"Please don't ask any more questions, my dear." He patted her hand. "Yes, you're a Carstairs, all right, I never doubted it for a moment. If Lenore only knew . . ."

She waited for him to go on, but he only stared out into the crisp, moonlit night as if remembering something that had happened long ago.

"Judge Hamilton, if you have any influence with Grandmother, and I think you do, tell her to give my share to Lenore. The money means a lot to Lenore and it matters little to me. I think I'm going away."

"Love him that much, do you?" He put his pipe in his mouth, but didn't light it.

She smiled ruefully. "Does it show so much? I can't stay and watch them marry, think of them together. And frankly, from what I've seen of this rich white society I've been thrown into, I don't think I like it, much less want to stay and be a part of it."

He grunted agreement. "Believe it or not, there's not a person who hasn't dreamed of running away to a happier place, a place free of restrictions, responsibilities, realities."

He was speaking of her father, she thought. Kimi shook her head. "I'm not running from reality, I'm facing it. I could only make Rand unhappy because I don't fit into his world."

"You're serious about going back to the Indians?"

Kimi nodded. "If Rand marries Lenore, eventually he'll forget about me. I'll only be a fond memory to think about when he's an old man bouncing grandchildren on his knee."

"Young Rand may have more guts than you think," the judge said, taking the pipe from his teeth, "he may want to marry you instead."

She shook her head. "Eventually, he'd regret it. His mother would see to it that he's disinherited, and besides, I would only be an embarrassment to him. I can't even read and I don't know how to needlepoint or which of a dozen forks in a table setting to use—"

"Those things can be learned."

"I know that, but as much as I love Rand, I don't want to live in a crass, superficial society that judges a person on things like that. Lenore was born to this life. She fits in well. Besides how would everyone treat Rand if he married me instead and was disinherited by his mother? I think he would end up regretting his choice."

"Well, if you have your grandmother's money—"

"If Rand's the kind of man I hope he is, he wouldn't live off a woman's wealth. Besides, I don't think he is willing to throw everything in his whole world away for me."

The judge sighed. "Young lady, he might surprise you. There are people who are willing to sacrifice everything for love."

"And I'm one of them," she said with conviction. "I won't put him in that spot; I'll make the choice. Before he has time to think about it, I'm going to tell him it's over. More than anything, it is important to me that he be happy."

"And you think that being master of Carstairs Oaks, having money and Lenore is what happiness is to Rand?"

"I don't see any middle ground. I'm not a white; I'm a Sioux Indian with pale skin. It's a very hard, dangerous life, but it's the one I know. It's insane to think that he would be willing to give up a life of ease and luxury and go back to the wilderness with me."

The judge sighed. "I reckon you're right, Laurel. A man would have to be crazy or hopelessly in love to throw all this away for a woman. All right, I'll not attempt to dissuade you. After all, you're probably as stubborn as your grandmother, a Carstairs to the bone."

The carriage pulled up before the palatial home. Lights streamed from all the windows and the sound of music and laughter drifting on the crisp October air:

Weep no more my lady, Oh! weep no more to-day! We will sing one song for the old Kentucky home; for the old Kentucky home, far away. . . .

The French doors leading out onto the third floor balcony of the ballroom were open with several couples visible standing out there enjoying the moonlight. Kimi wondered again why Lenore had driven herself as she looked around and saw the other carriages and buggies parked about the grounds. The buggy Lenore had driven stood off alone under a tree, almost hidden in the shadows.

If she could only get through this evening with dignity and grace, tomorrow she would make up some excuse and go away forever. She wasn't even sure she could tell Rand. Perhaps it would be better if she led him to believe that she had never really cared much for him. In the meantime, she would have to see Rand at this ball tonight, Lenore no doubt holding onto his arm possessively. More than anything, Kimi wanted to turn and run away, but she forced herself to alight from the carriage in a swirl of peach-colored skirts as they stepped out onto the flagstones that paved all around the entry drive and around the side veranda.

Then the judge turned and looked at Kimi. "Are you all right, my dear?"

"Certainly." She took a deep breath and pulled herself together. She had no idea what all that talk about inheritance had meant, but it didn't matter. Even she realized that Elizabeth Carstairs had strong family pride. She wouldn't leave a blood relative out of her will, no matter how angry she might get with her older granddaughter.

Kimi took the judge's arm, and they went in to be greeted by Mr. and Mrs. Erikson and then up the stairs to the giant ballroom on the third floor.

Rand must have been watching for her because immediately she saw his tall frame standing near the door. His eyes lit up and he came over. "Well, so glad to see you, Judge, and you, Kimi, or should I call you Laurel?"

She looked helplessly at the judge, but he only smiled. "I'll bet you two have a lot to talk about, so I'll get some punch."

Even as she opened her mouth to protest, he disappeared into the crowd. Rand took her arm. "Let's dance, shall we?"

"I really don't know how." She had to escape from him before her resolve melted away.

"Nonsense. This music is slow and there's a big crowd. No one will notice." He pulled her into his embrace and out onto the crowded dance floor. "This is called a 'slow waltz,' " — he grinned, — "considered quite daring only a few years ago because the man puts his hand on the lady's waist."

She managed to follow his steps, but her mind wasn't on the dance. His arms felt so powerful, so protective. Once again she thought of all those nights up in the Dakota Territory, making passionate love to him, sleeping safe in his embrace.

Everyone they danced past seemed overly polite,

nodding to the couple.

Rand smiled wryly. "It is amazing how peoples' attitudes change when word gets around that you're the missing granddaughter and entitled to half the Carstairs wealth, doesn't it?"

"You said that, I didn't." In spite of being in his embrace, or maybe because of it, she was miserable. She didn't like hypocrites who were friendly to her now only because she suddenly had wealth and social position. "I'm still the same person I always was."

"And that's what I love about you," he whispered close to her ear.

"Stop it, Rand, people will talk!" Was that her heart beating or his, pounding against her breast?

"I don't care if they do!" He sounded grim and determined.

They danced past his father and mother standing near the refreshment table. His father looked drunk and sadder than usual. His mother shot dagger looks at Kimi.

Kimi nodded politely to her. *Even if I am in for half the Carstairs estate, his mother would prefer Lenore.*

She must do this. Kimi managed to keep her body rigid, keep it from melting in surrender against him. She could only be thankful the chatter and music kept those nearest them from hearing their conversation. "Look, Rand, I don't know what you expect, but tomorrow, I'm going away."

He stopped in midstep. "Going away? You can't do that. I—"

"Oh, but I can!" She managed to keep her voice cool as if she didn't care what he thought. "Grandmother has offered to send me to a fine finishing school back East if I wish, so I can learn all the things a Southern belle should know."

"You at a finishing school?" He looked down at her as if he couldn't believe it.

She bristled. "Does it seem that preposterous?"

As if he realized people might stare at two people on the dance floor standing and staring at each other, he began to dance again. "It just doesn't sound like you, Kimi."

"Money changes people, Rand." She shrugged and kept her voice brittle so it wouldn't break. "I may come back in two or three years, or I may meet some suitor up there in Boston and never come back, but let me be the first to offer my congratulations on your upcoming marriage to my sister."

They had danced near the edge of the floor close to the balcony doors. Rand glanced around as if to make sure no one was looking, pulled her out through the open doors. "We have to talk."

"I doubt that we have anything to talk about, and anyway, what will Lenore say?"

He swore under his breath. "Damn Lenore."

If there was anything she didn't want to do, it was stand out here under the stars alone with him. She forced herself to turn away, looking out over the vast holdings of Randolph Hall. All this would be half his someday—if he weren't disinherited. And of course, if he married Lenore, he would have all the Carstairs fortune once Kimi went away. She tried to make sense of what Judge Hamilton had said in the carriage, and then decided it didn't matter.

It was chilly outside in the October night after the hot ballroom. Kimi shivered, and immediately he came up behind her, slipped his arms around her, and kissed her bare shoulder.

"We must go in," she said, trying to keep her body rigid, which was difficult with his warm lips caressing her skin. "Someone—someone will have seen us come out here."

"I don't care." He whirled her around. "Look, Kimi, I've made up my mind. I'm not going to marry Lenore."

"You're making a snap decision you'll only regret later." She tried not to melt as his lips moved along her throat. He held her so closely she arched against him, feeling his hard body down the length of hers.

"I'll be the judge of that." His eyes looked troubled. "Granted there'll be a lot of gossip, and maybe some homes we won't be invited to, but that doesn't matter. I just wanted to make sure you felt the same way about me before I created an uproar."

It would be an uproar, she thought—a scandal the likes of which the county hadn't seen in a while. It might embarrass her grandmother. It would certainly bring Mrs. Erikson's fury down on Kimi. She would never be accepted by that cold lady, never.

He kissed her, hot and deep, his tongue caressing the velvet of her mouth while his hand went to stroke the rise of her breasts. She loved him more than anything in this world, loved him enough to give him up. It took all the inner strength she had, but Kimi managed to pull away, laughing. "Oh, Rand, perhaps you didn't understand. What we had was nice, but there's a whole, big world out there waiting for a girl with money. I intend to take full advantage of it."

He looked stricken. "I can't believe you're saying this. What's happened to you, Kimi? You've changed."

"That's what I keep trying to tell you." She forced herself to shrug as if his feelings didn't matter to her. She straightened the lace of her ball gown. Her skin still seemed to burn with the warm passion of his kisses. "Now hadn't you better go back inside? My sister will be looking for you."

"Why you heartless little—! I've been three kinds of a fool! And to think I was ready to throw it all away when you care nothing for me at all!" He turned on his heel and went back into the ballroom.

Kimi clenched her fists at her sides to keep from running after him, declaring her love. She must carry this charade through for his own good. Tears began to run down her face. She would stand here a moment and compose herself. After all, if the announcement was made in a few minutes, Kimi would have to go forward, offer her best wishes to the two happy couples. Kimi intended to put on such a good show that Nana would be proud of her.

Shelby handed Lenore a cup of punch. "You are incredibly beautiful in that green satin gown. Must have cost a fortune."

She looked pleased. "Like it? I had Camelia's dress copied. You know, the one in the painting."

"Smart minx. Is that why you look like a cat who just cornered a mouse?"

She smiled with those golden eyes. "In a way, I have. Good news, future brother-in-law. We're going to end up with more than you think, and soon."

"Sweet Jesus. I don't think I even want to know how you know that."

She smiled back, mysterious, self-satisfied. "I'm not sure I want to tell you."

He looked down at her frowning face. "What's

the matter?"

"My feet hurt."

He chuckled and fingered his diamond stick pin. "You should stop trying to stuff big feet into too small shoes."

"Big feet?" Her golden eyes widened with outrage. "I don't have big feet. Small feet are a Carstairs family trait."

"Remind me to tell you something about that sometime, although I'm not sure you'll find the irony funny."

She looked bewildered and angry. "For pity's sake, Shelby, have you had too much to drink?"

"Hmm." He was only half listening. His mind was on the luscious Laurel. Vanessa danced by with her rum-soaked father and waved. He smiled and nodded, his mind still on Laurel. He wanted her, first chance he got. He wondered if she were still out on the balcony? He'd seen her go out there with Rand Erikson.

So Rand was plowing two fields at the same time, also, just like Shelby. Shelby looked toward the balcony, wishing he were in young Rand's shoes. Shelby wanted a sample of Laurel's kisses first chance he got. Pouty Lenore was more tiresome by the day. "So how are you and your newly found baby sister getting along?"

She made a slight face and lowered her voice. "For pity's sake, Shelby, don't you remind me. I was afraid I was going to have to share the Carstairs estate with her, but something's happened."

"Uh huh. Like what?"

"Remember you said I needed proof? I found the gun, Shelby."

Some friends of Lenore's danced past and they both nodded. Shelby nodded back and, without looking at Lenore, said softly, "What the hell are you talking about?"

"For pity's sake, don't swear. I'm a lady, you know." She fanned herself vigorously.

He fingered his diamond stickpin, deciding not to anger her further by pointing out that real ladies didn't roll in the dirt with their best friends' fiancées. "So some soldier dropped it during the war, so what?"

"A derringer?"

She had his attention now. "Sweet Jesus! Ivory-handled?"

"How did you know that?"

"Lucky guess." He shrugged and ran his hand through his perfumed, greasy hair. "Where is it?"

"Never you mind, I've got it safely hidden."

He managed to keep his face immobile as he sipped his punch, just as if he were sharing a few pleasantries with his future sister-in-law. "You got it with you?"

She fanned herself. "Don't be silly! I'm saving it for blackmail—if I need it."

The orchestra began to play softly: *Alas my love, you do me wrong to caste me off discourteously* . . .

Her words came in such a rush that he had a hard time making sense of them. "I think my mother was having an affair with a gambler. Suppose my father caught them and they killed him? They took all of the valuables like money and his watch. Then they took their bastard brat and left. I'll bet my Grandmother's been sending them money all these years to stay away and not create a scandal. Now their bastard brat is back trying to cut herself in on half the estate, but I've fixed that." She smiled smugly, evidently pleased with herself.

. . . *Greensleeves was all my joy, Greensleeves*

was my delight, Greensleeves was my heart of gold. . . .

Clint. Unknowingly, Lenore was talking about his brother-in-law, Clint. Did her theory make any sense? "Who knows about this?"

"My grandmother and the judge, I think. You should have seen their faces when I confronted them."

He shook his head. "Naw. No mother would help hide something like that."

"You don't know Elizabeth Carstairs! She would do *anything* to protect the family name. Besides something she blurted out suggested it wasn't murder, it was an accident."

Shelby stared out across the floor, but his mind wasn't on the dancers. Was it possible that Clint had gone West with the lady and died out there?

"Shelby," she said, "Don't you see? If what I suspect is true, I can blackmail my grandmother into cutting my bastard half-sister completely out of the will. Somehow, we're going to end up with both estates."

Out of the corner of his eye, he saw Rand Erikson come in off the balcony alone. He looked distressed. "Excuse me, dear sister-in-law," Shelby said politely. "We'll continue this conversation when I get a look at that derringer. Right now, I think I'll go out on the balcony and smoke a cigar."

"I'll go with you."

"What would people say?"

But about that time, Mrs. Erikson came up. "Oh, there you are, dear." She took Lenore's arm and smiled at Shelby. "Come along and we'll talk to Vanessa about when she thinks we should make the announcement."

Shelby nodded politely. "I'll leave all those decisions up to the womenfolk and go smoke my cigar."

He turned and limped out onto the balcony. Was there anything to Lenore's wild story? He wouldn't bet the farm on it. Laurel Carstairs was still out there, and there was no one else on the balcony. He could see by her silhouette that she was shaking with sobs. Vulnerable. That was just the way he liked them. Shelby had followed in his handsome brother-in-law's footsteps—except that Shelby had small feet. But he, too, made use of rich, beautiful women who liked the thrill of the forbidden. "Excuse me, Miss Laurel, may I be of service?"

Kimi looked up abruptly at the man bowing gallantly before her. She didn't care for Shelby Merson; the way he looked at her always made her want to cross her arms over her bosom. "I was just going back in; stepped out to get a breath of air."

"Yes, it is stuffy in there, isn't it?" He leaned against one of the big, white pillars. "Thought I saw Rand come back in a minute ago."

She didn't know what he expected her to say. She could smell his strongly perfumed hair oil from here. "We—we were talking about his and my sister's wedding, and how nice that it would be a double ceremony."

"And you got so emotional over the plans that you're crying." He sounded cynical. "I've heard of women weeping at a wedding, but not sobbing their hearts out over someone else's."

She took a step away from him, looking toward the open French doors. "What are you implying, Shelby?"

He grinned. "Did I say I was implying anything? My, you are a suspicious person, aren't you? We need to get a little friendlier, 'specially since we're

411

all going to be one big, happy family. Besides, I know something, that if you knew, you could cut Lenore right out of her share of the Carstairs money."

His tone sent shivers down her back. He seemed so incredibly evil. How could she brush past him and return to the ballroom without creating a scene? "I don't know what you're talking about, and I don't care about the money." She hadn't the least idea what he hinted at. Had he been drinking? All she could smell from here was that flowery hair tonic he wore.

"But I do care about the money and blackmail's a good way to get it." His mouth smiled but his eyes didn't. He advanced a step. Kimi backed against one of the large pillars that held up the balcony, and she glanced behind her. There was a three-story drop to the flagstones below.

What was Shelby hinting at? He must know about her and Rand. He was going to tell if she didn't pay him.

"I think I need to go inside." She started past him, but he caught her arm.

"Don't hurry off, we've a lot to talk about."

She hesitated. He was going to blackmail her. Everyone would know about her and Rand. Nana. What would Nana say if Kimi disgraced the Carstairs name by the affair becoming common gossip? "What do you want to keep quiet?"

For a moment, he blinked as if in surprise, then he threw back his head and laughed. "I do declare, everyone in the world, or at least this county has something to hide! What I want, my dear, is you."

She hesitated, almost speechless at his insolence; unsure what to do, how to bargain with this snake.

He snickered, but he didn't let go of her arm. "Like most women, you're more afraid of making a scene than you are of me. As long as women fear being ridiculed, what people might think, they will always be at the mercy of men who prey on that hesitation."

He was right, of course. If she screamed, or created a scene trying to get away from him, it would be both humiliating and embarrassing. What to do? If Rand were here, he'd know what to do. No, he'd probably punch Shelby in the mouth and there'd be even a bigger scene, more gossip. Kimi glanced around. There was a staircase at the end of the balcony that led down onto that flagstone veranda and on past that, into a rose garden. If she could reach the end of the balcony, she could go down the stairs and either go out and have her driver take her home or make a new entry downstairs and return to the ballroom without anyone knowing what had happened.

That would only buy her a little time. Now she knew that the decision she had been contemplating all evening was the right one. "Shelby, you're wasting your time. I'm going away. I won't be part of whatever scheme you've devised. You will not disgrace the Carstairs name."

"It's already been disgraced. I thought it was Rose, but the flower is Camelia. Pretty, rich, married, two children, Clint said. Yessiree, there's just all sorts of intrigue and blackmail possibilities in this county."

"I don't know what you're talking about," she snapped and tried to yank free.

"Don't be afraid, Laurel," he said softly and pulled her to him. "After all, I'd be a fool to do more than steal a few kisses with people liable to come out on the balcony at any time. But later, we'll have a lot of pleasure together, so I won't tell what I know, especially about your mother."

If he wasn't drunk, he must be crazy, but she had had as much as she was going to take. Kimi brought her hand up suddenly, slapped his face, and tried to break away from him.

"Why you little—!" He yanked her against him, his mouth covering hers as he kissed her so hard that she tasted blood from her cut lip. As they struggled, he pulled at the top of her peach ball gown, trying to get his free hand on her breasts.

Lenore stood talking to Rand, but she wasn't really listening. She was thinking that Shelby had gone out on that balcony some minutes ago and hadn't come back. She remembered Laurel was out there, too. Neither had come back in. Was her bastard half-sister capable of the same things Lenore was? Women would always forgive a little straying in a man, especially if they thought a woman had tempted him. However, the woman would be an object of scandal. Here was her chance to destroy Laurel.

"Lenore," Rand said, "you aren't listening to me. I said we need to go where it's quiet and have a talk. I've got something very important I must tell you."

"Hmm." She nodded, pretending not to hear. So he wanted to talk; no doubt to break their engagement. She'd have to be blind not to suspect there was something going on between him and her bastard half-sister. "Can't we talk later?"

"You aren't leaving me any choice." His face looked set, grim. "Believe me, this isn't something to be discussed on a crowded dance floor."

"Try me." He wouldn't have the nerve, not after she wept on Rose Erikson's shoulder.

"All right, Lenore, I want to discuss breaking

our engagement. It's not fair of me to marry you when my heart belongs to another, even if she doesn't want me."

What a humiliation that would be. Rand looked as if his mind were made up and couldn't be changed.

For pity's sake, what should she do? Lenore had seen Shelby go out on the balcony and hadn't seen Kimi come in. If there was even the slightest chance that something might be happening that Rand would misread, Lenore wanted to take advantage of it.

"Rand, if you want to talk, let's go out on the balcony where it's quiet." She took his arm, and with mincing steps she led him in threading their way through the crowd. She didn't care any more what else happened as long as she disgraced that gambler's bastard. The gossip would make sure Grandmother didn't include Laurel in her will. The real heir, that's who was going to get all the Carstairs wealth.

As Lenore steered Rand toward the balcony, she looked back and saw the judge standing near the orchestra with the local sheriff, and the judge frowned, watching her. She gave him a smug smile and fluttered her fan. She had Pierce Hamilton and Grandmother right where she wanted them, because of what they thought Lenore knew. The only thing left undone was disgracing her newly found half-sister and breaking up this romance.

Kimi struggled in Shelby's embrace, her heart pounding in terror and humiliation. He had both her hands in his, so she couldn't strike or scratch him while he held her against the pillar with his body. Even if she had dared to scream, she couldn't, not with his wet mouth ravaging hers. In the background, as she struggled against his strength, she was only vaguely aware that the orchestra had begun to play a loud Virginia reel, and the crowd danced and clapped their hands. The music reverberated through the mansion. Even if she did scream, Kimi thought, no one would hear her.

Abruptly past Shelby's shoulder, she saw Rand Erikson framed in the light of the doorway, looking angry and betrayed. He swore under his breath. "What's going on here?"

Even as Shelby craned his head to look behind him, startled, Rand grabbed him, whirled him around. "I said, what's going on here?"

Shelby quickly regained his composure. "The lady and I were just sharing a moment. You know how it is, brother-in-law," he winked broadly, "You two won't tell Vanessa, will you?"

Even as Kimi paused, uncertain what to say, Lenore feigned wide-eyed shock and innocence. "For pity's sake! I never saw such brashness. Why, my poor best friend would be so hurt to know—"

"Hush, Lenore," Rand snapped, "Kimi, what's going on out here?"

Shelby flashed her a warning glance, but from where Rand stood, she was certain he didn't see it. What should she do? Shelby obviously knew about Kimi and Rand. She didn't want to disgrace the Carstairs name or cause any more trouble. "Yes, that's right," she mumbled. "It wasn't anything, just a kiss."

She saw the fury in Rand's eyes and the amused triumph in Lenore's. The golden-eyed beauty had brought him out here deliberately for this, Kimi was sure of it. Probably Rand wouldn't believe her since he'd caught her in Shelby's arms.

Lenore grinned. "You little tramp!"

And in that split second, Kimi revolted. She slapped Lenore so hard it made the girl's head snap back, and the Southern belle dropped her fan. "Well, for pity's sake, did you see what that chit did?" Lenore wailed.

"Good night, everyone." With great dignity, Kimi turned and went down the steep balcony stairs.

"Kimi, wait!" Rand called behind her, but she didn't look back. She had known she didn't belong here and it could never work out. Kimi might have white skin, but inside she was a Sioux, and she was going back to her people. She crossed the flagstone courtyard veranda and went around the front of the house.

From the big mansion, lights streamed and the loud music and clapping still reverberated as Kimi ran across the lawn.

There didn't seem to be anyone else out here. Most of the drivers had gone around to the kitchen for refreshments, probably.

Kimi saw the judge's buggy tied under an oak tree. She ran for it, climbed in, and awakened the startled, snoozing old horse with the snap of the reins.

The Carstairs carriage was parked nearby, the driver half asleep on the box. "What happen, Miz Laurel? De party over?"

"No, I'm not feeling well. So I'm taking the buggy, and leaving early."

"Be glad to drive you, ma'am."

"No," she shook her head, "you bring the others when the party's over."

Kimi snapped the reins, drove away from Randolph Hall, shivering in the crisp autumn night. She didn't belong here. She had never really fitted in. Except for Rand's sake, she hadn't wanted to.

417

Now she wouldn't even have his love. Maybe that was for the best, too. Rand belonged in this society, and with Lenore, who was part of it. No doubt he thought the worst of her, but it didn't matter. It would be better if she made a clean break, got out of Rand's life. She had made her decision. Kimi was leaving Kentucky tonight.

Twenty-three

Swearing under his breath, Rand turned around to face Shelby. He'd go after Kimi later, tell her he'd been a fool; convince her to marry him. Of course he'd reacted with his gut feeling, seeing her in another man's arms, but he knew Kimi better than that. He doubled his fists and advanced on Shelby.

"Now, Rand." Shelby grinned with easy charm, backing away, holding up his hands in a placating manner, "Sweet Jesus. Who're you gonna believe? Your future brother-in-law, or that little tramp—?"

Rand hit him then, knocking him against the pillar. Shelby fought back and they meshed and struggled. In the background, the loud music and hand clapping of the Virginia Reel drowned out the fighting.

"You bastard!" Shelby snarled as they slammed against the wall and Rand hit him in the mouth. Shelby was a heavier man than Rand, and Rand realized abruptly that he was up against an experienced saloon brawler with no qualms about how he won his fights. Neither Southern gentlemen nor Indian braves went in for fighting with their fists. This put Rand at a distinct disadvantage.

"For pity's sake!" Lenore shouted, "you two stop it! This isn't what I had in mind at all!"

Lenore was behind this. Rand understood now why she had brought him out here. When he finished whipping the tar out of Shelby, Rand was going to finish breaking the engagement, go tell his mother off, and then beg Kimi on his knees to forgive him.

He hit Shelby again, knocking him against a potted fern that crashed to the balcony floor. He felt blood running from a corner of his mouth as the other man's fist connected with Rand's face.

They had fought their way back over to the railing of the balcony. Shelby brought his knee up and caught Rand hard in the groin. He had never felt such pain. Rand groaned, doubled up and stumbled backward. Shelby's nose sprayed blood when he breathed. "Now," he snarled, "I'm gonna throw you over the railing!"

Rand staggered weakly back against a pillar as Shelby charged him like a bull and they meshed again. The unholy gleam in the man's eyes in the moonlight told Rand that Shelby intended to make good his threat. Rand was too hurt to do anything but hang onto him, hoping to recover enough to continue the fight. He glanced over his shoulder. Three stories below was a flagstone veranda. The man who went over the railing was a dead man. In the background the music and loud clapping drowned out the noise of the fight.

"Shelby! Rand! Stop that!" Lenore screamed, "For pity's sake! That little tramp isn't worth fighting over; you hear me?"

Neither man paid the least attention. They were each fighting for their lives now, locked in combat against the balcony railing.

Rand slammed Shelby hard in the mouth, knocking him back against the pillar. He heard Lenore's angry scream and the rustle of silk, and he glanced up to see her coming at him, her golden eyes alight with fury. "No, Lenore!" Rand shouted, realizing she meant to push him over the railing.

His cry of warning seemed to alert Shelby. At the last second, even as Lenore's hands reached, Shelby dodged aside and gave her a shove.

Rand grabbed for her, but his hands caught empty air. For a split second Rand saw the horrified look on her face in the moonlight, the way she seemed to hang suspended in midair for a heartbeat. She tried to right herself, but her mincing step and her tortured feet caused her to lose her balance. She screamed as she fell in a billow of green silk skirts, all the way to the flagstones below.

The music had abruptly stopped. Rand glanced up, saw the judge standing in the doorway. The expression on the old man's face told Rand he'd witnessed the whole scene.

"Lenore!" Rand ran down the balcony steps. She lay crumpled on the flagstones. When he lifted her head, she smiled up at him, blood running down her pale face, which was pale as camelia blossoms. The green silk was soaked dark with it. "Oh, Lenore, hang on, we'll get a doctor!"

"Hurts . . . hurts so much . . ."

"We'll get a doctor—"

"No, don't move me . . . hurts . . . wanted to have it all; just like my mother . . ."

He turned and looked up. There was noise and confusion on the balcony. The judge had seen everything; no doubt Rand was going to be in trouble. He didn't even care anymore. There were several doctors at tonight's party. "Someone get a doctor!"

Lenore was breathing shallowly. Curious people

were coming out the doors, down the stairs. "What happened?"

"Lenore Carstairs tripped and fell off the balcony."

"Oh, my God!"

"Someone get a doctor."

Confusion, people crowding around, asking questions.

"Ask the judge, he saw it all."

"Yes, I did."

Rand cradled Lenore in his arms. He looked up. The judge was leaning over the railing, and behind him, the sheriff, the moonlight gleaming on his badge. "Sheriff arrest that man. He's wanted in several states."

Murder? No, he hadn't killed anyone. It dawned on Rand suddenly that Judge Hamilton was pointing at Shelby Merson.

Even as the sheriff led Shelby past in handcuffs, Shelby paused, leaned over Lenore. "Is she still alive?"

Rand sighed. "Just barely." He craned his neck and saw the plump doctor coming across the flagstones with his bag.

Shelby whispered, "Hey, Lenore, I've got something to tell you."

Her eyes fluttered open weakly. "Sh—Shelby?"

"Honey, the joke's on you. You're that kid."

Rand couldn't figure out what this was all about. Shelby grinned as if he knew a good joke. Lenore's golden eyes widened in horror as if she'd just realized something too terrible to comprehend.

"Bastard . . ." she muttered, "ironic . . . bastard."

Rand looked at the sheriff, cursing under his breath. Everything in him wanted to get up and slug Shelby for making Lenore's last moments so terrible. "Get him out of here!" he shouted at the officer.

The next few minutes were a blur of confusion, people crowding around, asking questions, Vanessa screaming.

Then they were all standing on the veranda, the sheriff questioning Shelby. "Did you push Miss Carstairs?"

"Who, me? Sweet Jesus, no!" Shelby shook his head. "The judge saw it, didn't you, Hamilton? Tell them I didn't push her."

The judge hesitated.

Shelby went livid. "I ain't gonna hang for a killing I didn't do! I'll tell you who's hiding a murder—the judge, that's who, the judge and old Mrs. Carstairs!"

"For shame!" The crowd muttered, "everyone knows those two have spotless reputations. He must be drunk or crazy to say something like that."

"The derringer!" Shelby shouted, fighting against the two strong deputies holding him, "ask them where they put the gun!"

The judge shook his head and looked around at the crowd. "Trying to shift attention away from himself, that's all. Does anyone here really believe his wild tale? Why, Elizabeth Carstairs is a paragon of this county." Everyone nodded agreement. "What really happened, judge?"

He paused and his gaze met Rand's. Rand waited, his heart pounding.

"Great Caesar's ghost," the judge said, "I had just found out that Shelby Merson was both a fraud and a killer. He's wanted in another state for strangling a lady he duped out of money."

Rand blinked, almost unbelieving, and the crowd muttered.

The judge cleared his throat. "I had alerted the

sheriff to meet me here at the party, and Shelby must have realized we had the goods on him and tried to get away. Young Rand here was brave enough to try to stop him. I stepped out just in time to see them fighting with Lenore Carstairs trying to break up the fight; poor thing never had a chance!"

Shelby protested, "No, she was trying to push him over, that's what she was trying—"

"Lenore was trying to save Rand," the judge said smoothly, "and about the time I came out with the sheriff, she went over the rail. Poor thing's a heroine. Isn't that right, Rand?"

He couldn't smear a lady's name—certainly not a Carstairs. "That's right," he said. "Lenore Carstairs was a real lady, trying to apprehend the crook."

"No, that ain't right!" Shelby struggled. "The judge is helping cover up an old crime, I tell you, won't someone listen—?"

The burly sheriff snarled, "You got your nerve, trying to smear two fine people like the judge and old Mrs. Carstairs. Why, everyone knows the Carstairs are the finest family in the county!"

The deputies dragged him away, still protesting.

Vanessa and Mother stood in the courtyard and Vanessa was wailing. "Mercy me, you mean I've been engaged to a killer? A thief? I'm disgraced! Disgraced!"

A murmur of laughter went through the crowd. Evidently no one was too upset that the two women had been made to look like fools. Rand got a little satisfaction out of that.

The old doctor had spread a blanket over Lenore's prone form. "She was so beautiful; just like her mother."

Rand tried to feel something for her, but all he could feel was pity and shock that he had ever thought he loved her.

Someone asked, "Where is Lenore's sister, anyway?"

What should he say?

He didn't have to say anything, the judge stepped in. "Laurel wasn't feeling well. She went home earlier in the evening, taking my buggy."

Rand hesitated a long moment, looking around. His mother and sister were sobbing; not for Lenore, he realized, but for their own disgrace. Jon Erikson had just the trace of a smile on his sad face. "Son," he said, "I want to have a little talk with you before you go over to the Carstairs."

"Jon," his mother wheezed indignantly. "You've had too much to drink. Rand, don't listen to him."

For the very first time in as long as Rand could remember, his father looked her straight in the eye. "Rose, shut up. I'm tired of your carping. When I finish talking to my son, we'll talk. No, I'll talk and you'll listen. I'm leaving you."

A murmur went through the crowd, and Rose Randolph Erikson turned deathly pale. "Please, Jon; I'll be humiliated—"

"Like you've humiliated me all these years? I made a bad choice, Rose, and maybe it's too late for me, but it isn't too late for Rand."

The judge put his hand on Jon's shoulder. "There are a few more things that have to be taken care of, questions that have to be answered. You and your boy go inside and have that talk. Then Rand and I will take the carriage and go tell Mrs. Carstairs and her other granddaughter what has happened here tonight."

A murmur of sympathy ran through the crowd. "Poor old Mrs. Carstairs. She's certainly had more than her share of tragedy."

Rand saw the judge breathe a sigh of relief, wondering about it. Perhaps Pierce Hamilton was worried about what Shelby Merson was going to say on the witness stand. It didn't matter. Who would believe a gigolo who was being tried for murder — especially considering the Carstairs sterling reputation. Shelby Merson would be lucky if this crowd didn't lynch him.

Rand had never felt so close to his father as he did now. He put his arm around the older man's shoulders and turned toward the house. "Maybe it's not too late for both of us to find a little happiness, Dad."

Elizabeth Carstairs stopped playing her piano and looked at the clock. Almost eleven. It was just about this time that long ago night. . . .

No, she must not think about that; it made her chest hurt. Certainly keeping the secret had been gradually wearing her down for almost sixteen years. Even Pierce and Nero were stressed because of it. *God is not mocked,* she thought as she stood up. Perhaps they were all three being punished for their part in it.

The house was so quiet she could hear the clock ticking and the old house squeaking in the chill October wind. If she listened really close, sometimes she thought she heard her daughter-in-law's laughter echoing through the halls. Beautiful and faithless Camelia.

She got up and went to stare at the big painting, remembering. She looked at the two little girls in the portrait and wondered how Lenore and Laurel were doing tonight at the Harvest Ball. Given half a chance, Laurel was going to outshine the older girl, but local society wasn't going to be kind to her. Young Rand would have to make his choice between the two half-sisters. Was he as weak as his father going the way of least resistance? Elizabeth hoped not, but tonight would tell.

The puppy lay by the sofa. Now it raised its head and its tail thumped. She went over, sat down on the sofa and patted its ears. "Tally Ho, you've created a lot of trouble for me with your digging. You're going to have to go live with the judge, but you'll like it there. I can't have you digging under the camelia bush. Bad dog, you dug up Clint Nutter's pistol. If you dug a little deeper . . ."

Nero stuck his head in the door just then. "Miz Elizabeth, I found it. She hid it in her bureau."

Elizabeth sighed with relief. "You take care of it?"

He nodded. "Nero always take care of you, Miz Elizabeth."

"Thank you, Nero." She dismissed him with a nod, relieved that the evidence was gone. If Lenore told her wild story now, who would believe her? Elizabeth settled back on the sofa. The clock ticked in the silence. She had lived with the secret a long time, she and Pierce and Nero. She would protect the Carstairs name, as would they. It had been a long, long time to carry the burden; it was telling on all of them.

With a sigh, she thought about the past. Her son had told her he was marrying the beauty in a whirlwind courtship because he had not behaved like a gentleman and had taken advantage of the lady. Camelia was with child. But the moment Elizabeth had seen the baby girl's eyes, she had known her son had been taken for a fool. Jim was the one who had been duped, giving the proud Carstairs name to another man's bastard.

Jim didn't seem to realize the truth, and he was so in love with Camelia that Elizabeth had kept her mouth shut, hoping for the best. For a while, it

427

seemed it might work out. Three years after Lenore's birth, Camelia produced a second daughter, and this one was definitely a Carstairs. However, that Memphis gambler, Clint Nutter, began to come around again when Jim was gone on plantation business. Elizabeth didn't know what to do, so she pretended she didn't know, although she confided the problem to her old friend, Pierce Hamilton.

The clock on the music room wall chimed eleven times. Yes, Elizabeth thought with a sigh, it was just about this time of night that it had happened. Jim gone on business, the two little girls asleep upstairs, Elizabeth playing her piano. She'd heard the stairs squeak and knew Camelia was sneaking out to meet that man. What could Elizabeth do? Would her son believe her if she told him?

It had been a warm spring night and the windows were open. Elizabeth heard the lovers' voices outside in the darkness and imagined them in an embrace. She thought she heard a horse approaching. Who could that be?

Alarmed, Elizabeth had run to look out the window at the east lawn. The lovers stood there in an embrace, oblivious to the rider as he reined in; watching. The moon had come out from behind the clouds and she saw the man on the horse and his expression. Jim had come home unexpectedly.

Mostly what had happened after that was a merciful blur. Elizabeth remembered running for the door. Knowing she must stop this fight, yet knowing she was not going to be in time. She would always remember how soft the grass was beneath her slippers as she ran to where the two men were fighting, how pale her daughter-in-law's face was in the moonlight as she watched helplessly. Pale as her namesake flowers.

The gambler had a derringer. Elizabeth saw the sudden gleam of it in the moonlight. Camelia screamed. Jim knocked it from his hand and it slid across the grass as the two men grappled.

Camelia was on it in a heartbeat, aiming the gun. "Stop it, Jim, or I'll shoot!"

Had she meant to fire or had the gun gone off accidentally? Elizabeth would never know. The men were still fighting. Even as Camelia fired, they moved, so that Clint took the bullet.

Jim let the dead man fall. "Camelia, give me the gun!"

She resisted, they struggled over its possession even as Elizabeth watched helplessly. And then it fired again.

"Oh my God!" Her son stared down at the gun in his hand, his face ashen. Camelia fell across the lawn, her green dress blending in with the grass, her red blood in such stark contrast to her pale white face, pale as the white camelias she loved. Jim fell to his knees, hugging her to him. "Camelia! Oh, Camelia, I love you so! Why did you cheat? Why wasn't I enough for you? I would have done anything for you; I loved you so."

Camelia looked up at him, smiling ever so slightly, the scarlet blood running down her snowy skin, the green dress. "You did something for me," she whispered with a one last bit of irony, "you gave my lover's child your name."

Camelia's final cruelty. Elizabeth would never have told him. Now she pulled him to his feet, put her arms around him. "Son, you didn't mean it. I know you didn't!"

"It went off," he said woodenly, blinking as if walking in his sleep and hoping any moment now he would awaken, "I was trying to take it away from her!" He put his face in his hands, sobbing.

Elizabeth sobbed, too. She would always remember how pale the beautiful face was in death. Camelia's golden eyes were open, staring at the dark sky. "Jim, we've got to do something. The law might not believe it was all an accident!"

"I don't care! She's dead! I want to die, too!" His green eyes were wild with horror.

It was like reasoning with a crazy man. "No, Jim, you've got to live. The children. Think of the children."

He laughed hysterically. "One of them's not even mine, did you hear that? I think I realized it from the first, but I loved her too much to care."

Elizabeth hugged him, her mind thinking fast. What to do? Pierce Hamilton dropped by just then, on his way from a party at another house. "Great Caesar's ghost! Anyone else witness this?"

Elizabeth shook her head. "What do I do, Pierce? We must protect my son. The Carstairs name must not be smeared."

"Get Nero out here. We can trust him and I'm going to need help."

By morning, Jim was headed West with his child. He couldn't bear to take the other man's daughter. All these years she had waited for word, and now she knew that her son lay in an unmarked grave near an ill-fated wagon train. It was ironic that he would never be buried in the Carstairs old family plot by the church. At least Elizabeth finally had his daughter back. She had a feeling God wasn't through with punishing Elizabeth for her part in the cover-up. What was she going to do about Lenore?

The sound of a buggy pulling up out front startled Elizabeth out of her thoughts. Were they back from the party already? She sat listening to Nero going down the hall to open the door. What choice had young Rand made? The girl he loved or the Erikson money? What was so ironic was that he would have the Carstairs much larger fortune—all of it—if he chose Kimi. True to her word, Elizabeth hadn't changed her will. The money was scheduled to go to the real Carstairs heir.

Kimi let Nero help her from the buggy, brushed aside his questions as she ran inside, her heart pounding. Nana came out of the music room. "My dear, what's wrong?"

She must not break down and cry; it would weaken her resolve. "Nana, I—I'm going away. Tonight."

"Young Rand announced his engagement to Lenore then?" She took a deep breath, almost as if she were in pain.

"I don't know, Grandmother," she shook her head. "I came to realize tonight that I don't belong here, that Rand would be better off without me, so I'm going away."

Elizabeth's eyes closed briefly, and then she turned and looked toward the painting. The beauty in the portrait almost looked as if she were smiling cruelly. "So Camelia, you had the last laugh after all—God's punishment for an old woman."

Was Grandmother losing her mind? Absently Kimi reached up to touch the medicine charm hanging around her neck. *Daddy,* she thought, remembering now how he had held her, trying to carry her to safety. "He loved me every much, didn't he?"

Elizabeth stared at the painting and the handsome man with the watch in his hand. "He loved you very much," she whispered, "almost as much as I loved my child and his father."

431

"Oh, Grandmother." She took the old lady's frail hands in her own. "I know this will hurt you, but I must go away."

"Back to the Indians?" Her mouth trembled, revealing how much she cared for her granddaughter.

Kimi nodded. "Please try to understand. That little girl in that portrait is gone, long gone with the passage of time."

Grandmother nodded. "Everyone gone, all but Camelia. She will be with me always. I hear her sometimes, her mocking laughter, the rustle of her skirts. I saw her reincarnated tonight; my punishment."

Kimi didn't know what the frail lady was talking about, but maybe it didn't matter. "It's just that, well, I love Rand, but I'll never fit into his life, not like Lenore would. Whatever Laurel Carstairs was, she was lost along with her father far away from here. In her place is a girl who is really Sioux in her heart and who will never feel at home any place else, so I'm returning to them."

Elizabeth Carstairs turned away, her shoulders shaking, stared at the portrait. "So Camelia, everything works out even in the end. This is my final punishment for what I did that long ago night, I find my granddaughter, only to lose her again."

Tears ran down her cheeks, and Kimi hugged the frail body to her own. "Nana, I don't know what you think you're guilty of and I don't care. I love you and I'm glad we found each other again, if only for a few days."

They put their arms around each other, and for a long moment they clung together.

The old lady looked at her, tears on her wrinkled cheeks. "How can you do this when you love him so?"

Kimi sighed and turned away. "That's precisely

432

why I'm doing it, because I love him and want him to be happy. I would only humiliate him and make him regret marrying me. No sacrifice is too great when you love someone."

"Spoken like a true Carstairs." Nana seemed to force herself to smile. "All right, if your mind's made up, I'll help you. I've got some cash in the house and I want to give you that mare you like, Onyx. Nero will take you to the train. Now get ready."

Her heart breaking, Kimi ran upstairs, changed out of the beautiful ball gown. For one evening she had been almost like the Cinderella she vaguely remembered from her story books that Daddy used to read to her a long, long time ago. Except this time, the girl didn't want the palace and the lifestyle that went with the prince.

In moments, she had a few belongings and was hugging her grandmother one last time. *"Pilamaya,"* she whispered. *"Thank you.* I love you, Nana; I love you so!"

As Kimi went outside, she paused, waiting for Nero to put her things in the buggy. No doubt Lenore and Rand were announcing their engagement now and everyone was drinking toasts of champagne. Kimi only regretted that she hadn't had a chance to say good-bye to the kindly judge. She turned one last time and looked off toward Randolph Hall, thinking about the man she loved. She would never, never forget him, but she loved him too much to stay and ruin his life. *"Wakan Tanka nici un,"* she whispered. *Good-bye and may the Great Spirit go with you and guide you.*

She was sobbing as Nero helped her into the buggy and tied the mare on behind.

Elizabeth stared after them long after her granddaughter had left. God had a way of dealing out justice after all. She almost seemed to hear her daughter-in-law's mocking laughter drifting through the house and the ghostly strains of her own piano echoing through the eerie mansion. *Alas my love, you do me wrong, to caste me off discourteously. . . .*

Almost blindly, she went to the French doors, opened them, and stared out into the shadowy plants of the conservatory. More than the pistol had been buried hastily in the east lawn. Ironic, maybe, that her daughter-in-law not have a respectable grave in the Carstairs family plot in the churchyard. The beauty slept forever with her paramour under the camelia bush in the conservatory Elizabeth had built later. She'd had to live with that secret all these years and the stress was gradually killing her. Elizabeth would do it again to protect her son and his child, but it had all come to naught. God is not mocked.

The sound of a carriage in the drive. Laurel had changed her mind and returned after all. With a glad cry, Elizabeth ran to the door and flung it open. It was Pierce Hamilton and young Rand Erikson. They both looked grim.

"What is it? Where's Lenore?"

Pierce took her arm. "I think we'd better go in the music room and sit down, my dear. Something terrible has happened."

Someone knew, she thought, but Pierce seemed to read her thoughts, shook his head. "No, not that. Let's sit down."

Woodenly, she let him lead her into the music room. She sank down on the sofa, waiting. Pierce put a goblet of sherry in her trembling hand.

She watched the judge pour himself a brandy

and offer one to Rand, who shook his head. "Lenore was a heroine tonight," Pierce said softly as he turned around to face her, "she did the Carstairs name proud."

Was he never going to tell her what had happened? She took a sip of sherry, looked questioningly at young Rand. He nodded agreement. "Yes, Lenore behaved like a true Carstairs, everyone says so."

Something terrible has happened, she thought, and abruptly, the sherry sloshed over her frail, trembling hand. "Tell me, Pierce."

"It was all over when I got out on the balcony. Shelby Merson's in jail and the sheriff will be over to question you later."

The clock ticked and ticked and ticked. Elizabeth seemed to hear her daughter-in-law's mocking laughter drift through the old house. "You're telling me Lenore is dead, aren't you?"

Young Rand's face twisted with pain as he looked at her, nodded. "She—she was trying to stop Shelby from throwing me off the balcony," he whispered. "Terrible accident."

Elizabeth tried to feel something, some hurt, but she felt only guilt because she had never loved Lenore, knowing she was not really her granddaughter. Lenore had had her mother's looks and Clint Nutter's morals. Elizabeth cleared her throat. "We'll give Lenore a beautiful funeral and headstone in the Carstairs family plot next to my James."

Pierce got up, poked up the fire so that it blazed brightly. "Are you all right?"

She nodded, although her chest was hurting again.

The young man made a helpless gesture. "I'm sorry, Mrs. Carstairs."

"It's all right," she answered numbly, thinking of all the people who would be coming, the flowers and food, everything she had yet to deal with. She saw the question in his eyes that he had been waiting to ask.

"Mrs. Carstairs, if I might see Laurel—"

"No," she shook her head. She must stall him, give Laurel time to make her train. "She didn't want to see you, young man. It was probably a wise decision. I'm not sure you care enough about her to make the sacrifice it would take to have her."

He swore softly under his breath. "Excuse me, ma'am, I sympathize with you on your loss, but I had already let Lenore know I was going to break the engagement, that I loved Laurel."

She looked into Pierce's eyes, back to Rand's pale blue one. She saw the truth in their eyes. She knew Lenore better than anyone. Lenore wasn't the heroine type. No doubt she had tried to push Rand off the balcony for jilting her and had gone over the rail herself. "Does anyone else but we three know the truth?"

Rand shook his head. "My father knows just that I'd made a decision to marry Laurel, if she'll have me."

So Jon Erikson had finally told his son about his own lost love. Would that affect the way young Rand looked at life?

Elizabeth sighed. "We'll not smear Lenore then. Let everyone think she was a noble heroine, a true Carstairs." She exchanged glances with Pierce, saw the puzzlement in Rand's pale eyes.

"Mrs. Carstairs," he knelt by her side. "I know this isn't the proper time, with this great tragedy and all, but I need to talk to Laurel."

She sighed, shook her head sadly.

436

"I love her," he insisted. "You must let me see her, explain."

"Somehow I think you really mean that," she whispered. "My James loved me that much. Such love is rare, young man, and for some people, it only happens once."

She looked into Pierce's eyes and saw the tears there. He had loved her as she loved James.

"Mrs. Carstairs," Rand said again, "I demand you let me see Laurel, or I'm going to go upstairs and break her door down. I won't leave here until I talk with her."

She looked at him a long moment, listening to the clock tick and wondering if Rand loved her granddaughter enough. Not that it mattered now. It would have been a difficult choice for him to make, giving up his whole world, turning his back on everything he'd ever known for a woman's love.

She shook her head. "It wasn't my decision, young man." A sudden look of comprehension crossed Pierce's face, and she nodded. This was the way Laurel had wanted it and it was not her grandmother's place to question that choice. She put her hand on Rand's arm. "You're too late; she's gone forever."

Twenty-four

Kimi sat on a windswept rise under a barren tree, staring out across the rolling prairies of the Dakotas. November. Moon of the Falling Leaves. The warm, cozy winter she had looked forward to sleeping in Hinzi's arms now stretched ahead of her as bleak and cold.

It was beginning to snow and she should go back to the Lakota village. Soon it would be dark and the snow would be falling harder. She shivered, pulling her buffalo robe closer around her and thinking tenderly of Rand Erikson. To her, he would always be the white warrior, Hinzi, Yellow Hair.

Had she made a mistake, returning to the Sioux? She had arrived yesterday and been greeted warmly. No, these were her people. She would never have fitted in with the wealthy, snooty friends of the Eriksons. They might have accepted her because of her grandmother's money, but they would have always laughed at her behind her back.

She could only pity them for their shallowness and lack of empathy. Kimi folded her arms on her knees, rested her small chin on them, remembering. She would miss Nana and the judge and old Nero. Most of all, she would miss Rand, the man who had once been her slave and then had made a captive of her heart.

Her soul ached at the thought of him, remembering his ardent kisses. Once she had been an innocent girl, and his passion had turned her into a woman. She didn't regret that. She regretted that she would have to spend the rest of her life without him. When she had returned yesterday on the black mare, Onyx, with gifts of flour and coffee and sugar bought with Grandmother's money, the whole camp had turned out for her. Many had asked about Hinzi, especially his friends, One Eye, Gopher, and Saved By the Wolf.

"Hinzi has chosen to remain with the whites." She had blinked back a tear. "His heart is there as mine is here."

One Eye nodded in understanding. "The easy white life is hard to give up."

"Yes," Kimi said, "I could not ask him to make that sacrifice, so I came alone."

Young Saved by the Wolf frowned. "You did not even give him a chance to choose?"

She shook her head. "There is a beautiful white woman with much money, who wants him. I made it easy for him by leaving without saying goodbye."

Gopher looked at her gravely. "Perhaps Hinzi will think you didn't want to be his woman."

"Perhaps. I think he will be happier without me, so I made that sacrifice."

Had she been wrong to do so? What was her future going to be? Tomorrow she would face all that. Possibly she would accept Gopher's offer to be his second wife. Tonight she could sit out here and watch the snow beginning to fall and think of Hinzi.

Was it snowing in Kentucky? She knew now that a part of her heart had been left there with her man, but she would manage somehow. After a while maybe she would finally stop hurting when she thought of him.

It was growing dark and the snow fell faster. Behind her, Onyx whinnied and stamped her feet. It was time to return to her lonely tipi fire, even the mare knew that. Still Kimi hesitated, remembering the times when he had been there waiting for her and she had run into the protective embrace of his big arms.

From the camp in the distance she heard children running and playing, dogs barking. The scent of camp fires and cooking meat drifted on the cold wind. Yes, she must return. Kimi stood up slowly. The mare whinnied again and a horse close by whinnied back.

Surprised, Kimi whirled around. In the shadows only a few yards away a big man sat a buckskin horse. The last of the daylight caught the gleam of yellow hair.

It was a ghost, she thought. She had wanted him so bad, she had conjured up a spirit. Her hand flew to the charm around her neck and she took a step backward.

And then the figure slid off the horse and walked toward her. "Kimi? They told me I would find you here."

For a long moment, she stared at him. "Hinzi?" She forced herself to disobey her impulse to run into his arms. He had only come to take her back to the white man's country, and she would never return there. When he knew that, he would leave again. No, she couldn't stand the pain of losing him a second time.

"Kimi, come to me," he commanded. And then he smiled ever so slowly and held out his arms. She forgot everything but the fact that she loved him and he was here. With a cry she went into his embrace, and he crushed her against him, holding her close, kissing her face, her eyes, her lips. "Kimi, oh, sweet butterfly, I don't intend to ever let you out of my sight again!"

His mouth was sweet and hot on hers, the feel of him warm and protective as he enveloped her. Only then did she realize he was dressed as a warrior, not a white man. She looked up at him, a question in her eyes.

He kissed the tip of her nose, holding her against his virile body. "Yes, I'm back for good, Kimi."

"But Lenore, all your wealth, your parents—"

"There's a lot to tell, but not right now." He kissed her again, deeply, lingeringly. "All you need to know is that your white warrior is back and I will never never leave you again."

She felt the tears on her cheeks. "Hinzi, you don't know what you're doing! There's been new trouble between my people and yours. They say the *wasicu* build new forts. They say Red Cloud will start a war—"

"Then we'll take whatever time we have left and be thankful to be together." He swung her up in his strong arms. "Even if we only have a few months, it will be worth it. Love is all that matters in this world, and I love you, Kimi, more than wealth or family or even life, I love you!"

"Oh, Hinzi, if you only knew how I've longed to hear you say that." She kissed him deeply and lingeringly as he carried her to his horse. He swung up on the buckskin, still cradling her against his broad chest. Snowflakes clung to his lashes over eyes pale as mountain streams. "Yes," she whispered, "if we only had tonight, it would be worth it!"

Leading the mare, Hinzi nudged Scout forward. Kimi clung to him, thinking of the ecstasy to come in their warm tipi. They rode through the snowy darkness toward the village of their people. The white warrior and his woman had finally come home.

To My Readers

Did a white soldier ever really turn his back on his own civilization and ride with the Indians of the old West? I did a lot of research in this area and found Comancheros, "squaw" men, trappers, and hunters, but the only white soldier I found is a vague legend among the Kiowas. There is a possibility that a black "buffalo" soldier rode with the Indians attacking Adobe Walls in 1874. I've already mentioned that in an earlier novel, *Comanche Cowboy.*

I know many of you have seen or read: *Dances With Wolves,* but may be surprised to know that the landmark novel on the subject of a soldier joining up with the Indians is an old novel published in 1950. It is called: *No Survivors,* by Will Henry, and was voted one of the best Western novels of all time by the Western Writers of America, of which I am a member.

What of white women, kidnapped as children and reared by Plains tribes who chose to stay with the Indians? I know of at least four and I'm still researching. The first was the well-known Cynthia Ann Parker, mother of the great half-breed Comanche chief, Quanah Parker. Both are buried here in Oklahoma at Fort Sill. Less widely known was little Millie Durgan, carried off during the Great

Outbreak of 1864 which I wrote about in *Cheyenne Princess*. Millie spent her whole life as a Kiowa and is also buried here in my home state.

A third was Lizzie Fletcher, stolen along with her sister, Amanda Mary, by Arapaho Indians from Wyoming in 1865. Her sister was later freed, but when she tried to reclaim Lizzie, now fifteen years old, the girl denied being white and would not leave the tribe that had reared her.

Yet another was a Spanish girl by the name of Tomassa. Recaptured and returned to Mexico, she ran away and went back to the Comanche. She married a half-breed Cherokee and spent the rest of her life in Oklahoma.

I've heard from some readers telling me that some of you are catching scorn from scoffers who say that Indian romances are "fantasy," and never really happened. Tell them about the four girls I mentioned or suggest two research books on the subject that back me up. One is *Comanche and Kiowa Captives* by Hugh. D. Corwin, privately printed in 1959. The Oklahoma Public Libraries have several copies. The other book is: *Women and Indians on the Frontier, 1825-1915,* by Glenda Riley, University of New Mexico Press.

If you'd like to do further reading about the Sioux Indians, there are many research books on the subject. Begin with one of my favorite authors, Mari Sandoz, and her classic: *Crazy Horse*.

As for the abandoned wagon train, it is one of those true and still unsolved mysteries of the old West. According to Captain Eugene F. Ware, in his book, *The Indian War of 1864,* he and an army patrol really did find a deserted wagon train of sixteen wagons all circled up in a desolate area about thirty-five miles above Julesburg, Colorado Territory. According to then Lieutenant Ware, the wagons appeared to have been there for years. There was no sign of violence, no skeletons of either people or animals. Although there was a lot of publicity concerning the discovery, no one ever solved the mystery.

The Crow and the Pawnee were indeed enemies of the Sioux and scouted for the soldiers. You've met Terry's younger brother, Asataka, as army scout Johnny Ace in my earlier novel, *Cheyenne Caress.*

Some of the other characters mentioned in the book you've just read also had their own novels. Rand's cousin, Quint Randolph, came from *Nevada Nights,* the Cheyenne Dog Soldier, Iron Knife, from *Cheyenne Captive,* and Cherokee Evans, the Galvanized Yankee who escaped from the *Effie Deans,* was the hero of *Quicksilver Passion.*

Some of you will wonder about the handsome Pawnee scout, Terry, or Wagnuka's missing half-breed son, or what happened to the beautiful slave girl that Jon Erikson's mother sold. They'll all turn up in future books of this very long saga.

You may be more familiar with the song, "Greensleeves," as the Christmas carol, "What Child Is This?" How old is the song? Shakespeare mentions it in *The Merry Wives of Winsor,* and it was ancient then.

As far as our country's most beloved national cemetery, Arlington, where both the Unknown Soldier and President John F. Kennedy are buried, it was indeed General Robert E. Lee's Virginia estate.

When the *Sultana* riverboat sank on the Mississippi in April, 1865, more people died than on the *Titanic,* but the tragedy is not nearly as well-known.

Yes, the Union army did get desperate enough in

1864 to recruit six thousand captured Southern troops into joining their army and going West to fight Indians. There's an excellent research book on the subject by Dee Brown: *The Galvanized Yankees.* The most famous of these soldiers was Henry M. Stanley, who would later become a reporter and go to Africa looking for a missing white man, and upon finding him, utter these famous words, "Doctor Livingston, I presume?"

As for the ship that carried the Galvanized Yankees to New York to catch their trains West, the *Continental,* history was not yet finished with her. In 1866, the *Continental* would again carry a unique cargo; a shipload of mail-order brides from the East coast on the long journey to distant Washington Territory. Washington at that time was wild frontier country, full of danger, hostile Indians, very few white men, and almost no white women.

The *Continental* and her cargo are the subject of my next Zebra novel. What kind of man would send for a bride he'd never met? Our hero was rich, moody, and darkly handsome; a half-breed bastard who craved respectability. He also wanted sons and an aristocratic lady to preside over his frontier empire. He didn't expect a love match and he didn't even care if she were pretty. What he did require was that she be from a fine family, have a spotless reputation, and be capable of producing children. In return, she would have wealth, position, and his name.

That's what he ordered. What he got was a pretty Irish whore, on the run in fear for her life. Only sheer desperation forced her to take another woman's identity and board the *Continental* for a place she'd never heard of to marry a man she'd never met.

Her name was Sassy Malone. For all you who

loved my short story in Zebra's 1991 holiday collection, *Christmas Rendezvous,* and wrote to ask what happened to Ginny's missing uncle, Mike Malone, and his family, this is their story.

Half-breed's bride. For Sassy, will this be a devil's bargain or a marriage made in heaven? One thing is certain, their passionate conflict will set those Washington woods blazing like wildfire. Should a woman try to hide her past from the man she loves? And if he learns the truth, can a proud man ever love her enough to forgive and forget?

I invite you to board the *Continental* with Sassy and share frontier adventure and fiery passion in the wilderness of Washington. That handsome, dark half-breed is waiting for you both.

To all you readers who have cared enough to write me or the Zebra editor asking for more of my stories . . .

Pilamaya. Wakan Tanka nici un.

Georgina Gentry